<u>**REA**</u>

ZIG / ZAG

GAR LAUGHINGLY TOLD URSULA,
"YOU OVER-SEXED BITCH.
IF SEX WAS AN OLYMPIC EVENT,
YOU'D WIN THE GOLD MEDAL."

Instantly on her bare knees,
Rio brought Gar to a great
overflowing. Keeping him
hard and erect to the very end.

PRESIDENT JOHN F. KENNEDY:
"YOU KNOW, I GET A MIGRAINE
HEADACHE IF I DON'T GET
A STRANGE PIECE OF ASS EVERYDAY."

"Can you really do it
for such a long time
without eating anything else?"

GAR HAD THE MOST DEEPLY
PENETRATING BLUE EYES.
MANY WOMEN THOUGHT
THERE WERE ONLY
TWO PAIRS OF EYES
THAT COLOR
IN THE ENTIRE WORLD.
PAUL NEWMAN
POSSESSED THE OTHER.

"I'll be in charge of
your temperature, baby.
As it rises, this chocolate treat
will melt in your mouth."

MARILYN MONROE:
"IT MEANS—WELL—IT MEANS
I'LL NEVER HAVE TO SUCK
ANOTHER COCK AGAIN."

"In a tumultuous all-inclusive
group orgy—no one was left standing."

URSULA FLUNG:
"YOU SELFISH BASTARD.
YOU *FEEL* ME
AND YOU *HEAR* ME TOO."
IT DIDN'T MATTER.
GAR'S RULES WERE
THE ONLY RULES.
YOU WERE THE PUPPET.
HE PULLED THE STRINGS.

Marlene Dietrich:
"In Europe, it doesn't matter
if you are a man or a woman.
We make love with
anyone we find attractive.

Based on New York, Chicago,

and international characters,

Robert Paul Miller

has woven together

a great read...

a scorching novel...

a spellbinding mix...

of startling true fact and exciting fiction

that runs through every page of this

original uncensored version of

ZIG / ZAG.

Spanning the years,

1917-1975,

the smooth, young, Chicago lawyer,

George Garfield Grey,

and his dominating Father-in-law,

James J. (Buck) McCormack,

become hugely rich from

the expansion boom of post

WW II Chicago.

And their backing from the

notorious Capone mob.

After a staggering Middle East oil

discovery, of questionable origin,

the new billionaire, Gar, gets caught-up

in the international jet-set with

Ursula, Cheryl, Rio, Ally,

and many other gorgeous
working women of his day.
Celebrities, like the womanizing
President, John F. Kennedy,
the infamous Aristotle Onassis,
Jackie O's Greek second husband,
and J. Paul Getty, the world's richest man,
romp through these fast-paced pages.
So, jump right into the pool.
New York, Hollywood, London, Paris
or the French Riviera,
you never know who you'll meet next.
Everyday, in every possible way,
the world simply loves to

ZIG / ZAG!

ORIGINAL UNCENSORED VERSION!

ZIG / ZAG

INTRODUCING
GEORGE GARFIELD GREY
IN
A VOLUPTUOUS NOVEL
OF
MONEY, SEX, AND POWER

ROBERT PAUL MILLER

STONEGATE PUBLISHING

This book is a work of fiction. Names, characters, places, and incidents, are products of the author's imagination or are used fictitiously. Any resemblance to actual events or locales or persons, living or dead, is entirely coincidental.

Cover design concept by the Author
Cover Art Director: Jay Casmirri for Cobalt Creative

ISBN: 0-9707168-0-X

Stonegate Publishing
P.O. Box 5953
Scottsdale, Arizona 85261- 5953

Printed in the United States of America

To Sally Magic.
From sunrise to sunset,
my raison d'être.

r.p.m.

ZIG / ZAG

IN THE SILENCE OF THEIR PERSONAL PRIVACY, WORLD WIDE READERS WILL VICARIOUSLY JOIN IN THE WILD ESCAPADES OF THE PROMISCUOUS BILLIONAIRE

GEORGE GARFIELD GREY

DON'T BE LEFT OUT OF THE FUN!

PROLOGUE

Many of our mutual New York friends had talked about it for a long time.

Ultimately, it grew to become a favorite dinner party conversation piece.

Of course, it had yet to be written, but everyone seemed to agree that it was only a matter of time until someone would write his blockbuster story. Not as a factually precise bio—but rather as an exciting work of 'fiction'.

After all, George Garfield Gray's life mostly resembled a prime-time soap opera. Much in the genre of the once high-flying television duo of *Dynasty* and *Dallas*. A deluge of glamour, sex, and elitism—but nothing in touch with our perception of everyday reality.

Then, somehow, the idea simply evolved into a popular guessing game.

Who *really* would write Gar's story?

That question always produced the same reaction.

Most eyes looked at me.

True, I had thought about doing the book any number of times.

However, no matter the reason, I had always allowed the idea to recede into the back of my mind—where it remained safe and untouched.

Coming to fruition as this particular novel, therefore, also included a bit of fate.

One day, quite by accident, I ran into Gar leaving the posh '21' club after lunch. Being with other people, we chatted only briefly but agreed to talk again soon.

As we were parting, I suggested we plan lunch or, perhaps, some weekend golf. Either would be pleasant—and golf would be especially easy. We belonged to the same country club.

Gar laughed, "Why can't we kill two birds with one ball? Let's do both."

I joked back, "Great. In the meantime, don't cheat too much on your handicap."

Again, that chance meeting triggered my thinking.

Should I actually write his story?

Subsequently, everyone I spoke with gave the same kinds of encouragement.

I heard lines like,

"People would just eat up a book about him."

Or—

"Once the word is out, they won't be able to print the damn things fast enough."

And—

"You know you can write it best, because you really know the guy."

Finally, a close friend said to me,

"Come on. Stop all this bullshit.

Just sit down and do it. I mean *really* do it."

Having exhausted all substantive reasons to delay,

I simply began to fill this apparent literary void.

BOOK ONE

ZIG

ONE

Flashback: New York City. Spring, 1969

Ursula's first American press conference attracted wall to wall media.

Editors-in-Chief, Fashion and Features Editors, Syndicated Columnists, all the famous Gossipmongers, and the cream of the television anchors—Huntley, Brinkley & Cronkite. At the last moment even a curious Johnny Carson quietly slipped in.

This disparate group of media kings and queens whose individual and collective power could shape the careers of headline-seeking wannabes, rarely found common reason to attend the same news-making event.

Their attendance today was a powerful expression of peer support for Ursula, who had been very explicit when stipulating the conditions for this appearance. For the first time, she wanted certain questions planted in advance with a few trusted journalists.

After thanking everyone for turning out in such large numbers, in her opening remarks Ursula was not at all hesitant about emphasizing her desire for a significant expansion in the scope of her career. Films. Serious Broadway. Musicals.

"Who knows—maybe I also have a voice."

Cautiously, she explained, "By itself, my fashion-modeling leaves me with the feeling that I am professionally underdeveloped." That remark produced knowing glances throughout the room.

During the closed press conference rehearsals in Paris, representatives of her American sponsor and her personal staff had spent hours attacking her from every conceivable angle. Repeatedly, they challenged Ursula's answers to their questions—planted or anticipated—endlessly trying to prepare her for the unexpected. They were especially rough on the embarrassing details of her highly publicized hedonistic lifestyle. No detail could be overlooked. Nothing left to chance. After all, this magnetic lady might well be the hottest current copy on the planet.

As usual, Ursula had peaked on cue today.

Joking, posturing—effortlessly roaming the platform with microphone in hand—she gave the performance of a lifetime. Dazzling her judgmental spectators.

Listen. Here she is answering another question.

"Sex? Maybe I didn't hear you right. I still get confused sometimes in my English."

"Oh—oh yes—I get it now. You just want my *view* of sex—right? Well, that's an easy answer. Here in America, sex is an obsession. Where I come from it's just an everyday fact of life. No big deal. Everybody should have good sex—even you guys. Okay?"

At twenty-four, the five-foot ten inch blonde beauty was deliberately raising her headline stakes with every provocative answer. Surprisingly, speaking in near-perfect English.

The fairy-tale focus of this packed media frenzy lived in a mostly artificial daily world of runways and photographers. Her live and photographic appearances could be financial life and death to the multi-billion dollar women's apparel industry. And everything allied to it. Whatever Ursula wore would be photographed, copied, and imitated—worldwide—producing enormous risks and royal rewards. With so much at stake, her fashion magazine sponsor had chosen her outfit for today's gathering with great care—finally, settling on a famous European designer's white, double-breasted, raw silk blazer suit, with uniquely crafted 14ct. gold buttons.

It retailed for $2,995. Outrageous for its day.

Far more than merely walking the raised platform, Ursula was sashaying back and forth. Marvelously succeeding at what she had purposefully set out to accomplish—to grab the audience's attention and slowly seduce it with a tempting illusion. The jostling crowd was being lulled into a dual fantasy. At once, watching a fashion model's runway performance—her normal milieu—and a risqué pre-war Berlin cabaret show. Both were alluring spectacles.

Too bad the mostly male crowd would never know that under her fabulous white suit was nothing more than a gauze-thin G-string.

For Ursula, the mere idea of her underneath nakedness titillated all of her erogenous zones. The feeling of total physical freedom energized her. It helped to propel her extraordinarily long legs—even more exaggerated in five-inch stiletto heels.

No matter what or where the event, unanimously—which then meant at least Diana Vreeland of Vogue—Ursula was acknowledged the epitome of high fashion.

A superstar.

Most of the reporters were standing on their chairs now—shouting, whistling, and wildly waving their hands for recognition. Adding to the disorder, photographers furiously raced around popping flash bulbs in her direction from every conceivable angle. The combined noise and confusion of this badly managed press conference had now broken all boundaries of restraint. The sedate Plaza Hotel, in its grand French Renaissance-Beaux Arts style, across the street from Central Park, seemed the most incongruous possible setting for this madding crowd.

Hold on. Here she is answering again.

"Well, everybody has to get noticed somehow. So we all did whatever we knew best."

A titter ran through the crowd. "Does it really matter how?"

With the instincts of a prowling tigress, Ursula knew she had them eating out of her hand. Winchell of the *Mirror*, urged Ed Sullivan of the *News*, "Ya really should invite her on your TV show, Eddie. That's what Carson's here for. She's gotta be the most spectacular piece since double M." For seven years the media had selfishly mourned the loss of Marilyn Monroe.

Finally, this foxy German beauty got the planted opening she had been waiting for. And fired off an answer that scorched every pencil in the room.

"People can think about me whatever they choose. Frankly, my dears, *I don't give a shit.*" With a lusty laugh, "Me and Clark Gable. Right? Okay—so he didn't say shit."

Whammo! The room erupted.

Adding their own twist to her sizzle, reporters frantically elbowed their way to telephones, screaming, "Get me re-write!"

In giving the best speaking performance of her career and behaving provocatively as she always did—which is what they had come to see—Ursula simply knocked their socks off.

On another day, in another place, she would have the opportunity to display her brain as well as her body. For now, the rush of stories and photos from today's hyped-up media event would turn into a virtual torrent tomorrow. Ursula's face and countless quotes would be splashed worldwide across the front page of every tabloid.

In fact, she was counting on the blaze of international publicity to be a crucial turning point in her flamboyant career, intending to cash-in on her incredible international celebrity. But it was not to be.

Completely irrational on the subject, George Garfield Grey railed on. Furiously, he demanded a much more subdued and submissive Ursula.

"You ungrateful, outrageous bitch," he screamed. "Grabbing the spotlight. Humiliating me. For an encore, you'll probably start to think that we're equals. And no way in hell will I allow you that. Forget it. There's only *one* person in control here. *Only one.* And that will never change. Got it?"

After that eruption, his angry silent treatment was her punishment. And he inflicted it on her for days on end. Unfortunately, this sort of emotional pain was nothing new. As a recalcitrant child, Ursula's father had used the same controlling technique. Then as now, she begged for forgiveness—would plead guilty to anything to ease the debilitating tension. Although, most often, she had no real idea of what she had done wrong. For reasons unknown, her father seemed to enjoy the spectacle of seeing his daughter grovel at his feet.

Ultimately, open psychological warfare developed between father and daughter. Later on, full-blown rebellion. Ursula could not deal with it any other way.

Despite the rage she was suppressing, while fighting back tears Ursula still managed a weak smile for Gar. But silently she promised herself, "No matter what he does to me. No matter how much he hurts me or frightens me, I will not surrender what I feel inside. I will never give up the *real* me."

Notwithstanding this vow, Ursula abandoned her quest for an expanded professional image. Yet, she dreamed on. "Someday, I'll find a way to use my mind more than my body. In the meantime, I'll continue to practice my acting—in bed—where he thinks I'm genuinely great."

A month later, Winchell ended an item in his famous syndicated column:

> "...and the personality contrast between these two is as deep as an ocean...a fertile spawning ground for irreconcilable differences. All their international pals are buzzing and concerned."

Unlike most printed gossip, this item was dead-on.

They rarely talked. He only kissed her in bed. And he *never* hugged her.

Yet, the exquisite Ursula patiently waited and desperately hoped. Telling every listener, "He'll change. It will take time, but Gar will change for me. Just you wait."

All contrary opinions aside, Ursula remained faithful to her wishful imagination. But many in their international set thought aloud that their entire affair represented an extraordinarily strange bonding. A male friend said, "If you engage her in any serious conversation, you immediately know that she is one very bright lady—not just another pretty face in the crowd." Indeed not.

This breathtaking blonde was the celebrated Ursula Von Ribbentrop, the most famous—the most sought after—the most envied—of all international fashion models. Her exquisitely lean face, high cheekbones, and narrow straight nose, was merely background for her ultra-spectacular violet-blue eyes. And a body that had made old men scream again. At least once. Indisputably, Ursula Von R. was the most heavenly creature to come out of Berlin since the consummate Dietrich.

Her entrance upon the international gossip scene had first been ignited by the discovery of a totally revealing nude photo spread which had appeared years before in an obscure European porno rag. When approached then, Ursula had jumped at the opportunity to do the shoot. Lying about her age, barely sixteen at the time, and posing under an assumed name, she willingly exposed her voluptuous nubile body—spreading her sensationally long legs to the North and South poles. And pushed her blonde bottom erotically into the close-up lens of the camera.

Since then, untold millions have stared at Ursula on the covers of every important international publication. And her worldwide fans continued to gobble up feature articles about every detail of her life—the more personal the better. They scoured *The New York Times Magazine, Der Spiegel, Le Monde,* and quite naturally, the scandalously untrue stream of gossip and innuendo fanning the circulation-rich tabloids—in every language of the western world. Wherever she appeared, she was mobbed. Yet, no matter how difficult the scene became, she constantly smiled and expressed her appreciation.

"Of course you can have my autograph. You made me. You are what I live for. All of you wonderful people. Thank you so much."

Even Women's Wear Daily trumpeted,

"URSULA HAS IT MADE!"

"Ursula," the single name by which the world referred to her, undeniably, was a woman most any man would kill for. But George Garfield Grey was not just "any" man.

Gar was the most storied and gloried icon of the corporate world. An unreconstructed male chauvinist, he was unalterably opposed to any notion of sharing his long-standing limelight. And nobody knew that better than Ursula.

Over six feet tall, Gar had thick sandy hair, straight nose, slim, and slightly suntanned. At fifty-one, he was handsome, virile, and a billionaire many times over. He ranked as one of the five richest men in the world according to the *Forbes 500 Richest list.* Reporters enjoyed writing, "That's 'B' for billions."

As one adoring Frenchwoman had remarked, *"C'est un enfer d'un homme!* That's one hell of a man!"

Gar had the most deeply penetrating blue eyes. Many women thought there were only two pairs of eyes that color in the entire world. Paul Newman possessed the other. He talked straight to your face. You always knew where you stood. That trait produced strong opinions of him. Those who knew him best liked him most.

More recently however, Gar's long-standing need to control seemingly had burst beyond any normal boundaries, causing much concern to family and friends. But no great surprise. On numerous occasions, he had been heard to say, "The secret is to keep people guessing—throws them off balance—makes them crazy." His control drive had now blown into total obsession.

Given his normal lack of sensitivity or any clear perception of reality, he now possessed one of the most difficult of all behavioral profiles.

But wait—hold on here.

If you also know George Garfield Grey, and it seems the entire civilized world does, you already know much about this world-famous billionaire. However, it is unlikely that you would have recognized the early manifestations, those unique signs that revealed his underlying true self. Such as, Gar Grey is much the charming chameleon. In any circumstance, he would do or be whatever was necessary to control the scene. He also has an intrapsychic conflict. On a daily basis, money and sex are equal-time competitors. Gold rules—but only by a thin margin.

While most women always had been mightily attracted to him, Gar was getting to an age where the very young looked better and better. And while a man with his high profile should be at least somewhat discreet, he did whatever he wanted—whenever the mood struck.

Once-in-a-while, together with some of his golfing pals at the Augusta National, Gar would relax with the inevitable martini and joke around a roaring fire in the Eisenhower Cottage. There, they concluded that when the 'Big Game of Life' was over the guy with the most fucks, *outside of his marriage,* would be declared the winner. After all, wasn't life itself merely another game in which to keep score?

So the guys decided that when they held their first meeting up in 'The Great Sky' the winner would be awarded a Lifetime Achievement Trophy. Not surprisingly, Gar was running far ahead of the rest of the pack. For years, to the most attractive women he met, he enjoyed saying, "Ordinary people do ordinary things—I don't. Does that grab you somewhere?"

Most often it did. And it was this forthrightness that earned him his prodigious sexual track record. Later, the entire group heartily laughed at another of their own ludicrous ideas.

They further decided that, inasmuch as the nickname *Oscar* was already taken, they would appropriately call their trophy, *Pussy.*

TWO

New York City. November 14, 1975.

Six years had passed. But only time had changed.

The immutable George Garfield Grey certainly had not.

Despite Gar's endlessly unloving behavior, Ursula was yet unwilling to surrender. In a highly agitated state, she sat alone twenty-nine stories above fashionable Central Park South, pensively contemplating the many offers open to her in her international universe.

As dusk slowly descended—capturing the last of a thin autumn sunset—Ursula hopelessly perceived the Lord's creative solar magic as only a successful celestial kidnapping. With the behavior of a hostile witness she immediately internalized, "And 'dusk' got away with his victim, too. All those bastards do." At this moment she had only one particular bastard in mind.

"Most women thrive on TLC and Gar knows that. So why doesn't he get it? Why has he *never* gotten it? Dammit, why don't *most* men get it?" Her anger provided her answer.

"Because they're all emotionally constipated—that's why. Their mothers emasculated them. I just hate all those mothers."

While totally out-of-character for the usually blunt and free-spirited Ursula, when it came to Gar it had always been easier to simply deny what she did not want to confront. Somehow, tonight seemed different. Tonight, she had the uneasy feeling that her years of self-deception had played out.

Anxiously, Ursula paced the length of her living room. In a moment, her intuition proved to be correct. Like a bolt of lightening, her true answer struck.

"The only thing he *really* cares about is between his legs. *That's why!*"

She felt the color rise in her face.

"It's not about me at all. I'm just a toy. His personal depository!"

Suddenly, Ursula's mind was invaded by past images. It was 1969. The year she met and quickly took up a dazzling liaison with the famous George Garfield Grey. Immediately, the scandal-hungry media turned it into a cause célèbre.

It might have come as a shocking surprise to many, but in her secret heart Ursula had wanted something more meaningful from their relationship. Something more beyond the frenzied jet setting and marathon sex.

Unfortunately, the always-preoccupied billionaire never reached out to her in any form of personal endearment. That urge was simply not any part of Gar Grey's genetic code. For Ursula, frustration and disappointment had rushed in to fill the giant void. And those two subjective responses became her constant companions.

When Ursula's conflicted rush overflowed the first time, the heavy spillage ruined most everything in her life. Her last refuge was her work. And when even that began to suffer, she had to finally admit, "I really am lost. Gar has me trapped. I can't even see light anymore at the end of the tunnel." Frowning, "Maybe there isn't any. Maybe there *never* was any."

Already fluent in transcendental meditation, the famous model had been calmed by repeating a mantra she invokes to this day.

"Stay in the moment."

It eased her current anxiety. But the confusion and anger clung to her like a second skin.

Aware that she was in need of immediate professional help, in the late fall of 1969 Ursula had flown off to Vienna to discuss Gar with a famous psychiatrist. An old friend of her Father.

In myriad versions, from both men and women, the renowned doctor had heard the same complaint countless times. However, having known Ursula since childhood he listened patiently. Extending all the comfort time she needed. They conversed in German—their first language.

"You do not bring to me a simple subject, my dear Ursula. You must understand, personality generates enduring patterns of thought, feeling, and behavior. These characteristics are highly influenced by genes ingrained for generations. Therefore, they are not subject to any significant modification. The same evaluation holds true for you—for me—for everyone."

Ursula scrunched her face, somehow hoping to change what she had just heard. At the end of a lengthy discourse on genetics, the white-bearded doctor leaned forward in his chair.

"Do you still want to go forward in a liaison with this complex man? Or maybe better, you should think about it—then we talk more tomorrow."

Cocking his head, "Yes?"

"I do not think so, Herr Doktor. As I had hoped, you have explained and clarified Gar for me. Before today, I really did not understand very much. I had thought it was all because of our age difference—an entire generation. Maybe now I can also help myself."

Suddenly free and unburdened, Ursula smiled. The entire room brightened.

"So, I will stay with Gar, for now. Tonight, I will meet up with him in Paris."

In the European fashion, she gave the elderly man a warm embrace. Her head darting to both cheeks. "Besten Dank" Thank you very much.

"Meine Vater sends his warmest regards.

Auf Wiedersehen."

As Ursula's plane approached Orly airport, the twinkling lights of the sublime Paris spread out below as a magic welcome mat. And to a new lease on a life she would do anything to maintain and preserve.

In addition to his lack of sensitivity, Ursula was soon to learn that Gar had a well-deserved reputation for at least two unquenchable thirsts. She already knew about absolute control. Now add unbridled sex. However, a supremely confident Ursula was unfazed. She interpreted Gar's reputation rather as a challenge.

Since she was a precocious fourteen-year old, she had thought of sex as her own personal invention. Her favorite sport. She had even ranked it ahead of skiing—and she enjoyed doing a lot of skiing. Nonetheless, she was startled to discover that Gar had been searching for something beyond the boundaries of ordinary lovemaking.

Finding her totally open and unquestioningly receptive to whatever he suggested, Gar quickly manipulated Ursula into far-out biopsychic experiences. And his libido was not yet up to full speed.

In self-amazement, the multi-orgasmic beauty became an insatiable sexual devotee. Gar laughingly told her, "You over-sexed bitch. If sex was an Olympic event, you'd win the gold medal. One of these days, you're probably going to fuck me to death—just for the pure joy of it."

But for the ever-willing Ursula, getting involved in his deviant sexual cravings also had produced an unexpected contradiction. Despite her new glow Ursula never lost her indissoluble fear that somehow Gar might threaten to use their fabulous intimacy to control her—or worse.

She already knew there was something about the very idea of vengeance that pleased some evil instinct in him. That very real fear continued to build. And led to Ursula's first all-out anxiety attack.

She confided to her male hairdresser, "I don't think Gar would hesitate for a second to destroy my career—and he could do it just that fast you know." She crisply snapped her fingers. "I will tell you something else that frightens the hell out of me. He will never let me go. He will do something very bad to me first."

With a frightening shudder, Ursula remembered overhearing Gar saying to someone during an overseas phone call, "In business or pleasure, total destruction in the pursuit of control is no crime. Just remember, I'm the guy who told you that."

She also knew that his unlimited international business connections led him to some very scary people all over the world. And they would do his bidding without question or hesitation.

Each day, in Machiavellian ways, Gar proceeded to tighten her emotional string. In his tunnel-vision mind he was fine-tuning a priceless Stradivarius. He had completely convinced himself that only a thin line now separated her anxiety from his dream of having sex with a monomaniacal woman. An especially exciting dream—if her phobia was fear—of him.

"If I could only raise her level of anxiety to overwhelming fear—" The obsessed Gar continued to scheme.

He gave some thought to using Spanish Fly. He had successfully used the aphrodisiac in Tangiers during a wild ménage-à-trois with identical twins. They had been a gift for the night from a Middle Eastern oil prince to help celebrate their fourteenth birthday. The gleaming black nubile beauties achieved erotic new heights. Simultaneously, doing all-possible things with him—and each other.

At this fever-pitch point, particularly now that he

believed Ursula was close to the edge, George Garfield Grey was not going to be denied. No matter what it took. And he was not far off the mark. At this moment, naked and on her knees, Ursula's anxiety closely bordered on sheer panic. Contrarily, Gar had no idea he had exacerbated her hidden inner anger.

"No plain vanilla for this sonofabitch," she muttered under her breath.

Taking him forcefully in hand, Ursula stimulated him there with a long suck. Manifesting lust, she again took all of him into her experienced mouth—then defiantly clenched her teeth. Gar rose with enormous anticipation. He thrived on rough sex.

Using her most explicit language, Ursula acted out all of the lascivious verbal descriptions of what she was doing to him. Careening on the wings of his favorite fantasy, Gar jerked—and trembled to climax. This was the moment Ursula chose to abandon her incredible self-discipline. Immediately, her amazing rosy-pink nipples transformed into elongated rocks. With copious wetness, she was already soaring. There was no more time! Unfortunately, the sated Gar was in no such hurry. Even his interest was gone.

Silent moments later, Ursula's miles of models' legs were locking her tall, blonde body hard against his muscular thigh. The celebrity still craved her moment. Pretending sleep, Gar still had not moved. Ursula flung, "You selfish bastard—you *feel* me—and you *hear* me too."

It didn't matter. Nothing mattered.

Gar's rules were the only rules. You were the puppet. He pulled the strings.

Take it or leave it. No questions. No options.

This psychodramatic role-playing was just one ploy Gar used to gain control.

Overwhelming generosity was another.

Cynically, his huge wealth had lost any other personal benefit. He had everything else.

Suddenly—without preface or warning—Gar bolted

up—exploding verbal abuse.

"Fuck the money! Fuck you too Ursula! Every woman has her price!

I bought you! I own you! Do—you—hear—me?"

Pouncing, he devoured her luscious fruit—top to bottom. Without pause, the obsessed conqueror rode his blonde beauty to victory.

Contrary to both her free lifestyle as well as popular opinion, Ursula was nobody's fool. She was the only child of an elite German family in Berlin. Her Father, a highly respected and powerful third-generation industrialist, had ties to the famous Krupp munitions family at Essen. Without a son and male heir, Gerhard Von Ribbentrop always pushed his daughter to have a firm grasp of money and business.

"I know your stubbornness only too well, my dear daughter. But just keep in the back of your head what I tell you now. One day your beauty no longer will support you. Be careful with your money. And do not tell me that you will always have your inheritance. You know only too well how I feel about that issue."

Surprisingly, finance had intrigued her. Ursula knew all about juggling money. Especially, interest rates. And the eighth wonder of the world—compound interest.

Swiss bank accounts? "What would you like to know?"

Not only did Ursula have what she was bought for, but she also had invested wisely during the oil embargo of 1973 with old friends—'insiders' on the floor of the Frankfurt Stock Exchange—and others who were trading in spot oil contracts in the Dutch city of Rotterdam.

She told a famous photographer friend in Milan,

"The diamonds may be in Antwerp, darling—but the oil is in Rotterdam. And these days the black stuff in the barrels is a girl's best friend."

The disheveled couple was finally spent from their non-stop thrashing on the priceless Aubusson rug, which covered the parquet floor in the master bedroom of Ursula's sprawling Manhattan apartment. The rug, "Had to be an Aubusson," according to the incomparable Parisian designer Pierre Montaigne—himself, a step beyond de rigueur. Ursula's apartment was another multi-million dollar gift from Gar. In addition, there was substantial cash, stocks and bonds—and much extraordinary jewelry from the likes of Bulgari, Cartier, Van Cleef, and Chaumet. All stashed and accounted for in her secret bedroom safe.

And Gar would madly travel her body again that very night—still pushing hard for control.

But not to hurry.

The night was young—and these two strange lovers had all the time in the world.

THREE

Two Days Later. New York City. November 16, 1975.

It was a dreary Tuesday. Overcast and damp. Just another routine November weekday in New York. But it didn't stay routine for long.

At 7:21 AM, the CBS Television Network was first.

In TV Master Control, the heart of the CBS Broadcast Center on West 57th Street, an engineer surrounded by banks of monitors in dimmed light had been smoothly handling network and regional feeds. Now, a director was answering a demanding red phone.

"Master Control...What?...When did it happen?... Okay, we'll handle it, Sig."

"Let's move it everybody—a 'Special Report' is roaring down the pike."

Hands went flying. Levers pushed and pulled. Opened and closed. Ready!

"O.K. people, we go on 'green'. Stand-by. Ten seconds."

Affiliates cued. Graphic up.

"A–n–d counting–5–4–3–fade to black. Take one."

The familiar 'Special Report' graphic filled TV screens all over America.

Millions of viewers abruptly stopped eating their breakfast—and held their breath.

"2–1–prompter rolling."

"Green!"

"This is a CBS News Special Report—

"George Garfield Grey, fifty-seven, Chairman of the Board and CEO of General Industrial Corporation, one of the largest business enterprises in the world, was found dead in his Fifth Avenue apartment in New York less than an hour ago. A household maid discovered his body.

"According to early word from the Homicide Squad of the New York City Police Department, the executive apparently committed suicide.

"Grey, one of the world's wealthiest men, was known simply as 'Gar' to statesmen, bankers, and employees, alike. Born in Chicago, a lawyer by profession, Grey soared to international prominence more than twenty-five years ago, when he masterminded an early bank take-over. That acquisition became the base for one of the the largest international oil and industrial conglomerates. And Grey became an important financial figure in money centers around the world. Both he and his wife Ellen have long been popular high-society jet setters.

"We will continue to up-date this important breaking story. Stay tuned.

"For CBS News—I'm Roger Cannon, in New York."

At the Grey apartment on Fifth Avenue in the mid-seventies, Detective Cleary turned to the hysterical maid. "Is any family member here, miss?"

"No, sir. Mrs. Grey is in Palm Beach getting ready for Thanksgiving. Mr. Grey was flying down there tomorrow," she sobbed.

"After you discovered the body, did you make any calls?"

"Yes, sir."

"Who'd you talk to?"

"Well, I—I didn't know what else to do," she stammered, "I was so scared. I never seen a dead body before. And he's so famous, ya know."

The detective interrupted.

"Please miss. Who…"

"…and it was so early. I just called Miss Henry at home."

"Who's she?"

"She's Mr. Grey's personal secretary."

"Why'd you call Miss Henry?"

"Cause in an emergency, she's the one I was always told to call.

Ya see—Miss Henry knows *everything!*"

FOUR

News of Gar Grey's death spread like wildfire.

And sheer bedlam was rapidly developing in the Executive Offices of General Industrial in New York's Rockefeller Center. Simultaneously, the news of Grey's death hit the AP wire; Reuters; The New York Times city desk; the New York Stock Exchange broad-tape; and The Wall Street Journal—worldwide financial centers only seconds later. The L.A. Times, Washington Post and every other news organization wanted an update. Down on the street, TV crews were setting up their equipment on the sidewalk.

In the private office of Clifford Blair, longtime Senior Assistant to George Garfield Grey, a frenzied conversation was taking place.

"Cliff, you just gotta put in a call to Ellen before she hears it on TV or radio. Or from some aggressively insensitive local reporter," shouted portly, cigar-smoking, Frank Templeton, GIC's well-respected Director of Worldwide Corporate Communications.

Now beet-red—the beefy, big man paused for breath.

"An' I gotta get a news conference set-up here—and damn fast. The phones are ringin' off the hook, and the reporters are screamin' that we're stallin'. They think we're tryin' to cover-up somethin'. Like was he alone? Maybe yes. Maybe no. Who the hell knows with Gar? This thing's gotta be handled right, Cliff. Our Gar was some importan' pisser." Templeton raced on. "An' our stock's getting fuckin' murdered downtown. Opened gap-down on a gigantic block—over two million shares. Been droppin' like a stone. Heavy institutional sellin'. Nothin' on the buy side."

"And to make it worse, that asshole floor-specialist is afraid to step in. Probably shorted big on the first up-tick he got—always breakin' every goddam floor rule. 'Buyer of last resort'—ain't that a crock. Report it to the Exchange Governors, right? Shit. He'll make a bloody fortune. Never did like that son-of-a-bitch. Never!"

"For chrissakes slow down, Frank," advised Blair.

"If Ellen's alone down there, and I think she is—well under these circumstances, I'm not sure I'm the right one to make that call. Maybe Arthur Pollack would be better."

Templeton: "Good thought. Arthur would be best." Then he added, "I know I wouldn't want to be the one—that's for sure."

Blair jammed the buzzer on his phone.

"Mary Etta, have Irene Henry get Dr. Arthur Pollack on the phone for me."

On Park Avenue, the phone rang softly in the posh medical office. "Dr. Pollack's office," the receptionist answered quietly.

"Good morning, Evelyn. This is Irene Henry. Is the doctor in for Clifford Blair?"

"Hello Cliff. What can I do for you this morning? Who's sick?"

"Arthur, have you heard the news yet?" Blair asked anxiously.

"What news, Cliff?"

"Gar's dead, Arthur," the executive blurted out. His voice high with emotion.

"Dead? What the hell are you talking about?"

"Just what I said. It seems that Gar committed suicide sometime last night—or early this morning. We're still waiting for more details from the police. But, while we're waiting and trying to make some sense out of this nightmare, Ellen's got to be told. She's down in Palm Beach. And except for staff she's alone at the house. Frank and I think it would be best if you made the call, Arthur."

Deeply shaken, the doctor slumped back into his leather chair. He and Grey, patient and friend, had been close for nearly twenty years.

"Oh my God. I can't believe what you're telling me, Cliff. I just saw Gar for lunch last week. He seemed perfectly fine—in good spirits. I'd checked him out recently. No serious medical problems. What else can you tell me, Cliff?"

"Nothing. Nothing's happened that's out of the ordinary—at least not here at the office. We're all just as stunned as you are. It's just plain crazy for Gar to go and do something like this. The man had everything in the world to live for—everything. But we've got to get that call in to Ellen. Will you do it?"

"Yes, of course I will. I'll put it through right now."

"Thanks, Arthur. I know I can always count on you."

It was one of those perfect Palm Beach mornings. The sun slowly breaking the sparkling Atlantic waters. Only a soft breeze coming ashore—gently caressing the magnificent estates along South Ocean Boulevard, some of the most valuable residential properties in the world.

Within the Grey compound, the giant lawn sprinklers arched their fountains of life to the perfectly maintained Bermuda lawns and lush gardens. The gardeners, themselves, moved about the estate in near-total silence.

The main house, which faced the endless ocean, was secluded from the other estate structures—two spacious guesthouses, huge swimming pool and terrace area for outside entertaining. And formal gardens bursting with color. Even further away, the bungalow residence of the estate manager, and several other small outbuildings.

A freshly rolled mauve-color clay tennis court, with crisp white chalk lines, patiently waited. Not even the hint of a footprint or ball-mark from yesterday. Perfection.

Inside the sprawling pink stucco Mediterranean-style villa, a low-ringing phone broke the long night's silence. A woman-servant's soft voice answered.

"Good morning. This is the Grey residence."

"Good morning. This is Dr. Arthur Pollack in New York. I must speak to Mrs. Grey."

"I'm sorry, doctor. I have not yet seen Mrs. Grey this morning."

"It's extremely urgent. Can you please get that message to her immediately?"

"Very well, sir. Please hold the line."

A gentle knock at the master suite. The servant opened one of the double doors.

"Sorry to disturb you madam. Dr. Pollack is calling from New York. Says it's urgent."

"Thank you, Maria, I'll take the call. Oh, Maria, tell Pascal only juice and coffee this morning. In about ten minutes please, on my bedroom terrace—too lovely to be inside this morning."

Walking to her white and gold-accented Louis XIV bedroom desk, the soft-spoken heiress picked-up her white French phone. At fifty-two, Ellen McCormack Grey was still a very beautiful woman. A few at the Colony and the Everglades had often mistaken her for a sister of her good friend, Dina Merrill.

Ash blond, medium height, soft elegant face, small athletic chest, Ellen had the body of a woman at least a dozen years her junior. She was well spoken and well liked. Unfortunately, throughout her life she was heavily burdened with all of the neurotic insecurities—and fragile psyche—common to many offspring of dominating, controlling, fathers. And the hugely successful, multi-millionaire builder, James J. (Buck) McCormack, was certainly those things. And a whole lot more.

Yet, in spite of, or maybe because of, her own background and a lifetime of emotional difficulties, Ellen had been a warm and loving mother to her three children. Always available and understanding of their needs. In return, all three had a deep and abiding love for her.

All in all, they had been a close and caring family, including Gar—whenever he had been home. Which was not frequently.

"Good morning, Arthur. Is something wrong?"

"Hello, Ellen. Sorry to break in on your morning. Are you alone?"

"Alone? Yes, I'm alone, except for the servants. But I'm fine. I'm O.K. You know there's always so much planning to do down here before the season really starts, and Gar will be down tomorrow. You know that makes everything so much more pleasant for me. We both so enjoy our rare private time together," she went on.

"If you are calling for Gar, Arthur, he's still in New York."

"No, dear. I'm not calling *for* Gar. I'm calling *about* him."

"Why? Is he sick? Has he been hurt? What's wrong?"

"No. Not sick or hurt, Ellen. It's worse—much worse. And I'm so deeply sorry to be the one to have to tell you this—and on the phone. But—Gar's dead, dear.

So far as we know now, it seems that he committed suicide at home—sometime last night. We're still waiting for more information. Cliff Blair just called me."

Ellen McCormack Grey shrieked, "Nooooo!"

And slowly crumbled to the floor.

Her maid, Maria, heard the scream—and came bolting through the door.

FIVE

Flashback: Portofino. October, 1969.

Captain Giovanni Auriello, commanding the second largest personal cruise ship afloat, Gar Grey's spectacular 325ft. gleaming white yacht, Emperor II, carefully guided his huge ship out of the crowded Barcelona harbor.

Spain's greatest seaport faces Southeast, across the blue-green Mediterranean toward the fabled islands of Majorca and Sardinia. Emperor II's next ports of call.

Aboard: A complement of 16 Officers, 123 staff and crew. *Two passengers.*

Two passengers on-board Emperor II was much the same as two people alone in the Empire State Building.

Finally, waved clear by the Catalonian harbor authorities, the meticulous sea captain relaxed, lit up his ever-present pipe, and thought about the likely activity taking place in his owner's expansive, mahogany-paneled, state-room-suite—then half-smiled to himself.

Ursula was not a new face.

He had carried these two before. Alone together.

Inasmuch as the Captain had arranged for some ship's mechanical work to be done in Genoa—three weeks later—Nice to Genoa, was the last leg of the glorious cruise.

The waters of the Gulf of Genoa were peaceful and calm. The early Fall Mediterranean air, somehow managing to delay summer's end, seemed more deliciously intoxicating than usual.

Captain Auriello slowly nosed Emperor II into this busiest of all Italian ports. At the very sight of this breathtaking, 325ft. floating mansion, on nearby vessels sailors gawked and ship's horns blew. As she slowly moved upharbor, nearby seamen stood rigidly straight and saluted. On his bridge, in acknowledgment, Captain Auriello politely nodded—and touched his cap's peak.

The Emperor had landed!

There, the two passengers aboard disembarked. The famous and handsome owner—George Garfield Grey. And his very much younger, frequent globetrotting companion, the celebrated international model, Ursula Von Ribbentrop. Yes—she was the great grandniece of the infamous WWII German Foreign Minister. And the paparazzi constantly searched for these two famous faces. They would not be found today.

By then—his car also had been put ashore. Freshly polished. Chrome gleaming.

With its two sun-tanned, sun-glassed, occupants in place, the sporty bright-red, two-door Lamborghini raced down the curvy Riviera di Levante headed for Portofino, described by Sir Winston, who loved to paint there, as perhaps the most beautiful stretch of coastline in the world.

On the left, timeless hills thrust up from the narrow roadway. The ultra-sleek driving machine flew by luxurious villas of Mediterranean, medieval, and art nouveau architecture—liberally sprinkled up and down those hills. Their pinks, yellows, greens and blues, creating exquisite images of Monet-like paintings.

Off to the right, the magnificent Mar Ligure, as the Italians call that part of the Mediterranean Sea, sparkled like diamonds.

But scenery was not much on the mind of today's high-spirited driver—whose destination choice was not an accident. Almost nothing in Gar Grey's life was accidental. Portofino was one of his favorite hiding places.

The smiling owner of the exclusive hide-a-way for the very rich, a long and trusted friend, greeted them at the door. He was expecting his near-royal guest and knew a public restaurant was not on Gar's short-list.

Immediately ensconced—his most wanted food and drink were waiting on an incredibly beautiful table set with crystal, silver, and linen the cool color of the sea below. Including two bottles of his favorite vintage Cristàl champagne—chilling in their buckets.

Of course, it would all wait. Ursula would satisfy him first. That's what she was there for—had even trained for—and had no false illusions.

She had heard his philosophy myriad times.

"Fuck the money—everybody's got their price—anything you want can be bought."

Ursula cringed whenever he carried on. Educated at the best schools, the sophisticated Ursula was extremely intelligent in the old European tradition. Ways that most Americans simply do not even begin to comprehend.

Perhaps as an act of defiance against the old ways, Ursula lived a fast and glittering life. And no apologies offered. In profusion, Gar heaped all the material things of life upon her. In turn, she indulged herself in every possible way.

Someday—when their biopsychic tugs of war ceased—Ursula knew she had to lose. The name of the game was "Rich Man's Choice."

The partner with the most gold wins. No exceptions.

But, Ursula also knew that that would not be the end of her world. There were others before Gar—and there would be other rich men in her life after him.

If you traveled in the right circles—they would find her. They always did. They always would. Ursula would make sure of that.

1970. Cap d'Antibes.

Ursula? For sure, gorgeous. And that incredible body! Maybe the best sex Gar ever had. But there were many Ursulas—everywhere in the world. Other names. Other international watering holes. But they were there.

Their type was only about gifts—generous and often.

Furs. Jewelry. Designer-clothes. Skin tight jeans—mostly white.

Lots and lots of shoes. And cash to stash or to do all the silly little things that seem to please exquisitely beautiful models—when not on their backs or knees.

Keeping your current fella happy is the cardinal rule some girls learn, certainly by fifteen or sixteen, if they have their eyes set on a certain kind of future lifestyle. You have to become really great—world-class—at your chosen craft.

Sort of like the famous mob moll, Virginia Hill, back in the '50s, who appeared before the Senate's McClellan Investigating Committee. A member of that committee, Senator Charles Tobey of Vermont, was not satisfied with Hill's responses as to why so many hoods continued to give her big-money gifts over such a long period of time.

Then, in a media-closed session, Hill, finally pushed to the wall by Senator Tobey, loudly answered for all to hear—and for the Congressional Record,

"Because I'm the best cocksucker in the world. That's why, Senator—sir."

And all kinds of sex are still the service-of-choice in determining gifts between friends who keep score.

For Ursula that was easy.

At home in West Berlin, she had learned to be the best 'everything' by age fifteen. Even a favorite man-friend whom she called 'uncle' readily agreed. A high British diplomat posted to the former German capital.

Money was easiest for Gar, too.

No questions. No strings. No guilt.

And always—total control.

1972. Biarritz.

Even for the problems of the ultra-rich, life has never provided easy answers. Gar's need to totally control every detailed facet of his life, business as well as personal, lay deep in his psyche. Not easily surfaced without years of psychotherapy—even psychoanalysis. A long road.

Since he was a youngster, he had known that 'control' was a big part of his emotional core. Even with childhood playmates, it always had to be his choice—his game—or he didn't play. "But why? He asked himself. Genetic?"

He thought about his father. "Like Father like Son?" Someone once said, "It could be insecurity, you know." Gar Grey emotionally insecure? Now there's a hooter.

Once more, Ursula reached for him.

In her gently pumping hand, Gar started to get hard again. Ursula's nipples had stretched to their fullest. She pushed one into Gar's mouth. He sucked like a baby. It was warm and comforting. But, only prelude to the night's sexual symphony to be performed in a key of multiple orgasms—and many encores. Two bodies in perfect harmony. Bravo!

1975. Mykonos.

Aboard Emperor II, anchored near the fabled Greek isle, lying softly in each other's arms, Gar and Ursula, these extravagantly drained lovers, drifted off.

For the moment, George Garfield Grey had found peace.

SIX

Beverly Hills. November, 1975.

In her ultra-spacious condo on the posh 'Wilshire Corridor,' Cheryl Blake was hurriedly finishing dressing. Tall, raven-haired, and strikingly chic, the very successful executive recruiter was already running late for an early-morning breakfast meeting at the Polo Lounge.

Surrounded by an expensive collage of mauves and soft greens—set against linen-white walls—life for Cheryl had become wonderfully sweet.

For many years now, most often with Gar's help, Cheryl had ranked high on the annual Partners List—the heavy-hitting rainmakers—among the eighty-seven world-wide partners in Kramer-Franklin, one of the largest executive recruiting firms in the world.

And this morning she was meeting with her Board Chairman, Larry Kramer, to discuss a new search she had just taken on—an international search—that would again take the glamorous, well-traveled, Cheryl to London and Paris.

She was about to open the door for a mad dash to the garage elevator, when she was stopped in her tracks by the ringing phone on her private line.

"It must be Gar," she thought, as she dashed back to answer.

"Hi darling," in her sexy, husky, voice—a voice that always thrilled Gar. He heard it as a siren's call. Simply sent tingles down his spine. Down his cock, too—with appropriate positive reaction. It had been that way for the nearly five years they had been 'together.'

Of course Cheryl had no knowledge of his long-standing affair with Ursula—and vice versa. Gar always told Cheryl she was the world's best 'voice-fuck.' They spent hours on the phone, from everywhere in the world. Talking dirty. Getting each other 'off.' Her pussy constantly 'creamed.' Nipples hard. Cheryl loved their long distance phone sex, desperately needing her daily orgasms.

Ever since she was only thirteen, she had been the masturbating champion of her class. Young girls do count, and they do talk—to all of their best friends.

Gar had the same driven body. The same physical needs. The more, the better. Time never mattered. The two of them could hardly keep their hands off each other.

"Good morning, Cheryl. Cliff Blair here. Sorry to be on your private line, but—"

Cheryl cut in, "It's O.K, Cliff. I just automatically thought it was Gar. But I know you've got the number for an emergency. So, what's up? Has Gar changed his travel plans?"

"I'm afraid so. I—well. I might as well give it to you straight, Cheryl. Gar's dead. He committed suicide last night. We just heard a few minutes ago. And I wanted to reach you as quickly as possible."

"What did you say, Cliff…?"

The phone dangled crazily on the end of its cord.

In Manhattan, Sal Bellini had just entered his law office on Centre Street, across from the Criminal Court Building, through his private side door. This allowed him to take a few minutes to make-ready for his always-crowded daily schedule. But, almost immediately, his secretary burst into his private office. She looked as though she had just seen a ghost.

"Oh, Mr. Bellini! I'm so glad you're in a little early this morning. Mr. Blair just phoned. He asked that you get uptown as soon as possible.

He said—I'm quite sure he said—Mr. Grey committed suicide last night!"

Salvatore Antonio Bellini was not a man easily moved, or quickly shaken. He had seen too much of life for that. Remembered too much from his early days of struggle and fighting, just to survive, on the filthy streets of New York's Little Italy.

The suave, seventy-five year old, Bellini had been both lawyer and confidante to George Garfield Grey from the beginning. Having played a key role in the big corporate takeovers that put Gar on the fast track.

As both General Counsel and a Director of General Industrial, he and Gar shared many top secrets. Corporate and personal. Secrets that these kind of men silently take to their graves.

The distinguished gray-haired lawyer, wearing aviator-style glasses, whose dark tint and steel rims strongly suggested his good friend, Carmine DeSapio, the Democratic boss of New York City's Tammany Hall. As always, Bellini was attired in a custom-made dark blue suit; light blue shirt monogrammed on the left cuff; small-print blue tie; soft-blue silk square in his upper-left jacket pocket. Picture-perfect.

The lawyer firmly commanded, "Cancel all my appointments. Tell Rocco to bring the car around to the side door in five minutes. Call Blair. I'm on my way uptown. He can reach me in the car and he's not to do or say anything to anybody till I get up there."

As soon as the secretary closed the door behind her, Bellini walked over to a handsome Italian walnut cabinet, its rich patina glowing, and unlocked the doors.

Inside, the cabinet held a secret, voice-activated, recording system, and a disguised wall safe buried into the concrete wall behind. The cabinet could not be moved. Always at the ready, the combination opened with only a half turn. From a smaller inner-locked compartment, Bellini withdrew an envelope he had placed there many years ago. On the front, in Grey's unmistakably childish handwriting was scribbled,

"Sal—
Open this, when you get the news.
G.G.G."

The lawyer reached for his letter-opener.

High in a towering Chicago office building on LaSalle Street, inside the World Headquarters of McCormack International Construction Corporation, seventy-four year old Founding Chairman and CEO James J. (Buck) McCormack had arrived only moments before to preside over a crucial financial meeting.

In global construction circles, McCormack International was world-ranked second only to the even more-renowned San Francisco-based Bechtel Corporation.

Today's confidential agenda centered on the highly complex $4.3 billion global-financing of a state-of-the-art steel mill his company was planning to build for Mitsubishi Heavy Industries in Japan. Volumes of Plans and Specs were already signed-off and leather bound. So once the financing was set, construction could begin.

As usual, Buck, was just itching to get the huge project moving. He had been ready for six months—pushing his project managers, designers, engineers, and draftsmen. After many rounds of negotiations in New York and Tokyo, today could signal a final green light.

Everyone at the meeting was anxious and tense

The 'boss', as everyone who knew Buck McCormack referred to him, was naturally seated at the head of the huge conference table, surrounded by international bankers, his corporate financial advisors—and Gar's father.

The near-eighty year-old Lucien Smith Grey was still Chairman of First Illinois National—Buck's longtime American lead-banker, personal investment advisor, and one of his oldest friends in Chicago.

With nearly all of the attendees dressed in dark blue or black suits, the scene mostly resembled a United Nations Security Council meeting.

An aide quietly handed the boss a folded note. It was a message to call his wife—marked urgent! Silently he thought, "Maggy's too smart to mislead me." The burly, ex-steamfitter excused himself from the boardroom and hurried back to his massive corner office. On a private line, he personally dialed his home in suburban Kenilworth.

His butler, Charles, answered.

"Where's the Mrs.?" The boss barked.

"I'll get her for you immediately, sir. She's waiting in the library."

"Buck, dear," she said softly.

"Maggy, what the hell's so important to get me out of that Jap meeting? You know how goddam sensitive those little bastards are!"

"Buck—it's terrible," her voice trembling.

More gently now. "What's wrong, Maggy—what is it?"

"Ellen just called from Palm Beach, sobbing like a baby. She said—oh Buck, she said Gar committed suicide last night at home, in New York. She's just falling apart. You know he's her whole world."

"Holy shit," the 'Boss' automatically reacted.

However, to himself: "Some gorgeous whore probably fucked him to death."

Out loud, again: "That crazy son-of-a-bitch," he now roared.

"Maggy stay right where you are!

I'll call New York. Then I'll call Ellen. Try to stay calm.

I'll call you back just as soon as I can!"

The line went dead in Maggy's ear.

Buck was already banging on his intercom button—and shouting,

"Get me Cliff Blair in New York."

Almost simultaneously—it hit him.

"Jesus, his Father is sitting in my Boardroom—and he doesn't even know yet.

Cancel that call!"

Lucien Smith Grey, the banker—had literally created James J. (Buck) McCormack, the builder. Some thirty-five years back, when Buck had badly wanted to get a start in the construction business he had great ambition, but no money. After many bank rejections for a small loan, it was Lucien Grey's bank that gave him an unsecured $250 loan to buy his first truck—very used. And Buck never forgot.

Whatever his corporate financial needs grew to be, and his requirements became enormous, he never did business with another Chicago bank. And, over the years, Buck and Lucien had become close personal friends.

They were both from the old school, and shared old-fashioned common values. Like loyalty, honesty, and integrity.

Lucien had often told his loan officers,

"Buck McCormack can have the keys to this bank, on his word alone."

Such was their shared trust.

Buck hit his intercom again.

"Somebody go into the boardroom and whisper in Mr. Grey's ear that I'd like to see him here in my office.

"And I mean whisper!"

SEVEN

It was preordained that Gar ultimately would gravitate toward money and power. He would never know another way.

When he was born, in 1918, in the big Tudor house in suburban Kenilworth overlooking Lake Michigan, his father, Lucien Smith Grey, was already the President of First Illinois National, the family's powerful Chicago bank. As such, he had a great deal of influence in the city's ruling circles.

His mother, the former Mary (Molly) Garfield, was the only daughter of James Abram Garfield of Ohio, the 20th President of the United States. Politics had been an integral part of Molly's daily life for as long as she could remember. Consequently, money, power, and politics were in the bloodlines—on both sides.

Gar, and his sister Charlotte, two years younger, grew up in an atmosphere heavy with lavish society dinner parties and elaborate political receptions. All attended by the rich industrial and political leaders of the city. The very top Chicago Democrats. And the strongly Republican downstate lions from the capitol in Springfield. And, very often, by famous visiting dignitaries from Washington and New York.

In 1932, the Democratic National Convention was held in Chicago. Only fourteen at the time, Gar got his first close-up look at what power and politics was really all about.

The panic and depression set off by the 1929 Wall Street Crash had considerably deepened. The mood of the nation was now grim and growing desperate. There were no jobs to be had. Nowhere to turn. No benefits. Nothing!

Sell an apple on the corner. Who cared? Certainly not Uncle Sam. The Federal government was simply not in the 'people' business. Never had been.

Continuing a longtime Republican philosophy, Hoover followers still preached, "People are responsible for themselves."

On the other hand, Lucien was constantly referring to the fact that, "Someone has to do something to stop the run on the deposits at the banks or we'll all have to close our doors. Things are so bad, it might even cause a revolution in the streets—damn near unthinkable."

Then he added, "This New York governor, Roosevelt, might be the right man to do the job."

Gar had great difficulty trying to understand what his father was talking about. Any fourteen-year old would have been bewildered. Nevertheless, Gar had been completely caught-up in the excitement of it all. He never imagined that politics could be so interesting. His school classes surely hadn't prepared him for anything like this.

His father took him everywhere and encouraged him to learn and understand that this was the reality of life. These were the things that counted most. Gar knew, right then and there, that this was the way he wanted to be involved when his time came.

Absorbing it all like a brand new sponge, he loved every minute of it.

As the convention opened, he met some of the most important Democrats in the country at a meeting that took place at the Drake Hotel. It was held in Lucky Luciano's suite. The Mafia boss held a lot of votes in his pocket—and in the final analysis conventions are only about votes.

Gar was introduced to the popular Mayor Curley of Boston. The Mayor was busy introducing everyone to a very rich and important Beantown friend—an aggressive, bespectacled Irishman. His name was Joseph P. Kennedy.

Other big-city bosses were there too. Men like tough Frank Hague, the Mayor and 'owner' of Jersey City. And 'Boss' Tom Pendergast of Kansas City, who also had friends with him. An unknown haberdasher named Jacobson, and a small quiet man who wore old-fashioned glasses and liked his bourbon. They called him 'Judge.' His real name was Harry Truman.

Gar also met a very loud, brassy pol from Louisiana, who talked with an accent that Gar found funny—like his mouth was full of cotton. Even his name sounded funny.

It was Huey—Huey Long.

But all the pols called him 'Kingfish.' The boy thought that was even funnier.

But the most important thing to Lucien was that all of these men, clean or dirty, were for Roosevelt—for a political price, of course. Everybody had a price. But the price had to be paid, and a deal was struck. Shortly after that, all hell broke loose.

Jimmy Walker resigned as Mayor of New York City. And quickly sailed off to Paris.

Tammany Hall was shattered. All the NYC wise guys pissed and moaned, "The good old days are gone forever. All the easy money's gone."

Maybe. Maybe not.

Either way, for fourteen-year old Gar, that brawl, called the 1932 Democratic National Convention, made a huge impression.

Power. Influence. Dealing.

Cut any kind of a deal. Do whatever it takes.

The name of the game is winning—nothing else counts! And this became the criterion, carved in stone, for the rest of Gar's life.

"I'm going to be a winner—that's for sure. Anything less is bullshit."

In 1936, when Gar graduated from New Trier High, it was just assumed that he would enter Northwestern University, in nearby Evanston, then go on to Harvard Law as did his Father and Grandfather before him. However, by 1940, with Europe already at war, his parents felt that their only son should remain closer to home. So Gar did not go East, but rather entered Northwestern Law School.

There was one big change in his life, however, to which his parents did not object. Gar moved out of the big family Tudor and into a fraternity house on campus.

On December 7, 1941, with the attack on Pearl Harbor, everything changed for Gar—and all of America's young men. After much thought, one Saturday while visiting his parents, Gar announced that he had made up his mind to volunteer for the Air Corps, and was planning to do it the coming week. As fate would have it, during his physical exam, it was discovered that he had some hearing impairment in his left ear. He was turned down for service and placed in 4F.

This unexpected turn of events would loom large and lucky in his future. It meant that while others would be off fighting a war, Gar would be allowed to get his law degree on schedule. In time to take full advantage of the boom he felt sure would take place when the war was over.

While naturally bright, as an undergraduate Gar had mostly loafed along academically. However, law school was now quite another matter. He was determined to make 'Law Review' as both his Father and Grandfather did at Harvard. He wanted to be first in his class. For the law to become almost an extension of himself.

In Gar's mind, mediocrity and failure were the same

thing. And being just another journeyman lawyer was not at all what he had in mind for his future. So the law library became the new focal point in his campus life.

As the fall semester wore on most of the same guys became daily library 'regulars.' And it was there that Gar started a casual talking relationship with a fellow student, David Ross, a very intense young man from the Westside slums of Chicago, who was at Northwestern on a full scholarship.

A pleasant-looking, slim young man of medium height, brown hair, and burning brown eyes, David was the first Jewish friend Gar ever had. And he often thought something unusual must have been driving his new friend.

Gar had never met anyone who was so dedicated to learning. To achieve his lofty goals, David was more deeply committed to learning the law better than anyone else.

Were Jews really different?

As their friendship grew, Gar learned that David never had the time or the money for a real date. Though, secretly, he did have a crush on Rachel Stone, who had been in his class at high school.

He also learned that David had worked in his Father's grocery store from the time he was old enough to handle a mop and a broom. Later on, after school, making deliveries on his bicycle. But Gar recognized that these hardships had also built a strong character and generated fierce ambition.

David already had decided that he would devote his future legal career to fighting for social justice. That he could help, perhaps even lead, the fight to change some of the world's outrageous conditions—such as the terrible acts of anti-Semitism in Germany. Nobody, then, would have ever believed the Holocaust that was to follow.

In time, he hoped that he also would be able to help his long-suffering immigrant parents, as well as downtrodden people of every race, creed, or color.

The two budding lawyers were rapidly expanding their

friendship, quizzing each other for exams, having a common professional goal—but for very different reasons.

Gar was already planning his law future with great care. He saw something very valuable in David. In their second year in law school, Gar began planting the seeds for the two of them to form a law practice together. Gar, with his well-established family connections, knew that becoming a top-notch 'rainmaker' would become his most productive area. A great 'outside' man.

On the other hand, he felt David would be a perfect 'inside' man for the partnership. Impeccably honest, a brilliant law scholar, a tireless worker. It was a great team for all that Gar had spinning in his mind.

Throwing his head back and laughing, Gar would shout over and over again to David,

"Look out world—the partners are coming!"

EIGHT

Gar had matured into a handsome six-footer with a cool smile and an easy-smooth personality. He had become one of the most sought-after 'dates' on campus. And while his social life was a constant whirl with many weekend conquests, by Spring he had begun to concentrate on Nancy Lee Hendrix, a vivacious hazel-eyed brunette, who had come north to college from the deep-south. Magnolia Springs, Alabama.

They had met at a fraternity-sorority party during the winter and the chemistry between them seemed to ignite from the very first moment. It had been an informal party, and Nancy, in a matching turquoise skirt and sweater, had attracted Gar's attention from the instant he had spotted her on the dance floor early in the evening.

He was greatly taken with Nancy's soft southern drawl and, even more, with her full-blown southern body.

With his usual aggressiveness, he had 'cut in' on her dancing partner and introduced himself as they started to move to some Tommy Dorsey music. Frank Sinatra was singing.

"My name is Gar Grey, and whatever your name is I think you're the prettiest thing at this whole party," he opened. Charm oozed from every word.

He held her just a little too tightly.

"Ah'm Nancy Lee Hendrix—and ah must say Mr. Gar Grey that you Yankees do come right to the point now, don't you?" Then laughing, "And ah also must say that my Daddy does the same damn thing. So he'd probably agree with your course of action."

Instinctively, Nancy seemed to know the perfect way to snuggle up against Gar's strong young body. His manhood had an immediate response that did not embarrass him in the least.

Not Gar Grey. Not then. Not ever.

And his hardness did not go unchallenged by Nancy Lee either. She adjusted her body—in the right direction.

While dancing to Glenn Miller's romantic theme song, *Moonlight Serenade*, their adolescent hormones shifted into high gear. Nancy Lee and Gar were now only aware of each other. The music sounded very far away and the other couples seemed to have disappeared from the dance floor.

"How does a pretty Nancy Lee from warm Alabama feel about our northern winters?" Gar breathed into her hair.

"Cold—damn cold. Ah just seem to be cold all the time," she replied, faking a slight shudder for Gar's physical benefit.

"Well then, young lady, your Dr. Grey prescribes a roaring fire as the perfect remedy."

"Ah give in Doctor—you all just might lead me now to your remedy," she encouraged.

Gar lead the way off the dance floor into the adjoining lounge, a comfortable room with a heavy beamed ceiling and a rugged stone fireplace that stretched all the way up to the beamed ceiling. He motioned to a large leather couch that faced the fireplace.

Nancy Lee curled up in the far corner tucking her shapely legs underneath, then looked invitingly up at Gar who immediately put himself down so comfortably close to her that he could feel the delicious shape of her soft thigh through her skirt.

The fire was warm and crackly. They stared hypnotically at it for a long time, without speaking—with Gar studying Nancy Lee out of the corner of his eye. He could already imagine what that soft tender body would feel like underneath him.

While not a virgin, Nancy Lee had only been with a boy once. In High School, on a dare, back in staid Alabama where 'nice' God-fearing young girls just didn't do those kinds of things.

Her Father would have 'killed' her.

And her older brother? Don't even think about it.

She remembered it as nothing much. Frenzied. Quick. Over. And it hurt too. Not the kind of experience young girls dream about and look forward to with great expectations. Nancy Lee thought to herself, "Gar would be different," and she would be willing—she knew that the minute they had started dancing.

"Nancy Lee, I live in Kenilworth. That's not very far from here. And my parents are in Florida." Then, laughingly but hopefully, added, "Would you like to see my etchings?"

"Ah didn't think you were a collector already, Gar."

"Not real art, Nancy Lee, but certain pretty Alabama girls—well that's a whole different kind of artistic story. How about it?"

Looking over at him from her corner of the couch, and with a flirty look, Nancy Lee softly coooed, "Do you think ah might be cold?"

Gar, now standing, looked down at her lovely glowing face and then sat down again. Moving very close to her lips. "Not tonight, my sweet Nancy Lee—no way."

On the drive out Sheridan Road in his new Packard convertible, Gar had the heater on high, and the radio on low. Nancy Lee sat wonderfully close.

Neither talked, but their silence could have filled a lover's dream book. Soon Gar turned into the familiar driveway leading to the big Tudor house. The house was dark. The servants long asleep. Expecting no one—least of all, 'Mr. Gar.'

As soon as he had turned off the motor, Gar took Nancy Lee into his arms kissing her long and tenderly. Her lips parted. Gar's hands worked their way under her coat, sweater, and bra. Over her full, round breasts.

They both heard their song—but the radio wasn't on.

Gar found his keys and they were inside the house.

He quietly led the way into the library.

Turning on a small lamp he moved quickly to Nancy Lee and again took her into his arms. This time kissing her harder and pulling her tightly against his very hard erection. From deep down Nancy Lee was tingling with anticipation.

Convinced the moment was now, Gar took her hand and headed for the huge curving staircase. At the top they walked down the long hall to his old bedroom. From the time he was an infant until he moved into the fraternity house, it was the only bedroom Gar had ever known.

He smiled to himself. His fantasy in that bedroom was to be on a Little League championship baseball team. And then to play for the Chicago Cubs.

Sitting on the edge of the bed, Nancy Lee slowly pulled her sweater over her head. Turning her back to him, he unhooked her bra with fingers that Nancy Lee was sure had undone many bras before hers. Actually that reassured her.

"One of us should know what we're doing," she said silently.

Naked now from the waist up, she turned to him, her breasts squarely in front of his face. Gar leaned down and took her nipple into his eager hot mouth and applied slight pressure. He heard her catch her breath.

Gar said, "Let's get undressed."

Totally naked, she pulled back the spread from Gar's bed and stretched out fully.

A naked Gar slid into the bed next to her.

"Nancy Lee, you're the most beautiful girl I've ever known. Honest."

Completely on fire, the two young bodies were exploring each other everywhere, without the slightest hesitation. Gar touched and played with her in all the 'good' places. Nancy Lee held him firmly. Thrilled by his size and strength.

In one motion, he suddenly mounted and thrust himself inside. In less than twenty seconds, rocking furiously and breathing heavily, Gar wailed,

"Nancy Lee—oooohhh Naaancy."

Nancy Lee vaguely remembered hearing a wail.

But there had been *two* of them.

In the afterglow, she silently vowed,

"I'll never leave him—*never!*"

NINE

Because of his genuine affection, as well as his planning for the future, Gar saw to it that he and David became inseparable during their first years in law school—Gar always being the leader. Whenever there was a moment to be spared from studying, Gar made sure that David did not lack for outside friends or activities to busy himself with.

The fact that David was Jewish had long since vanished from Gar's mind. The rare times that the thought still entered his head brought a smile to his face. Whatever had made him think that Jews were different?

Of course he knew the answer.

His parents. His church. His friends.

Gar smiled. David was terrific. And that was that.

He took a special delight in the fact that David was such a brilliant law student—ranking second in their class for the first two years. And never missed an opportunity to push that fact.

If any fellow law student was having a problem, and it came to Gar's attention, he would always suggest to David that a little bit of tutoring from him might solve their friend's difficulty.

To please Gar, and his own ego, David would be more than willing to lend an academic hand. And rarely did he fail in getting things back on track.

A fraternity brother of Gar's, Billy Mason, was David's most chronic case. A pleasant young man, slight of build and mild mannered, he would very often seek David's help. Yet, somehow, David had the strange feeling that Billy understood the legal material far better than he would ever admit.

David told Gar at lunch one day, "As a matter of fact, sometimes I have the feeling that Billy asks for help a lot more often than he really needs it."

Gar shot back, "What the hell for?"

"Damned if I know," replied David, "but he sure can be a pain in the ass."

Noting David's genuine irritation, and feeling responsible for Billy in the first place, Gar suggested, "If he really bugs you, tell him to fuck off."

David smiled back, "O.K. Boss,"

A few nights later at the fraternity house, Gar and David, along with others, were having a bull session in the lounge, when Billy came down from his room.

"David would you come upstairs for a minute? I really need some help on an assignment." Remembering his recent conversation with David regarding Billy, Gar was about to say something, when David shot him a glance. Gar said nothing.

"I don't have too much time Billy, but come on let's see what your problem is."

With that he followed Billy up the stairs. David sat down at the desk and started to read the case problem. Billy was sitting on the bed listening to David's explanation, asking some questions.

As before, David had the same uneasy feeling. "Billy knows enough about this assignment. He doesn't need me." His anger was rising.

By this time Billy also was at the desk, his arm draped loosely around David's shoulder. "Well, Billy, that about does it," David said as he pushed his chair back and stood up.

"David you know I always appreciate your help—I really do."

Without another word, Billy moved closely up to David, put his arms around his neck, and kissed him full on the mouth.

At the very same instant, deciding that he'd better come upstairs and bale his buddy out, Gar opened the door and burst in on what seemed to be a mutual embrace.

Stunned at the sight of Billy and David, Gar muttered,

"Well, I'll be a son-of-a-bitch. Sorry for butting in on the romance fellas—have fun."

Slamming the door, he was gone as quickly as he had appeared.

David vehemently shoved Billy away from him, screaming, "You goddam little fag—you fucking little fag bastard. I should break your fucking head."

Aggressively, David pulled the door open and raced down the steps after Gar.

Wildly disoriented from the entire incident, David found the lounge completely deserted. Up the stairs two at a time, he bolted into Gar's room and found his friend casually sitting, tapping his foot, obviously expecting David any second.

"And what do we have here," Gar smart-assed, "Lady Chatterly or her Lover?"

"Cut the shit, Gar. You know damn well that I thought Billy had something else on his mind besides law. That crazy little fag bastard just put his arms around me and kissed me—before I even knew what was happening."

Gar, already a people-user, sensed he had something valuable here and wanted to squeeze just a little more future juice out of the incident.

Smiling cynically, "Look David, just think what you'll

be able to tell your children. Boys will be boys—only some will be girls—*some* of the time."

Belly-laughing at his own lines, "Forget it kid—see you in class in the morning."

The summer before the start of his senior year in law school, Gar's Father got him a vacation job as a law intern in the office of the City Attorney of Chicago. A job that brought him into contact with the real workings of the city on a day-to-day basis.

Chicago was running as wide open as in the days of the 'roaring twenties.'

Bookie wire rooms were visible from the streets and political hacks were in control of many city agencies. The Bookie's main revenues came from horse racing. And the founder of the number-one racing news wire in America was the wily Moses Annenberg. His rag sheet, *'The Daily Racing Form'* was the original source of that gigantic family fortune.

Introduced to the mob at their famous Atlantic City Conference in 1929, by his good friend the murdering Al Capone, Annenberg's Nationwide News Service, was actually a partnership with Mafia bosses Lansky, Luciano, and Costello.

Many years later, Annenberg's son, Walter, a widely respected philanthropist, was appointed Ambassador to England by President Richard Nixon, who always had a great eye for gift-givers.

And it also was at Walter Annnenberg's opulent Palm Springs estate, that President and Nancy Reagan always found so much peace and comfort.

An old New York pol once said, "You can go to bed with dogs—but if you have enough money—spread it in the right political places—and keep it long enough—you don't get up with the same fleas as ordinary people do."

Meanwhile, Lucien Grey's old friend, Richard J. Daley, already a member of the State Legislature, was given the most politically-sensitive, non-elective, job in the Cook County government—that of Comptroller. Gar's summer job brought him into only fleeting contact with Daley, but the rising pol certainly wanted to please Lucien Grey, one of the most powerful bankers in Chicago.

Gar was given total clearance.

He had access to much valuable information.

For example, he was able to find out which contractors were being favored with big public works contracts, and which suppliers were 'in' with the Purchasing Managers of the city hospitals.

And it didn't hurt to understand how and why rate increases were so easily granted to utility and transportation companies; and most importantly, how rezoning and a few choice variances, could send the value of a piece of property sky-rocketing with the stroke of a pen.

Handy stuff to know for a soon-to-be Chicago lawyer. Gar stored it all safely away—like a squirrel.

Of course, in most all of these machinations some loyal Democrat got a piece of the action. However, meaningful rewards also found their way into his Republican Father's bank. There was room for all. And forget that all this hanky-panky was occurring despite the terrible pain of the Great Depression.

Roosevelt and his 'New Deal' notwithstanding, the Depression dragged on until the start of World War II. Someday, New Deal economic history will need a serious reality check. Many of FDR's pronouncements and much historical economic fact simply don't wash.

A friend told Gar about FDR's plan to 'pack' the Supreme Court? Somehow, he had not heard about it. And his response was typically forthright.

"Stop jerking me around—no president would get such a screwball idea."

In young Gar's mind, it was the 1932 convention all over

again. All of this information was mind-boggling to him. It excited him even more than sex—and that was saying a lot.

And it was only ten months now—only ten months until he would graduate from law school. Then he would fight like hell for a chance to put his own finger in that big—fat—bottomless—public-pie.

Gar started to count the days. He could hardly wait to get his tires down on that fast track.

"David can you believe it—only ten more months. Wow!"

Ever the pragmatic one, David responded, "Think you'll pass the bar exam on your first shot?" Grinning broadly, Gar answered, "I'll cheat, if I have to—but I'll pass—*nothing's* going to hold me back."

Not at all sure if Gar was serious or not, David didn't reply.

From Gar: "Hey Mr. Straight-Arrow, don't be so damn serious."

But David was very bothered. Honesty had always been a cornerstone of his core value system. But you just never knew with Gar Grey. He always wanted you off-balance.

"Was he for real? Would he really cheat?" David had to admit to himself, he wasn't totally sure. Was Gar just being flip?"

"Shit," David muttered to himself, "why is he always muddying-up the water?"

It was not an accident.

It was never an accident with Gar.

'Control' was everything. To be achieved by any method—at any cost—to anyone.

But, David constantly challenged him.

"You want to control the whole world. Dammit. Maybe the whole fucking Universe."

In a patronizing voice, Gar said,

"For openers, let's just start with Grey & Ross"

David shot back, "Fuck you. How about Ross & Grey?"

TEN

From the beginning of her memory, Ellen McCormack's life had been a series of disappointments and conflicts with her Father. It had always been a difficult and painful relationship. Rarely fun. Never happy. And those memories had left their indelible mark. She would emotionally suffer for the rest of her life.

In fact, many years later she would tell her psychiatrist that she had felt rejected by her Father as far back as she could remember.

Neither Father nor Daughter changed.

In the end, the genes always control. They never change.

When Ellen was born, Buck was already an iron-giant of a man, twenty-three years old. Her Mother, Margaret, whom everyone called Maggy, was just eighteen, and typically planned on having a large family. She told Buck, "The five er six children'll be helpful in supportin' ar family—n' evry family is surely needn' all the help it could get."

But Ellen would be the only child Buck and Maggy would bring into this world. Her birth had almost cost young Maggy her own life.

The near-tragedy only being averted by last-minute surgery which finally stopped the massive post-natal internal hemorrhaging.

However, the surgery performed by a relatively unskilled doctor, left Maggy unable to bear anymore children. That confirmation produced a serious depression lasting several months. And an unusually fierce protective bond with her new little baby. Maggy never took her eyes off of Ellen. Her constant fear was terribly stressful—and edged close to phobic.

Buck added to her stress. The straw-haired infant, with the soft emerald-green eyes, was an exquisite child. But if Maggy tried to put the baby into Buck's powerful arms, the big-man would turn white-as-a-ghost and as helpless as the baby he was juggling. Baby Ellen would smile and coo to her Daddy. Even then his huge strength generated her instinctive love.

But what was love?

Buck never knew what to do with the emotion of love. He was totally confused by Ellen's very existence. Yes, she was his daughter—flesh and blood—so he would protect her and provide for her. But 'love' was just another word to him. Emotionally, Buck was totally incapable of forming any positive response. Having never received any love, how could he respond? Obviously, he had no idea that he was damaging his child forever. Tragically, he didn't even have a clue.

Buck silently wondered, "For crissakes, how can a guy give somethin' away if he don't even knows what it is. Kin' I buy some love? Is it for sale in a store? Shit—it's confusin' as hell."

James J. (Buck) McCormack had been born and raised in a violent neighborhood on New York's teeming West Side, infamously known as Hell's Kitchen. An area disfigured with brick and lumberyards, slaughterhouses, and warehouses of every kind and description. Mixed in were blocks and blocks of squalid festering slums.

When Buck was born in 1901, it was one of the toughest sections of the city. Even the beat cops patrolled in fear. Only in daylight—and as little as possible.

The Hudson River Railroad laid tracks right down the middle of Tenth and Eleventh Avenues. And the poor neighborhood residents, mostly tough Irish and black laborers, ate that filthy soot and breathed that polluted smoke everyday of their lives.

Interracial gangfights were just another daily occurrence. As a young boy growing up in Hell's Kitchen, if you couldn't fight for your life—and win—you had no worry about becoming a man.

Buck McCormack learned to fight by five or six, but he never learned when to stop. He only knew the rough and tumble life that he had grown up with. He could not remember his Father, Tim, other than either half-dead from working or half-dead from drinking.

When Buck came into this world, Tim was a laborer in the construction gangs that worked on many of the huge projects that were changing the face of New York.

In 1904, Tim had been on the gang that carved out the tunnel for the city's first subway. Tim also had worked on the building of some of the fancy new hotels that were springing up all over upper Fifth Avenue.

The Plaza. The Savoy. And The New Netherland.

So, when Tim came home, no matter how cold the day had been, he was so wet with sweat that his first move would be to peel off his filthy shirt and undershirt and plunge his face and arms into a tub of cold water.

Working six or even seven days a week, Tim got home so late that there would be weeks on end when Buck did not see his father at all. That was what a growing Buck McCormack saw. That was all he ever knew about family life.

The McCormacks were a large family of seven children. Life was a constant struggle just to keep going. His Mother, Kate, was haggard and old looking long before her years. Just doing the cooking and laundry for her brood was enough to keep her going from sunrise to midnight.

As a result, she was in a continuing state of exhaustion

and sick most of the time. Tim paid scant attention to her or the children. It was everyone for themselves. These difficult family circumstances forced young Buck to go to work as soon as he could earn a nickel. After school, he did odd jobs in the lumberyards in the neighborhood.

He was nine years old.

Three years later, Tim brought his son with him for his first real job, laying new tracks for Commodore Vanderbilt's New York Central. The Central's tracks extended right up the middle of Park Avenue—all the way from the Commodore's new and breathtaking Grand Central Terminal. Buck never went back to school after that.

It was a typical New York summer—hot and humid. Carrying steel track and the enormous ties were enough to fell an animal leave alone a man. And a mere boy? Then, after work Tim would take his son with him as he joined the rest of the men at their favorite saloon. In those early years, it didn't take much cold beer to send Buck's head spinning. But just like street fighting—he learned fast. Now, strong as an ox, Buck could hold his own anywhere—including the brass rail at the bar.

Kate McCormack might not have had the time or ability to show her family any love, but she was always concerned about their moral well being. She still attended Holy Cross Roman Catholic Church on 42nd Street, as often as she possibly could.

And Kate was furious with Tim for taking Buck with him to the saloon and would upbraid him severely when Father and Son would come staggering home after many hours at the saloon. Greatly worried, Kate decided to talk to Father Duffy to seek the holy man's help and guidance.

It had been Father Duffy who always worked so hard to uplift Hell's Kitchen and break up the tough gangs that gave the area such an unsavory reputation.

Kate also knew that Father Duffy was well acquainted with many of the famous theater people who were bringing fame and fortune to the new 'Great White Way' of

New York. Not too far away—just over on Broadway & 42nd Street.

So, with a heavy heart, but determined not to let her first-born fall from grace, Kate entered the Church Rectory one August morning. She had to wait a bit. But soon, Father Duffy, who knew practically all of his flock by name, smilingly emerged to greet her. The mere sight of him made her feel better.

"Ahh, top o' the mornin' to ya Kate," the Father welcomed her. "What brings ya over this lovely day?"

Kate looked down at her soiled dress and clasped her hands together in her lap. Hesitant for a moment to speak badly about Tim to the Holy Man.

"Oh come now daughter—out with it—just come right out with it. Cain't be all that bad now," the Father said in his gentle rolling Irish tongue.

"Well Father, it's about my Tim and what I fear he's doin' to young Buck—now that the lad's workin' regular with him over on the tracks."

Father Duffy raised his eyebrows high into his forehead. "Now Kate, the boy's strong as iron, and a little hard work never hurt a person. It's a lot better'n fightin' in the streets ya know."

"It's not the hard work that's bothern' me, Father, it's what's goin' on after that's hurtin'. Ya see, Tim is takin' young Buck with him over to the saloon most every night and the two of 'em is draggin' in drunk as two skunks. And Father, he's only thirteen now ya know, strong though he be. I'd be mos' grateful to ya if ya cud help me wit this worry, Father?"

"Sure an ya know I will my dear Kate. So put yur mind to rest. Buck's a good boy, Kate, so go on home now and let me tend to the matter."

Father Duffy telephoned his good friend Father Kean, well aware that one of Father Kean's old friends, and a member of his church, was now the powerful and newly elected Assembly Speaker in Albany, Alfred E. Smith—

later to become a four-time Governor of New York and 1928 Democratic candidate for President.

Now climbing the tough political ladder, Al Smith was certainly in a position to lend a bit of help to a deserving young Irish Catholic boy. And Smith had a reputation for not being able to say 'no' to his old friend and confessor, Father Kean.

About ten days later, Father Kean phoned the good news. Smith had arranged a job for Buck at the Fulton Street Fish Market. Kate was overjoyed.

Buck would work from three o'clock in the morning until business ground to a halt in the afternoon. His pay would be two dollars a week and he would be allowed to take home some slightly spoiled fish. Otherwise, just, "throw the shit in the garbage," his boss would say.

Tim said, "What the hell's the matter with the job he's got? If it's good enough for me why isn't it good enough for the kid?"

Buck, on the other hand, was thinking about the word powerful.

He liked the way it sounded. Maybe it would be a word that would describe him someday. Ambition had struck. Soon, he was reading everything he could get his hands on. And the more he learned, the more he wanted to know.

"There's a powerful world out there," Buck told himself. "And I want to be powerful too."

In 1918, two very important things happened.

His Father's health finally broke after all the years of hard working and hard drinking. A short while later, Tim McCormack died. And Kate was left penniless. Through the charity of friends, the funeral expenses were paid.

Walking back to their flat, after the brief service, Kate muttered, "I jus' don' know where ta turn, wha' ta do."

Buck overheard his Mother's nearly inaudible words. Reacting, he took her arm, and said softly, "Don't worry Mama, I'm here. I kin take care of ya."

The other crucial event was even more important to

Buck. He now had a good friendship with Al Smith, the newly elected Governor of New York. Smith suggested a new job. Through mutual friends, Buck was steered toward a Manhattan trucking company that had tight political connections throughout the entire metropolitan area.

Buck was now earning three dollars a week. He was seventeen years old.

The trucking company did a lot of work in the construction industry. Best of all for Buck, he was becoming exposed to the building trades again, which is what he liked best of all ever since he worked as a ten-year old in the lumberyards of 'Hell's Kitchen.'

Building anything fascinated Buck. He hoped that someday he would get into the building business for himself.

In 1923, Buck met and married Margaret Riley, a nice quiet Irish Catholic girl from his own neighborhood. Kate was pleased to have Maggy for a daughter-in-law and felt sure that she would make Buck a good and faithful wife.

As for Buck, he simply thought it was time for him to get married. Maggy was a good, clean girl. And Buck thought he liked her.

What else was there to think about?

"Love? What the hell was that?"

ELEVEN

On January 16, 1919, the Eighteenth Amendment to the Constitution was ratified.

It banned the "manufacture, sale, and transportation, of intoxicating liquors and beers."

But Americans were not about to stop drinking.

They would just look elsewhere.

So the 'Roaring Twenties' were cued-up and Americans were ready to play.

The wannabe stars of a new and looser America were about to take center stage.

On the warm night of September 14, 1923, more than 82,000 people were stuffed into the New York Giants' venerable Polo Grounds to watch the popular heavyweight champion Jack Dempsey go against the Argentinean, Luis Angel Firpo, the 'Wild Bull of the Pampas.' Firpo knocked the Champ through the ropes into the laps of ringsiders. But Dempsey came back to floor Firpo nine times and destroyed Luis in just two rounds.

Charlie Luciano, by now the leading bootlegger in America, was hosting more than a hundred other hoods, judges, and assorted politicians, at ringside.

Buck McCormack was there too. With two friends from the trucking company. He was way out in the bleachers—but he was there. As Buck would excitedly tell Maggy when he got home, "Everybody was there, Maggy."

Then, proud as all hell,

"All the big shots in New York—and me, Maggy.

Even me!"

The age of the speakeasy had arrived, and arrived king-size in New York City.

Texas Guinan, with her cheery, "Hello Sucker," was the top hostess in town. Soon she became an early mentor of an unknown writer for the New York Graphic—Walter Winchell. Winchell was a true newspaper 'original.' Nothing like him ever existed before.

He created American 'gossip'—American 'celebrity'—and American 'cafe society.'

If W.W. were alive today, most likely he would be the editor/host of 'Hard Copy'; 'Current Affair'; and 'Entertainment Tonight.' Simultaneously!

Without his battles with his famous boss, the vindictive publisher, William Randolph Hearst, most probably none of that excitement would have come into existence for years—if ever.

In addition to his column—and for an astounding twenty-eight years—W.W. was the best-known voice on American radio. *He had the largest listening audience of any radio program in the world!*

Every Sunday night, Buck and Maggy, along with countless millions, sat glued to their radio speakers to hear W.W. bark in his famous rapid-fire, staccato—and his storied trademark, the ever-present clacking telegraph key—

"Good evening Mr. and Mrs. North and South America—and all the ships at sea—Let's Go To Press!"

His crowd discovered Harlem. And began going up to the Cotton Club to hear the fabulous music of a young Duke Ellington. Then on to Connie's Inn, and of course, to the wonderfully exciting Savoy Ballroom.

He made the musicians famous, and the nightclubs they worked in became legends. Nobody cared that the 'speaks' were owned by the hoods. Who else could smuggle in the good booze from Canada? The Purple Gang in Detroit? Moe Dalitz in Cleveland?

Buck yearned to drive for those big-time bootleggers, who paid top dollar for the dangerous work—despite the fact that some drivers never came home again.

Larger and more garish movie palaces were being built all along 42nd Street.

The Shuberts built 'Broadway' and Florenz Ziegfield's 'Follies' were the big draw. His stars became superstars. The likes of Eddie Cantor, Fannie Brice, and Al Jolson.

Soon—the 'fun express' was highballing down every fast track in every fast city.

Just name it.

Chi, Philly, Beantown, Motown, and Cleve—all over Dade County (Miami).

But nothing important yet had grown west of the big 'Sippi.

L.A.? Water and WW II came first—people later.

S.F.? Lots of water—no bridges.

DFW—Zillions of real cowboys. What football?

PHX—Just a big empty desert.

But back East, populated America was having a post World War blast. And so many marvelous new treats for American consumers were born everyday.

In 1922 alone, Americans got: Postum, Canada Dry, Campbell's, and Kellogg's. To say nothing of Maytag, Greyhound, Thom McCan, and The Reader's Digest.

Henry Ford made more than $264,000 per day. And the Associated Press declared him to be a billionaire.

As the 'Roaring Twenties' roared on—anything seemed possible.

NBC in 1927.

CBS the next year.

By 1929, Americans were paying over $100 for elaborate radio sets so they could listen to Amos n' Andy, Rudy Vallee, and The Goldbergs.

TWELVE

Minneapolis. 1959.

By any reckoning, it's a long way from the biting cold and heavy snows of Minneapolis to the sun and palms of Beverly Hills. Even longer if you don't take a direct route.

Channa Bernstein couldn't have taken a direct route because she wasn't sure exactly where it was. She didn't even know anyone who had ever been there.

A girlfriend, with whom she worked at The Dayton Co. store, had told her, "I think it's somewhere near Hollywood, but you'll find it. If anyone can find it it's you Channa, because it's your dream. Oh how exciting!"

Twenty-two year old Channa Bernstein was an 'accredited' dreamer—had always been a dreamer. For years, her mother complained to her father, "Sam—why don't you talk to her. You can tell her there's nothing wrong with dreaming—if you're sleeping. But Channa dreams all day long. And you mark my words, Sam, that girl will never find a husband because a 'nice' Jewish boy isn't going to want a dreamer on his hands. He'll want a helper, not some foolish make-believe girl. Enough with those movie magazines already.

"Believe me Sam, 'his' mother will never stand for it—*I know.* We'll probably have her on our hands for the rest of our lives. Now, take Marty. There's a child to be proud of. He'll end up a lawyer or even a doctor, maybe. Something substantial. But Channa—Sam—Sam are you listening to me?"

Of course, Sam Bernstein, was not listening to his wife.

Forget listening, he had not even heard her for years. He had totally tuned her out. And he was not about to change at this time of his life.

As he would quietly confide to a few old cronies, "If I had listened all these years—if I had paid any attention—I would never have survived."

So, contrary to his wife's pleadings, Sam not only listened to Channa's fantasies, but also encouraged her to dream bigger and better.

"If you dream big, you'll be big, sweetheart," he told his daughter. And then he would give her a reassuring hug. He adored Channa, and never missed an opportunity to shower her with his affection. Of course, she thought he was the very best Papa in the world.

"For Godsakes Bessie, leave Channa alone—stop nagging her. I think she's terrific just the way she is. So stop. Enough is enough."

One Sunday afternoon, when she was only fifteen, "Papa—Papa can I tell you something private—just you and me?"

Of course, my sweetheart, what is it?

"Well, I keep having this dream—the same dream, over and over."

"What's the dream about?"

"Oh, Papa, I dream that I'm all dressed-up like a fairy princess. All in white sparkles, I'm dancing a beautiful Russian ballet, all by myself, across the whole stage—in New York. And now Papa, now I'm holding a big bouquet of roses and I'm bowing to the audience, and they clap and clap. Then they stand, and they keep on clapping and cheering until I leave the stage. And Papa, they're clapping for me—for me Papa. *Only for me!*"

And so in the midst of a blinding Minneapolis blizzard on a late winter day in 1959, Channa Bernstein made the biggest decision of her twenty-two years. She would change her name for the 'movies.'

She would become Cheryl Blake.

And as Cheryl, she would soon begin a new life.

She would begin her climb on the stairway to the stars and turn her dreams into reality. She would never allow herself to see snow on the ground again—in Minneapolis.

"I think I should plan to leave around the end of August, Papa. That should give me time to find a room and sort of get settled by Labor Day."

"So let's see now where that puts me for money. Mmmmmm—not so great."

To herself: "Oh, how much I want to be famous and really rich. Have people look at me—and be somebody. Just like in my dreams."

THIRTEEN

In Beverly Hills, several hours after she had gotten the call from Cliff Blair telling her that Gar was dead, Cheryl Blake was still in a daze.

Somehow, she had remembered to call Larry Kramer at home to cancel her breakfast meeting, saying something about, "not feeling well." Took a Valium, laid down on the chaise in her bedroom—and fell asleep.

Slowly opening her eyes now, it was difficult to accept what she knew to be true. Denial can help for a moment, but she knew Gar was dead.

But was that actually possible? Gar—gone just like that—and a suicide? How could she possibly live in a world without Gar Grey? Without his strength.

She wondered, "Did he leave a private note or letter for me—anything?"

So many questions, but no answers. Her eyes desperately wanted to close again—to sleep—to allow escape. There would be a big funeral in New York. Somehow, she would try to finesse an invitation. But how?

Irene Henry would know the answer.

Irene knows *everything.*

"What I need right now is a scotch." And Cheryl headed

for the bar in her living room. As she poured, a little voice in her head cautioned, "Don't do Scotch on top of Valium."

She left everything on the bar untouched. Settled instead for a cup of steaming black coffee. It warmed her and helped to take off some of the edge. But, her skin still felt too tight.

Thankfully, as if on cue, the phone was ringing—on her business line. The first ring sounded very far away, the second brought Cheryl up quick. "Oh, shit, I completely forgot to call the office." She canceled out the rest of her day.

Then, thirty-eight year old Cheryl Blake again fell into the safety of her overstuffed chaise—and a sobbing reverie. The street outside her window was Wilshire Blvd.—L.A.—November, 1975. But the street drifting through her memory was Park Ave.—NYC—August 1969.

Any August in New York can be a bitch. The weather is not one of the city's best features. The temperature and the humidity compete to see which of them can make people more miserable. The result is usually too close to call.

At five, on a late Wednesday afternoon, at least a day too soon for those still in town to head for the Hamptons, every stool and table in the bar at the Regency Hotel was occupied with the usual crowd of heavy hitters.

George Garfield Grey, at fifty-one, already the Chairman and CEO of General Industrial, was in conversation with the President's National Security Advisor, Henry Kissinger, when owner Bob Tisch stopped by to greet his two friends.

Now—entering the elegant bar, with enormous panache, was a tall, stunning, raven-haired, beauty in an equally stunning black and white Halston summer suit, topped by a huge-brimmed, black straw hat. Très chic.

Trying to locate whomever she came to meet, expressionless, the woman paused and posed. Her gaze imperiously swept the room.

Maybe business. Maybe monkey business.

Gar, whose seat faced the entrance, looked up. And for a fleeting second their eyes made contact. Now, finding whomever she was meeting, the stunning one quickly moved to a tall smiling man, who was rising from his chair.

In response, he received a European two-cheek buss. And the two immediately became engaged in animated conversation.

Gar's eyes had followed her all the way.

With his famous poker-face, Kissinger growled, "Dat's a good-looking voman."

To Tisch, Gar inquired, "Do you know who she is, Bob?"

Turning half around, "That's Cheryl Blake, a dynamite head-hunter. She's with Larry Kramer, out on the Coast. We've used her. Sharp. Does her homework. A real pro. Has a sometime relationship with an older man in L.A. Some other guys have tried, but I hear they all struck out. That's the whole sheet on her, Gar. Happy hunting."

His private conversation with the former Secretary of State concluded, Gar had one more pleasurable task to initiate on his way out. Sidling up to the maitre d', and in a lowered voice, "Henri, would you please hand this card to the woman right over there," nodding in the direction of the stunning one in the big black straw hat. "No, there's no message."

Worldwide, Gar knew if any man or woman did not instantly recognize his name, any message would be superfluous. Simultaneously, he palmed a twenty-dollar bill into Henri's hand. "Thank you, Mr. Grey." At once, the tuxedoed host headed toward his target. Quite naturally, Gar headed for the door—his bait already in the water.

In the familiar pattern of the Regency, Gar's limo was double-parked outside, near the corner of 61st and Park. His chauffeur held open the rear door and he easily slipped into his seat. As the long, black car slowly eased into the rush-hour traffic, Gar wore a pleased expression.

"Good morning, Mr. Grey's office.

I'm sorry Mr. Grey is not presently available—may I ask who's calling? Yes—Yes—and you say it's personal, Ms. Blake? Please hold, I'm going to transfer your call to Ms. Henry's office."

"This is Irene Henry. Yes, of course I understand Ms. Blake—you're leaving tonight. Well, he does have an extraordinarily full schedule today, but I will get your message to him as soon as I possibly can. May I have a number where you can be reached? The Regency. Thank you, Miss Blake. I will do my best. Goodbye."

In her suite, still in a robe—Cheryl Blake looked at her watch. It was ten-fifteen.

She had more calls to make before her one o'clock lunch appointment. Had to call her L.A. office at noon. Had to bathe and dress. But a cunning smile was spreading across her face. She was dialing her N.Y. office.

"Marcy Newman please. Hi Marce—Cheryl. I need a favor."

"You always need favors when you're in New York—what now? You need a *what?* Hey girl, this may come as a big shock to you. You know I'm no kid, but even I haven't seen a hatbox since I was a teenager in Boston. And just for kicks, if you needed one, Cheryl dear, why the hell didn't you bring one from home? Okay, okay. It's for business and you had no idea. And I'm Florence Nightingale.

"Well, hang in there, love, I'll give it a full-court press, but as of this minute—An hour? And a very big one? Why? Are you planning to deliver yourself naked in this box to get a new search? Know what, Cheryl? You're so damn good at what you do, because you're completely crazy!"

"Irene—Mrs. Grey is in Southampton—right?

Well, anyway, there's a lady's hatbox here for Mr. Grey. I'll bring it in."

Fifteen minutes later—

Gar: On the intercom. "Yes Irene, I know the time.

Into the dining room in a moment. I'm just signing some mail. What? Well—whatever—it can wait. No? O.K.—bring it in. Put it anywhere, Irene, I'll open the damn thing later."

"Mr. Grey, one more thing. You might want to know a Cheryl Blake called?"

Looking up, "Lady—that's the most interesting thing you've told me so far today. Well, let her twist until tomorrow."

"We can't do that this time, Mr. Grey—she's leaving tonight. And, if it matters, Miss Blake is stopping at the Regency."

Gar repeated, "The Regency." Mmmm.

With Irene Henry gone, and half out of his chair to head into his private dining room, Gar looked over at the hatbox sitting pertly on a small sofa—then glanced at his watch.

Aloud, "Now or later?" He opted for now, and quickly untied the wide gros-grain ribbon. Not at all a surprise, inside, without any card or note, reposing majestically all by itself, was the black straw hat with the great big brim.

Do black straw hats with big brims talk? Gar thought this one did. On his private line, he was dialing her hotel.

"Cheryl Blake, please."

After three rings, a voice that was to thrill him for years, answered hurriedly and business-like. Despite the rushed tone, in those wondrous romantic beginnings, when physical chemistry is crackling, voice recognition is instantaneous, and even small-talk takes on big heat. Like combustion. After that—except for making passionate love—nothing else much matters.

Gar opened with, "Seems a very familiar-looking hat managed its way into my office this morning. I plan on returning it, in person, and a little birdie…"

"Oh shit. It's you—hold on. I'm on long distance. But don't go away! O.K.—I'm back, but I'm running late for lunch—later would be better."

"For me, too. Where are we having dinner?"

"Dinner?"

"You know most of us do it every night."

"What," she teased, "do most of us do every night, *Mr. Grey?"*

"Don't be a smart-ass Cheryl—neither of us has the time."

"Something tells me, we'll always have the time. Isn't that why you sent your card over to my table?"

Bingo.

Maybe it was what she had said. Maybe it was just the way she said it. In either event, something special had been exchanged between these two.

He said: "The bar—7:30"

She said: "No. Let's have a drink up here—1902—and 7:30 is fine. Bye."

Gar put the dead phone down, smiled, and buzzed Irene Henry. "Irene, take a look at this hat. I want red and white duplicates of it delivered this afternoon to Cheryl Blake—1902 at the Regency. No, no. This one I will hand deliver."

Heading for lunch, Cheryl's voice was still saying sexy things in Gar's head.

He loved it.

As his car drew-up in front of the Regency, the doorman said, "Good evening Mr. Grey. You know, sir, that's the third large hatbox I've seen today." Gar smiled to himself, all the way up to the nineteenth floor. He looked at his watch—it was 7:40.

Two experienced lovers were about to play.

Quietly, he placed the large hatbox on the carpet in front of the door to Suite 1902—rang the buzzer—and stepped about six feet back against the corridor wall. The door opened.

Two elegant bare arms picked up the box—and without so much as a glance in either direction closed the door. He broke into a wide, knowing smile.

To himself: "Gar Grey, playing games in a hotel corridor. Hell, what next?"

This time, planting himself directly in front of her door, Gar pressed the buzzer.

Footsteps—then the husky voice through the closed door, "The delivery has already been made."

"Okay. Then, have a safe flight home—or wherever you're going."

But he didn't move.

The door opened with purpose.

Framed in the doorway was the stunning 'hat lady'—backed only by a soft lamp. Raven hair severely brushed back into a soft French bun accenting her great cheekbones. If she had had a rose in her teeth, Cheryl looked ready for a performance of *Carmen*.

She was wearing a sleeveless black Saint Laurent summer-silk accented with a single strand of substantial pearls, which warmly picked up the creamy glow of her skin—as all good pearls do. The diamond clasp, turned to the front—sparkled. So did her diamond stud earrings.

She—was positively radiant.

He—was instantly captivated.

Stepping into suite 1902, Gar swept Cheryl into his arms. His kiss was long, warm, and tender. Maybe even from his heart. Her bare arms around his neck held his kiss. Long, warm, and tender. Parting at last, they moved into the living room.

"If this is your standard opening, Mr. Grey, do you also have a prepared encore?"

Squaring to her and looking seriously into her eyes,

"I don't do anything standard, Ms. Blake—and nothing is ever prepared. What's more, I think the very idea is rather insulting—to you."

Smiling and nodding her head toward a sofa, "We really shouldn't quarrel in front of the children, they know more than you think."

Silently, taking in the entire scene, much like small

children, were three identical straw hats. Red, white, and black—all with marvelously huge brims.

Gar laughing, "Yes, of course, the children. Now, let's uncork this wine."

Raising their glasses, Cheryl said: "To all the unprepared encores."

Gar followed: "And none of them ever standard."

And for five years now, in all the loving places of the world, Cheryl and Gar, true to their very first toast, engaged in every conceivable unprepared sexual encore. They were the most creative couple—driven by their most erotic fantasies. And, as Gar had told her that first evening—nothing was ever standard or prepared.

If they could dream it—they would do it.

Nothing was off limits.

One more. Two more.

Any gender. Dream any number.

And they did!

Of course, his thing with Cheryl did not restrict or limit Gar's other extramarital activities. His worldwide circle of friends and acquaintances knew what they knew—and the international media that closely followed his every move, expertly guessed. At his core, George Garfield Grey simply was an incorrigible philanderer.

Cheryl burst from her bedroom chaise.

"Oh my God—I—I must have been dreaming."

Now remembering reality—she cried, "Gar! Why? Darling—Whhhyyy?"

Moments later, she found the phone number. Cheryl was dialing New York.

"Hello, is this Irene Henry? Irene—this is Cheryl Blake. Sorry to bother you at home. I know it's late—but, I'm sure you will understand. Yes—we'll all miss him very much.

Now, Irene—about the funeral—"

FOURTEEN

New York City. November 21, 1975.

A celebrity funeral service at New York's majestic St. Patrick's Cathedral is never an ordinary event. This morning, George Garfield Grey's funeral certainly was not going to be an exception.

An important figure on the world stage had fallen. And the great and mighty were coming from around the world to pay their last respects.

On every continent his death received maximum print and broadcast exposure. 'Urbane,' 'Shrewd,' and 'Ruthless,' were adjectives the international media had used for years to describe Gar Grey on both pages. Front and Financial.

Now add a third page: Obituary.

The Chicago lawyer turned brilliant businessman and financier had been extremely well respected in the financial stratosphere, where the rules of the elite game were set centuries ago by the likes of the Rothschilds, Hapsburgs, and Medicis.

Gar, Chairman and CEO of General Industrial Corporation, was an admired wizard in financial markets. Personally controlling what Gar jokingly called, "our counting house," in London. There, all of the world markets were monitored on a 24-hour basis. Stocks, bonds, currencies, commodities, metals—all were under close watch.

Gar's complicated financial strategies were initiated, but not necessarily executed, from this carefully guarded room. Sometimes secrecy necessitated order execution away from normal channels. A known currency rate hedge in Hong Kong could be crushed into worthlessness in Zurich, Frankfurt, or London. Sometimes in mere minutes. Or less. Consequently, counting house personnel had instant access to him wherever he might be working or playing. That instant access to Gar was crucial.

Larger than most banks, GIC was as much in the money business as in any other. At all times, worldwide corporate cash on hand, or in negotiable equivalents, ran to the billions—in every imaginable local currency. Funds, in excess to local operating needs, were transferred or translated to freely traded currencies.

All globals, GM, GE, IBM, British Pete, Royal Dutch, vigorously work their cash flow. Investment income is an important profit center.

Going forward even without George Garfield Grey to call the financial shots, GIC, one of the largest industrial enterprises in the world, would remain for its millions of shareholders what Gar had created. It was listed for trading on the New York Stock Exchange and all the important international stock exchanges around the world.

Yet, as they entered Saint Patrick's, the financial gain which freely flowed to those with close personal ties to Gar, certainly had to be uneasy. The dominant question of the day was, "Who would become Gar's successor?"

Hence it was only fitting that the funeral of an international powermaster of Gar Grey's stature would take place in Saint Patrick's, the largest Roman Catholic cathedral in America. The seat of the mighty Archdiocese of New York—lovingly known to millions simply as "St. Pat's".

Built in the imposing Gothic Revival style, as are any number of European Great Grays, St. Pat's, with soaring twin spires and huge nave accommodating nearly twenty-five hundred, has been standing on its present site for nearly one hundred years—covering an entire mid-town Manhattan block. Fifth Avenue to Madison. 50th to 51st Streets.

On this typically cloudy fall morning, the cathedral's three sets of bronze doors facing Fifth had been open since nine. The funeral would have all the trappings of a state ceremony—with admittance by invitation only. But not to worry. If you played anywhere in Gar's world you had an invitation. Gar's longtime personal assistant, Irene Henry, indelibly knew that world. Intimates constantly said, "Irene knows everything."

The service was called for ten.

By nine-thirty the long black line of waiting limousines stretched more than five blocks up Fifth Avenue—extending to fifty-sixth and fifty-seventh streets. Appropriately, only Bonwit-Teller and Tiffany occupied that entire block.

Media coverage was intense. International deadlines were pushed to the limit. Approaching 4:00 PM in London, the BBC people were getting anxious. "Don't these bloody Americans ever do anything on time? For sure it's not Buckingham."

As celebrities and dignitaries emerged from their secluded back seats, reporters, photographers, and TV camera crews didn't know where to look or point first. Not wanting to miss anyone of note, they were madly running helter skelter for the entire world to see. The concrete apron in front of the great cathedral produced a fast-forward scene straight out of an old Mack Sennett silent movie. If the occasion were less somber, it would have been pure comedy.

The crowd of thousands pushed hard against NYPD's familiar light blue barricades. Set smack in the middle of the famed metropolis, the size of the crowd and this congested location, created special concerns for the Secret Service agents.

Their choice was for President Ford to make a hurried entry into the cathedral. So as to be exposed to 'daylight' for as short a time as possible. Consequently, they preferred to wait until the other invitees had cleared the cathedral's entrance areas. With so many focal points to coordinate, their 'squawk boxes' communicated at a loud and furious pace.

Two maximum-security cars—a 'lead' and a 'chase'—were directly in front of and behind the President's limousine. A receiving team already was in place in front of the cathedral. Sharp-shooters, with rifles at the ready, could be seen leaning out of windows of the surrounding buildings whose names sounded like the text from a "Tourist's Guide To New York City."

Saks Fifth Avenue across 50th Street to the south.

Best & Company across 51st Street to the north.

Rockefeller Center across Fifth Avenue to the west.

To say nothing of any number of agents who cordoned off the entire square block. Many were also stationed inside of Saint Patrick's. When asked, the Secret Service Agent in-charge ignored all questions regarding which of these procedures were new since 1963 Dallas.

Air Force One had landed on time in New York.

Informed of the continuing congestion in front of the cathedral, the start of the presidential motorcade into Manhattan had been held on the tarmac at the Marine Air Terminal at La Guardia for about nine minutes.

The Secret Service prefers no public announcement detailing the route of a presidential motorcade. However, in this case, only two ground routes existed. Grand Central Parkway over the Triborough Bridge—and down the East River Drive. Or the Long Island Expressway through the Mid-Town tunnel.

On dry runs, the Service times everything surrounding a presidential appearance. Down to the minute. And nine minutes can be a long time if you are responsible for the life of the President of the United States.

Endlessly longer if you are tied up in the unbelievable traffic jam presidential appearances create for New York City dwellers. Taking no chances this day, NYPD, "New York's Finest," allowed nothing to move along either possible route.

Rolling easily down upper Fifth Avenue, approaching St. Patrick's the motorcade had slowed to a crawl. Every agent clearly heard the anticipated command.

"All agents on guard!"

The time was nine-fifty.

Cabinet officials headed by Kissinger and Simon had entered. Vice-President Rockefeller had arrived. On his home turf, the former New York governor had many friendly hands stretched out to him. His trademark, "How ya doing," the infectious wink and smile had made him a longtime crowd pleaser and a formidable vote getter.

One could spot former Supreme Court Justices Arthur Goldberg and Abe Fortas, along with Chief Justice Warren Burger. Hollywood pals, Cary Grant, Bill Holden, and Greg Peck had arrived together. Next, UN Secretary General Kurt Waldheim, and CBS' still handsome, seventy-four year-old founder, William S. Paley. And, surely, it was not hard to recognize Leonard Bernstein. The famous conductor wore a loden-green wool cape over his shoulders.

Lawyers, bankers, politicians, foreign dignitaries—famous faces everywhere.

An impressive list.

A glittering crowd.

The important Otto Carl Freylinghausen, Chairman of Germany's Central Bundesbank, known to his international banking colleagues as 'Otto The Terrible' for his fierce financial defense against possible German inflation, had been a late cathedral entrant. And was quickly seated in the last row of pews.

His arrival, with a special guest, had set off quite a stir—and an unexpected seating problem. Even the normally cool Irene Henry lost her confident patina for a brief moment. It was she who determined the last-row seating.

"There was just no alternative," she anxiously whispered to an assistant.

The left and right Fifth Avenue cathedral entrances were immediately closed. Only the center entrance remained open.

The bulletproof presidential limousine, with the two familiar small presidential flags fluttering above the front fenders, approached the curb. As always, the tension mounted. Everyone would feel much relieved once the President was safely inside the cathedral.

And now he was.

Replacing the President's limousine, the hearse inched to a soft stop. The six Pallbearers, including Sal Bellini, Cliff Blair, and Frank Templeton, in traditional cut-a-way morning coats and gray striped trousers, were waiting at the curb.

Suddenly, from out of nowhere, a lone woman dressed in all black emerged from within the crowd. Eyes forward, she quickly mounted the cathedral steps—and was promptly stopped. NYPD officers and the Secret Service asked all the necessary questions.

Cheryl Blake had not received her invitation from Irene Henry. But rather from Sal Bellini. As Gar often had said, "Sal always knows the right thing to do."

Her late arrival, however, had produced exactly the opposite of what Sal had requested. "Keep a low profile, Cheryl. It will be best for everyone."

Along with the other pallbearers, Bellini, with much trepidation, watched Cheryl's entire entrance unfold. He felt his pulse beat at his left temple. Turning, the lawyer could see Ellen and the rest of her family just inside the remaining open door waiting to escort the casket in the long processional to the front of the nave.

Cheryl produced her invitation and apologized to the authorities for her lateness. Directed to enter the same center door—Cheryl froze. Her throat went bone dry. Her thoughts were racing.

"Oh God, Ellen must be waiting just inside that door."

But, if she turned to leave now, Cheryl was certain she would be detained. That would provoke a frightful scene. Without a viable alternative, she took a deep breath and started to move through the center door. With eyes focused hard forward—and butterflies in her stomach.

As she passed within just a few feet of Ellen—she heard an audible gasp.

Instinctively responding, their eyes made contact.

Ellen turned ghost-white. More than that—she looked horrified—her face contorted.

Ellen had recognized Cheryl!

Sometime back, an anonymous source maliciously sent her a photo of Cheryl.

"This is what she looks like with her clothes on," said a small yellow post-it note. Ellen had kept the picture. When she held the 8x10 next to her own face, tears rolled down her cheeks.

Ellen—ash-blond.

Cheryl—raven black.

Lucky Gar. They were both quite beautiful.

Unfortunately, Ellen never saw herself that way. Diagnosed as depressed, and under continuous psychiatric care since her college days, Ellen often cried into her pillow. Sleep visited only after she took medication. Acutely aware of his dual life, Gar's highly publicized infidelities only worsened Ellen's problem.

After receiving the photo, she had called Sal Bellini.

"In Gar's position, Ellen, you know he meets a lot of people. So have you. Comes with the territory. Be smart—forget it. Any direct confrontation would be a grave mistake."

But Sal felt obliged to tell Gar of Ellen's call—cautioning him about the existence of the photograph. Once again urging his client and friend to be more discreet.

"It could cause problems Gar. Nasty problems you don't need. Watch your back, my friend."

For selfish reasons, Gar told Cheryl about the photograph. She frowned in disbelief. Now, her invited presence today had confirmed Ellen's worst nightmare.

Suddenly—she felt light-headed—dizzy—faint.

Beads of cold perspiration. Head to toe.

Ellen was fighting, but losing, her physical control.

And now—this very minute—the pall-covered casket was nearly beside her.

From a long-ago church ceremony, she heard Gar promise, "To be a true and faithful husband—till death do us part."

At that terrible moment, life had become more than Ellen could endure. Her body was shutting down. As she lost consciousness, Ellen folded in a strange kind of slow motion.

Sissy, standing next to her Mother, shrieked *Mothhheeerr!*

Only a few feet away, the pallbearers stopped in their tracks.

Secret Service agents covered the President.

Terence Cardinal Cooke quickly rose.

Grabbing wildly, Dr. Arthur Pollack caught the falling Ellen. The entire scene became a blurred freeze-frame.

Ellen McCormack Grey was dead where she fell!

In the ensuing confusion, Cheryl placed a hand-kiss on the cold metal casket. And for the last time whispered, "I will always love you, my darling Gar."

As Sissy's piercing scream tore through huge cathedral, the German banker's escort, craning for a better view, questioned, "Do you suppose someone fainted from the emotion?"

Then, through a crack in the midst of the confusion, she glimpsed Cheryl's tender cameo. A stunned Ursula Von Ribbentrop quietly wept on the understanding banker's shoulder.

As the highest financial official of his government, Freylinghausen had often hosted the powerful billionaire,

Gar Grey, and his young celebrity companion, at gala West German state receptions. As personal friends, Gar and Ursula spent any number of pleasant weekends at his country estate outside Frankfurt am Main.

On this last day of her life, how unfair for the fates to have condemned the sublime Ellen to this complicated web of deceit. To her dying moment, forcing her to share her husband with two other women.

It was cruel. And cynical. But all genuine Gar Grey, the original misanthrope. The Ultimate Controller, cold in his casket but not yet in his grave, remained the supreme master of the mind game.

In fantasy or reality—in death as in life—it didn't matter.

Gar's rules were the only rules.

You were the puppet. He pulled the strings.

Take it or leave it.

No questions. No options.

Ellen.

Ursula.

Cheryl.

None of them had a choice.

They could only react.

Puppets have no power of their own.

FIFTEEN

Flashback: Chicago. 1944.

Having volunteered for military service and been rejected, Gar felt absolutely no guilt at what turned out to be a very lucky break—graduating from law school without any military service interruption.

So he and David, who had received a family hardship deferment, had their college diplomas and law certificates framed, and hung out their shingle in modest offices on North Michigan Avenue. One month after passing the Illinois bar in August, 1944, and a full year before war's end, these two cock-eyed optimists were ready to conquer the legal world.

Amazingly, only a few years later, the word was already out in Chicago's business community. If your company was planning to do anything that required city, county, or state regulatory approval, the current law-firm-of-choice clearly was Grey & Ross. And there was hardly a Chicago company of note that was not in that hungry category. Immediately after World War II, every company needed to build something.

What a time to be a lawyer—or almost anything else.

Out of nowhere, G&R had not only landed some of the most prestigious companies in the city as new clients, but they were doing a bang-up job for them in their chosen area of legal specialization. They were moving complicated projects through various municipal and county agencies and courts as if on a magic carpet. It seemed that this young firm knew just what moves to make while their competition was still sound asleep.

Relaxing early one evening after a typically hectic day, Gar was recalling to David, "You know that summer job I had in the City Attorney's office our last year in law school, was the luckiest thing that could have happened to us. The stuff I learned and the guys I met have turned out to be pure gold for us. I mean guys like Hank Brady and Phil Sosno."

David quickly added, "And don't forget Pete Argus, the best clerk a judge ever had. I can't imagine what more a Clerk of Court could have done for a couple of rookies like us."

Along with the rest of the country, in those post-war years, Chicago was booming. In order to meet the pent-up demand of the country's second largest city, Chicago needed more roads, expressways, bridges, viaducts, and schools—more of everything. And there was another important plus.

With all the restrictions on private business during the war, banks had little loan demand. Now they were all rushing to convert their huge war bond portfolios into commercial loans. Consequently most sound loan requests at First Illinois National Bank & Trust were being granted—especially from corporations represented by the law firm of Grey & Ross.

Not to forget. First Illinois was founded by Gar's grandfather before the Great Chicago Fire of 1871—and still controlled by the Grey family. Gar's father, Lucien Smith Grey, being its long-time Chairman and CEO. Not unlike the Mellon National in Pittsburgh, or the Chase National in New York—controlled by the Rockefeller family.

David Rockefeller headed the Chase for many years. He and Lucien Grey were longtime friends. And two of America's most influential bankers.

Through his financially and socially prominent family, Gar had many natural important contacts—and he wasn't hesitant about using them. He aggressively followed up on every possible new-business lead with much legal knowledge and an equal abundance of smiling charm.

He worked the dining room at the Union League Club as effectively as any politician did. A handshake here, a wave over there. Some began to call him 'Senator' Grey.

He was becoming very well known. And he liked that.

Hence, at the incredibly youthful age of thirty, and all rolled into one formidable talent, Gar Grey had become the hottest rainmaker in Chicago legal circles.

In recognition of his new importance, floods of offers to become a member of the Board of Directors of some of Chicago's biggest and best were almost getting to be embarrassing. He accepted only the choicest directorships including the Chicago Symphony and the Art Institute. On both of those prestigious boards, he was the youngest person ever to serve. Of course, obvious conflict of interest problems prevented his serving on the First Illinois board.

But these days the biggest problem at G&R was not attracting new clients—but rather finding enough hours to continue doing a top-notch job for their already bulging client roster.

There was not a night when both Gar and David did not leave the office without an overflowing brief case of urgent work. Weekends only meant more working hours.

From the beginning, the two founding partners had recognized the necessity of not allowing the firm to become a Gar Grey one-man-show. As a counter-balance, David, as well as a number of talented new associates he now personally directed, had also become critical to the firm's burgeoning success.

And David was a tough legal taskmaster. If a document was not of superior merit, with foundation and citation in law beyond challenge, he would be furious. And his younger associates knew it. They knew David Ross. They knew his standards. And were betting their future on him.

His troops made their point one-day by composing a limerick and leaving it, anonymously, in the most conspicuous place on his desk—spiked on his marble-based fountain pen.

"David Ross is a tough tough boss—
For sure he's not a honey.
But that's okay—cause one fine day—
He'll make us lots of money."
—Your devoted slaves.

David's laughing reaction when showing the paper to Gar, "They're sure as hell better lawyers than poets. We must be doing something right." Naturally, Gar agreed. Then, David proudly pointed to a small frame on his office wall.

His own composition.

THE GREY & ROSS CREDO.
If you're not interested in
Doing your best—Being the best.
Every day—for every client.
Quit these premises now.
WE DON'T WANT YOU!

The lawyers who were running legal affairs at client firms knew all about this striving for excellence and had formed a tremendous level of professional respect for David—who by now had acquired a solid reputation as a lawyer's lawyer.

It was obvious that he had not been appointed Editor of the Northwestern Law Review without reason.

Even Gar had to admit, “David was simply the best.”

It was especially obvious to the Clerks of the Courts of all the various jurisdictions. These veterans were in the best position to compare the work of all the top lawyers. Of important consequence, they would make their opinions known to all the judges.

Of course, clients already were well aware of the significant edge they had with the quality of work turned out by G&R. And that edge was reflected in the hourly billing rate they accepted—already equal to the highest in Chicago.

As Gar had thought and planned years before, he and David did make an extremely powerful business combination.

And they had only just begun.

SIXTEEN

"Mr. Grey do you know a Hank Brady?"

His secretary's voice was coming over the inter-com squawk box.

It was November, 1944. Only three months after they first opened their law practice.

"I sure do—why?"

"He's asking for you on the phone."

"Hello Hanko, how the hell are you—how's the family—still shagging your ass off for the City Attorney?"

"I'm fine. My family's great. And, yes I'm still in the C.A's office. Now my turn, Mr. New Lawyer. Since you probably have more time on your hands than you have clients, how about lunch one of these days?"

"Great idea Hank. It's been too long."

"But not at the Union League Club, Gar. Better at an out-of-the-way place where we can talk more privately."

"Right. Let's meet at Enzo's, Hank. Tomorrow about 12:30. Okay?"

"Sounds good. See ya then."

Gar made sure he was a little early, got a corner table and waved Hank Brady over when he saw him enter the quiet old Italian family restaurant.

Despite the fact that Hank was more than ten years older, they had liked each other ever since they met when Gar had his summer job in the City Attorney's office. They greeted each other warmly.

"Ya know, somehow, even for a rich kid, you don't look any smarter since you passed the bar," Hank joked when they were seated—and had ordered a beer.

"You're right, wasting time with you is not smart at all," Gar shot back, "I should be spending my time with people who can generate some business for me."

"Well, ya just might have gotten lucky, old buddy, because potential business is really what I wanted to talk to you about."

"You've got my full attention, Hanko."

"Have you heard about what's going on these days at the Department of Public Works?"

"Can't say I have. Something both of us might be able to chew on?"

"Better believe," Hank went on, "What those guys are cooking up over there is beyond anybody's imagination—and the money. They're gonna be spending hundreds of millions, maybe even billions, on every kind of infrastructure imaginable. Bridges, tunnels, water systems, airports, schools—you name it. And they're working on a lot of the plans already. Some projects are even scheduled to start soon. And you know plenty of legal has to come first."

Hank paused to catch his breath.

"Every company in the city that's in any facet of the construction business, or even remotely allied to it, Gar, is gonna bust ass to get on that gravy train. And the kind of set-up I've got in mind will get you so goddam many new clients you won't be able to hire new lawyers fast enough to grind out the work."

"Sounds like real music, Hank. You got a plan in mind?"

"Yup, but I didn't take anything for granted. I had to know your reaction first."

"Well you know David and I are brand new—just odds

and ends so far. Mostly family referrals—a few wills and trusts—things like that. Nothing that's covering the overhead. And whatever little does comes in I'm letting David take it all. He and Rachel need it much more than I do—they've got a brand new baby. And you well know, Hank, I'm never going to go hungry."

"If you ever are, I know a bank that might give you a small loan." They both laughed at the reference to Gar's father's bank. Looking at Gar with a mock straight-face Hank said, "Hey—maybe this check should be Dutch?"

They both laughed again. Then, ordered another round of beer.

"Let's get down to business, Hank. Lay out your plan."

"Okay. Here's where it's at right now. First, you should know, we'll have a third partner—an inside connection I have at the PWA—which is how this whole thing got started. This person will deliver all the critical confidential info we'll need on their projects."

Gar broke in, "Like what ?"

"How's plans, specs, a–n–d advance numbers on competitive bidding? Believe me when I tell you, Gar, we'll always be in the catbird seat. And, you damn-well know, I would never bullshit you. How's that for a sweet set-up, old buddy?"

Very deliberately, Gar replied, "I'd say it was pretty... damn...sweet."

Hank continued flat-out.

"With that kind of head-start, how much dough you can generate for your law partnership is your part of the deal. And we split the money three ways. This deal is very simple, Gar. It's like straight fucking. No kissing. No talking. It's only about money, money, money.

Even better, I don't want to know any of your details. And I don't need any receipts. I can also tell you that I haven't talked about this to anyone else, because I know I can trust you, Gar. And that's essential. Because this entire arrangement can only be based on trust. If we go forward on this, I don't plan to reveal your name to my 'connection'—or that individual's name to you. I'll be the only one who'll know the names of all three partners."

Hank continued, as he slid a slip of paper over the table. "And Gar, when you call me, use this number—it's my secured extension.

Now, let's order something to eat—I'm starving."

Then with a wink, "But I hope not for long."

For most of that afternoon Gar stayed alone in his office. He couldn't think of anything else but his conversation with Hank Brady. He was completely taken with the entire proposition. It was going to give him an early opportunity to play with the big boys. Yet, he pondered. Was he really as good as he thought he was?

Smiling smugly, Gar smacked a closed right fist into his open left palm, and said out loud to himself, "Goddam right I am."

However, he was still hung up on how to approach David, "Mr. Straight Arrow."

"Could I possibly handle this deal without telling David?" Then, frowning deeply, "But what the hell do I do if I tell him and he says, 'no'?"

That thought set off a long soliloquy.

David's voice echoed through his head. He heard, "Gar, if you want to run the risk of being disbarred before you even get going, that's your decision—but count me out. That's not what I beat my brains out for. Not why I wanted to become a lawyer. For chrissakes, Gar, if something leaks out it could even mean more than disbarment, it could mean prison—*federal* prison."

"These are federal funds you're screwing around with. Are you really prepared for some insane catastrophe like that? And what about your family?"

In his secret heart, Gar knew the entire deal was not going to fly with David. It would bug his conscience. It would stick right in the middle of his throat. In David's crystal-clear legal mind, the sort of deal that Hank was proposing, that had Gar's adrenaline flowing, was not only way down on the legal ladder—it was in the sewer!

Still quietly thinking about David, Gar had to smile. He knew David dreamed of someday trying a complicated case before the U.S. Supreme Court. They had talked about that back in law school.

Not every lawyer in the country is admitted to practice before the High Court—but David yearned to be one of the chosen few just as soon as he could file a petition request. A true legal knight in shining armor.

On the other hand, Gar knew that Hank's proposal might well be the chance of a legal lifetime. And in his gut he was sure that this opportunity was too big to pass up—despite whatever ethical qualms David might raise.

Gar also knew that no matter what he did to put a better face on Hank's proposal, David certainly would turn it down. That is, if he knew the whole story.

All of Gar's wheels were now spinning at full speed.

He had been rapidly pacing back and forth in front of his desk. Abruptly—he stopped.

He had reached his decision. Jaw set—his chin raised and jutted forward—lips tight and determined.

"David will get his fifty percent of our share of the money—no matter what. I'll figure out those details later. But, shit, he really doesn't have to know *everything.*

I'm not ready to break up this law firm—yet."

SEVENTEEN

Flashback: New York City. 1929.

Buck McCormack finally got his chance to be a wheelman on a bootlegging truck working for the notorious duo of Lucky Luciano and Longy Zwillman. That chance occurred in the latter part of that terribly unsuccessful social experiment—prohibition. Near the end of the Roaring 20s.

For obvious reasons, booze runs were always done at night. That meant Buck was able to keep his day job at the Manhattan trucking company.

The trucking company's owners, themselves Mafiosi, supplied the trucks for these illegal trips. That meant constantly switching license plates, which had to be stolen from other trucks. This became another of Buck's many regular assignments. But, if something went wrong on a run, and he was gone longer than planned, it didn't present any problem at the trucking company. His bosses knew what was going on.

The whole idea was the cash Buck received at the end of each successful trip. Successful meant he arrived back home alive. Some didn't.

When he gave the money over to Maggy, she was always thankful for, "The good Lord's extra blessing." But, knowing full well where the money was coming from, each time Buck was gone Maggy worried herself sick until he returned.

With the cash in hand, she would immediately cross herself, and quickly squirrel the green bills away. Routinely, she stuffed them into a special jar, which she shoved out of sight on a high kitchen shelf. Superstitiously, Maggy touched the hot money no more than was absolutely necessary—then hurried to wash her hands in a serious effort to erase the tainted source.

Looking up at her husband with overflowing eyes, Maggy would say, "Thank you my darlin'—that'll keep us a month ahead of the rent collector." But she didn't want to tempt fate by discussing the subject any further.

The good money notwithstanding, Buck was smart enough to know that his luck would not hold up forever. He remembered some close calls—plenty of running shoot-outs. It was dangerous work, but he never discussed those dangers with Maggy. Although it was no secret that the government agencies were sworn to enforce the law. And they kept the heat on high.

In New York City, the heavy bootlegging operations belonged to the top banana—Charlie Lucky, as his pals called Luciano. Longy, who hated to be called by his real name, Abner, was in complete charge in Northern New Jersey. Both men were greatly feared. Any number were killed to enforce their orders. But many small-time hoods were constantly being arrested and roughed-up. To cop a plea bargain, they would sing whatever song the Feds wanted to hear. And those federal agents could be menacingly tough. After all, the government had the big stick—the threat of long federal prison sentences—which intimidated all but an arrogant few.

Making it even tougher for the bootleggers, most Federal courts were beyond the reach of the big cash payoffs the Mafia was successfully throwing at lower level judges and small-time, local politicians. The higher the mob tried to push their money—the tougher and more expensive it became. Not impossible—just tougher.

Which always brought up the name of the patriarchal, but crafty, Joseph P. Kennedy.

He, alone, had the highest connections on both sides of the law. He also was well known to talk out of both sides of his mouth—and was never fully trusted by anyone. Most insiders believed the timely opportunity available in bootlegging to generate so much tax-free cash would have proven irresistible to Old Joe.

Some wiseguys even thought they knew about meetings held in out-of-the-way places—like on boats in choppy Atlantic waters off his Hyannisport compound. Or in warmer waters off his Palm Beach estate on North Ocean Boulevard. None of that gossip was ever proven.

During those hectic days, Buck had managed to make some good personal connections of his own. One of them was a young Italian attorney, Salvatore Bellini, who had an impressive diploma from Harvard Law—and many questionable friends.

When Buck's luck finally did run out, it was Sal Bellini who showed up to post bail. And it also was Sal who advised Buck to promptly leave New York in order to protect himself and his young family, saying, "Buck, you'd best be out of New York before next Monday. A friend has asked me to represent you that day, but I can tell the judge you left town without advising me. I'm quite sure I can get the charge dismissed. They're really not after you, Buck. They're after Charlie and Longy."

Sal added, "That same friend also says you're one hell of a stand-up guy, Buck. And he told me to tell you the construction business might be right for you now in Chicago. He also asked me to give you this envelope. It'll help until you get connected there. Be smart—take his advice. Leave town."

"Who was the guy, Sal?"

"Sorry, Buck. I've never been very good at remembering names."

Buck, Maggy, and five-year old Ellen, got off the bus in Chicago in the afternoon.

It was Tuesday, October 29, 1929.

Struggling out of the Union Bus Terminal, the rag-tag trio had no idea of why young newsboys were running about the streets, shouting,

"Extra! Extra! Read all about it! Read all about the Big Crash!"

Turning to Maggy, Buck said, "Must've been a big accident here today."

Indeed—there had been a very big accident.

But it happened in New York, not Chicago. The Roaring 20s stock market finally fell out of the sky.

Billions were lost.

Panic ruled.

On Wall Street, men jumped out of windows.

An era had crashed to a terrible end.

Forget construction.

Forget *any* business.

The Great Depression would now begin.

Hello, Buck McCormack.

Welcome to Chicago!

EIGHTEEN

Washington, D.C., March 4, 1933.

Turn on your radio America—it's time for Roosevelt's Inauguration!

Gar questioned his Father. "Dad you don't look very well. Are you O.K.?"

In the big Tudor house, facing Lake Michigan in suburban Kenilworth, Gar's father, Lucien Smith Grey, wearing his favorite old Harvard sweater, a crimson button-front, sat huddled near a warming fireplace in his walnut-paneled study. By contrast, the crimson-color sweater only increased his almost waxen pallor.

And the cold Northeast wind whipping off the lake, combined with a gloomy overcast sky, had produced a brooding late winter day—which fully matched Lucien Grey's mood.

Fifteen-year old Gar was sitting on an ottoman at his Father's knee. In a subdued voice, a broken and despondent father finally replied,

"Son—this is the worst day of my life. And while I have been in fear of its coming for a long time now, I never really expected to live to see this day. And I'm sorry I did. Our bank is closed. Only the Almighty God can save us now."

Lucien's voice trembled. Unsteady in his chair—now he was badly slumping.

Frightened, Gar loudly called, "Mom. Mom come quick. I think Dad's sick!"

The nightmare had started in Detroit on February 14th.

Alfred P. Sloan of General Motors, Henry Ford, and Walter P. Chrysler—all tried in vain. After much talk and agony, but without any realistic alternative in sight, Governor Comstock ordered an eight-day bank holiday for the State of Michigan.

Then, the panic took on a life of its own.

The anxiety was overwhelming.

People started running and screaming in the streets.

"Trouble's coming! Get your money out of the bank!"

"Hurry up! Hurry up—don't wait! Get your money out of the bank!"

"Sell everything—get cash. You'll need cash!"

Unbelievable. Impossible. *But it was true.*

America's safe and solid banking system was falling apart! But there was more oil for the fire.

On Monday, February 27th, Charles E. Mitchell, Chairman of the powerful National City Bank in New York, resigned amid disturbing rumors of official misconduct.

Even worse, simultaneously joining Michigan and Maryland—Ohio, Indiana, Kentucky, and Pennsylvania went down. More states quickly followed. Americans were in a daze. Moreover, the entire world was gripped in turmoil.

On that same night, the 27th of February, the Nazis burned down the Reichstag in Berlin. German democracy was doomed for more than five decades. Japan, seizing the moment, stepped up its barbaric invasion of Manchuria.

Everywhere—the world order was crumbling.

But America was helpless.

The last strongholds, New York and Chicago, also battered, struggled mightily to hold on. But the spreading panic was causing more runs against shrinking deposits.

Secretly, under cover of night, armored trucks raced from city to city carrying cash from the regional Federal Reserve banks to the beleaguered local banks.

But it was too late.

At 4:30AM, in the pre-dawn hours of that momentous Inauguration Day, March 4, 1933, Governor Herbert Lehman of New York proclaimed a bank holiday. With New York gone, Governor Henry Horner immediately closed the banks in Illinois.

All hope vanished.

Together, with all the other banks, Lucien's family bank—the once-mighty First Illinois National Bank & Trust, founded by Gar's Grandfather in the last century, closed. Everywhere—only gloom and doom.

Paradoxically, the only remaining group of people in the country still flush with abundant cash was the Mafia. Their illegal cash flowed in an endless green torrent. By this point in time, these once-starving street thieves had amassed untold fortunes. Hundreds of millions. Maybe billions. No one really knew.

Not trusting anyone, the hoods couldn't possibly know their combined wealth. Even more, that stash was tax-free. It never had been reported as income in the first place. Since that cash had never been near a bank, it was strewn about everywhere—in trunks, drawers, and attics.

And, at this critical point in our history, this illegally acquired cash was the country's most readily available money supply. How ironic.

Over time, this cash seeped into many legitimate businesses. But in that horrendous depression no one cared. Cash was King. And if it hadn't been such a national tragedy—it could have been quite funny. Something like a wild Marx Brother's comedy.

Picture this—if you can.

Groucho (using a cigar), imitating Dutch Schultz (with a machine gun), imitating J.P. Morgan?

Would you believe, killers, pimps, whoremasters,

extortionists, and racketeers—the absolute dregs of the country, had now become America's bankers!

Nothing like this had ever happened before. It was too painful to believe that it was happening even now.

NINETEEN

From the October, 1929 crash until Roosevelt's Inauguration Day, three and one-half years later, March 4, 1933, seemed like a long and terrible nightmare.

It certainly was that.

The Great Depression had gone from bad to worse.

People scavenged in garbage cans—ate horseflesh—and incredibly, right here in America—some even starved to death. Then, the country heard the message that it desperately needed to hear—from what would become one of the most famous voices in all of recorded history.

"The only thing we have to fear—is fear itself," FDR said on Inauguration Day. Representing new hope—his word beamed forth from the Capitol steps. Better yet, most who heard him believed him.

Gar, his Mother and Father, and his sister Charlotte, were all gathered in front of the walnut floor-model Philco radio in the library ready to listen to the new President deliver his first "fireside chat." It was Sunday, March 5, 1933. Just one day after Roosevelt's Inauguration.

FDR, calmly explained how the re-opening of the banks would be managed. The President told the people there was no reason to panic again, and asked for their help in making the process orderly.

With that news, Lucien Smith Grey exploded out of his armchair and, clapping his hands, danced a jig around the room. Overjoyed—ecstatic. They all jumped up, and joined in the dancing and laughing.

Lucien shouted, "Happy Days are here again, everybody—our bank is going to re-open! I didn't do all that fund-raising work to get him elected for nothing, after all."

FDR, was true to his word. Monday, March, 13th, the banks began to re-open. And Lucien's bank now would struggle to eventual normalcy.

For nearly four years, the Hoover administration had been waiting for the economy to cure itself. Fine chance. On the other hand, and contrary to what many honestly believed as gospel for generations that followed, the incoming Roosevelt administration only *outlived* the Depression.

All the hyperbole and charm of FDR, notwithstanding, economic history has proven beyond any doubt, that it took the industrial expansion provided by World War II to solve the suffering. How tragic.

But he certainly and successfully soothed and comforted working-class America—his core constituency.

On that same day, in the Halsted Street ghetto, it was a far different story. A dejected and bitter Buck McCormack was sorry he ever came to Chicago. And that feeling didn't change for years to come. Following the great crash, the construction business died. So did everything else.

In the '24 campaign, President Coolidge said,

"The business of America is business."

"So, an angry Buck wondered, "Where the fuck did all that business go?"

Buck and Maggy had rented a tiny one-bedroom cold-water flat, in the West Side Irish ghetto. Miserably inadequate, it was even worse than what they had left behind in the squalor of Hell's Kitchen in New York.

Day after day, Buck walked the streets, asking strangers if they knew of any available work. It was all in vain. Everybody in the ghetto was in the same boat. And no matter how carefully they watched their small expenses, the envelope Sal had passed to him back in New York was growing thinner with each passing day. And so was Buck's dream of a job in construction—or a dream of any kind.

"We don't have a choice Maggy. We're in Chicago two months now—and I've not worked a day. We can't go on this way."

Just before he fled New York, the same day Sal had given him the envelope, the lawyer also had given him a name and phone number in Chicago—if he needed help.

Looking at the name, Buck started out the door for the phone in the hallway. On second thought, "It would be too easy to get rid of me on the phone." He would go in person.

A few days before that bleak Christmas of 1929, Buck McCormack found himself standing on a South Michigan Avenue corner staring across the street at the imposing Hotel Lexington. The hotel's entire fourth floor was the headquarters of Al Capone, the Chicago crime lord.

As he came through the Lexington's main entrance, and looked around the ornate lobby, which rose to a luxurious shopping gallery, Buck stopped dead in his tracks.

His eyes turned big as saucers.

Never before had he seen, much less been in, such a magnificent place.

Even the people moving about contrasted so enormously with the desperate people he saw everyday—the masses of hopeless poor in the Halsted Street ghetto.

As though snapping back to reality, Buck, quickly and respectfully, removed his grimy, dark-brown cap, which he clutched in his right hand, as though he was holding a hot potato. Buck bent the visor in the same place he had done so many times before—and hurriedly jammed it into his rear pocket. Yet, he stood frozen—not quite knowing what he should do next.

At the same time, with great embarrassment, he looked down at his disheveled clothes. While they were his best, Buck knew his rumpled clothing did not qualify him to walk through this elegant lobby and casually hop aboard an elevator. Dejected, he thought it best to leave.

As he slowly turned, an arm grabbed him—and held on tightly. "What the hell ya wants here?" A menacing voice barked at him.

The voice belonged to a tough-looking guy wearing a dark-blue suit with wide chalk-stripes, a hard-starched collar, topped off with a snazzy white Homburg hat. He looked like an imitation of Edward G. Robinson—right out of the movies. But this guy was real—very real. He was Al Capone's notorious chief Enforcer.

"I'm Frank Nitti," he growled. Who the hell are ya? And I awready asked ya what youse wanted here."

"My name is Buck McCormack—an' somebody in New York sent me here."

"Who from New York—and what fer?"

"Well—I'm not sure who really sent me—but Sal Bellini is the guy what told me."

The greatly feared Frank Nitti, broke into a broad smile.

"Sal Bellini—the mouthpiece? How the hell is my miserable buddy? That sonofabitch."

"He's fine. Well—he was fine a coupla months ago, when I last seen 'im."

"So, Mr. Buck McCormack from New York City—ya looks like youse needs some help."

"I sure do Mr. Nitti—I need a job, real bad. I got a wife, a kid—and I'm broke. Sal told me to get in touch here. Ya see, I had ta leave New York fast—real fast."

"Well—I gotta go to a meet now, said Nitti, so lissen ta me real careful. Tamarra aftanoon ya comes here at tree—ya gives yer name to dat guy ova by da elevata door—da guy what's holdn' the Tommy gun—name is Tony—Tony Accardo.

He'll tell ya what to do—an ya do esactly what he tells ya to do. Capisce?"

"Yes sir, Mr. Nitti," a pleased Buck replied, "three tomorra—I'll be here. You can be sure of that Mr. Nitti. Thanks again Mr. Nitti."

But, The Enforcer no longer could hear Buck.

Nitti, and his bodyguards, had already disappeared through the revolving door.

TWENTY

"No bullshit David, Ellen McCormack is the most beautiful girl I've ever known. And—well I think I'm going to propose to her."

"Fine pal you are. How long has this been going on?" inquired David.

"Not long at all. I've only had two dates with her."

"And you're in love—already?"

"Come on, David, how many times have I listened to you tell me how you fell in love with Rachel the first time you laid eyes on her."

"You're right, Gar. I did."

"So?—"

"Wait 'till I get home. Rachel will be thrilled. Hey, when do we meet her?"

"I've booked a table for the four of us for dinner, Saturday night at the Pump Room."

"You've got yourself a date, partner," said David.

"Damn right I have," laughed Gar. "The best."

Only four months later, in a huge church ceremony, attended by every important person in the city, the two powerful Chicago Catholic families were united in holy matrimony.

And raising more than a few cool eyebrows, was the groom's Jewish law partner, who was also his Best Man. Many of the guests already knew David. The others did now.

A near religious oddity. The Cardinal and the Best Man were the only ceremonial participants who wore skull-caps. One red. One black.

At the sumptuous reception that followed the ceremony, a well-known judge, toasting the two happy fathers and long-time close friends, Lucien Smith Grey and James J. (Buck) McCormack, raised his champagne glass and intoned, "To Big Banking and Big Construction—may they always remain as close as they are now." Then jokingly added, "Inasmuch as this marriage merges so damn much money, I think that it should be first submitted to the SEC for approval." Everyone laughed.

With a straight face he added, "And, inasmuch as the SEC has not yet approved, accordingly, I rule this wedding night to be 'illegal entry.' Turning toward the Cardinal, I hope Your Eminence doesn't take any of this seriously." Everyone roared with laughter.

At that point, the two mothers, Molly Garfield Grey and Maggy Riley McCormack, smilingly arrived on the scene, newlyweds in tow. Maggy quickly asked, "What's this about illegal? There aren't any crooks here," adding a wink, "Just good old-fashioned politicians."

On the fringe of the party, a most attractive hazel-eyed brunette pondered. "Married or not, I wonder how long Gar can stay out of my bed?"

A man walked over to her, "And you are?"

"From the groom's side, I'm Nancy Lee Hendrix, an old college friend of Gar's."

The man continued smiling, eyeing her up and down. Then moved a little closer.

"And also quite obviously from the South."

"Yes, I'm originally from Alabama, but I've lived in Chicago for a long time now. Perhaps not long enough to completely lose my accent, but long enough to know that I no longer wish to speak to you—whoever you are. So if you will excuse me."

Nancy Lee quickly moved on to a buffet table.

The man watched her walk her walk, and, as most men do, he loved what he saw. Nancy Lee moved in the most imaginative way.

Again, the man moved to her side.

"Look, I'm Arthur Hill, the new op-ed page editor at the Chicago Tribune. I'm also drunk. But drunk or not, I just love eating anything Southern. So why don't we just get the hell out of here."

Nancy Lee Hendrix flushed hot pink. Her head turned stone cold. Her eyes hard steel. "Listen, you insulting sonofabitch, I'm going to walk away from you again. If you even—"

"Hi Nan—everything all right?" It was David and Rachel Ross. Rachel said, "You look terribly upset, Nan." Angrily, looking straight at Arthur Hill, then back to Nancy, David questioned, "You having a problem here, Nan?"

"More of a misunderstanding, David. But I'm O.K. now."

Understandingly taking Nancy's arm Rachel suggested, "Let's go freshen our makeup."

As the two lady-friends headed for the Powder Room, David turned his attention back to Arthur Hill.

"Listen, fella—whoever you are. Stay away from Nancy Lee Hendrix. Just don't even go near her—or you're going to be in very deep shit. Got it?"

Arthur Hill, now sober enough, and without a word turned and headed for an exit. A moment later David turned, and very nearly ran into a steaming Gar.

"What the hell was that all about? I saw Nan hit the ceiling. What happened?"

"Some jerk made a pass at her—she's okay now. Rach went to settle her down."

"Who was he?"

"I don't know who he was. It really doesn't matter, he's gone now."

"But it does matter, David—and you've known that since school."

Startled, David responded, "But you're married now."

Walking back to join Ellen, over his shoulder Gar shot back, "What's that got to do with anything else?"

TWENTY-ONE

Chicago. 1939.

"Maggy, I tell ya, it's now or never. I jus' gotta try construction on ma own," Buck said to his frightened wife. "Ya jus' hav ta trus' me."

"Oh, darlin', it has nothin' ta do with trust. Ya know I'd trust ya with ma life."

"Then what the hell is it, woman? It's the only way we might get a little real money. And we haven't had none since I was drivin' the bootleg trucks back in New York."

"I know yur right Buck, but all three of us is now earnin' a little. Even Ellen works some after school."

"Ya, she does. She's a good girl. But besides rent an' food mos' everthin' else goes fer things ya want Ellen ta have. Forgitin' me, when do *you* git, Maggy?"

"That's not importin'. Ya gotta remember she's fifteen now an'…"

The storefront was small and shabby.

A badly hand-printed sign was hanging unevenly from a wire in the dusty window.

The words, tilted slightly upward, read:

JAMES J. MCCORMACK
GENERAL CONTRACTOR
I CAN DO ANYTHING

To the fledgling proprietor, that ugly little home-made sign might as well have been one of the brilliant, multicolored, neon spectaculars in New York's Times Square.

Buck McCormack had survived!

Even more, his little sign meant that, finally, he would realize his boyhood dream. Now was his time. His chance to reach out and grab the brass ring. At last he was in the construction business for himself.

He was thirty-eight years old.

The Capone gang, mainly Frank Nitti, had been his only important contact and source of support during the entire decade of the thirties. And that was tenuous at best. Nitti had never given him a steady job. Nothing that Buck could ever depend upon. Consequently, his economic battle lasted the entire time since he arrived in Chicago.

He would never forget memories of hundreds of backbreaking menial jobs. More than once, he had been thrown out the back door of some grubby hash house without being paid for washing stacks of dirty dishes. Or mopping filthy floors in some fleabag rooming house. And only paid part of what he had been promised.

He still felt that anger and pain, deeply embedded inside his powerful body, it would stay there forever. But his struggle also had created an emotionally and physically tough giant.

The federal government's unemployment figures showed more than twelve million out of work. Of course, no person in their right mind ever believed that statistic. Most economists believed the more accurate total was, at a minimum, twice the admitted figure. If twenty-five million were out of work, one out of every two American breadwinners was out on the street.

And in those days, long before unemployment benefits or any other social safety net, that meant total disaster. Go sell apples on the corner.

Who cared? Certainly, not the federal government.

'Uncle Sam' was not in the 'people' business. Never was. And nobody knew that better than Buck McCormack. So, his sign in the storefront window said it all—with fierce determination.

"I can do anything."

But willing to do "anything" in the construction business, first required, at least, one minimum thing—a truck. Buck had tried every small bank he could think of.

Yet. No loan. No truck.

Out of sheer desperation, and with Maggy's fear of failure still ringing in his ears, Buck headed downtown.

He got off the bus at LaSalle Street and looked up—slowly turning around.

The sight of the tall buildings in Chicago's financial district always disoriented him. But, somehow, today was different. Today was his point of no return. Resolutely, Buck pushed through the revolving brass door of First Illinois National Bank & Trust.

To himself: "Shit, man, this is some fuckin' marble palace—nothin' but money here."

As he passed the bank's platform in the middle of the main banking floor, the historical place where stern-faced men wearing small eye glasses and dark suits have always sat, Buck stopped to look at two men in muted conversation across a rich walnut desk.

One of the men looked up, eyebrows rising.

"Yes, may I help you?"

"I sure hope so," Buck replied, and walked closer to the heavy marble rail.

"Ya see I need a small loan to buy a truck. I'm jus' startin' a new business an' I have to make a livin.' An—"

"I think you had better stop to take a breath, Mr....?"

"The name's McCormack—Buck McCormack. What's

yurs?" Extending his hand, the banker responded, "I'm Henry Fowler."

Gaining confidence, Buck asked, "Are you a guy here that kin make a loan?"

"Sir, it would be better if you came around and sat down here next to my desk."

"Ya sure dat's okay wit the guy dat's wit ya?"

The second banker: "First and foremost we're here to help our customers."

Buck asked the second banker, "Are you the boss around here?"

"You might say that. My name is Lucien Grey—I'm the Chairman of the Board."

"Holy shit, sir," Buck blurted. "Sorry—I didn' mean ta be outta line."

"Perfectly all right, Mr. McCormack, Mr. Fowler will try to help you now."

"Maggy, Maggy—I got it—I got it!"

"Whatcha got darlin'?" Maggy replied?"

"The loan, my girl, the loan to buy my truck." Buck bubbled.

"Oh my." Maggy said, "Jus' las night I asked the Lord again 'bout the truck."

"Well, this time he heard ya. Here's the check—$250. We're off ta the races."

Once Buck started—he never looked back.

And he never would.

TWENTY-TWO

Would the trifles of the summer of 1939 come back to memory some day as incidents of the happy lull before the storm?

King George VI and Queen Elizabeth of England visited the Roosevelts in Washington and Hyde Park.

Clark Gable and Vivien Leigh starred in *'Gone With The Wind.'*

Robert Donat won an *Oscar* for *'Goodbye Mr. Chips'*.

Then—August 24th produced these unexpected headlines in New York.

VON RIBBENTROP IN MOSCOW;
GERMANY & RUSSIA SIGN 10-YEAR NON-AGGRESSION PACT;
HITLER REBUFFS LONDON;
BRITAIN AND FRANCE MOBILIZE!

The world held its breath—waited—and prayed.

The stock market hesitated, sold off a little,—then wobbled to the closing bell. Most Americans stayed glued to their radios to hear the latest bulletins.

Early on the morning of September 1, 1939, the terrible waiting ended.

Hitler's armies had marched into Poland.

But still an important question remained.

What would be the response of Britain and France?

Two days later, on Sunday morning, September 3rd, that answer was delivered.

Over the crackling radio from London came the frail, unsteady, monotone of a fatigued Neville Chamberlain—the beaten British Prime Minister. He was about to make one of the most important public pronouncements in history. More than thirty-five years later, let's listen again to Chamberlain's fateful words.

"This morning, the British Ambassador in Berlin handed to the German government a final note; stating that unless we heard from them by eleven o'clock, that they were preparing at once to withdraw their troops from Poland, a state of war would exist between us.

I have to tell you that no such undertaking has been received. And in consequence—this country is at war with Germany."

World War II had begun!

Earlier that year, in January, President Roosevelt had asked Congress for heavy increases in armament production. A few months later on Easter Sunday, as he left 'The Little White House' in Warm Springs, Georgia—where, six grueling war-years later, he would die—Roosevelt called out to the crowd at the station,

"I'll be back in the fall—if we don't have a war."

Along with many other small-businessmen, Buck McCormack could measure the true start of his construction business from that time.

At long last—but for the wrong reason—happy business days were here again. But America could not convert buildings, or manufacture the equipment and supplies of war fast enough.

Meanwhile, Hitler's Panzer Divisions were streaking across Europe as though opposing forces were not even there.

Poland, Austria, Czechoslovakia, the Low Countries, Norway, Denmark—then, shockingly swift—France.

They all fell like so many dominos.

Next. The Soviet Union.

The absolute future of the Free World was now totally dependent upon the production ability of the U.S. "The Arsenal of Democracy," personified now by "Rosie the Riveter." America's new working woman.

And Buck told his wife,

"Ya have ta come down to the store full-time now, Maggy, I can't be answerin' the damn phone, out workin', an' hustlin' jobs—all at the same time. It's jus' getting' ta be too damn much."

Maggy effervesced, "I luv ya—ya big galoot. From here to County Cork."

As if on some magical cue, the phone rang. Buck answered.

"Ay Buck, it's Frank Nitti," began the most important phone call of Buck McCormack's life. "Der's a guy goin' ta call ya—name's Harry Potangeleone. Harry's a ingineer wit da Public Works Administration. Bin der for years. A good fren' a mine. An' he kin be a good fren' a yurs—*a real good fren.* Capisce?"

"I got it, Frank—I hear ya—we'll be good friends—ya kin' coun' on it."

"I'll keep in touch wit ya, Buck."

The receiver slammed down.

Buck and the diminutive Harry Potangeleone, who Buck quickly re-named Harry 'Potato', did become good friends over piles of corned beef and cabbage for Buck, and much pasta for Harry. Washed down with good Irish Whiskey, cold mugs of beer, and many glasses of Italian red and white wines.

The little 'Potato' knew everybody and everything there was to know about public works contracts in Chicago. For the right people, Harry was a potential gold mine.

In short order, Buck and Harry Potato, who stayed on

at the PWA to be the 'inside' man, together with Frank Nitti, Paul 'The Waiter' Ricca, and Tony Accardo—the three top Chicago mobsters who took over the Capone empire—after Big Al went to prison for income tax evasion, formed a construction business partnership.

They continued to call it McCormack Construction. Their combination had it all. And it worked like a charm from the beginning.

Harry, the fox in the hen house inside the PWA, plus his impressive engineering skills; the mob's contacts at City Hall; everybody who was anybody was 'in the pocket.' And Buck's surprising business skills, aggressive determination to succeed, and his amazing ability to find and keep the best sub-contractors. Everybody liked him.

Quite naturally, their firm had the best 'protection' in the city. With Harry's advance knowledge of what was going on inside the PWA, Nitti, Ricca, and Accardo, in a bewildering series of threats, favors, payoffs—whatever was necessary—took care of the rest. Their powerful influence completely blind-sided the Chicago construction establishment, who were already counting their own huge profits on the gigantic State Street Subway Improvement Plan—in advance.

When the PWA rather miraculously, awarded that juicy plum to the comparatively unknown McCormack Construction Corporation, the Chicago establishment construction firms howled to the sky. But they never had a real shot. The mobsters had it 'covered' right off the bat.

The Chicago Tribune ran screaming headlines like:

"The Real Power Behind McCormack Construction"

And, "McCormack Performance Bond Questioned!"

While these illegal activities increased costs, the McCormack partners always found ingenious ways to recapture. Like mutltiple deliveries of the same order. And drawers full of signed delivery receipts for which no material at all was ever delivered.

This hanky-panky provided more than enough political grease for all the wheels. Most union leaders openly accepted their stuffed envelopes. A few judges and politicos sent trusted bagmen. None left empty-handed.

A handful of disruptive canaries were left lying with the fish at the bottom of Lake Michigan. The only live singers still to be heard in the Windy City were performing at places like the *College Inn* at *The Sherman*, the *Camellia House* at *The Drake*, and the *Chicago Opera*.

But, the unfamiliar publicity made Buck nervous.

Despite all the noise, Harry calmly assured him, "Relax, my friend, I've got it all under control." And he did. Completely.

Next came the huge contract for the extension of Lake Shore Drive to Belmont. Again, almost overnight, the partners made more millions. And the contracts kept right on coming.

A few months later, at Buck's urging, little Harry Potato finally resigned from the PWA and officially came to work with Buck. He stayed for the rest of his life.

Their huge local success did not go unnoticed at higher levels. Ricca and Accardo, with their national crime syndicate connections, and hefty contributions to important Democratic politicians, saw to that.

Quickly, McCormack Construction began to acquire an impressive national reputation.

TWENTY-THREE

Over the next few years, Hank Brady pushed a tremendous amount of valuable advance information Gar's way. And he was able to convert most of it into new clients for his burgeoning law firm.

In other instances involving existing clients, he continued to astound them with his uncanny ability to steer them in the right direction—and always well before their competition.

Equally important, staying his own course, Gar had still not told David about the deal he had cut with Hank. From the beginning, he had been paying David's share of the profits into an account he opened at a New York bank which had nothing to do with Grey & Ross.

Seated at his desk late one afternoon, Gar heard the muffled ring of an unlisted phone he kept in a locked walnut box. Only Hank Brady knew that phone number.

Picking up, "Yes Hanko."

"Just a fast question, Gar. Does your Father's bank do business with Buck McCormack?"

"Why do you want to know?"

"Cause almost every job we lose—we lose to McCormack. There's a smarter way, Gar."

"That's for damn sure. To answer your question, Hank—Dad and Buck McCormack do a lot of banking business together. They're also good friends."

"So, do you think you can ask your Dad to arrange a lunch or something."

"No problem Hank. Consider it done."

Despite the age disparity, Gar and Buck McCormack were a business match made in heaven. From their first meeting over lunch at the Imperial House, these two chauvinistic men's men clicked because they seemed to instinctively trust and understand each other. They arranged to meet several more times to discuss matters of mutual interest. It all went well. Gar kept Hank updated.

A few months later, Gar volunteered to his Father, "You were right on, Dad, about Buck McCormack. Not only is he a nice guy, but his word is his bond."

Lucien replied, "Absolutely true, my boy. Buck McCormack is a gem of a man. And I've known that for many years now. So do all of my senior loan officers. You don't normally find a lot of honesty and integrity in construction."

New York attorney Sal Bellini remembered that about Buck, too, as he asked his secretary to get "Mr. McCormack" for him in Chicago.

It was October, 1945—two months after Japan's surrender.

Buck came on the line. Bellini's secretary wisely asked if he could call back on a secured line. A moment later Buck was back and Bellini picked up.

"Buck, how are you my old friend?"

"Hey Salvatore, long time no hear. What's goin' on—what's up?"

"First, how is Maggy and your daughter? Good—Good.

Buck, I hear from our mutual friends in Chicago that you're doing well and they think you're ready to take a very important trip."

"Where to, Sal?"

"I'll tell you when I see you."

"What's the big fuckin' secret? Are we gonna stick-up a bank?"

"I'll make it short. Just listen—and don't say a word about meeting me, Buck—okay—not even to Maggy. Meet me at the Miami Airport tomorrow at noon—all alone—no gophers. I'll be alone too. I'll be waiting for you at Eastern Airlines. Gate 8. You can tell Maggy you'll only be gone for one night Buck—but that's all. You got it?"

"I got it. But gimme a chance to write it down for chrissakes. Mus' be goddam importin'."

"It is Buck—very important. Noon. Eastern. Gate 8. O.K.? See you tomorrow in Miami."

"Ladies and Gentlemen, may I have your attention, please. This is Captain Erickson. We've just turned on the seat-belt sign and ask that you extinguish all smoking materials at this time in preparation for our landing at José Martí International Airport in Havana."

The stairway was rolled up to meet the Eastern Lockheed Constellation and locked into position. As they descended the steps into the sub-tropical humidity of Havana, Buck and Sal were pointed out to the driver of a black Cadillac limousine parked importantly near by—directly on the slightly sticky tarmac.

They were getting the full VIP treatment, which was boringly observed by the Cuban authorities. They had witnessed this scene countless times before—and could not have cared less. The limo immediately took off—no questions—no customs inspection.

Walking through the ornately-elegant lobby toward the registration desk of the world-famous Nacional Hotel, hearing a mixture of many languages, predominantly English, Spanish, and Brazilian Portuguese, the two Americans were politely intercepted by a distinguished-looking man who nodded his head slightly and extended his hand.

"Good afternoon, gentlemen. Permit me to introduce myself. I am the hotel manager, Enrico Hernandez. If you will please follow me, your suite is ready."

Looking at Buck, Sal touched a warning forefinger to his lips and shook his head, ever so slightly. Buck wisely remained silent. Their two-bedroom suite was perfection—comfortably large, plush, and both bathrooms were loaded with piles of thick white bath towels.

The manager wished them a pleasant stay. The bell captain refused any tip. Both bowed their way out.

As the double-door to the suite silently closed behind them, and an electric lock automatically engaged, Sal held up his hand and silently motioned to Buck to first read a note he had just written.

It said, "The room is probably bugged. Don't talk. Write."

As if on cue, the phone rang.

Sal moved quickly to answer. "Yes."

A deep-throated male voice said, "Please come to the lobby promptly at 6:30. You will be found and escorted by the manager. Follow his instructions. White dinner jackets, black trousers, and all other accessories, will be provided and delivered promptly at 5:45. We have all the necessary measurements. Don't be late." The phone abruptly clicked off.

At precisely 6:30 a smiling and gracious Enrico Hernandez again greeted them in the lobby. "Good evening, gentlemen. Please follow me."

He led them toward a white, half-louvered door on which a mini brass plate engraved with black letters discreetly proclaimed, "Private."

As they approached, the door emitted a soft buzzing sound. Without breaking stride, Hernandez pushed through with Sal and Buck on his heels.

The door closed behind them.

They were in a small walnut-paneled room—the size and shape of a hospital elevator.

Almost immediately, the little room began to climb.

Not only was the room the *size* of an elevator—it *was* an elevator!

Hernandez said nothing.

Sal and Buck were certainly not the first passengers to be caught off balance by this moving magic carpet. Wherever they were in the hotel, they had reached their destination. The door opened without a sound.

As Sal and Buck walked off the private elevator directly into a large and impressive apartment, a short, slightly-built, middle-fortyish man with a pleasant yet serious expression, also wearing a white dinner jacket, extended his hand to Sal, saying simply, "Good of ya to come on such short notice, Sal."

"Always at your service my friend."

Turning to Buck, their host said,

"Hi ya Buck—I'm Meyer Lansky."

If the diminutive New York mobster and killer, only five foot-five and one-hundred forty-five pounds, had worked his way up in the legitimate corporate world, little doubt by now he would carry the title of Chief Financial Officer—or even CEO—of an important company.

Such was not the case.

The reality was that Meyer Lansky, a founding director and the acknowledged financial genius of the 'National Crime Syndicate' in the United Sates—the Mafia—and now the czar of all gambling in Cuba, rose with a gun in his hand from New York's squalid Lower East Side.

His youth was spent running from the police, mostly as the operator of back-alley floating crap games. Ultimately, Lansky hit gangland's bigtime as a close pal of the most feared gangster of them all—the super-notorious Charlie 'Lucky' Luciano. Then, add to his resume, that Lansky was the mastermind behind the original concept of Murder, Inc. The enforcement arm of the Mafia.

Back in the mid-30s, Lansky was looking down the road for ways that the mob could expand from their historical roots. Prostitution, illegal booze, labor racketeering, and robbery. Later on—came murder-for-hire.

A long-term planner, Lansky invited Colonel Fulgencio Batista y Zaldivar, commander of the Cuban Constitutional Army and absolute dictator of the island since 1933, to his Havana hotel suite. After simple greetings, he quickly got down to the purpose of his mission. Opening a suitcase stuffed with five million U.S. dollars—in 100s, 50s, and 20s, Lansky told the Cuban dictator, "This is our earnest money for the gambling franchise for all of Havana."

Without counting it, Batista replied, "Done." They shook hands.

For nearly twenty-five years after that meeting, until the 1959 Castro revolution, Meyer Lansky was the unquestioned ruler of all Havana gambling. And he ran it as a tight-fisted business.

With Black Tie requested at the tables, the rich and royal from all over the world could hardly wait to donate their money to the Mafia. And they did—by the millions. Also in gold and diamonds.

Thereafter, while Lansky regularly traveled to Europe, South America, and the Far East, opening gambling operations all over the world, he regularly dispatched his trusted payoff man, Doc Stacher, to deposit countless sums in various Swiss numbered bank accounts for the Cuban strongman. Batista reportedly received one-third of all gambling revenues as his cut of the action.

As always, Lansky's longtime partners Lucky Luciano, Frank Costello, and others were all cut in. Knowing when to share was just one of Lansky's many smart traits. It ensured short-term survival and long-term life.

Buck later told Sal in the men's room, "I dammed near shit when 'the little guy' told me who he was." Quickly, looking to his left and right, Sal whispered into Buck's ear, "Don't ever use that expression again, Buck—*absolutely never.*"

Buck raised his right hand as an oath. "Gottcha."

Moments later, Sal was served his Scotch.

Buck drank Irish.

Their host had milk.

Lansky began, "Buck, I've heard a lotta good things about ya from some of our mutual friends in Chicago. That's why I asked Sal to bring ya down. Ya see, I'm going to help an old friend to do some buildin' soon and I, myself, don't know that much about buildin'. But I guess that as far as yur concerned a buildin' is a buildin'—construkshun is construkshun—right?"

"Yah, pretty much so, Mr. Lansky."

"Call me Meyer."

"Yah, Meyer, a plan is pretty much a plan—unless there's somethin' unusual about it."

"As a matter of fact, there are two unusual things about this job. First of all, it's gonna be built in the middle of a goddam empty desert, which I personally consider stupid. The other unusual thing is my friend, hisself.

Ya see, he's never built a damn thing in his life. But all of a sudden he thinks he's a construkshun genius—like he built the fuckin' Empire State Buildin'—or somethin'. An' we're talking about some serious money here—like maybe two big ones. Things ain't cheap anymore."

Taking a quick glance at Sal, Buck said, "Meyer, I think ya left out part of yur story. Whether or not yur friend has any experience ain't importin' ta me. But if he's gonna build whatever he's plannin' ta build, an' he wants ta run da job alone—what the hell does he need a general contractor like me fur?"

The mobster nodded his head in the affirmative and replied, "Ya know, yur O.K. McCormack."

Looking over at Sal and waving a thumb like a hitchhiker in Buck's direction, Lansky said, "This guy's real good, Sal. Picks up fast. Talks straight. I like that."

"He is straight, Meyer. I'll vouch for Buck any day. And that's not chopped liver."

Turning back to Buck, "Yur right, Buck. He doesn't need ya—and wouldn' wantcha either. But I do. Ya see, I wanna protect the guy from hisself.

His name's Benny Siegel. A hot-headed, stubborn bastard if there ever was one. Sal knows 'im too. He can tell ya plenny stories about Benny's crazy temper. We bin friends an' partners since we was punk kids knockin' over pushcarts on da Lower East Side. The kid's always hadda very short fuse—specially if somebody calls 'im 'Bugsy'. That wild temper kin git him killed someday—an' I don't wan' that ta really happen."

"So whaddya want me to do, Meyer?"

"I wancha ta to look over da plans an' estimate da job fur me. I gotta know da real score. Ya see my Sicilian and Irish partners are lookin' over my shoulder all da time on dis deal. They tell me they're goin' for it only because Benny's my boy—like a son. So they make like it's my own personal deal. Sure, I'm strong for Ben on da one hand—but it's business as usual on da other. There ain't no other way fur me ta play it. Ya unnerstand what I'm sayin', Buck?"

"Sure I do, Meyer. Jus' lemme know when the plans are ready."

Lansky nodded his head toward one of two ever-present bodyguards who had been silently listening to the conversation. The thug immediately disappeared into an adjoining room.

Lansky's full-floor apartment was conservatively furnished by gangster-garish standards. And was surrounded on all four sides by a wide, beautifully landscaped terrace. A number of hidden cameras monitored every inch of space. The floor-to-ceiling windows were double-plated and bulletproof. Nevertheless, four armed toughs, each assigned to one side in four-hour shifts, also kept a twenty-four hour watch.

Meyer Lansky's safety was a matter of great concern to everyone interested in the gambling activity in Havana. Beyond his partners, that group also included his many enemies, who envied his gambling stranglehold over the entire tropical paradise. And from time to time, through various channels, some of those enemies had the balls to make direct overtures to Batista. His response never varied.

"I only trust Meyer Lansky. Do not waste my time."

The bodyguard quickly reappeared with a heavy roll of blueprints held together by several monster rubber bands. Another goon carrying a large picture and a display easel followed him.

Lansky barked, "Set da easel up over here an' roll da prints out over der on da big table. Augie, you an' Joey hold down da ends."

Sal and Buck stared at the large picture standing on the ledge of the easel. Both were completely dazzled.

Lansky remained silent and expressionless.

The subject captivating the two visitors was a large-scale color rendering of what the front elevation of a sprawling, ranch-style, hotel-resort-casino would look like.

Even the background of huge mountains topped with scattered snow was startlingly different. Nothing even remotely like it had ever been seen before. Nothing like it had ever been dreamed before, either.

It was very impressive.

A huge and jazzy bright pink neon sign, with a highly stylized script logo ran across the entire facade—seemingly floating in the air.

It screamed, *'FLAMINGO'*.

At last, the darkly handsome, maniacal New York killer, 'Crazy Bugsy' Siegel, thirty-nine, a co-partner with Meyer Lansky when they ran the murderous 'Bugs & Meyer' mob—and the same guy who had been assigned to the relative safety of Los Angeles in 1937 by the N.Y. Mafia, had become a Hollywood big shot. Running around with Gable, Cooper, and Harlow, Siegel was now the best pal of his lifelong friend and former bootlegger, actor George Raft. As well as the publicly-praised lover of actresses Wendy Barrie and Marie 'The Body' McDonald.

Yet, he was always up to his eyeballs with the mob bag

lady, Virginia Hill, "the bait to my shark." He also affectionately called his long-legged Alabaman mistress, "My flamingo."

Now—this very same 'Crazy Bugsy' Siegel, against everybody's best advice, was single-handedly about to invent the most famous gambling resort in the world—in Las Vegas, Nevada. With a population of less than 8,000 people, Vegas was nothing more than a dusty Southern Pacific Railroad water-stop in an otherwise barren and scorching desert.

Yet, Buck and Sal, together with the notorious Meyer Lansky, were not looking at a mirage. Not a figment of their imagination. All three men were looking at the very beginning of what would become the most famous and glamorous Mafia-controlled street in the world.

The Las Vegas 'Strip.'

While the unknown Del Webb of Phoenix was doing the actual building, Buck was passed off as one of his top men. They both knew they each had a job to do. But despite their many meetings in Las Vegas, building the huge casino-hotel for Bugsy Siegel was proving to be far more difficult than either man had bargained for.

Buck had estimated the original cost at more than two million dollars. But he also burned up the long-distance wires keeping Lansky updated on the insane cost overruns being forced, even threatened, by the headstrong Bugsy Siegel.

Webb told Buck that he overheard Siegel barking orders to have this person "fixed" or that person "hit."

Noticing the contractor's apprehension, Siegel gave Webb his boyish, toothy grin and simply stated: "Don't worry, Del. We only kill each other."

By the tens of thousands, the construction was spinning out of financial control. By this time, Siegel was feeling intense pressure from back East. Principally, from Lucky Luciano.

Despite having been convicted on ninety-one counts of extortion and compulsory prostitution by the ambitious Thomas E. Dewey—yet to become Governor of New York and Republican candidate for president in 1948—Lucky had secretly flown to Havana to confer with his partners.

There, Luciano and Lansky were battling daily over the cost of building the *Flamingo,* which finally had a very inauspicious opening in December, 1946.

The public was curious, but failed to appear in the droves Bugsy had predicted. That news angered the syndicate bosses—again, particularly Luciano.

Ultimately, the *Flamingo* would cost Bugsy Seigel more than money.

On the evening of June 20, 1946, he was assassinated as he sat in the living room of Virginia Hill's Beverly Hills mansion. The hit came on orders from Luciano after Siegel told him to, "Go to hell," when the East Coast mob boss demanded the return of more than five million dollars, which had been loaned to build Siegel's fantasy.

Lansky had suggested to Siegel, "Ben, at least begin to knock down the loan. Like in installments."

Lansky then told Mickey Cohen, Siegel's bodyguard, "Don't let Ben out of your sight."

Obviously, the order came too late.

TWENTY-FOUR

From an open phone booth at the Miami Airport, the connection was less than perfect.

"Gar, it's Buck."

"Where the hell are you, Buck. I can hardly hear you?"

"Well—let's jus' say I'm not in Chicago. But, I'll be back tanight. An' I gotta see you, Gar. How 'bout first thing in the mornin'?"

"Sure. My office at eight?"

"I'll be there. Have some coffee fur me."

Promptly at eight the next morning, "What's up, Buck? Can't be here in Chicago or both of us would know about it."

"Gar, you got any conflict of interest problems representin' me as my attorney?"

"You personally, or the company?"

"Jus' me fur now. We'll talk about McCormack Construction later on."

"Buck, is what you want to discuss related to wherever you've been?"

"Yup."

"Well, whatever it's about would be considered privileged information—and I would be bound by the confidential lawyer-client relationship rule. So you can tell me whatever you want. Then, I can commit to being your attorney or back off. Either way I can assure you that our conversation will not leave this room. So fire away."

After listening silently for most of an hour, Gar responded, "That's one hell of a story."

Holding up the first two fingers on his left hand, he continued, "Two important points here Buck. Number one. It's only your personal expertise and integrity that Lansky wants. Number two. The current project will not be in Chicago. So I have no conflict—for now."

Wasting no time, the following week Buck invited the sophisticated Sal Bellini to Chicago to meet young Gar. Over a private lunch in the 'Danny Thomas' suite at the swank Ambassador East Hotel, the two lawyers had an unusually frank first discussion with their mutual client.

Then, Buck had to rush off. "You two guys can sit and bullshit as long as ya wanna—but I gotta go back to work so I can afford to pay ya. I awready told Maggy she has to cut down on da food bills."

They all laughed at the very idea.

With Buck gone, the experienced Bellini baited and tested the much-younger Gar.

Sal had quickly realized in Havana that Buck could still be naive. And any slip-up with this Havana crowd, including this young Chicago lawyer, could be fatal.

These guys wouldn't hesitate for a minute to lose Buck in the Nevada desert or bury him in the poured concrete of the *Flamingo.* And Sal felt it was his primary job to protect Buck.

As to this sharp, but still-green, lawyer—well, you just never know. Sal decided to push further.

"As you've already discovered, Gar, my practice covers a wide spectrum of clients. I know many people who are engaged in all kinds of businesses. And I'm never judgmental about whatever people do for a living. It's not my business or concern. What they do need from me is a lot of steering, strategic legal advice, and tons of personal attention. And they get those things from me. Like Buck. He calls—and here I am. Same thing with my clients in Havana. And all my clients, wherever they're located. Even in the Middle East. The world's getting smaller every day."

"My people get the same from me," bragged Gar. "Looks like we're reading off the same page, Sal. Of course, I'm not in your class yet, at this point in my career. But with a little more time...."

The pair continued to parry and thrust, avoiding any number of direct answers—skillfully hedging for more than an hour. Buck could not have chosen two more dissimilar lawyers. The maturely smooth, New York born and bred Bellini. And the thirty-year old tall, sandy-haired, and upcoming Catholic Chicagoan, George Garfield Grey.

Shaking hands at the curb, a shiny black limo belonging to an important local friend was waiting for Sal.

"Talk to you soon my new friend, but don't forget to give a holler the next time you're in New York." Adding with a smile, "I'd be pleased to hear from you, Gar."

Despite their full dialogue, the skillful Bellini had yet managed to save a little something. As he started to enter the limo's back seat—he stopped.

Turning back to Gar, "By the way counselor, I nearly forgot—please extend my best regards to your Father."

As the Packard pulled away, Gar quickly made a mental note of the license plate number.

And wondered, "Does Sal Bellini know *everybody*?"

On his way out to Midway Airport, Bellini planned to make two stops. The first was merely good business.

He wanted to say hello to the co-chairmen of the Chicago Mob at the Lexington Hotel—Paul Ricca and Tony Accardo. The two men, Buck's remaining silent partners, seemed truly glad to see him. Off in a corner, the three engaged in quiet conversation.

Next, the long black car headed for the western suburb of Cicero, and came to a stop in front of a narrow, old, red brick house on 22nd Street. Only three blocks from the infamous Hawthorne Inn, which had been the suburban headquarters of the killer Al Capone in his glory days.

It would be hard to imagine a more unlikely place to be meeting an Irish prince of the Roman Catholic Church—His Eminence, Eamon Cardinal Shanahan.

Sal had not seen his old friend from college, since before the young priest traveled to Rome to study canon law at the Gregorian University.

The vast historical scope of the Eternal City completely mesmerized the mid-western Shanahan, who had had every intention of returning home, to work or teach somewhere in the sprawling Archdiocese of Chicago. But, in his own words, "I just got trapped."

A temporary summer job at the Vatican's Secretariat of State so impressed the under-secretary Monsignor Giovanni Battista Montini—later to become Pope Paul VI—that he was taken on permanently. He had sadly come home now to officiate at the funeral of his widower Father. They warmly embraced in fond recollection of their years of friendship.

Wearing the impressive black robes of a Bishop of the Church, the red-capped Cardinal was an imposing figure. At six foot three, he still had the husky build of the former star football player that he had been. Since his teen years, by sheer size alone, Eamon Shanahan had always dominated every physical space he had occupied.

But, he also had a towering intellect to go with his great bulk. Over the years, that intellectual capacity grew in direct correlation to his meteoric rise in the hierarchy of the Vatican Curia—the governing body of the Holy Roman Catholic Church.

After directly serving two Popes in many important posts in the Curia, Eamon Cardinal Shanahan was now the powerful Chairman of the "Instituto per le Opere di Religione," created in 1942, according to the personal decree of Pope Pius XII, "to manage cash, shares and property." Assets owned by the worldwide Catholic Church.

Strictly translated it meant:

"The Institute for Religious Works."

More prosaically, it was simply known as 'The Vatican Bank'.

Even more informally—The IOR.

TWENTY-FIVE

Six Years Later. Zürich: October, 26, 1951.

From Milan, Umberto Ben-Levi Goldmanni had come to Zurich on two important matters. From New York, but more importantly by way of Havana, so had Joseph 'Doc' Stacher, a portly middle-aged man.

Precisely at noon, Goldmanni, a classically handsome twenty-six year old Italian with black wavy hair, had begun to carry out his instructions.

He had been assured that there was nothing illegal involved. No risk of bodily harm. And he had been well paid—in advance. All by someone representing a certain Count Carlo of Bergamo. Although, in point of fact, he did not know whom he legally represented. He also knew that he would need this money, most likely, quite soon.

Holding a folded copy of the Paris Herald-Tribune and being purposely hatless, Goldmanni was leaning against the railing in the middle of the Quaibrücke, the southern-most bridge crossing the River Limmat. The river cuts the ancient Swiss financial capitol in two. That day, as on most days, the bridge had a steady flow of walkers and talkers. Residents and tourists.

Goldmanni had arrived in Zurich yesterday after having driven his powerful Ferrari like a madman all the way from Milan—crossing the Alps via the Simplon tunnel.

Stacher had arrived only a few hours ago via overnight rail from Paris, but had already completed the first of his assignments.

On this trip it was a stop at the palatial headquarters of Crédit Suisse on the elegant Paradeplatz, where he made a substantial cash deposit into one of the many secret numbered accounts to which he had access. On other trips deposits were made in many other banks. A long-time Mafia bagman, Stacher preferred to think of himself more as a trusted courier.

Regardless of the bank, however, Stacher's routine never varied. He punctually arrived at his previously scheduled time. In a private room, he would script-out the four or five-digit number of the particular account to be credited on this trip. In Switzerland, that number was considered to be the depositor's signature.

Before touching the deposit, however, Stacher's receiving bank officer would first leave the room to re-confirm with a senior official that the written numbered account was still valid. This was a mandated bank procedure according to the world-renowned secrecy clause, 47(b), of the Swiss Banking Act of 1934, which specified that any bank director or employee, or anyone involved in auditing or controlling banks, who violated the depositor's secrecy may be fined up to 50,000 SFr. or imprisoned.

Legend has it that this clause was written into the revised banking act so that when Nazi agents came searching for funds which had been deposited in Switzerland by German Jews, the Swiss would rally round the persecuted minority. History debunks this legend. In the fullness of time, 47(b) had protected the anonymity of all depositors.

Upon re-entry the banker's slight affirmative nod would indicate all was well.

Stacher would then hand-over his black Gladstone case. Expeditiously, the banknotes were tallied. The count was witnessed. Attested to by another bank employee. And receipted.

"Frisch und gesund." Safe and sound.

Squinting left and right into the bright noonday sunlight as he left the bank, Stacher also made his way toward the Quaibrücke. His part of the instructions were etched in his head. Casually, Stacher walked toward the middle of the bridge. The instructions called for Goldmanni to make the first move. If Goldmanni had known the identity of his opposite number's employer, he might not have felt so safe.

As Stacher approached, Goldmanni slowly turned to face him. Proffering the newspaper, he said in Italian-accented English, "Good morning, signore. Buon giorno. Would you like to read the *Paris Herald-Tribune*? It's a timely copy."

Knowingly, Stacher replied, "I don't have the time."

Simultaneously he raised his hand to look at his watch.

That was good.

Their first hurdle had been safely passed.

Stacher asked, "Do you know if Rome and Milan have the same time?"

Goldmanni again held out his newspaper—this time switching to his left hand.

"Here—you can look for yourself."

When Doc Stacher also switched to his left hand—both men were satisfied.

Quickly shaking hands, "Umberto Goldmanni?"

"Yes—and you are Doctor Stacher?"

"Just plain Doc will do fine."

The mere fact of this bridge meeting would signal that a mutual interest existed to go forward in a possible international business deal. By using this sub-rosa device, neither party would have any publicly rejected egg on their face. And in this complicated international deal that was extremely crucial.

On the buy side, there were two parties.

In Chicago, a wide-awake Gar Grey stared at his watch. It was 4:30 A.M. In New York, Sal Bellini stayed cool, and waited for a cable that would be faster than an overseas call.

On the sell side—only a single seller.

The I.O.R.—the Vatican Bank.

In the Vatican, Eamon Cardinal Shanahan paced, and looked at his Rococo clock.

For sale: The I.O.R.'s majority interest in the offshore Atlantic Overseas Bank in Nassau.

It was half after noon as Goldmanni and Stacher walked off the bridge. They already knew the location of the nearest cable office. In minutes, the three-word coded cable that Bellini was waiting for was on its way.

"Everyone is happy." It was signed, "Santa."

Immediately upon its receipt, Bellini called Gar.

Both understood the message.

"Try to catch a flight for New York this morning, Gar. Tonight we'll fly BOAC to London—then on to Rome. Charlie said he'd come up from Naples. I'll book all the arrangements.

More than thirty-one hours after taking off from New York's new Idlewild Airport, with a three-hour layover at Heathrow in London, an exhausted Gar and Sal finally landed at Rome's Ciampino airport.

"Is Charlie also staying here at The Excelsior, Sal?"

"No. No—way too public for him. According to the Italian police, he's not even supposed to leave Naples. So he's staying privately with a ladyfriend. But we're going to meet for dinner."

The Mafia's top banana, Charlie 'Lucky' Luciano, even as a deportee from the United States, still had powerful contacts everywhere. And let it be known at the Banco di

Napoli that he would be interested in the availability of a bank—especially in Italy, Switzerland or "Offshore anywhere."

When he received a confidential call from Rome, it was from an old and trusted friend. Carl Conti, an American who looked like the actor Vincent Price. Conti was long married to the widow of an Italian nobleman. A true Countess, who preferred that her down-to-earth American husband be known as Count Carlo of Bergamo. Consequently, as they say in Italian—he was *ben introdotto*—well introduced. He knew everybody that counted money—clean or dirty.

When the Count informed Luciano that there might be a bank for sale, even the world's most notorious mobster, who had not been surprised at anything in years—was very surprised.

"Did I hear ya right Carlo—da seller is da Vatican? Da Church owns a fuckin' bank in Nassau? Nassau—like in da Bahamas?"

"That's my information Charlie. The Church is the seller—but you never heard that from me. O.K? An authority at the I.O.R., an old personal friend from back in America, asked me to find a buyer. But the Church did not want their identity revealed until I was satisfied I had a legitimate buyer. So we'll set up a little shuffle. Charlie—you and I know we can deal."

Still shaking his head in disbelief—"I'll be a—dem sneaky priest bastards. Well—I don' really give a shit who da seller is. I'll call ya ta set up a appointment in Rome, Carlo. Still got da same number?"

"Still the same number, Charlie. Call anytime. I'll understand your message."

"Grazie tanto, Carlo. Ciao."

"Prego, Charlie. Arrivederci."

TWENTY-SIX

The first evidence of the appearance of Jews in Italy were the emissaries sent by Simon Maccabeus to Rome in 139 B.C.E to conclude an alliance with the Roman Senate.

Over the many intervening centuries, besides Rome, Jewish communities also came to exist in Milan, Genoa, Palermo, and other Italian cities.

The ability of the Jews to live normal lives fluctuated widely—from total freedom to great suppression. Such as during the reign of Pope Innocent III (1198-1216) who originated a series of restrictive measures, including an order that all Jews had to wear a distinctive yellow badge.

On the other hand, the influx of Jewish refugees from Spain after the expulsion of 1492, had a stimulating effect on Italian Jewry. Inasmuch as many of the newcomers were men of scholarship, they obtained the protection of several rulers including King Ferdinand I of Naples.

Nevertheless, in 1516 Venice established the *Gietto Nuovo* from which the word 'ghetto' is derived. And Jews were herded into the ghetto in Rome, established by Pope Paul IV, in 1556.

Undoubtedly, the worst of times for Italian Jews occurred during the highly anti-Semitic, Fascist regime of Benito Mussolini, during which many Jews found refuge in religious institutions.

Until less than six months ago, Umberto della Ghassi, the first-born and only child of Bernardo Levi Goldmanni, was not able to be known by his patronymic name. His true identity was known only to two people. One of them was still alive.

This was especially astounding in view of the fact that the Goldmanni family went back more than three generations in Florence and Milan. As his father and grandfather before him, Bernardo's family had been prominent art and antique dealers. And well known for their expertise and fair-dealing in a trade historically short in these traits. Over many decades, they had acted as principals for their own account and also as agents for the most famous European collectors. Nobility, royalty, and most of the great moneyed families of Europe.

Nevertheless, as a young Italian-Jewish father in the early nineteen-twenties, Bernardo became obsessed with fear for the safety of his only child and son. And an only child to be forever. His wife had died in childbirth.

When Benito Mussolini and his suppressive, anti-semitic Fascist regime came to power in Italy by 1923, Bernardo's fear grew to hysterical proportions. It began to consume him. Convinced that there was only one way to save the little boy's life, he gave the child over to the nuns at the convent of the Sisters of Santo Domenico at Brescia, begging them to give the child up for adoption to a loving and devoted Catholic family.

Baptizing the child, and after much praying for divine guidance, the Mother Superior had allowed Umberto to be adopted by a successful local family by the name of della Ghassi. Childless, they deeply loved the boy, and raised him as a good Catholic. A bright student, Umberto's adopted parents sent him off to the University of Florence, then, graduate school at The London School of Economics. He graduated second in his class with a major in "Money and Banking."

As prophecy would have it, during World War II, along with thousands of other Italian Jews, Bernardo Levi Goldmanni, his Father, and every other member of his large family, were rounded-up and sent off in sealed railroad boxcars—first to be starved and near-frozen—then murdered in the gas chambers at Auschwitz in Nazi-occupied Poland.

The only person still alive who knew of his Jewish birth was the retired Mother Superior at the convent, Sister Maria Pagliani—by now well over ninety. And, while her eyes and ears were no longer perfect, Sister Maria's memory was as clear and sharp as ever.

Sal answered the late-afternoon phone in the two-bedroom suite he was sharing with Gar. A woman's voice said, "Prima colazione alle otto." Breakfast at eight. Not another word. The line went dead. Not uncommon in Rome—but this click-off was intended.

To Gar's quizzical look, Sal said, "Charlie will be here for dinner at eight." And he was. Materializing out of the thin air. Certainly without a call from the Excelsior's front door or front desk.

That kind of public entrance for Charlie Lucky would have produced—first a buzz—then the immediate appearance of the Rome politzia in the middle of that grand lobby. Obviously, that was not how he entered the hotel. He had his own ways and means.

As the clock struck eight, there was a single strong knock at their door.

"Hey Charlie—benvenuto," whooped Sal. "It's good to see you, old friend." After a crunching bear hug, Sal turned to the waiting Gar.

"Charlie, this is our friend Gar Grey. He's a lawyer from Chicago whose done a lot of work for our pal Buck

McCormack there, and—"

Charlie Lucky quickly interrupted.

"Wayda minute Sal, I remember his Father. Owns a bank in Chi—right? Isn't he da guy who helped us at da '32 Convention at dat stinky Stockyard place? Ya, we was all fur Roosevelt. Your Dad, he raised a lot of money ta get FDR 'lected."

Extending his hand to Gar, "Glad ta meetcha, kid."

"Same here, Mr. Luciano."

"Jus' Charlie, Gar. All of us are on da same side—like always. Like me an' your Papa. And Salvatore, what da hell duz a guy have ta do 'round here ta get some food? A little vino, some pasta asciutta, maybe vitello al forno."

"I remembered all your favorites Charlie. The food's on the way up—any minute.

"Bene. Mi scusi." Good. Excuse me. "Think I'll take a piss." In surprise, Gar looked at Sal. In embarrassment, Sal looked away.

Over the course of his infamous career, Charlie Lucky had been called every name in the book—pimp, racketeer, extortionist, killer—while wearing the most expensive tailor-made suits money could buy in New York, London, and Rome. The one thing Luciano really wanted, but could never buy—was Class.

The luxurious suite included a large formal dinning room. A server announced in halting English, "Dinner is served, gentlemen."

In Italian, Sal asked both servers to leave, explaining, "Questo è privato." This is private.

Still standing, the three men raised their wine. "Salute." Glasses were clicked.

As they began to eat—Luciano began to talk.

"Well gents, I had a meet dis afternoon wit da guy what brought me da bank deal. I also have ta tell ya I still can't get over da fact dem Vatican priests own a goddam bank in Nassau—but they sure fuckin' do. Anyway, here's da deal:

Twelve million—denominated in Swiss francs—deposited inna secret Panamanian nominee account fur da 87% of da shares dey own. An' dey'll deliver da certificates anywhere in da world we want—guaranteed, genu-wine, wit' da proxies attached, an' in street name a' corse—when we pay over da dough. An' cash is O.K. too. Wouldya believe dat? Dem guys in da long black dresses reports nothin' ta nobody. An' dey don' pay no taxes ta nobody neither. Yu'd think like the Vatican is maybe a sovern' place.

An' der's still two more importan' points. Dey ain't gonna let us cherry-pick. If we wanna deal, we gotta take 'em outta der total position. Lock, stock, an' barrel—jus' da way da loan portfolio exists. No provision fur bad debts. Nothin'. An' dis one'll kill ya. The fuckin' price ain't even negotiable. Twelve big ones—take it or leave it. How 'bout dem balls?" Adding, "Dem virgin celibate guys mus' really be getting' their orders direct. Shit—it's like we're tryin' ta cut a deal here with God hisself."

Sal asked, "How about a balance sheet, Charlie—an operating statement—a listing of the bank's loan portfolio? No way we can go forward completely in the dark."

"My guy told me, if we're serious, dey'll work up somethin' fur us ta look at. Dey ain't never done them financials before 'cause da Pope wouldn' unnerstan' dem numbers anyway. He jus' wants ta give da dough away ta da poor people. But da big guy at the I.O.R. knows better. He told my guy, "Sure da Pope is infallible, but the Church can't run on a bunch of Hail Mary's."

Finishing, "Dat's one smart dude, I tell ya."

Complicated international law, made even more difficult by the Vatican's predilection for ambiguities, brought the negotiations to near-end several times. Charlie Lucky's view was classic gangland. "Some guys I had iced was easier ta do business wit den deez religious guys."

When Sal was past the point of exhaustion and ready to throw in the towel, Gar hung tough. With the crucial eleventh-hour intervention by Count Carlo of Bergamo the purchase of the Atlantic Overseas Bank at Nassau was finally accomplished. The final agreement, written in English, had to be translated into Italian, French, German, and Latin. Then proofed by four devoted Catholic translators.

In Nassau, no one would have believed that those sinister-looking men in rumpled brown suits and crushed felt hats—talking in emasculated English—were Gar's original founding partners.

On the other hand, anyone who knew the intensely competitive Gar Grey, never would have doubted that this relatively small purchase would ultimately represent the beginning of one of largest business enterprises in the world.

Perhaps, one should believe in God's miracles—after all.

TWENTY-SEVEN

On a recent night during the tense negotiations for the purchase of the bank, Gar felt quite brittle. Sal reacted. "I don't know where your head is tonight, Gar, but sure as hell it's not here. I'm going to bed. Why don't you go out for a walk—or something? We'll pickup our conversation right where we are in the morning."

"Good idea. Think I'll wander around for a while. Be back—whenever."

Sal joked, "Hear no evil. See no evil. Do no bed check." They both laughed.

Once outside, Gar started away from the huge white palace that is the Excelsior Hotel, whose driveway was bumper-to-bumper with shiny black limousines. Some were filled with robed Arab sheiks wearing their traditional kaffiyeh headdress. Others were carrying important looking European diplomats.

Beyond the odious fumes of the driveway, the night air felt good on Gar's face. Without an agenda, he began to stroll aimlessly down the Via Veneto. In 1951, the Veneto was already the most alive and elegant street in all of Rome. The epicenter of what would become known as 'la dolce vita'—the sweet life.

Turning right into Via del Tritone, and not until he was nearly there, did Gar realize he was approaching the Trevi Fountain. As he came closer, he smiled to himself. Had he unconsciously come this way for a special reason? The last time he had visited Rome—with his back to the Fountain, he had tossed a coin over his shoulder into the water. Having done that, legend has it that the magic of the Trevi will bring you back to Rome. That was before his marriage. Before he knew Ellen McCormack even existed.

Had she ever realistically existed for him? Was he fulfilled? Was he a completed man? His thoughts were suddenly interrupted by an alluring feminine voice over his shoulder.

"Another penny for your thoughts, Mr. American Man."

Turning toward the source, at once Gar was eye-to-eye with a most striking woman. Equally tall—stylishly slim—dusty-blond—striking green eyes. The flirtatious lady was wearing a textured, creamy-color Chanel suit. The narrow skirt topped by Coco's classic single-breasted box jacket—this one trimmed in a luscious sea green. And the trademark gold buttons.

"My name is Rio Roundtree," she announced. "What's yours?"

Gar replied, "Can I lie?"

"Sure you can. Tonight, you might be able to do anything else you want."

"Rio—if it's your real name—that's not one of the smartest things you ever said."

"Maybe I don't want to be smart tonight. Maybe I just don't want to be alone."

"Neither do I. By the way, my name is Gar Grey.

"Of course it is," she teased.

"Hey lady—if your parents could have named you Rio—"

She finished his thought, "...then your parents could have named you Gar." Quickly adding, "Let's stop all this bullshit? We're not a couple of teenagers."

"Don't know about you Rio, but I guess I'm out of practice."

"Well, Mr. Gar Grey, you sure do look married right this minute. For your information, that's a special kind of guilty look. Like you just got caught with your finger in the cookie jar—or somewhere much more interesting. But more to the point, you surely didn't have a wifely look in your eye before I broke up your reverie. So who's the other lucky lady?"

Ignoring her question, Gar asked, "Harry's Bar or Caffè Doney?"

Putting her arm softly through his, "It really doesn't matter, Gar. The important thing is that I found you—and for tonight I'm all yours."

"Come on Rio, let's go into Harry's and just talk for a while."

"Since I'm older, Gar, you have to answer all my questions. Or do what I ask."

"We'll see."

"Do you like older women?"

"Don't really know. I've never been with one."

"How about starting right now with this forty-one year old Texan?"

Gar added, "All six feet—small hard tits—very sensitive nipples—right?"

Rio finished, "And a starving pussy that can't wait to swallow you—whole." He clearly heard her last line—but pretended he didn't.

"Where in Texas are you from, Rio?"

"Rio Grande Valley. Can't you tell by my name? My Father was a rich cattle operator down there. Dead now. My Mom's gone too. Dad was a hard drinker who had a bunch of old cronies and a house full of Mexican servants. So he had plenty of Chicanas. The younger the better. But he was devastated when my Mom died—missed her dreadfully. He always said I reminded him of her. So when he was drunk, which was most of the time, he would burst into my room—and try to jump me. He succeeded once. I was only a fifteen year-old virgin. And I'll never forget it for the rest of my life.

I don't think my Dad even knew what incest meant. Or, if he did—he didn't give a damn. Later on, some of my girl friends told me that they had suffered a similar fate. Some of them were regular victims for years. Fathers, Uncles, Brothers. But they were too scared to ever snitch.

Anyhow—my Dad died of cirrhosis of the liver shortly after I graduated from Radcliffe. I was his only child—only heir. And if it makes any difference Gar, I've been married three times. Never was able to pick right. Mostly, I think I was always too scared to ever feel safe with a man in a legal marriage. Guess I tried because I thought that was what my Mother would have wanted."

Rio was deeply lost in the yesterdays of her mind.

"That one night with my Dad made me hate all men. So when I first went East to college, I experimented with a few lesbian affairs. It was safe. And I liked it."

Rio looked Gar straight in the eye, adding, "Sometimes, I still get that hankering—but then, I've always been a rebel. To hell with conventional society."

Aggressively, Rio put her next words straight in Gar's face. "You ever been with a man?"

"Never."

"They say there's some gay in every man. If you decide to try it, I'm also an experienced voyeur."

With equal curiosity Rio shot, "Ever made love with two women at the same time?"

"That I have, Rio."

Gar's answer excited her. She felt a rush—everywhere. Seated side by side on a red velvet banquette, turning to face Gar, Rio sensually brushed his lips with the tip of her tongue. They both had an instant reaction.

Hoarsely, "Are you ready to fuck me now, Gar—or are you getting off this way?" Without waiting for his answer, Rio hastily seized his hand under the table. "Here—feel this," she commanded.

There were no panties under that chic Chanel skirt—only Rio's clean-shaven pussy—stimulated by every step she took. Gar now knew why Rio always was at fever pitch.

Naked, constantly wet, and, above all else, king-size—Rio's exciting aggressiveness fulfilled every man's fantasy of what a sexy six-foot woman was all about.

Gar responded by sliding his entire middle finger into her now vibrating vulva. Startled by his unexpected insertion, Rio moaned softly. And closed her eyes.

By now, Gar was saturated with the very thought of making unrestrained love to this sex-starved mega woman. To pay the tab, he threw a hundred-dollar bill on the table—and grabbed Rio's hand. On the street, she somehow managed to direct their way to her magnificent near-by appartamento where their clothes quickly flew in every direction. Neither could wait any longer.

Instantly on her bare knees, she brought Gar to a great overflowing. Keeping him hard and erect in her mouth to the very end of his climax. Gar felt drained. As though he had just emptied the very core of his being.

In bed, Rio's tan, well-toned body and strong tennis legs, coupled with the world's most disciplined vaginal muscles, took Gar to a sexual level he had never known—or believed existed.

More than exhausted, he was now spent beyond his wildest imagination. But the insatiable Rio, still determined to reach her Promised Land, held Gar's cock so tightly inside her, that she continued to generate uncountable orgasms. Near faint, she was sated.

Upon his return to the hotel, a disheveled Gar drew a look and an attentive word from the Excelsior's doorman.

"Are you all right, sir?"

Weakly, "Yes, thank you. I'm perfectly fine."

The experienced doorman smiled to himself. "Americanos." And shrugged his shoulders.

For the first time in more than a week, Gar Grey had no trouble falling asleep.

Unbeknownst to Gar, earlier that evening as he and Rio were heatedly finding their way to her appartamento, another couple was walking just behind. The thirtyish woman stopped short. So did her escort.

"What's wrong, Nancy Lee?"

"It's—it's nothing. I thought I recognized someone I knew back in Chicago."

"Did you?"

"No. I guess I was wrong. His wife is nowhere near that tall."

But Nancy Lee Hendrix, a senior aide to the U.S. Ambassador to Italy—knew she was right. Ever since that first long-ago college night at Gar's boyhood home in Kenilworth—and a minimum of two times each week after that first time—she never forgot Gar Grey from any angle—with or without clothes. She also had never lost her yearning for him.

At four the next afternoon, an overseas call was directed by a secretary to the switchboard of the U.S. embassy in Rome, which had been originally built in 1890 as the Palazzo Margherita. The embassy was the former residence of an Italian Queen. The palace and the adjoining rose-colored consulate building are now part of the carefully guarded American embassy complex.

"Miss Hendrix would like to speak with Mr. David Ross—Grey & Ross—Michigan Avenue—Chicago—USA." Where it was nine in the morning.

"Operator, when you have Mr. Ross on the line, please call Miss Hendrix on this extension. Record if you must. Otherwise just monitor. It's nothing official—just a short personal call."

"Hi David—it's Nancy Lee."

"Hi, Madam Ambassador," he joshed. Any plans yet for Secretary of State?"

"You'll have to ask President Truman," she laughed. "But I think Dean Acheson is doing a great job. Seriously, how are all of you back there? That's great.

Listen, David, I need to reach Gar. If it's O.K. for you to tell me, I'd like to know where he is."

"As a matter of strange coincidence, Nan, he just happens to be in your town—and almost next door. He's stopping at The Excelsior. Give him a call. You know he's always happy to hear from you."

"Thanks, David. Love to Rachel and the children. I'll see you guys at Christmas."

In one motion, Nancy Lee hung up the overseas line and dialed locally. 4-7-0-8.

"Buon pomeriggio. Good afternoon. The Excelsior."

"George Garfield Grey of Chicago, please. Yes, I do know him. Please ring his suite."

"Gar Grey, here."

"Hi baby. It's me."

"Nan! Where are you?"

"I'm right here in Rome at work where I'm supposed to be. I guess that makes at least three of us here—right?"

"I hear you Nan, but I don't understand what you just said."

"Would you understand better if I told you that I was right behind you last night as you were racing to take some six-foot blonde broad to bed? And I don't have to ask if you scored. For a moment there, I thought you might even do it right in the middle of the Veneto."

"Oh."

"Don't sweat it, hon. I hear the same routine all the time. Something about being away from home for a longtime and so lonely. Right?"

"Come on Nan—knock it off. Are you free for dinner tonight?"

"Would you have called me, if I hadn't called you?"

"Don't start with the same old routine, Nan. We've plowed that ground before."

"Can you really ditch the big blonde for tonight?"

"Stop all this crap Nan—and I mean it. Just give me your address. Okay?"

"This minute, that's none of your business. Where should we meet for dinner?"

"For crissakes you're really up a tree over something that hasn't any meaning."

"We all react differently, Gar. Nine o'clock. Where?"

"Okay—have it your way. How about George's? Know where it is?"

"Everybody does. Do you think I've become some kind of a Roman dummy?"

"I'll be at the bar Nan—alone."

"Well, bully for you. See you there at nine. Ciao."

Gar was sitting at the piano bar when Nancy Lee came into his view, escorted by the owner Michele Pavia in his customary Black Tie, with a white silk square casually tucked into his upper left tuxedo jacket pocket.

Raising his hand in Gar's direction, "Le presento la Signorina Hendrix."

Gar was not prepared for what he saw. It had been nearly five years. And her international exposure at the Embassy was readily apparent. Rome had turned the always-attractive Southern co-ed from Magnolia Springs, Alabama, into a stunning European beauty. This night she looked very sophisticated in the latest Dior basic black, with fashionable blonde highlights streaked through her hair. Nancy Lee still walked the walk, like no one else he ever knew. Gar rose slowly as she approached. And simply stared.

"My God, Nan—you're a sight for these sore eyes."

"Everything of yours must be sore from last night—kiddo."

Gar moved the next empty chair at the piano bar closer to him. Nancy Lee nudged it still closer. The scent of her Arpége quickly enveloped both of them. And played with their heads.

The lovely lyrics to 'Unforgettable' faded from the piano into the background. Other people seemed to melt away. They were alone—with their pounding hearts. All else obviously forgiven, Nancy Lee leaned her radiantly smiling face to his.

"Married or not, the only thing that has ever really mattered to me since I've known you, is that I love you madly, George Garfield Grey—and I'll never let you go!"

But the object of her affection had a fleeting priority conflict. Having already forgotten what Nancy Lee had just said, Gar suddenly remembered he had forgotten to return Ellen's calls.

Two days later—his wife was still waiting

TWENTY-EIGHT

In the aftermath of the purchase of the Atlantic Overseas Bank and understandably hoping for an infinite series of finder's fees and other tokens of appreciation, Count Carlo of Bergamo threw an elaborate celebration dinner in Rome.

In attendance were all of the important Roman personalities—mostly bankers, various judges, and assorted politicians. The guests of honor—Gar, Sal, and Charlie Lucky. Joined by Gar's law partner, David Ross, who flew over from Chicago.

Meeting Charlie Lucky for the first time, predictably, David was not enthused. Privately saying to Gar, "We should talk about your relationship with this guy."

But Luciano was having a ball. He had known most of these people for years. At one time or another, they had courted his powerful international favor. And, at one time or another, he had had most of them safely in his pocket. This night, many of them seemingly glad to see him, were carrying on and laughing. Repeating stories they had not told in recent memory. Others kept to their own space.

Lucky's very existence rekindled memories they would have preferred not to recall. Earlier greed for material wealth was gained through unsavory partners—like Charlie Lucky—who never forgot the dirty details of any deal he ever made.

Near the end of the evening, Count Carlo discreetly mentioned to the three lawyers—Gar, Sal, and David—"If you gentlemen need any assistance in choosing resident legal counsel, anywhere in the world—perhaps in locating the legal ownership of your new bank, or any other matter, I would be most pleased to make some recommendations. Kindly remember, both our God in Heaven and the Catholic Church—are everywhere."

Two days later, showing the extent of his immediate sphere of influence, the good Count caused an impressive private luncheon to be held in Turin. Hosted by none other than 'Gianni' Agnelli, the dashing Chairman of automaker Fiat—and the most influential industrialist in Italy.

Others at the large oval table, in addition to Agnelli's brother, included: Leopoldo Pirelli, CEO of Pirelli Tire; Prince Ahmad ibn Saud, one of the many sons of the oil King of Saudi Arabia, who flew down from Paris; Dr. Franz Josef Ritter, an important lawyer from Vaduz, the capital of the tiny Principality of Liechtenstein; and, not to forget, the Prime Minister of Italy—who "just happened to be in Turin today." Gar, Sal, and David, were duly impressed by their initiation into 'The Club.'

A Fiat corporate plane had them back in Rome by late afternoon, where Gar found three messages.

"Call Rio Roundtree—5279."

"Miss Hendrix, U.S. Embassy—5100. Ext. 41."

"Please call your home—whenever you get in."

A guilty Gar reached for the phone thinking, "It's about ten this morning in Chicago."

The hotel operator came on the line. "Sì signore."

"Operator, I would like to place an overseas call."

"I will get the overseas operator. Momento por favore."

After a short hold, "I am sorry sir, but right now all of the overseas operator lines are busy. I will call you when a line first becomes available."

A reprieve of sorts. With so many conflicts going on inside his head, Gar's mind could hold no more. At that moment he could not even recall his home phone number in Chicago. Setting the phone back on its cradle, he fluffed-up a pillow on his bed and turned off the light. The soft gray quiet of dusk was soothing. Gar closed his eyes.

Almost immediately, he was assaulted by one long loud ring on his phone. "Signore Grey, I now have the overseas operator for you."

"Operator, I would like to speak with Mrs. Ellen Grey, Chicago, USA." By now, he remembered his home phone number.

"Signore, I would estimate that it will take about an hour to complete your call. It is a very busy time of day. I will call you back as soon as possible."

"I will be waiting, operator. Thank you."

Once again Gar fell sound asleep.

In less than an hour, he heard Ellen's voice, which sounded like she was in China.

"Gar? Darling—darling can you hear me?"

"Yes, Ellen, I can hear you just fine. He couldn't, but—
How are you and the children?"

"We're all fine. But we miss you dreadfully. How's everything going—whatever business you're doing there?"

"Quite well. But everything takes so darn long. They don't work very fast here."

"I spoke to Rachel yesterday. She told me David is over there too. Do you have any idea when you'll both be coming home?"

"I'm not sure yet, but I think David will make it back before me. I may have to go on to Zurich with Sal Bellini when we're done here. We'll wait and see. I'll keep you informed. Stay well—kiss the kids for me. I'm also anxious to get home," he faked.

"Hugs and kisses, darling. Remember that I love you."

"I'll see you soon, Ellen. Bye."

With far more enthusiasm, Gar contemplated the other two messages he was still holding.

TWENTY-NINE

Proper introductions have always been a most important—sometimes crucial—consideration to the smooth-flow of two of Europe's most inbred societal functions. Royal marriages—mostly arranged for political and economic benefit. And the perpetuation of the status quo in business—for the same reasons.

So, it was not a complete surprise to the lawyer, Dr. Franz Josef Ritter, to have received a phone request to consult with Gar and Sal in Zurich—after meeting the two Americans at the Fiat luncheon in Turin.

Both the call to Ritter in Vaduz, as well as the proper introduction to Gar and Sal, was made by Count Carlo of Bergamo—a professional at benefiting from this sort of thing.

Ritter, a man in his mid 50s, could more than hold his own. He just happened to be one of the most renowned lawyers in all of Europe. And one of the most influential lawyers in the world.

Promptly at nine on the appointed morning, Ritter presented himself at the front desk of the swank Hotel Savoy Baur—on the prestigious Paradeplatz, where it crossed the equally elegant Bahnhofstrasse.

For symbolic reasons alone, nothing could be better located in all of Zurich. Three of Switzerland's five major banks were also located on the Bahnofstrasse.

While the tiny Principality of Liechtenstein covers only sixty-one square miles, squeezed between Switzerland and Austria, it is the registered resident country to more than 25,000 tax-advantaged foreign holding companies. Now it had one more. The Atlantic Overseas Bank of Nassau.

The 'Liechtenstein Attraction' as international financiers chose to call it, was not terribly complicated. Underlying the entire structure was an entity called an 'Anstalt.' It roughly translates into English as 'foundation' or 'institution.' But any similarity ends there.

The Anstalt was a financial creature that was neither required to list its true ownership, nor to reveal any of its dealings or records to anyone—not even to the government of the Principality. Even further, no matter how much it earned, its taxes would always be the same—only five thousand francs a year—about three thousand dollars.

As the skilled Dr. Franz Josef Ritter carefully pointed out—it was for good reason that some of the world's richest men used Liechtenstein as the hub for the 'most private side' of their business and amatory affairs. But the advantages did not come cheaply. The two most expensive aspects were the fees that had to be paid to men with prestigious resumes or titles who would front as 'directors.' As well as to the lawyers who administered these 'foundations,' under a blanket power of attorney. Herr Doktor Ritter would supply a slate of properly positioned directors. And estimated an annual cost for all services, expenses, and board fees, of one million Swiss francs.

"Zoh gentlemen—let us now get on wiz our buziness. Firsht, you must pick a name for your Anstalt. Usually a generic vord is used—in any language." Momentarily stumped, Gar and Sal looked at each other.

"I think I've got one," Gar exclaimed.

Turning to Ritter, "What's the German word for money?"

Ritter, already nodding his assent, smilingly answered, "Geld. Pronounced gelt."

Sal enthusiastically agreed. "Money it is."

'Geld' went into the proper space on one of the many forms Ritter had before him.

"Next. Do either of you haf any bank preference for ze numbered Swiss account? Ah—Mr. Grey, I undershtand from Count Carlo zhat your family owns a bank in Chicago. If I may make a suggeztion, 'Geld' should not use a Swiss bank zhat might, even indirectly, be an associated or a correspondent bank of your Father's. Too great a pozzsibility of zome kind of accidental discovery. To be absolutely safe, ve vill extend our layers of secrecy—pozzibly to South America. Zoh, how much, und from vhere, can I expect to receive ze initial funds?"

"Twelve million U.S. will be wired from the IOR—the Vatican Bank in Rome," Sal calmly told Ritter.

In his mind, Sal quickly threaded and rolled a tattered, sepia-tone film of an important conversation he had had with Meyer Lansky years ago in Havana.

"Jus' remember Salvatore, da IOR was da bes' place we never invented fer launderin' our casino stuff. Ya see, Charlie's got dis guy in Rome—a 'Count Somethin' or Other'—an' da Count he knows a big religus guy at da IOR. Dat guy takes a little action on da side—but dat's O.K. We send da dough ta Rome from da Atlantic Overseas Bank in Nassau—we is der biggest depositor. Den we put it away in dem secret banks in Switzerland. It kin stay der or dey invest it fur us in legit things. An' we never paid no taxes ta nobody—on nun of it. Howda-ya like dem der apples, Mistah Lawyer? Woodja ever gess I never finished da six grade?"

It was also against Italian law to export hard currency. And the authorities in Rome constantly fretted—to no avail. They had no jurisdiction over God's money.

Gar jumped in, "Which bank for a Swiss account? We can tell you that tomorrow."

"Goot enough. Mozt likely I vill file zhese papers in Vaduz sometime tomorrow. However, I haf a special account to accommodate ze cost of zhis sort of interim financial situation. Oh yes—another important item of business. It vould be mozt inadvisable for you to identify yourzelves by name in any phone conversation vit me—no matter ze circumstance. You muzt choose a code vord. I repeat—no personal identification—no matter ze circumstance—und vithout exception. Am I correct to undershtand zhat ve three vill be ze only parties to zhat code vord?"

Gar answered, "You are correct Herr Doktor Ritter."

"Goot. Zoh—if ve can now eztablish a code vord."

Slowly waving a forefinger, Ritter warned, "Und chooze carefully. Vonce adopted, ze code vord should never be changed. Much too rizky."

This time it was Sal who had the inspiration.

"Our code word will be 'Santa.' Okay with you, Gar?"

The younger lawyer replied, "Great. That's been a lucky name for us already."

Ritter: "Zoh—listen carefully. I haf written zome numbers on zhis card. Zey identify a private phone line. Use zhis number to contact me. Use no other means. I vill answer immediately from vherever in ze vorld I might be. If engaged, at vorst, by ze end of zhat day. Und as zoon as I leave here, it is my strong zuggestion zhat you both memorize zhis number. Even rehearse each ozzer a few times. Burn it into your brains—zhen burn it vit a match. Und flush ze ashes down ze toilet. Under no zircumshtance are you to leave zhis room vit zhat card intact. I take it zhat I have your vord on zhat."

Gar and Sal both nodded their assent.

"Zoh gentlemen, it haz been my pleasure to serve you. Until tomorrow zhen—"

Formally, Ritter bowed ever so slightly from the waist. One also might have imagined hearing a slight click of his heels. Then he was gone.

All smiles, the two Americans vigorously shook hands. Gar enthused, "Well Sal, our shopping list has just expanded. Now we'll have to include suntan lotion and swimming trunks."

Sal questioned, "Do we also include wives?"

Hunching his shoulders, Gar merely replied, "That's an interesting future question."

To celebrate, from somewhere Sal produced a bottle of good Rhine wine. Touching glasses, Gar challenged, "Hold on to your straw hats Nassau—here we come."

Pretending to be dancing with someone, Gar started to waltz around the room by himself. To music only he could hear. Shouting with excitement—"Look at me, Sal. I'm really Fred Astaire—dancing on top of the world."

"Just remember, Gar, when you're riding that high every other bright guy in the world wants to take a pot-shot at you. If they hit, it's a long and painful fall. I know guys who've taken that plunge."

"I really don't give a damn about those poor bastards, Sal. It's only numero uno—number one—that counts. Me, myself, and I. Screw the rest of the world—before they screw you. That's my motto."

Sal was so dumbfounded by Gar's outburst, he didn't utter a responsive word.

Silently: "Oh well my young friend—at only thirty-three you've got plenty of time to change."

THIRTY

Nassau, The Bahamas. November 23, 1951.

At Oakes Field, just west of Nassau, the new Chairman of the Board of the Atlantic Overseas Bank of Nassau bounced off the small charter from Miami.

It was 10 AM.

In his crisp blue-white seersucker suit, George Garfield Grey was in a big hurry.

"Why are you guys crawling on such an important day? Come on—let's move it." Three, were trailing. Sal, David Ross, and a last-minute passenger—Umberto Ben-Levi Goldmanni, Gar's new resident manager for Nassau. Recommended by Count Carlo of Bergamo.

With two large British-built taxis in tow, meeting them was another new partner—Meyer Lansky. The financial genius of the Mafia, now spent full-time as the gambling czar in Havana. The entire concept of the Atlantic Overseas Bank was originally Lansky's brainchild.

Enthusiastically, Gar extended his hand.

"Meyer—thanks for coming out—it's good to be able to put a face to the voice."

"Likewise."

Old friends, Sal Bellini and Lansky exchanged greetings. The others were introduced.

Twenty minutes later the two taxis turned into Bay Street. After several blocks, they pulled into the circular driveway of an imposing three-storied, pink and white Georgian mansion—the former residence of a high British government official. A small brass plate, located to the right of the double-door entry simply stated,

"Atlantic Overseas Bank of Nassau."

Inside the former residence nothing much had changed. One felt as though he had stepped back in time. Back through Alice's famous looking glass. It still was a beautifully furnished mansion. Gar had never seen a bank like this before. Nothing here to remind him of his Father's marble mausoleum—the First Illinois Bank & Trust in Chicago.

Using the massive curve of the walnut staircase that floated down to the elegant double-ceilinged foyer as a backdrop, waiting to greet Gar was the current bank manager. Thurwin Drevescraft, stood tall and slim, with slicked-down jet-black hair parted down the middle, wearing a navy blue bespoke Saville Row suit—the very formal Brit stepped forward.

"Welcome to the Atlantic Overseas Bank—Chairman Grey. I trust that you will find all matters in satisfactory order." Drevescraft turned and nodded: "Mr. Lansky—gentlemen—greetings all."

On the way in from the airport, Lansky had told Gar, "Drevescraft's a good man. Ya might want to think about keepin' 'im in some kinda job. He's a dependable thief. Knows ev'ry trick in da book—an' a few he makes up on da way." Gar chuckled.

"We'll see what happens, Meyer. Who knows?"

Inasmuch as the Atlantic Bank did not seek nor have any retail customers, there were no tellers and no waiting lines. Nothing whatsoever in this mansion gave one to believe that, indeed, this was a bank. The relatively simple banking business was mostly carried out in a large paneled library and two adjacent rooms. The only sound was the constant clacking of the Telex machine.

In point of fact, the Telex was the vehicle of choice for most of the deposit transactions of the Atlantic—except for the huge suitcases overflowing with U.S. currency constantly being lugged in from Havana, New Orleans and Las Vegas. The advantageous secrecy laws of The Bahamas were as tight as those of Switzerland or Liechtenstein.

As the group moved into the library, a strikingly beautiful light-skinned woman, in her mid-twenties, intently watched a message moving on the Telex wire. Obviously, she was the beauteous product of generations of much mixed Caribbean blood.

Gar's experienced eye locked onto her curvaceous but slender body. Looking up at the same moment—her timing was perfect. For an instant, their eyes met and held. She felt immediately undressed. Not a bad guess.

Drevescraft beckoned her over.

"Gentlemen, may I present Miss Victoria Tracy—my—your assistant manager. She is the person who makes my job here at the bank a lot easier—without exception."

Silently, Gar thought, "I'd bet on that."

As they mounted that marvelous staircase to the second floor of the bank building—again nothing had changed from the mansion's residency days. There were a number of apartment-suites. Some had sitting rooms. Drevescraft lived in the principal apartment, which included a small kitchen and a private dining room. The main kitchen and formal dining room were downstairs on the first floor.

The manager patiently walked them through the entire floor. When finished, he waved at a narrower stairwell that gave access to the third floor. "Vikki—Miss Tracy—occupies a small apartment on the third floor." Quickly adding, "With two other staff—including cook."

"These Brits do think of everything," Gar mused.

Drevescraft told them, "Our house steward, Mr. Johns, will have you all settled presently. If it is satisfactory to you Chairman Grey, after you have time to freshen up, I've arranged for a buffet lunch to be served on the terrace. I've not invited any staff. And, sir, there is a most important subject only we two should discuss in private."

"Good. We'll make a point of talking about it later."

Before lunch, Gar invited Lansky into the sitting room of his apartment.

With Sal and David present, "Meyer, I want to update you on an important change of ownership I worked out with Charlie before I left Rome. I have purchased a majority fifty-one percent of 'Geld' for $6,120,000. That money is already in the Anstalt's account. And Dr. Ritter has accomplished all the necessary documentation in Vaduz. I have never really worked for anybody else—and I didn't want to start now. Also, I wanted you to know where we stood before we chat at lunch with the others."

"Dat's a smart move on yur part, Gar. An' its okay wit me. Besides, you better lookin' den da rest a us. So yur pictures kin be gud for da papers. I even like ya better awready. Now, let's go down an' have some chow. Ma stomik thinks ma troat's been cut—an' dats not so gud in my kinda bizness." Laughing, they all headed downstairs for lunch.

Gar had taken the six million plus from the ten million inheritance he had received on his twenty-first birthday from his Grandfather, the first Lucien Smith Grey—the founder of the First Illinois Bank & Trust in Chicago. Gar's Father had been the legal trustee until Gar reached the age of thirty. Now all ten million was at his command with no strings attached.

With control of 'Geld' securely his, Gar moved swiftly. At lunch, in a quiet but firm manner, he immediately dismissed Thurwin Drevescraft and appointed Umberto Ben-Levi Goldmanni as his new resident manager. The Englishman was not the least bit surprised.

"Chairman, I wrote my resignation letter the day I heard we had new ownership. I know how the game is played."

Gar, then proceeded to surprise everyone at the table—except Lanksy. "While you're no longer the manager here, Drevescraft, you still work for me—if you want to."

"Thank you, Chairman. I will be honored to serve in whatever capacity you choose."

"Good. We'll talk later—or tomorrow. Now tell us all about this bank we own."

Before another word, however, a black server appeared at Gar's elbow, wearing red silk pants with a wide gold stripe down the side of each leg—topped with a white, vest-length linen jacket held together by two large brass buttons on a short chain. It was a typical British colonial uniform—a resplendent sight.

"Begging your pardon, sir—but there is an international operator on the phone for you. Permit me to show you to a private room."

Seated comfortably in warmly paneled privacy, Gar reached for the phone.

"Hello. Yes, operator. You need a code word? And do I understand what that means? Yes. Yes, I do understand. If the calling party can hear me—this is Santa."

Gar knew only one person could be calling for a code word. Then he heard the German-accented voice on the line asking, "To whom am I now shpeaking?" Gar replied again, "This is Santa. You're on the right sled. Proceed to slide forward."

Without any salutation, the voice delivered a stark eight-word message.

"Very important. Paris Ritz. Forty-eight hours. Alone."

Together in a bank limo, Gar and David went alone back out to Oakes Field.

David was saying, "Gar, you know I understand your conflict, but when you get back to Chicago we have to talk about the future of Grey & Ross. I can't handle your clients and mine with you gone so much of the time. Besides, your clients want you—not me."

Smiling, and giving Gar a slap on the shoulder, "You still charm their pants off, kid."

Upon his arrival in Paris, Gar checked into the fashionable Ritz Hotel in Place Vendôme. In less than fifteen minutes there was a knock at his door. Standing in the corridor were two guests. The expected Dr. Franz Josef Ritter and, to Gar's surprise, the affable Count Carlo of Bergamo.

"Welcome gentlemen—please come in. May I offer you a refreshment?"

Ritter: "It iz better, Mr. Grey, zhat ve proceed immediately to our buziness. Ve have a mozt shtartling piece of information vor you. Az you know, both the Count und myself haf done much vork vor ze Vatican over a number of years. Carlo, iv you vould now take up our shtory."

"Mr. Grey, a few days ago in Rome I had a conversation with a Vatican representative. An important person, but somehow not yet familiar with your purchase of the bank. He asked about the current status of the bank's option on a certain petroleum reserve. He recalled that it was owned through a Panamanian subsidiary—which turns out to be an oil refinery in Venezuela.

Of course, I knew nothing before of this matter. A fact, which I naturally kept to myself. Immediately, I called Franz in Vaduz and requested that he thoroughly review the many files of Vatican Bank documents in his underground vault."

Ritter broke in, "Und I found ze original of ze option agreement. Accurate und valid. Zoh. Now, Mr. Grey, inazmuch az you are ze majority owner of 'Geld'—az ve shpeak, you are alzo ze majority owner ov one-zhird of one ov ze vorld's largest known petroleum reserves. Vhile shtill an undeveloped property, ze virst official geological estimate iz zhat ze reserve contains, at a minimum, more zhan 150,000,000 barrels. If ve azzign only ze current 1951 value ov approxzimately $1.80 per barrel, ve are talking here ov a property vorth at least $180,000,000. Und, zooner rather zhan later, I am most reliably informed—double—triple—und even more."

After a quick glance at Count Carlo, Ritter continued—but now in a conspiratorial tone. "Mr. Grey, ve too did zome discreet checking. Vit ze exception of zhis Vatican celibate—nobody knows ze existence of zhis mozt valuable option—I repeat my dear sir—*nobody.*"

Trying to sound cool and calm, an astonished Gar asked, "So?"

With eyes now as big as extra-large saucers, Ritter exploded, *"Zoh?*—You now ask only *zoh?* Zoh, I vill answer you az plainly az I possibly can, Mr. Grey. Unless you have zoh much personal money zhat you don't give a damn—und zhis is big money—I ztrongly zuggest zhat you keep zhis valuable piece of information to yourzelf."

"Does 'myself' mean only myself, Herr Doktor Ritter—or do you two now consider yourselves some kind of partners in propria persona—as in *my* person?"

"Come, come Mr. Grey—ve are talking here az three professionals, nicht kinder—not children. Are you pozzibly zuggesting zhat vee all zhree agree here und now to handle zhis kind of potential money pro bono—vithout any compenzation?"

Gar replied, "We'll deal with that subject shortly, Herr Ritter. Right now, I have more important questions that need answers."

Ritter, quickly deflated, "Vhatever qvestions you azk, sir—I vill reply in my best."

"Good. For starters, I have two questions. One. Where is this reserve located? And, two. Who owns the other two-thirds? Who are my partners?"

"Zhis petroleum reserve, Mr. Grey, underlies a vast barren desert in Northeashtern Zaudi Arabia—near its borders viz Bahrain und Qatar.

Und here, I pause to collect myself for ze answer to your second qvestion, Mr. Grey. Vhich, I assure you, vill have ze greatest possible impact on ze rest of your life."

"The rest of my life? Strong words, Herr Ritter. What makes you think that?"

"Becauze it vill prove to be ze most financially und emotionally rewarding ov all your possible life's exzhperiences. Particularly vor a man zuch as you—ov ze Vestern Vorld. You zee, Mr. Grey, ze fact ov ze matter iz—you don't have partners—in za plural. You only haf *one* partner—in za zingular. Und I might add—*very* zingular."

"For God's sake Ritter—enough is enough—what the hell is his name?"

"Your partner's name is Abdul Aziz ibn Abdul Rahman Al Saud.

"Who's he?"

"He just happens to be ze King ov Zaudi Arabia!"

THIRTY-ONE

As the inevitable consequence of Ritter's earlier disclosure, Gar was unable to sleep. He spent most of the night strolling the streets of Paris. Thinking mostly about oil. He gave short shrift to the situation with Ritter and Bergamo. "We'll work something out," he said to himself. "I'd probably pull the same card if the tables were reversed."

Back in his Ritz suite, Gar waited for first light—then picked up the phone. In Rome, a sleepy Nancy Lee Hendrix, thinking it was the Embassy calling, groped in the dark. "Hendrix here."

"Nan—Nan wake up—it's me—Gar."

"I know who it is. But jeez, hon, it's still dark. Why the crazy hour?"

"Cause it's urgent, Nan. So try to shake the cobwebs."

"Okay, okay. I'm up—sorta. What's so urgent? Where's the damn fire?"

"Today is Friday. Are you free to spend the weekend with me here in Paris?"

"Is this your weird idea of a proposal—or is it more like a proposition?"

"Nan, I don't have time for any of your nonsense right now. Just listen to me carefully. The subject is oil. With a capital 'O'. By the end of today, what material can you get your hands on that you can bring with you tonight to Paris? I need to learn everything I can about oil. Like... Who?—What?—Why?—When? Including everything there is to know about the current situation. Particularly with all the double-crossing that's going on between Iran and Britain. In other words, Nan, I need you to provide me with a fast tutorial on oil. Got it?"

"Why don't you just go to the library—it's all there?"

"Come on—this is big and it's serious. I'll tell you all about it tonight."

"Hold on, hon—if what you're looking for is more than what's available in any library—what are you *really* asking me to dig up?"

"I'm not too sure of that answer myself. But oil is big stuff—and I'm sure that the State Department as well as the CIA must have truckloads of information on all the players—and you must have plenty of that information in your Embassy files right there in Rome."

"We probably do. But it's all classified material. Gar, my honey-bunch—and I hope this doesn't shock you too much—but I never included 'spy' on my work resume. What would I tell my family as to why I'm in a federal prison for thirty years? You got any great answers to that kind of question?"

"Hey, I'm not asking you to go that far."

"Just how far *are* you asking me to go?"

"I guess I'm asking you to push the 'safe' envelope as far as you possibly can—but short of getting into serious trouble. You know damn well, Nan, I would never ask that of you."

"Well, I *think* I know that. But you have never given me a lot of reasons to totally trust you. Anyhow, where are you stopping in Paris? You...you...international spy handler?"

Laughing uproariously, "I'm at the Ritz."

"I'll get back to you later in the day. But don't you dare leave your suite—cause I won't leave any message.

There's a flight out of here tonight about seven. I'll try to get on. Bye."

First it was announced in French. Now, the public address system at Orly airport was announcing in French-accented English. "Your attention please. Alitalia—Flight #4—from Rome—is now arriving at Gate 8."

Recognizing her walk before he saw Nancy Lee's face, Gar had to laugh to himself. Walking across the tarmac, her wrist chained to an official-looking briefcase, and wearing a fashionable trench-coat pulled tightly at the belt, collar up, slouchy black felt hat with the brim way down in front—Nancy Lee was doing a super imitation of Ingrid Bergman in Casablanca. Her grim expression turned into a big smile as she threw herself into Gar's arms.

"Even in this goddam rain—and surely headed for jail," she joked, "I still love you madly. Here, take my tote bag—that's all I brought. And this briefcase, which weighs a ton with what I 'borrowed' from the Embassy files, is so tightly locked to my wrist it's been hurting like crazy ever since this afternoon. See—it's marked 'United States of America. Department of State. Official Diplomatic Pouch.' And there's our Seal too. Hon, would it sound corny if I said this pouch and all the stuff that's printed on it makes me proud to be an American?"

"Not at all. You're the kind of grass-roots person that makes America great."

"Ya—and a spy too—right?"

"That's a completely different thing. Let's change the subject."

"By the way, I was officially cleared for Paris from the Rome Embassy—so no customs."

"Good. I've got a limo and driver out front—let's get the hell out of this airport."

In his Ritz suite, "I've ordered dinner sent up, Nan. Thought that would appeal to you."

"Right on, hon. Get a fire going. I'm heading for a hot

bath. Should be a cold shower."

Reciprocally, Gar's instant reaction to Nancy Lee was rigid and ready. Despite the chilly and rainy Parisian night, he already felt hot and horny. A condition that occurred whenever Nancy Lee was in his orbit. The scent of her Arpège which filled the room, made Gar's nostrils flare. He felt hyped-up like a racehorse getting ready to run the Derby, the Preakness, and the Belmont—all in one day.

Two hotel servers smiled pleasantly as they set up dinner for two. But, Nancy Lee did not hear them come into the suite.

To tease Gar, she entered the living room totally naked swinging a hand towel overhead in the manner of a stripper walking across the stage.

"Hey there big boy, I know we have a lot of work to do but if you wanted to eat me first as an appetizer, I wouldn't put up too much of a fight."

Without waiting for an answer, in one simultaneous movement Nancy Lee was on the carpet—with her legs spread open.

"How about raw like this, hon? Like oysters. Supposed to be healthy."

For all to see, the marvelously well endowed Nancy Lee Hendrix—daughter of a lifetime member of the ultra-conservative Daughters of the Confederacy—lay provocatively reposing, with every luscious part of her on full display. As Gar turned to look, Nancy Lee spotted the two lasciviously smiling servers in a far corner waiting to serve dinner. For an instant everyone froze. Red as a beet, she raced back to the bedroom—with Gar following.

"Hey, Nan—these guys have seen everything before—so don't give it a second thought. I'll have them put dinner on the table and send them on their way. You won't have to face them again. Okay?"

Gar took the still naked body into his arms. "And you're still the sexiest broad in the world with the sweetest body of all time. And I'm going to screw it right into this mattress—as fast as I can get rid of those guys out there."

As she fell onto the goose-down comforter, Nancy Lee ran her tongue ever so lasciviously around her glistening lips. "I've really come all the way from Rome to fuck you, hon. So, don't disappoint me." Over his shoulder, Gar shot back, "Not a chance in hell."

After love and dinner, Gar was up to his eyeballs reading the important Oil Position Papers that Nancy Lee was able to temporarily 'borrow' from the Rome embassy files.

"The United States—Our Current Position In The World Of Oil."

"The Soviet Union—First in Oil Reserves."

"Options In A Worst Case Scenario—When Our Wells Run Dry."

These papers and more were scattered all over the living room floor. Suddenly, Gar was attracted to a copy of a letterhead simply engraved 'The White House'.

Date: July 15, 1951.

Addressed to: Ambassador W. Averell Harriman.

Stamped: 'Top Secret'

In a "Dear Mr. Ambassador" letter, President Truman, citing the critical Iranian nationalization of her oil industry, abrogating a 1933 concession treaty signed with Great Britain, requested the former Ambassador to the USSR to make an emergency trip to London to urge a settlement.

"Nan—Nan just look at this letter from Truman to Harriman! If I can get myself appointed to Harriman's staff for this conference, I'll get to know most of the big oil players. And I know just the man who can get me there—my Dad. He's known Harriman for years. Even their Fathers were friends."

"Hon, if you can get me hitched on too—maybe as a liaison officer—then we can go to London together." Gar reached for the ornate French phone.

"Operator? I'd like to speak with Lucien Grey, Chicago, U.S.A.…the number is—"

On the long flight from Paris to Chicago, Gar mulled over the two important endings that he would have to put into place—before any of his new beginnings could become realities.

Entering his Law Office for the first time in months, his secretary said, "How nice to have you back, Mr. Grey—I almost don't know where to begin. But first, there was an urgent-sounding call from your Father this morning. He said to call him back before you do anything else."

"I'll call my Father—you ask Mr. Ross if he's free? I need a few minutes with him."

On his private phone, "Dad, what's the good word from Harriman? Great—absolutely super! I knew you could do it. What? Briefings start next Monday in Washington? Wow—today is Wednesday, already. Dad we have to talk about some things. I'll run over to the bank in a little while."

As he made his way to David's office there were shouts of hello—and handshakes from every side. Watching from his office doorway, David was smiling from ear to ear.

"Hail the conquering hero. Welcome home, partner."

With both men seated, Gar spoke first.

"David, the future of Grey & Ross, which you brought up in Nassau, is our most important subject. Can you manage some conversation time during lunch?"

"I'll shuffle things around. How's one o'clock?"

"Perfect. I'm going to run over to the bank to see my Dad now." Starting for the door, over his shoulder, "Union League at one."

"Look Dad, I know you and Mother are upset over the way my marriage has pretty much fizzled out. And I'm sorry for that. On the other hand, if I told you that Ellen and I are a happily married couple you certainly would know that I was lying through my teeth."

"I certainly would. And we both know that. Nevertheless, I believe you should have a talk with Ellen before you go off to London with Harriman. And I also feel that with the way you have been openly carrying on with other women, the time has come for you to be totally frank with her. Do we agree on that?"

"Yes, we do agree on that."

"She's deserving of that, Gar. These long absences of yours simply devastate her."

"Yup. I guess that's true too."

"But she is still your lawful wife, and as good Catholics, she always will be. Do whatever you feel you must do—but be gentle, my boy. What Ellen has *thought* is one thing—*knowing* is quite another. And outright rejection is going to be a big pill for her to swallow. If she can handle it at all. Remember that she still loves you from the bottom of her heart. Any idea what you'll say to her?"

"Yes, I pretty much know what I want to say to her. And as far as the children are concerned, this is not exactly out of the blue for them either. Since they were old enough to verbalize their feelings, they've asked, 'Why is our Mommy different?' Instinctively, Dad, they knew something. And Buck and Maggy, from whence all of Ellen's problems flow, surely were not strangers to their daughter's emotional difficulties."

Lucien, with a deep sigh, "Yes, I know that's all true enough."

"I'll do my level best. Oh—and will you talk to Mother for me? I really don't want to go through the whole story again with her. She only sees it from a woman's point of view."

"Of course I will. By the way, David and I have talked some in your absence. He knows you're leaving—says the hand-writing's on the wall. Good man, that David."

At The Union League Club, Gar was effusively welcomed by the maitre d'. "Ahh—good afternoon, Mr. Grey, so nice to see you home again. We've missed you here.

Mr. Ross has already arrived. For more privacy, I've seated you two in the far corner."

David said, "I've already ordered drinks—thought we might need a little support."

"My Dad told me you've already guessed my decision, David. But a few more thoughts are in order. From a financial standpoint, any value you want to place on my share of the firm is okay with me. And you can also name the payout period. I think there is good reason for you to allow the firm's name to remain the same. And it might also be a good idea for my name to appear on the letterhead as "Of Counsel." Continuity means a lot. And then there is another matter. Our business relationship with Hank Brady."

"We don't have any business relationship with Hank, at least none that I'm aware of."

"That's true. You're not aware, David. Nevertheless we do." Listening intently to Gar's full disclosure, David's reaction was typical.

"You've got some kind of balls, Gar, to have me involved in this kind of mess. I really am pissed at you."

"Before you go all pious on me, think about how rich this deal has made you. Let's both of us talk to Hank. There's a lot of money and a lot of clients involved here."

After downing the last of his vodka martini, Gar continued, "The two of us go back so many years, David, and we've been through too much together to really part. So we'll always be partners—right? I need to know from you that that will never end. That I can always count on you—you and Rachel."

"Of course you can—and you should know that. We'll never be more than a phone call away. No matter what." Raising his glass, David made a toast. "To the two of us—from the beginning to the end."

Upon arriving home that evening, Gar knocked on Ellen's bedroom door.

"Come in."

She was resting and reading on an elegant Louis XIV chaise lounge. After a dutiful peck on Ellen's cheek, "Can we spend a few minutes together?"

"Of course we can, dear. Come sit here beside me. Is there something in particular you want to talk about?"

"As a matter of fact there is. First of all, I want you to know that I've made some important changes in my business affairs. As a result, I've sold my partnership in the firm to David—and we are going to be moving to New York. I've already arranged to put the house up for sale. Assuming that you are willing to move."

"You know that I'd follow you anywhere, dear. If it's New York—so be it."

"There's more. Although we have not been man and wife for some time now, I'm willing to keep up the pretense so long as that pleases you. But I will be away on business most of the time—and most likely not alone. And even when I'm in New York, I plan on having a place of my own. I wanted you to know all of this up-front before we move East."

Ellen froze. Dazed and shocked at what she had just heard, she remained motionless. Only a fixed, vacant stare out the window toward her beloved garden.

"Ellen—Ellen are you listening to me?"

Getting no reaction, Gar gently reached for her.

"Ellen, can you hear me?"

Abruptly, in sheer panic, Ellen clutched both his arms, begging, "Dear God, you're not going to leave me here all alone are you? Wide-eyed, *are you?"*

Gar had gone through this kind of crises with Ellen many times. She couldn't help herself. Every neurosis Ellen had fought since childhood had simultaneously surfaced.

Insecurity. Anxiety. Depression. Irrational Fear. Totally traumatized, Ellen was in a cold sweat.

Over time, in addition to her current psychiatrist, Gar

had encouraged her to see some of the foremost psychiatrists and psychologists anywhere in the world. Including the legendary psychoanalyst, Karen Horney. Same conclusion. Ellen was beyond emotional improvement.

"Please—please don't leave me, Gar. Please don't do that to me after all these years."

Hysterically screaming, *"Promise me you will never leave me—never!"*

Knowing the scene was hopeless, Gar put in a call for her current psychiatrist.

Without answering, he left the room.

THIRTY-TWO

Washington, D.C. July 25, 1951.

As Gar arrived inside the terminal at National Airport shortly before noon, an attractive auburn-haired young woman aggressively approached him.

Wearing a celery-colored silk Eisenhower jacket and matching slim stick slacks, she appeared to be nearly six feet tall. Mostly legs.

"Mr. Grey? Good morning, sir, I am Alayne Benning-George from Ambassador Harriman's office. If you'll give me your claim checks, I'll have your luggage retrieved, and we have a car waiting. The State Department has made arrangements for all of the Ambassador's personal staff to be put up at a Safe House in Virginia during the oil briefings. Security you know."

Not at all concerned about security, disinterestedly, Gar mumbled, "Of course."

She quickly added, "The CIA and FBI have picked up all sorts of threatening rumors from everywhere in the world. Seems to be a lot of unhappy people out there—on both sides."

But Gar's thoughts had logically followed his eyes. His focus was riveted upon Alayne Benning-George's most prominent feature. In-your-face king-size nipples. Nipples protruding straight-out from equally oversized breasts, whose total proportions were well beyond any others Gar had ever sucked on. And he had had numerous mouthfuls of every size, shape, and color, upon which to base his judgment.

Anyone, with even less than 20/20 vision could only describe Alayne's breasts as stupendous. Gar dreamed those breasts reflected her generally stimulated condition.

Instantly thrilled that Alayne was obviously not wearing a bra, Gar immediately hoped she would never wear one. He mused, "If she ever did, it would remove one of the great sights in all of Washington. With those headlights, she could create a traffic jam at midnight in the middle of the Tidal Basin."

And he was also very much taken by a wishful notion. That at least one of those humongous nipples was about to break through her thin silk blouse—right here and now—in the middle of the air terminal. Gar was serenely floating in tit-man's heaven.

All this daydreaming had brought him to a rock-hard condition. However, without any immediate use for his splendid erection, his biggest problem was finding enough space in his trousers to hide the long hardness of his cock.

Despite the fact that Alayne was talking directly in his face, Gar made no attempt to divert his fixed gaze. Neither did Alayne. His daydreaming continued.

"Those nipples are just begging to be sucked. And at the top of those long legs her wet pussy is hungry to be fucked. And, would I ever love to oblige this broad."

Inasmuch as Alayne had completely blown his normal cool, Gar was already spinning a strategic follow-through—once they all arrived in London. Naturally, he would orchestrate the entire scenario. For Gar, the thrill of control played a dominant part in all of his sexual conquests.

For her part, Alayne had been so completely caught-up in her organizing duties for the oil conference that, uncharacteristically, she had put her own highly-active sex life on hold for nearly a month now. A new record for her.

She joked with close friends. "Long abstinence from sex does terrible things to my complexion."

Her closest friends knew she had never taken that chance—never would. Without any embarrassment, she often regaled them with vivid accounts of her sexual adventures with many of the rich and famous. To this day, Alayne continued to offer easy sport sex to most any man she thought able to advance her career.

That inclination was never lost even on her boss, Averell Harriman. Although the famous patrician statesman was long since quite married, he carried on a well-publicized war-time affair in London with Prime Minister Winston Churchill's captivating daughter-in-law, Pamela. Twenty-eight years Harriman's junior, she was trapped in a loveless marriage to Churchill's only son, the alcoholic Randolph. Pamela, a well-known seductress all of her adult life, was referred to as, "That bitch," by Harriman's wife, Marie, who remained home in New York throughout the war.

But with sex out of her mainstream thinking these days, Alayne was quite unprepared for Gar's aggressively suggestive behavior. Not put off—just unprepared. Until only moments ago he was just another name she did not know, on her diplomatic list. Nevertheless, Alayne was deliciously turned-on. And was internally reacting to the point where she began to worry that her super-lubrication might prove to have an embarrassing result—like showing through her thin silk outfit. But with her usual aplomb and discipline, she managed to finish without any obvious hitches.

"By the way, Mr. Grey, regarding those briefings which were supposed to start at lunch today? Well sir, Ambassador Harriman was scheduled to arrive at the Safe House in about an hour from now—but he's running late. I was told that he had been called back to the White House for further consultation. So you'll have plenty of time to settle in and freshen up. Incidentally, you should also know that Nancy Lee Hendrix, a newly appointed staff officer for liaison has been assigned to act as your personal assistant during the conference. She's awaiting your arrival at the Safe House, as we speak. I'm quite sure you'll find her to be a pleasant choice."

Despite all the global security threats, the huge U.S. military cargo plane, together with its Air Force fighter plane escort, safely touched down at a military air base near London. Predictably, through a steady rain from a leaden sky. But the weather did not dampen the spirit or excitement of this group, including Gar, Nancy Lee—and Alayne Benning-George.

It was not everyday that one got included on a mission at the direct request of the President of the United States. To say nothing of serving on the personal staff of such an impressive international figure as Averell Harriman, who had served his country in a number of posts, including four years as our Ambassador to the Soviet Union.

The important Harriman negotiating team of nearly fifty top American oil and legal experts, with supporting staff of more than twice that number, were immediately herded onto U.S. Embassy bulletproof buses and dropped off at their hotel.

Inasmuch as the front desk had been alerted that the buses were en route, all the attendees were quickly escorted to their pre-assigned rooms. Gar drew a modest room with a double bed—and no roommate. Nancy Lee was assigned a double occupancy. Her roommate turned out to be an attractive, thirty-year old, whom Nancy Lee very briefly knew when she first arrived to work at the American Embassy in Rome. Friendly and spontaneous, everyone simply called Alayne Benning-George—"Ally."

This unexpected room pairing, however, presented significant logistics problems for Gar's planned social service agenda.

"Dammit. These room assignments are going to wreck all of my plans," he muttered to himself. "On the other hand, if necessity really turns out to be the mother of invention, who knows what unexpected goodies may lie ahead?" Laughing to himself, 'The shadow do'."

The London phase of the Anglo-Iranian International Oil Conference lasted from August 8th to the 15th and resumed in Teheran on the 22nd. But Harriman was not able to bring home a negotiated settlement. To the contrary, the talks dragged on, indeterminably, until 1954.

Despite the apparent failure of the oil conference, Gar achieved great personal success. He was properly introduced to every important international oil celebrity in attendance. His oil networking had gone from zero to nearly one hundred per cent. Although he had been disappointed by the arrogant standoffishness of the two Saudi Arabian princes who had been sent to London as interested observers by their father, the founding monarch, King Abdul Aziz ibn Saud.

More than disappointed, Gar had been confused by the royal behavior. "Don't they know I'm a major partner in their Father's largest undeveloped oil reserve? If they know who I am, how come they're not even a little curious? Maybe Kings don't discuss their private business affairs with their children."

If Kings did talk, at least to their male children, this monarch could certainly qualify for an exemption. King Abdul Aziz ibn Saud had prodigiously produced forty-three sons, to say nothing of twenty daughters, in fifty busy years. No other reigning monarch had ever come remotely close to that record. Yet, in spite of that awesome achievement, rumors still persisted in various parts of the kingdom, that the king may have sired as many as twice that number. That said, obviously, a little family chat was out of the question.

Shunted aside, Gar was devising a different approach to meeting the royal sons, when a most impressive handwritten note arrived. Sealed with hot wax, in the old royal tradition, it was hand delivered to his hotel by a driver wearing a dark oxford-gray suit, black gloss-visored cap, and white driving gloves.

"Mr. Grey, if you do not mind, I have been requested to wait for your response. With your kind permission, sir, I will wait in the outside corridor."

Withdrawing the note from the impressive envelope, Gar proceeded to read.

> "Dear Sir,
>
> Their Royal Highnesses, Prince Barkah ibn Abdul Aziz and Prince Mukhtar ibn Abdul Aziz, cordially request the pleasure of your company at dinner this evening at 8:00. If you are able to accept, you will be called for at 7:45.
>
> Please feel free to include as many female guests as you choose to escort."

To the waiting driver, "Kindly convey my acceptance to their Royal Highnesses."

The first thing Gar did when the driver left was to show Nancy Lee the royal invitation. Her reaction was typical. "Gee, hon, I didn't bring anything with me dressy enough to wear to a royal dinner party."

Making his decision on the spot, Gar responded, "Don't sweat it, baby. I think I should show up alone tonight, for all kinds of good business reasons—starting with the fact that I've never met these guys before. And I'm sure that I can get a better read on them if I'm there by myself. Don't forget, Nan, that you're one of the few people who have any idea of the size and scope of this oil stake. So you know that I can't risk any kind of a mistake. But you've got a first-class rain check. Okay?"

"Well—not really, hon. But, you probably are right. Then joked, "If you promise to tell me all the dirty details of the Arabian Nights in the morning, I won't make too much of a fuss right now."

Promptly at 8:00, the custom-fitted, silver cloud, Rolls-Royce limousine with two small Saudi Arabian green and white flags fluttering from its front fenders, smoothly arrived at the entrance to the London hotel quarters of the royal brothers.

George Garfield Grey, thirty-four, about to dine with royalty for the first time, eagerly alighted from the plush back seat.

And eagerly bounded toward the front door.

THIRTY-THREE

Supremely confident that the evening had gone well, a stimulated Gar arrived back at his hotel shortly after 11PM, feeling a surge of physical and mental energy.

The Saudi princes, contemporaries in their thirties, who had both dressed in western business suits for this evening, were surprisingly cordial and friendly. Having been educated in America, they spoke perfect English. Consequently, dinner conversation had flowed freely.

There were discreet questions about Gar's family, his personal background, and his company that held the oil reserve option.

Satisfied with Gar's answers, the royal sons volunteered the opinion that their Father would welcome a meeting with his new American oil partner. Pleased, Gar came away from his dinner with an official invitation to visit Riyadh, at his earliest opportunity.

His triumphal dinner also seemed to have wetted his sexual appetite. He had paused in the lobby for a moment to consider a detour to Nancy Lee's door.

"Damn. I almost forgot—she's got a roommate."

In the alternative, the exciting possibility of a ménage à trois quickly crossed Gar's mind, but he dismissed it as too much and too soon. Without any viable option at hand, a reluctant Gar proceeded directly to his room. As he inserted the key into his door lock—he stopped up short. "What the hell—"

Through the still closed door, he perceived the scent of flowers—more likely perfume. It triggered more than his senses. Carefully, Gar opened the door.

"Don't turn the light on just yet, Mr. Grey. Let's play awhile in the dark."

For years, the overriding priority in Gar's constant prowling invariably centered on his insatiable need to control every relationship. Typically, he would first send the new object of his attention a strong signal of his interest. Flowers. Gifts of all kinds. After which, he fully expected every woman to come to him—be at his beck and call. A contrary response never would have even occurred to him. Ultimately, in Gar's mind, every chase came down to a simple unromantic truth.

"The one who cares the *least* is in control."

With a deep sense of pure ego satisfaction, he instantly recognized her voice. "What a pleasant surprise, Ally. What took you so long? I was beginning to think that I had made a serious miscalculation about you. By the way, how did you get in here?"

"Slow down, Gar. I'll answer—while you get undressed."

"Great idea. Just what I had in mind."

Ally went on, "First, I had to know if your original interest in me was still intact. You confirmed that every time you looked at me during the conference. And better believe, I've known that look since I was a teenager.

You also should know that for me to get into a man's room is about as difficult as getting into his pants. If you know anything about hotel managers, I can tell you that it didn't take too long and it wasn't too hard. But, that's only a small detail. The only important thing, right now, is that from this point on you proceed here at your own risk. After all, our night is still very young."

By this time a very naked Gar, led by his enormous erection, had come to sit on her edge of the double bed. Bathed in the soft moonlight shining through the window, the full extent of Ally's voluptuous, nearly six-foot body was on total view. Large and luscious.

As an offering and a reminder, she held her breasts up to him. "I presume these are what grabbed your attention the other day in Washington. Here, lover man, suck 'em good and hard. That really turns me on."

Without a moment's hesitation, Gar's anxious mouth found the stupendous nipples. The vision of these two engorged mammillae, were freeze-framed in his mind as two red-hot clitorises. Fanning his original vision that they were just aching to pop out of her blouse.

Alternating his attention from one exciting mouthful to the other, Gar was subtly applying more pressure as he increased his sucking rhythm. Ally was moaning her reaction from deep within her sexual soul. And now her hips were beginning to grind—pushing—trying desperately to find her reward.

Gar put her hand on his massive cock.

"Is this what you're looking for?"

"Damn right I am."

Then, abruptly, in one heaving motion, Ally turned him over on his back and had the full length of him deeply into her mouth. Instantly, Gar knew this was not going to be any ordinary blowjob—which proved to be an understatement.

Ally proved to be a highly skilled cocksucker. She easily deep-throated him. That sensation nearly drove him overboard. Then, her hands, tongue, and lips, manipulated his erection as never before. Gar shuddered and gushed. Not to be denied a single drop, Ally kept her mouth glued to his cock. She sucked and swallowed him bone dry—finishing with a little kiss on the tip of his cock. In the soft afterglow, she asked, "Now will you do me like that?"

Gar's answer was his long middle finger firmly pushed into her lavishly dripping cunt—up to his knuckle. In an automatic response, Ally audibly sucked in her breath. Her legs spread-eagled. Gasping, "Push your whole fist in Gar—please. I can take it all. Oh, *please.*"

More than willing to oblige, Gar knew exactly how to proceed. Ally's huge and copiously wet cunt, easily accepted Gar's fist, transporting her in an ecstatic trance somewhere beyond the realm of her wildest dream, from where she cried out to him, "Oh, baby, that feels so sensational. Now fuck me with your whole arm. Do it, baby. Please. Do it like you mean it. Make me come all the way up to your elbow."

She was bucking and thrashing as though trying to rid herself of whatever she was impaled upon. Engaged in the greatest sex experience of her life, Ally started to scream every description of herself she had ever fantasized.

"I'm your cunt. I'm your whore. I'm whatever you want me to be. You can do anything you want to me—anything. Take all of me! It's all yours. Oh—Oh I'm coming. I'm coming, baby. Oooohhh!"

Seizing the moment, Gar quickly withdrew his soaking arm. In full stride, he leaped into her spread-open saddle, shoving his rock-hard cock up to the hilt. Ally automatically reacted, "You're built like a goddam bull, baby, but I love every inch of it."

Not only did Ally have king-sized nipples, all of her equipment was similarly sized. Never before had Gar known a woman with genitalia of her dimensions. In fact, he had the immediate sense that he might quickly drown inside her limitless canal.

Amazingly soon, Ally was building yet again. Talking and taking Gar higher and higher. "Harder, lover—harder and deeper. You've got it. I need it."

Now she was screaming at the top of her voice, "Use that big cock you selfish bastard. Push harder and deeper.

For chrissakes, are you hard of hearing? Push it in deeper. Slap me with your big balls."

Moments later, her orgiastic litany began again.

"I'm coming," she shrieked. "I'm coming for you, baby. Take it. Take it again. Now! Oooowww!"

Her incredible internal pressure finally forced her dam beyond the bursting point. But she would never remember how many orgasms she produced. Her climactic flow was much like white-water rafting on the Snake River. Violent and exciting.

In quick succession, she flipped her body over on top of him, for the second time. And greedily sucked him to orgasm three more times. Gar could not believe himself—or her insatiable hunger. Lying back, more dead than exhausted, the inevitable conclusion struck him.

"No question," he told himself, "This broad is a certified nymphomaniac. She probably could go on all night like this." And he was right. Unbelievably, with her eyes still closed, again, Ally's body was slowly beginning to move. This lady wanted still more!

Tweaking a nipple to get her attention, Gar told her,

"Ally, you are truly exceptional. But I'm wiped-out. And I need a little sleep before a 7AM breakfast meeting with Harriman at the embassy."

But, silently, Gar's mind was racing ahead. "I know just the place where she can be fully-appreciated—with a little quid pro quo left over. After all, in certain environments, gratitude can be even more valuable than money. It also would give me an invaluable marker."

Cynically smiling over his latest diabolical scheme, Gar was quite pleased with himself.

Not to forget, however, Alayne Benning-George, was nobody's fool. Despite her driving ambition, Ally was always on guard, cautious—not easily boxed in. Even by the smooth demeanor of the likes of George Garfield Grey.

Using it as a convenient springboard, Ally took full advantage of her important position as a senior aide on

Harriman's permanent staff at his White House office. Before that, she was also with him at the Commerce Department.

In both sensitive posts, she had used all of her wiles and charms to establish a solid network within the complicated web of the international diplomatic community. The hush-hush, overindulged, world of extravagant living the public is almost totally unaware of— although it foots all the bills.

Within her worldwide network of equally ambitious friends, were strange bedfellows of both sexes. They spoke every possible language, and were privy to much privileged information, for which they constantly squeezed each other. "Milking," they laughingly called it. Consequently, a request for help on obtaining inside information usually began with, "Can you spare some milk?"

Depending on the working level of the network source, milk glasses came in many different shapes and sizes. And tonight was a perfect example of a very large glass. Ally, who understood some Arabic, had succeeded in finding out who had hosted Gar for dinner. Knowledge not easily come by. In fact, Gar's invitation to the royal dinner was not known by anyone outside of the princely duo's personal staff. And Nancy Lee.

Yet ambition runs high even within Saudi government ministries. Particularly among those young bureaucrats who had been sent abroad to be educated at the best universities. Most of these young Saudi men enjoyed the social freedom of the West. And they looked forward to serving their government in the most favorite posts.

Washington—London—Paris. Where the oil action was always at fever pitch.

Typically, in long Arab tradition, the Saudi princes, handshakes and smiles notwithstanding, trusted no one outside of their royal family. A possible exception, at this early date, might—just maybe—include, their new oil partner, George Garfield Grey. In this instance, Ally became involved in a quid pro quo—an equal exchange. By sheer coincidence, a friend, a young man at a mid-level staff job in the Saudi Ministry of Petroleum, and present at the London conference, learned of the invitation from an unusual source, the calligrapher assigned to write it. A woman at the Saudi's London Embassy.

In turn, the young man made a deal with Ally. He would reveal to her where Gar was dining that evening, in return for a later advance tip on the date of Gar's expected first trip to Riyadh. The 'milk' had been exchanged. It was a done deal. Therefore, her timing in Gar's bed, was not any mere coincidence.

In hot pursuit, she threw another question at Gar.

"How about cocktails? Just the two of us. I have some free time late this afternoon. Say about 5:00 at the Emerald Club? A guy like you should know the Emerald, anyway. That's where all the international power brokers hang out. It's just up the road from the Ritz. You can't miss it."

THIRTY-FOUR

Gar hastily showered off all traces of the night's heavy love making. And with an exhausted sigh, fell into bed and some much-needed sleep. Unfortunately, in less than five minutes, he was rudely awakened by the loud ringing of his phone. The hotel operator was on the line.

"Mr. Grey, there is a long distance call for you from Caracas, Venezuela. But the long distance operator says the calling party wants to confirm something about "Santa." Do you have any idea of what the caller is talking about?"

"Yes I do operator. Tell him he's on the right sled—and put the call through, immediately." Dr. Franz Josef Ritter had learned to be super cautious many years ago. This morning, with the important contents of his intended conversation with Gar, he wanted to be doubly sure he had the right party on the line before he proceeded with any further conversation.

The overseas cable produced strange noises and echoes. Despite the distortion, the already familiar German accent of the caller was unmistakable—and perfectly natural. German was the national language of his home country of Liechtenstein.

Accordingly, he began, "Zir, iv you can recognize my voice, please call me by name."

"Yes, Herr Ritter, I do recognize your voice."

"Goot. Mr. Grey, perhaps you may recall vhen ve organized 'Geld' I told you, under zertain zircumshtances, it might be verthvhile to add yet another layer of protective secrecy. Maybe Panama or Venezuela. Vell, a zubztantial purchase opportunity haz become available to uz here in Venezuela, und zhat is ze reason for my being here."

"Sounds interesting, Herr Ritter. Please go on."

"I vas asked by old vriends, vrom ze original I.G. Varben Trust, if I might know a pozzible buyer vor an oil produzing property und a refinery zhey vould now like to dizpoze of. Und zhey vill alzo be vorzed to divezt additional azzets in ze not too diztant future. Zoh, it vil be to our benefit to remain on cloze und friendly terms viz zhem vor zome time to come.

By ze vay, Mr. Grey, you might not know—but now it iz time. Varben, together vis Krupp, vas ze voundation of Hitler's vor machine in Vorld Vor II. Varben Chemicals had alzo been ze developer und manuvacturer of ze deadly Zyklon B—ze poizon gas ze Nazis used to kill zix million Jews. Vortunately, zhat iz now all in ze pazt. Let uz better to get back now to ze prezent time."

Gar added, "By all means, Herr Ritter."

"Zoh—I haf already had a preliminary converzashun vis ze Varben people here, und I believe, Mr. Grey, zhat vee should pursue zhis oil acquizishun vigorishly."

"I have already learned to trust your judgment, Herr Ritter. If you are in possession of all the relevant facts and figures, just tell me when and where should we meet?"

"Inazmuch az you are already in London, Mr. Grey, und if it is zatisfactory to you, vhy don't vee meet zhere? I can make arrangements vor a Varben plane to fly me. Und I believe vee can meet on Friday. Let uz plan vor 3:00 in ze afternoon. Kindly come to my zuite at Ze Zavoy."

"I will look forward to that pleasure, Herr Ritter."

Gar was on a roll. As soon as he hung up—he was back on the line. "This is the London overseas operator. Do you wish to place a call?"

"Operator, I would like to speak to Mr. Salvatore Bellini in New York City. His number is—" After a long delay, Sal came on the line.

"Gar, good to hear from you, my friend. I was beginning to think you were becoming a full-time diplomat."

"Not a chance, Sal. It's very interesting, and I've met all the big oil players at the conference here, which is good for us—but now it's back to business. Which is the reason for my call. I just had a call from Ritter. He's down in Caracas, but he's coming to London on Friday for an important discussion regarding an oil acquisition.

Can you possibly get away on such short notice and be here by then? You can? That's great. One other favor, Sal. Get hold of our two guys in Nassau—Umberto and Thurwin Drevescraft. You should be able to find them both at the bank. As a matter of fact, Dreve is still waiting for a new job assignment from me. Make arrangements for both of them to join us. We need an update from Umberto on the bank's operations since he took over as manager. And Dreve might as well start to learn the oil business from our beginning.

So, I will see you Friday morning. When you arrive at Heathrow, call me here. I'll send a car out for you. Safe flight, pal."

Comfortably seated in front of a large Chippendale desk in Ritter's Savoy Hotel River Suite, Gar, Sal, Drevescraft, and Umberto Ben-Levi Goldmanni, were ready to listen to their German-speaking attorney.

"Gentlemen. Vor zome months now, I haf been drafting ze nezzazary documents to form General Industrial Corporation, S.A. in Venezuela. Ve vill be mozt comfortable und velcome in zhat country. Ov course, you can haf ze phyzical corporate headquarters anyvhere. Und I zuppose you vill vant zhem to be in New York. For which I cannot blame you. Alzo, I haf been zending out acquizishun feelers all over ze vorld. Vhat ve haf here now is ze opportunity to create ze beginning of our international pyramid.

On our table of organization, just below 'Geld' ve vill haf ze General Industrial Corporation, S.A. However, unlike 'Geld', vich vill never zee ze light of day, G.I.C. vill be our main public vehicle. Zhen, ov course, ve alzo haf ze Zaudi oil rezerve—vich vee haf not yet completed. But zoon ve vill.

Vhat I haf ready to go now iz to acqvuire ze oil vells und ze refinery in Maracaibo from I.G. Varben. Zhat vill give uz ze impetus to set up a General Industrial Oil Corp. Here iz ze deal."

More than two hours of questions and answers flew back and forth. Strategies and Counters. Amounts in the tens of millions of hard curriences were discussed and considered. The money was made to seem as available as so many multi-colored jellybeans in an oversized jar.

At last, Gar made the decision. "Herr Ritter is right. We should do this deal. I'll admit the financing is a huge undertaking, but we can swing it. I have a few ideas already."

He looked around the room. No one was about to disagree with the Chairman and majority stockholder.

I.G. Farben, which dated back to 1925, was no amateur seller. In order to retain the proceeds of the sale, which, legally, they were supposed to turn over to the Allies for reparations, Farben had proposed an enormously complicated transaction. It now took the sophisticated international legal expertise of a Franz Josef Ritter, aided by Gar and Sal, to untangle the proffered web of deceit.

Gar began to outline his own strategy. His idea for the financing would take a circuitous, and highly unusual route. Later on, it would be hailed by the Wall Street crowd as "ingenious" and "creative." And it would mark the beginning of what would become George Garfield Grey's legendary financial trademark.

"OPM." Other Peoples Money.

For any number of reasons, Gar wanted to keep the cocktail date with Ally. Using the pretext of a dinner appointment at the Embassy with Harriman, and several foreign oil ministers, Gar was able to duck dinner and the evening with his colleagues. Even more, a thoroughly disappointed Nancy Lee, finally lost her cool, and turned her feeling of rejection into a blast of fury at Gar.

Despite the havoc he left in his wake, a few minutes after 6:00, and already an hour late, a very self-possessed and unruffled Gar appeared at the Emerald Club. And looking for all the world like a man without a care in sight.

Amid the din of the noise and music, he quickly spotted Ally hailing him from a far corner table. As he approached, Gar froze dead in his tracks, growling to himself, "That dirty little bitch. She set me up for this."

For there was the triumphant Ally sitting with the two handsome Saudi princes—Barkah ibn Abdul Aziz and Muktar ibn Abdul Aziz. To make it an attractive foursome, her oil conference roommate, Nancy Lee Hendrix joined the group.

To say that it was an extraordinarily awkward moment, for both Gar and Nancy Lee, was a gross understatement. Both would have given anything to be somewhere else. Anywhere—but here at the Emerald.

Until now, having been so late in arriving, Ally had felt sure Gar was going to be a no-show. And she did so want to put Nancy Lee on display for him. Now, trying hard to contain her exuberance, she decided to play the part of the great innocent. But, no way could she hide the gleam in her eyes. This was a conquering moment. She had the gained temporary control!

The Saudis, quite naturally, expected that the next time they saw Gar Grey would be in Riyadh. Not the following evening. And certainly not at the Emerald.

Without a clue as to what was going on around them, the two Princes were simply perplexed by the obvious tension between Gar and Nancy Lee—not knowing the long and intimate relationship between the two Americans. On the other hand, not surprisingly, both Gar and Nancy Lee were deeply embarrassed and uncomfortable. This scene took the two college-days lovers into uncharted waters.

Fleetingly, Gar wondered if this accidental meeting would have any bearing on his future oil relationship with King Ibn Saud. Changing course in his mind, on the spur of the moment, he muttered to himself, "Why the fuck should I be the only one to worry about appearances? These guys are married, too."

To add an even crazier dimension to this unlikely grouping, as the conversation moved icily and laboriously along, Gar looked—but could not believe what he saw.

Whenever she thought it would go unnoticed, Ally was happily stroking Nancy Lee's thigh. And her hand went higher as she grew bolder. For her part, Nancy Lee was fully aware that Gar had seen where Ally's hand had been traveling. And she did not seem to mind. Either the stroking or his viewing.

Shortly thereafter, when the Arabs decided the party was over—the party *was* over. Cheerfully, Ally invited Gar to move along with them to the Connaught Grill for dinner. Gar pleaded exhaustion and begged off—returning directly to his hotel room.

Inside, he loosened his tie and stretched out on the bed. For once he knew how it felt to come in second. And he didn't like it. Since childhood, he had always been a terrible loser. However, it triggered his motivation. And that was all Gar needed.

As he fell into a deep sleep, he was already plotting his revenge against Ally.

THIRTY-FIVE

Caracas, Venezuela. September, 1951.

To conclude the Farben oil acquisition, Gar arrived in Caracas accompanied by his newly formed entourage. Franz Josef Ritter, Sal, Thurwin Drevescraft, Umberto Ben-Levi Goldmanni, and his ex-partner from Chicago, David Ross.

Gar still considered David the best legal technician he knew. And he felt secure with the loyalty, as well as the competence, of everyone on this newly assembled staff. And of nearly equal importance, for the first time in his brief exposure to oil, Gar felt a new level of confidence in his own knowledge. Confidence born of the fact that his oil education was nearly complete.

Remembering his law board exams, he smiled. For him, this learning experience carried a certain sense of déjà vu. He had crammed much into a compressed time frame. And none of his newly acquired knowledge had come easily.

After the Harriman conference was over, Gar chose to remain alone in London, spending many hours in reference libraries, pouring over every oil fact, story, and legend. Then, more hours of discussion with Ritter, during which he asked endless questions. At times their intense dialogues dragged on until the wee hours. A few even lasted until dawn.

But, no matter the hour, or the complexity of Gar's queries, or the subtleties and redundancies, Ritter remained extremely patient. Always providing the correct answers, with particular sensitivity to their legal nuances. Nothing seemed beyond his intellectual reach. Ritter possessed knowledge that could not have been accidentally come by. From Baku to Beaumont, he simply knew everything there was to know about oil.

Forecasting even brighter days ahead for Gar, the Liechtenstein lawyer took great care to make sure that the rising entrepreneurial star from Chicago had all of this information totally straight—instantly usable in his head. Yet, despite all of the time they spent together, and for whatever his reason, there remained some crucial background material that Ritter purposely withheld.

Gar, ever on the alert, did not let the apparent void go unnoticed. Instinctively, he had felt some blank space existed all along. At some point, however, he knew it would become necessary for him to put that important query to Ritter.

From ground zero, Gar quickly absorbed oil history, geography, and politics. As well as where and how all of the powerful past and current industry personalities had helped to shape the world oil picture as it now existed. And to his surprise, he discovered that there were many men who had significantly added to the critical history of world oil. Like most Americans, when Gar began his quest, the only oil name he recognized was John D. Rockefeller.

But Ritter told him about the significant contributions of other oil pioneers. He told Gar about men, such as: Alfred Nobel, the famous Swedish inventor of dynamite and blasting gelatin, who, in 1873, financed the refinery at Baku, in Caspian Russia. Where, in fact, the world's petroleum industry began in 1823. Although 'the eternal fire' of natural gas holes had been known, at least, since the time of Alexander the Great in the 4th century B.C. Gar gave Ritter an incredulous stare.

"The dynamite guy—the Nobel Peace Prize guy—was also in oil?"

"Ja, he vas. Und der vas more."

For example, the single event that had made Texas the number one oil state, had nothing whatsoever to do with anyone named Bass or Hunt. Rather, it was a one-armed lumberman, with the unlikely name of Patillo Higgins, who located the Beaumont Field that produced the sensational "Spindletop," the world's first oil gusher, in 1901.

It tumultuously roared in spouting 110,000 barrels per day, and flowed wild for more than a week before it could be brought under control.

Then, Ritter finished in rapid order. Noting: Joseph Cullinan, who founded Texaco in 1902; Marcus Samuel, an English merchant banker, who founded Royal-Dutch-Shell; William Knox D'Arcy, a New Zealander, who, in 1908, first found oil in what is now Iran; and the Armenian, Calouste Gulbenkian, who negotiated the biggest oil deal of its day, between Anglo-Persian and Royal-Dutch-Shell.

Later on, of course, there was Howard Hughes, whose father revolutionized the oil drilling industry when he invented the steel-toothed rock-drilling bit, and created the Hughes Tool Co. in Houston in 1908. And who could forget the legendary curmudgeon, J. Paul Getty, whose 1949 concession to drill for oil in the Neutral Zone, between Kuwait and Saudi-Arabia, made him the world's richest man.

All of this oil history poured out of Ritter as easily as water over Niagara. Almost fiercely, Gar soaked it up—always wanting more. His profound insight and substantial thirst for such information greatly impressed Ritter, fundamentally changing his original impression of Gar as merely a rich playboy who had temporarily found a new toy.

As a direct consequence, a genuine bond of friendship began to grow between the disparate two men. Ritter even went so far as to allow a mild thawing of his stiff and formal manner and began calling Gar by his given name. Gar reciprocated in kind.

Shortly thereafter, in order to accommodate Ritter's travel time, they decided to change their venue to Paris. And it was at lunch at the Ritz that Gar decided to put the all-important background question directly to him.

"Franz, how is it that you came to be this fount of oil knowledge?"

Ritter smiled. "Vrankly, Gar, I haf been vondering vhen you vould ask zis qvestion? Zoh, I vill anzer you—here und now. In nineteen zhirty-eight, upon ze reference ov a highly rezpected British mutual vriend, King Abdul Aziz ibn Saud, summoned me to a private audience in Riyadh. Zhere, he reqvested zhat he vould like me to shtudy und appraze ze vorld oil zituation—und report back directly to him. No von else vas to know. Und zhere vas no time frame involved. It took me almozt a year. Und much travel all over ze vorld.

Everyvhere I vent, in ze king's name, I met und shpoke to ze most important und powervul people. Vhen ze report vas vinished, ze king vas mozt pleazed—und I had learned a lot about ze oil buziness. Ov course, it alzo vas highly remunerative."

Gar, who had carefully listened to every word of wisdom that had come his way, paused, only to quickly put another question. "I cannot imagine, Franz, what the king could possibly have expected to find out that he did not already know?"

"Zoh, my boy, in ze end, you fall into ze zame trap az all ze rest. Ze king, in vact, knew very little about oil. Vor exzample, in nineteen zhirty-zree, he handed over a sixty-year exzclushive concezztion to Shtandard Oil ov California to exshplore for oil on an unbelievably large 320,000 shqvare-mile tract ov desert. Und, you vil be zurprized vhen I tell you, Gar, zhat vat all he got in return vas only a loan ov $170,000. Mind you, not only vas ze amount nozhing much—but it vas only a loan. Ibn Saud didn't have a clue az to ze real value ov ze riches under zhat blazing dezert.

Ov course, ve all now know, zhat dezert turned out to overlie ze vorld's largest petroleum rezerve—billions und billions ov barrels. Zoh, zince King Saud now had more black gold zhan anybody elze, he vanted to learn much more about vhat ze outzide vorld of oil vas all about.

But you muzt remember, Gar, at zhat time, hiz country, Zaudi Arabia, vas shtill dirt poor. Und camels ver ze bazic mode ov tranzportation. Nobody in ze rezt of ze vorld gave a damn about Zaudi Arabia."

Trying to absorb all that Ritter was throwing at him, Gar followed up with a final question. "And, Franz, is it really true that the whole oil thing started in Russia—of all places?"

"Ja. Zhat iz a hiztorical vact. It vas in Baku, on ze Caspian Sea. Ze capitol of Azerbaijan. Und ze Soviets shtill do not know how much oil zhey really haf under all zhat vasser. Maybe more zhan ze Zaudis. Only Gott knows."

Meyer Lansky, one of Gar Grey's original partners, quietly landed at Caracas using a Cuban passport, and immediately headed for Gar's hotel. Per usual, Lansky had not traveled from Havana empty-handed.

In fact, he had brought two very different surprise gifts for Gar. The first was an old black Gladstone, a beat-up suitcase that he never let out of his possession. His second surprise was in the person of the milk-chocolate skinned beauty from the Atlantic Overseas Bank of Nassau—Victoria Tracy.

Despite the blazing Caracas sun, Vikki Tracy, a native of Jamaica, British West Indies, looked coolly stunning in a double-breasted, white linen blazer suit. As was her custom, Vikki never wore a bra. So her gold-buttoned jacket was worn directly over her ample bare breasts, which exposed luscious deep cleavage. Her only adornment—a single strand of exquisite quality pearls. Compliments of an oft-sated Meyer Lansky.

As usual, the statuesque Caribbean beauty was hiding behind her trade-mark—oversized round sunglasses—years before anyone had ever heard of Jackie O. Her long jet-black hair pulled tightly back into a stylish chignon at the nape of her neck. Her Las Vegas show-girl legs were even more enhanced by glossy white patent-leather pumps set-off by sexy five-inch heels. Coupled with her oh-so-short mini-skirt, the exciting scene rose almost to the beginning roundness of Vikki's rock-hard shapely buttocks. North of which was nothing more than high-cut, thong-style, silk briefs—now pulled deeply into her moist crevices. She could have covered more of herself with a fig leaf.

Taking her usual three-foot long strides as she quickly moved across the rose-pink marble floor of the hotel lobby, Vikki's gait also had a deliciously sensuous effect on the rolling movement of her hips. Her sensuous hips had attracted much male attention ever since she had been a well-developed adolescent back in the slums of Kingston. Now, her fast pace was pushing the short, transplanted mobster from New York to his limit. In no uncertain terms, expressed in a deep growl, Lansky commanded,

"Slow the fuck down, Vikki. Yur makin' me look like some kinda dumb schmuck. Ya hear me?"

With an annoyed frown, from the product of native Jamaican haughtiness came a barely audible, "Yes."

Looking neither left nor right, moving at her slower ordered pace, it was not at all surprising that Victoria Tracy was now creating a mild form of male erotomania throughout the hotel lobby, as well as a different problem for Lansky, who detested this particular kind of notoriety. Over the years, the diminutive mobster had said, "Publicity—any kinda publicity—jus' ain't no good for my kinda business."

Vikki was the exact opposite. Much as a dry sponge, she quickly absorbed all of the attention directed at her in the lobby, but it was never enough. Given her childhood, it was perfectly natural that her bottomless psyche could never be filled. Vikki constantly craved ever more attention. As one of many children in a poverty-stricken family grinding out a pitiful existence in the cruel slums of Kingston, she had been mostly ignored as just another unwanted mouth to feed.

But that misery was all in the past. These days, using every tool in her physical arsenal to the utmost advantage, this spectacular new version of Vikki Tracy was able to turn the head of every man under ninety. Even with their walkers and canes. She was certain that her magnetic feminine allure would surely entice some important big fish. Until then, her ultimate game plan was constantly striving for maximum exposure.

Mercifully, at last, the mismatched duo entered the protective custody of the elevator. As she turned to face the sliding door, Vikki felt positively exhilarated in the knowledge that her lobby performance left behind any number of male gawkers scarcely able to suppress their fondest hopes and strongest desires.

From time to time, whenever those gawkers reached sexual climax, their most vivid sexual fantasies would be the centerfold image of Vikki Tracy.

Without any advance notice, Lansky had arrived at the suggestion of the exiled Mafia chief, Charlie 'Lucky' Luciano. Charlie's verbal message was delivered by a mutual friend, recently arrived in Havana from a visit with Charlie in Naples. Even stashed away in far-off Italy, Charlie Lucky was always up-to-date and he wanted to help Gar make the oil deal in Caracas. Consequently, he had urged Lansky to reveal his extensive past business dealings with the powerful and corrupt military elite who ran Venezuela.

Dirty money from gambling casinos, or just plain dirty

from "black gold," made little difference to those "officially" elected crooks. They had been lining their pockets with graft from the powerful international oil companies since 1922. In that year, led by Royal-Dutch-Shell, the first oil well near the shores of Lake Maracaibo in northwestern Venezuela gushed. For nine days, it dumped nearly a million barrels into the murky lake before it was capped. And those who were loyal to President Juan Vicente Gomez, in power for twenty-seven tyrannical years, found themselves hugely rich. Overnight.

Gulf Oil and Standard of Indiana, who held adjacent leases, were equally generous to the military locals. And neither the oil nor the largesse ever stopped flowing.

If someone ever thought that the natural resources of a nation should bring aid and comfort to its beleaguered people, certainly did not have Venezuela in mind. In point of fact, it never happened anywhere for the betterment of the commonweal. Perhaps, the world only wishfully imagined some leader, somewhere, would think in such social high ground. Consequently, amidst the newly found cash waterfall for the few, the wretched Venezuelan poverty rolled uninterruptedly along.

Gar, happily welcomed Lansky back into his fold. Although he was quite obviously startled to see Victoria Tracy. Not unhappy—just startled.

However, Gar could not help but peek out of the corner of his eye in the direction of Thurwin Drevescraft. Being quite sure, all along, that the smooth Englishman and the fluent Spanish-speaking Vikki had long been lovers. All of this body linkage went on, of course, before Gar's crowd showed up to buy the bank in Nassau. But, Drevescraft, ever the perfect gentleman, ever the team player, never so much as blinked, when Vikki came into his view. Rather, he silently philosophized, "She must have been brought here for Chairman Grey's diversion and pleasure—and I bow to his rank."

Lansky, not willing to talk in front of everyone present, asked for a moment alone with Gar. Behind a closed bedroom door of his suite, Gar motioned Lansky to face-to face chairs.

"I'm glad to see you here, Meyer. Must be something important on your mind to fly all this distance. Does it have something to do with our deal with Farben?

"Right. But, Sal tol' me about da deal awready—and it sounded kosher. So I sent word wit a trusted guy over ta Charlie in Naples. An' it wuz really his idea dat I fly over here. Ya see, Gar, it's like dis.

Back in da 30s, I come here ta Caracas ta set up some gamblin' joints. Here, an' in Columbia, and den down in Bolivia. Nuthin' was goin' right—nuthin' waz happenin'. Once I figured out da angle it didn' take me long ta figure out who I had ta do business wit if I wanted a deal.

The key man in any big money deal down here was the dictator hizself, President Juan Vicente Gomez, who'd bin runnin' dis country like it wuz his private candy store. He died in 1935. It wuz da same story wit both presidents what came after—Contreras and Jiminez. Dey both had very sticky fingers so dey wuz always open ta a little brown bag on da side. Sorta goes wit da territory down here.

Farben may want ta do a deal wit us directly tru Ritter. But take my word fur it, Gar, yur jus' goin' ta get jacked aroun'. Nuthin—I tell ya absolutely nuthin'—will happen till da top brass here gets cut in on da action. Mark it down in yur rulebook. I know it. Charlie knows it. Now you knows it too.

So, if ya really wanna make da deal, let's stop da bullshit and get started by tellin' Herr Ritter da faks of life here in Caracas. But before we do dat, me and Charlie thought ya might have some trouble findin' enough 'green' ta start da ball rollin', so I brung ya a little cash help."

Lansky opened his old Gladstone bag. Gar's eyes nearly popped out of their sockets. "I brung ya five mil. It's da same amount I originally brung down to Batista when we bought inta Havana. When ya start ta spread dat stuff aroun' down here, it'll help give ya da proper intro ta da right gents. By da way, pal, I'd like da old Gladstone back. It's my good-luck bag. Maybe yurs too."

"Well, Meyer, I've got to hand it to you, my friend, you sure put it all face-up up on the table. No dirty dancing. Now everyone will be able to read off the same page. And I think all my guys should be told what the score is at the same time. Like right now.

I have no reason to distrust any of them—at least so far. Let's go back and get started. But first, I think it might be wise to suggest that Umberto take Vikki out to dinner. I'm sure they are no longer strangers to each other."

"Yur right agin'. Ya see, I bin spendin' a lotta time on business in Nassau fur a cupala months now. An' I bin' staying in one of da apartments on da second floor in da bank buildin'. So I kin tell ya fur sure, Gar, dem two young ones ain't no fuckin' strangers."

THIRTY-SIX

Shortly before 6AM, Gar's dormant hotel room phone violently burst to life.

It was the morning after Meyer Lansky laid out the facts of life for Gar's staff, who had assembled much economic data on their own regarding Venezuela. However, now they had the inside lowdown from Lansky, who had told them how Venezuela's military rulers truly conducted its government's business. In pure, genuine, 100% green cash. Preferably in US dollars.

And the money gushed forth in endless tandem with the oil so generously embedded in the rock far below the floor of Lake Maracaibo. This precious natural resource also flowed in only one color—black. Black Gold.

Gar mumbled a sleepy, "Hello."

"Good morning, Gar. Do you know who this is?

He immediately recognized the voice of the caller. It was Alayne Benning-George, most likely, calling from Washington.

"Of course I know who it is."

"Great. That pleases me."

"I'm for anything that pleases you, Ally—but do you know what time it is?"

"Sure I know what time it is, lover boy—but this call is not for fun. It's strictly business. And when I start, don't ask me how I know that what I'm about to tell you is true—just you believe. Because what I am about to tell you is from one of my best "A" list sources. Unimpeachable. Got it? Absolutely unimpeachable."

"Okay, you've made your point, Ally. It's obviously something important. So far, I've got that part of it straight. But what could gossip from one of your, so-called, unimpeachable sources possibly have to do with me?"

"Only everything. You must know that Venezuelan crude is absolutely essential to our current effort in the Korean War. And we are using a lot of oil in the Far East. The Japanese have no oil of their own, so they cannot loan us any. Even you must know all that by now.

But, overall, you're still pretty much of an international innocent. So, this will probably come as a big shock to you. Nevertheless, you should be aware that all of official Washington seems to know that you and your staff are down there to acquire IG Farben's South American producing and refinery operations. Do you read me, Gar?"

"Sure I read you, Ally—but so what? The war is long over. And I don't need any official approval to do the Farben deal or any other deal I might want to do. It's simply none of Washington's damn business. Besides, since when do the things I do get to be so important? I'm not tied in with the guys in the federal bureaucracy. And you know that."

"Well, fella, when you started hobnobbing with the likes of Averell Harriman, then got on a first name basis with the top oil ministers all over the world, to say nothing of chumming around with a couple of Saudi princes, let me assure you, my boy, you wind up being important."

"That's a crock," Gar cracked.

"Not so. In media parlance, you're a 'newsmaker'—whether you like it or not. And everybody starts poking around trying to find the dirty linen in your closet. All of your affairs become public—business, private, or romantic. Especially the sleazy stuff. The public simply binges on sleaze."

"Fuck the public."

"You can think that. You can even say it. But you can no longer do it. Those days are gone for you forever. Better start trying to get used to it. And here's some more free advice. Be extra careful, especially in front of whomever you're dropping your Jockey shorts for these days. And, don't leave your room anymore without first checking your waste basket. Destroy any phone messages, and make sure the last writing on your bedside notepad cannot be read on the next few pages by the impression you left behind. Ballpoint pens have a tendency to do that."

"What the hell is your real point here, Ally?"

"Well, even though a lot of this sounds like cops and robbers nonsense to you, let me assure you that people snoop absolutely everywhere. And most will do anything for money. True or false. That's my point. Sometimes, that even includes me. Does that message carry some interest for you?"

"Okay, you're probably right about these warnings. As for whatever it is that you will do for money, you're right, that does carry a great deal of interest for me. As a matter of fact, you might be interested in knowing that I've already planned some social events that definitely include you—in various important capacities. But, we can talk about that another time."

"Always at your service, Mr . Grey."

"Now, let's get down to the nitty gritty. Just who has their sensitive Washington nose out of joint about the Farben deal?"

"For starters, how about General Walter Bedell Smith. And if you're not up to date on his bio, Bedell was Ike's chief-of-staff in London during the war. Then, he followed Harriman as our ambassador to the USSR. And, just for good measure, he is currently the Director of the CIA. Does any of that open your sleepy eyes?"

"Sure it does. But what's his beef about the Farben deal?"

"How about the fact that you didn't clear a damn thing with anybody—anywhere. Not the White House. Not State, Treasury, Defense, the CIA, or FBI. Not even the Bank for International Settlements in Basel, or the UN Secretary General in New York. Must I go on?"

"Wait a minute, sister. There are plenty of things all those guys don't know a goddam thing about. They just assume they are on the inside of everything—and that's plain bullshit. What's more, I am legally advised by esteemed international counsel, that I don't have to spill my guts all over the world just to cater to the egos of a bunch of bureaucrats. And I don't think I will either. What's your response to that monologue, young lady?"

"That's easy. I'd say you're doing a genuine Gar Grey. Carrying on like a brash, inexperienced, foolish, arrogant, smart-assed, know-it-all, unmitigated prick. Did those carefully chosen words help to make my response perfectly clear to you?"

"Perfectly." Sarcastically adding, "But aren't you concerned that all of those gaudy compliments just might give me a swelled head? Seriously, Ally, I still don't get it. Why all the fuss? Is it about Farben, in particular, or something personal about me or my family back in Chicago?"

"As far as my source knows, you're personally clean. You haven't had enough time on the international stage yet to draw personal enemy fire. But the word around this town is that you are either an innocent dupe, or maybe, just a rich kid who hasn't done his homework on the treacherous Nazi background of IG Farben, their duplicitous executives all over the world, and their American Nazi cabal. Which, by the way, include many of America's corporate ruling families—such as the most outspoken of all anti-Semites, Henry and Edsel Ford.

That shame list also includes many others: The Rockefeller family with their principal holdings in the Chase National Bank and Standard Oil of New Jersey; the Du Ponts led by Irénée; and ITT's Sosthenes Behn. And you also may not know about the infamous Sterling Drug Company."

"Wait a minute," Gar fairly shouted. "You're not going to tell me that when Americans bought *Bayer* aspirin or *Phillips Milk of Magnesia*, during the war, that those purchases were actually contributing to the Nazi war effort?"

"Took the words right out of my mouth. That's exactly what I was going to tell you. Now do you understand the depth of the furor you're causing back here? 'IG' is bad news, Gar. Real bad. Always has been. Their file at Justice is one of the oldest and longest in the department.

By the way, while you're thinking things through, try to think of any possible suspects who might want to see you get your tit caught in the wringer. Remember, that out of nowhere you're playing in the world's biggest poker game. And these big boys play down and dirty. Who knows, you just might want to give the entire deal a second thought—or even pull out altogether. There are worse decisions you could make. Best you think about it—but please be careful. I really want that delicious body of yours to stay safe and sound. I'll try to keep you informed. You have my home number, so stay in touch. Bye, lover boy."

As he put the phone down, more than simply stunned by the entire conversation, Gar was also terribly suspicious of the contents of the call. And, especially the caller.

He was already planning his personal revenge against Ally for what she did with Nancy Lee and the Saudis in London. "Now, she wants to do me the biggest favor in the world?" There was no longer any question in his mind.

"Obviously, Ally has no scruples whatsoever. Nymphomania and personal ambition are both exciting stimulators, but maybe I can turn those traits around and make them productive."

More than an hour had passed. Now, a little after after 7AM, Gar reached for his phone.

"Hotel operator? Señor Salvatore Bellini. Por favor."

"Sal, it's Gar. Sorry to wake you, but jump into some pants and a shirt. I need to talk to you. No it can't wait for breakfast. *Right now!"*

In less than ten minutes, Sal knocked on his door.

"You sounded so damn upset. What's up?"

"I just had a one-hour phone call from Ally."

"Where from? What about?"

"From Washington. She says that everybody from The White House, State, Treasury, and Defense, and over to General Bedell Smith at the CIA, not only knows that we're down here, but that they're all having a fit about our doing this deal with Farben."

After a thoughtful moment, Sal said, "Seems to me that someone very high up in Washington probably has a strong incentive to rock our boat. And that someone is manipulating, maybe black-mailing, Ally to encourage you to give up the Farben deal.

My guess would be that she's not on her own in this scheme. Even worse than that, Gar, I think there's a leak in our own backyard.

Somebody here is a double agent."

THIRTY-SEVEN

Elsewhere in Caracas that evening, U.S. Senator Warren Baxter Bascombe 3rd, the wealthy beneficiary of a Texas oil windfall, together with his wife, the former Rio Roundtree, the only heir to a Texas ranching fortune, were the guests of honor at a small but glittering dinner party at the Saudi Arabian Embassy. The dinner was hosted by their Royal Highnesses, the Princes Barkah and Muktar ibn Abdul Aziz.

Both the Senator and his wife had something in common with Gar Grey. But very different perspectives. He was the Chairman of the Senate Foreign Relations Sub-Committee on Resources & Minerals, which included oil. His wife Rio, had spent an extraordinarily erotic night with Gar in Rome.

Most surprising, was the solo appearance at the dinner table of a new face on the Caracas oil scene—Count Carlo of Bergamo, O.I.P., in full white-tie regalia, including a left upper chest replete with ribbons and medals. Count Carlo also wore the widely impressive over-the-shoulder, red, white, and green sash of the Order of Italian Patriots, symbolic of his high rank. In point of fact, his adornments were acquired by his wife's inherited fortune.

The Saudi royal sons had been dispatched by their father, King Ibn Saud, specifically to learn everything possible about the proposed Venezuelan activities of the King's new oil partner, George Garfield Grey, with whom they had just recently become familiar with in London. And who they expected to see soon on an invited visit to Riyadh.

The Saudi King had learned about the Farben deal from his well connected ambassador to Washington. The ambassador had been confidentially briefed on a country week-end walk as the guest of Senator and Mrs. Bascombe. The setting was their sumptuous estate in the rolling hills of Virginia.

Having traveled halfway around the oil world, the grapevine had now entwined even Count Carlo, the trusted old friend of Lucky Luciano in Naples. In a highly controversial international business deal of this magnitude, especially involving oil, the obvious was bound to happen. Suspicion regarding the advisability of making the Farben deal was spreading in every direction like the plague. Without an early solution, it would ultimately grow to include even Carlo's longtime associate, Dr. Franz Josef Ritter—the originator and principal architect of the potential Farben acquisition.

Sal was sitting closest to the phone in Gar's suite.

"My immediate thought, Gar, is we need to talk to Meyer. I'd like to call him now."

Gar peeked at his watch.

The quick peek brought a sharp reaction from Sal. "Forget the time. Meyer is an early riser and we've got a four-alarm fire here."

"You're right. Give him a call."

Lansky picked up the ringing phone. "Start talkin'."

"Meyer, it's Sal. I'm with Gar. We need to talk to you as soon as you can get here."

"If it's top stuff, Sal, we don' wanna talk in da room—it could be bugged. Gimme fifteen minutes—den meet me on da corner across from da hotel. Da corner by da park."

Always a brilliant strategist, the diminutive mobster found a nearby bench and listened intently to Gar's retelling of the morning's events. Before speaking, Lansky first paced back and forth in front of the bench.

"Dis iz a big deal an' I think Sal's right on da money. We bin sold out by some fuckin' insider. Dat's nuttin' new. I bin der plenty times before an' all dem bastards iz sleepin' wit da fish now. An' yuz kin coun' on me ta find dis bastard too."

The gravel voice of bloody experience finished, "So I'm gonna go back ta my room an' start off by talkin' ta all our guys—one by one. Yu guys don' say nuttin' ta nobody till yuz hears from me. It'll take me a cupala hours. Yuz guys don' even answer yur phones till yuz hears from me. Okay?"

In far off Naples, just as he was about to leave for an 8PM dinner appointment, Charlie Lucky's private phone rang. He answered, "Ya."

"Charlie, it's Meyer."

"Where are ya?"

"In Caracas, like we agreed. We got a stoolie in da Farben deal who's really fucknin' things up in Washington. I awready talked ta all da guys here. Dey iz all clean—so far. Jus' ta cover all da bases, why don' ya call yur buddy, Count Carlo. He might know sumpin'. An' den call me back at da hotel here. I'll hang aroun' wit Sal n' Gar. We'll wait ta hear from ya."

Hours later—shortly before 9PM, Lansky's ringing phone startled all three men.

"Ya might be right, Meyer," Charlie Lucky said. "Somthin' could be rottin'. I knows Carlo's butler fur years an' he knows he kin trus' me. So he tol' me dat Carlo is in Caracas—dat I probably jus' furgot abou' it. It's on a oil deal dat he tinks I'm in on. So yuz better get a hol' of Carlo. Tell 'im ya heard from me an' dat he'll never leave Caracas alive if he iz da stoolie. An' ya kin also tell 'im dat he should call me cause I'm waitin' ta hear from 'im. Keep in touch, Meyer."

THIRTY-EIGHT

By late 1945, Paris had become a favorite holiday destination for the well-known German industrialist, Gerhard Von Ribbentrop. The forty-two year old bachelor was the third-generation family member to be the Managing Director of their vast industrial empire.

As his father and grandfather before him, his life had been totally dedicated to the growth of the family dynasty. Accordingly, he is said to have once sternly lectured a budding young plant manager, "Under any circumstance, you must never again make a rash decision, if you want to grow in our organization. That sort of nonsense is simply out of the question. No matter what else. Stop—take your time—think the situation through."

He could have easily added, "The same warning applies to any subject dealing with personal emotion. And simply forget about passion."

A stoic aristocrat of Prussian background, Gerhard reminded many of his friends of the famous German character actor, Erich von Stroheim—including the famous monocle—who last year starred in the smash film remake of *Sunset Boulevard* opposite Gloria Swanson. That same icy, frozen image was the face Gerhard presented to his world.

In reality, however, Gerhard had been a shy child who had become an almost painfully shy adult. Accordingly, he had simply found it easier to keep mostly to himself.

Not surprisingly, in his very limited social circle, he was nicknamed, "The Iceman."

This night, together with local friends, he was attentively watching the floor show at the Moulin Rouge, the world-famous cabaret in Montmartre.

Gerhard, whose late uncle, Hitler's Foreign Minister, was found guilty as a war criminal and hanged in 1946, was fortunately sitting at a table close enough to be almost a part of the spirited and suggestive Moulin Rouge floor show. However, for the third consecutive night, his eyes were absolutely riveted on just one member of the high-kicking chorus line—the tall and vivacious blonde on the far left. She was the highest kicker in the show. And Gerhard's imagination was running wild over her.

Finally, summoning all of his limited social courage, a bouquet of red roses in hand, Gerhard went backstage and introduced himself. Her then unknown name was Willi Eschweiler, an eighteen-year old coal miner's daughter from the industrial Saarland near the border with France.

While the subject was never spoken about in family circles at home, more and more the business community began to assume Gerhard was probably a closet gay. Obviously, at this moment, the bachelor was unmistakably heterosexual—and overloaded. With all of his sex hormones madly careening down an emotional autobahn, Gerhard was more than ready and trembling with desire. He could barely manage to wait the few minutes it would take to invite the physically mature teenager back to his Ritz Hotel suite.

Without a moment of hesitation, Willi replied, "Ja—I would be happy to give you great pleasure, Herr Von Ribbentrop."

An hour later, Willi wiggled onto his ample lap, and snuggled up tightly. "Since we are here in Paris, Gerhard, first we do the French kisses. Yes?"

Between those deeply passionate kisses, Willi helped him drop each article of his clothing. After both were quickly naked, Willi continued kissing Gerhard everywhere—routinely performing every sex act as she had done many times before—down to each toe—where she deeply sucked ten times. Of course, Gerhard had no idea that it was Willi's standard procedure.

From that moment on, Gerhard helplessly stumbled beyond his previously known emotional borders. Pleading, "Do whatever you want to me, Willi—*anything*—just please don't stop."

The impoverished chorus girl from Montmarte had no intention of stopping. Street-smart, she put on a convincing act. "But I must go back to my room soon, Gerhard. After all…"

Gerhard panicked.

"No, no—you cannot leave me like this! You must spend the night here with me. I will make it more than worth your while. Whatever you ask for—I will give you double. In Francs, marks, or dollars. Just don't leave me, Willi—I beg you!"

Willi Eschweiler became speechless. No one had ever wanted her that badly. "Mein Gott, such an offer," she said to herself, "What else could I get?" Her actions now became far more intense. Willi blew Gerhard's mind—orgasm after orgasm.

Truly seeing him for the first time, she suddenly found genuine interest in the size of Gerhard's overdeveloped breasts, which were nearly the size of a female "D" cup—strongly suggesting gynecomastia. Willi had never seen male breasts of such proportions. Happily, she later found, that Gerhard also reached climax when she aggressively massaged his huge breasts, and painfully bit hard on his protruding nipples.

Inasmuch as she also loved similar rough stuff, Willi wondered just how many other female traits might be buried inside this rich man.

For Gerhard, the line of demarcation between pain and ecstasy rapidly blurred. To this point in his life he had been a captive of his own limited libido. Now that captive emotion was frantically pushing for total emancipation.

As Willi's touchings became stronger and harder, a devious idea burst to fruition in her mind. Willi rolled the totally lost Gerhard onto his stomach. And furiously began to spank his ample buttocks. The sturdy coal miner's daughter swiftly increased her punishing attack until she now beat at him as hard as she could.

Enraptured by his own punishment, with tears of joy trickling down his cheeks, Gerhard weakly whispered, "More. Much more." Obligingly, Willi continued her whacking. Gerhard's entire rear end turned bright crimson. Moving sorely, but utterly turned-on by the entire episode, Gerhard slowly sat up and willingly offered up his hard, thick, uncut, cock to Willi—who accepted it as a kind of sacrificial offering. A sadistic ritual had begun.

More sure of herself, Willi viciously slapped three eager times at Gerhard's erection. In a moment, his gratitude arrived. A great shudder, followed again by a huge orgasm. What she had suspected, Willi now knew as a certainty. Gerhard wanted to be punished. More than that, Gerhard *needed* to be punished!

Willi Eschweiler was a good amateur actress and thoroughly enjoyed being cast in the role of a dominatrix, which she had played several times since her arrival in Paris. On each occasion in which she was involved in sadomasochism, it had occurred during outrageously unrestrained group sex. Marvelous orgies of equal gender opportunity.

While admittedly desperate for the easy money, Willi also experienced great pleasure in the perverse evil of S & M. It beckoned to her. And she was more than willing to enter the darkness.

The next day, Willi invited Gerhard to join her at a secret S & M dungeon she had previously known. The very idea caused his eyes to light up.

After Willi quietly spoke her credentials to a strange-looking woman of indeterminate age, Gerhard handed over several large banknotes. Cleared for passage, they entered the dimly lit, windowless, dungeon room. As his eyes slowly adjusted to the low level of lighting, Gerhard suddenly realized he was alone. Cautiously, he touched the blood red, fabric-covered walls. In contradiction to their burn-in-hell color, they were surprisingly cool to his touch. Immediately, he knew that any possible screams would never be heard beyond these soundproof confines.

A look around the large space also revealed ominous sex toys and tools that would shortly carry Gerhard into a new dimension of lifestyle. Whatever fears he might have had were instantly overcome by a potent erection. He was shivering in lustful anticipation.

Without warning, the vast silence was violently broken by the crash of giant cymbals. The hugely amplified sound reverberated from and into every corner of the dungeon. It caught Gerhard completely off balance.

Before he could regain his focus, an intoxicating chemical mist descended over him. He felt dizzy, but also stimulated. The clinging vapors also caused his nostrils to flare and his eyes to burn. Simultaneously, Willi appeared only a few feet in front of him. In every way, she was perfectly cast as a dominatrix.

Her long blonde hair cascaded below her shoulders. Her full mouth promised fulfillment to all genitals she commanded to be presented. Her skintight black leather costume, with steel projectiles attached everywhere, had disturbingly allowed her hard nipples to fully show through the intended round cutouts. Her hip-high leather boots, had five-inch heels, and a spiked wheel. That wheel would force much compliance. So would her pointed metal toes.

Then, there was her whip. Brandishing it brought her great cunt to the edge of orgasm.

Convinced beyond all doubt that Gerhard needed to be her love slave, Willi began an exquisite series of carefully orchestrated humiliations designed to introduce her novice to the painful pleasures of sadomasochism.

Preceded by a sharp crack of her whip in the air, Willi sternly commanded, "First, you unworthy bastard, remove all of your clothes. You won't need any in here. Leave nothing—nothing at all! When you are naked, get down on all fours, like the miserable dog that you are. Then, I will put a collar and a leash on you. Now move!"

Never before in his life, had anyone spoken to the venerated industrialist, Gerhard Von Ribbentrop, in such a manner. Stunned beyond any comprehension, the still-proud German did not move. Willi's whip did.

Thus, both stung and hurt—his new life had begun.

Once they returned to Gerhard's hotel suite, Willi's abusive treatment continued.

"Dogs sleep on the floor. From now on you will sleep on the floor beside the bed. And you will wear your collar and leash unless we leave the hotel—and only if I give you my permission. Which I may or may not."

Gerhard was never again allowed into their bed without first begging Willi for sexual release. Mostly she refused him. When he cried out that he could wait no longer, Willi commanded him to first masturbate in front of her.

She wanted him to perform standing, stark naked, in front of a large mirror. To be on top of the action, the voyeuristic Willi, moved in closer, happily exclaiming, "Now, we can both watch you jack-off."

Only when his semen was already dripping on the carpet, would she finally relent. Only giving Gerhard permission to briefly mount for his finish. All the while, Willi repeatedly screamed out every four-letter word she knew—degrading him to zero. It pleased him. In unspeakable ways, Willi continued to inflict pain without hesitation.

Her stated goal was Gerhard's unconditional surrender.

"I will own you, my pet. Heart and soul—your very life—will belong only to me."

In a matter of days, Gerhard's suffering seriously escalated. Yet, both of them seemed to thrive on their sexual perversion. Now at the vicious crossroads of sadism and masochism.

Day after day, Willi's focus continued to be concentrated on Gerhard's enormous cock. She had become hooked on a contrarious phallic worship. The harder his erections became, Willi's slapping, biting, and whipping, similarly increased.

Yet, despite these hurting conditions, on her command, Gerhard, unfailingly continued to produce gigantic erections and multiple orgasms—four and five times daily. This ability controlled her imagination. Clearly, by now Willi had become totally crazed. As she spiraled toward sadistic heaven, Gerhard entered his dreamy masochistic paradise.

Their ecstasy notwithstanding, from the intensity of both his pain and his pleasure, on the fifth day of non-stop inflictions, and suffering from asphyxia, Gerhard fell into a state of suspended animation and lost consciousness. Willi looked on in sheer disgust.

Miraculously, a totally dedicated Gerhard, apparently determined never to deny her anything, returned to this world. Somehow, for reasons that made perfect sense, but only to himself—the novice love slave had no regrets. Gerhard found the insatiable Willi to be an irresistible treasure—an absolute wonder he had no intention of ever giving up.

Casting aside every safe emotional instinct he had followed for a lifetime, shocking his elderly parents, friends, and colleagues, Gerhard proceeded to marry Willi within the month. For the first time in his adult life, Gerhard Von Ribbentrop felt genuinely loved.

When she bore him a beautiful blonde baby girl they named her Ursula, for her paternal grandmother. Including exquisite blue-violet eyes, the infant was a picture-perfect clone of her gorgeous mother.

At her fully staffed home in Berlin, Willi took to her new high station with gusto. The same went for her other new mansion at Cannes, on the French Riviera. In no time, one would think her to the manor born. Gerhard was constantly amazed by her. His favorable reaction to her every move pleased the aggressive Willi. It was the good life. But Willi also knew there was more—of everything. And she wanted it all.

In her new environment, she knew that Gerhard was no longer enough for her. A certifiable nymphomaniac, Willi was fast becoming perfectly sure that no one man would ever be enough for her libidinous psyche. She wanted to reach for the stars. And it no longer mattered how many twinkles there might be. She needed many. The more, the better.

Back in the gritty coal-mining town where she was born, her drunken father had forced-sex with Willi beginning when she was about twelve. After a time, when she had forgotten her original pain, knowing it was wrong in ways she couldn't understand, Willi began to actually enjoy sex with her Father. Even the oral part. And the incest continued as much as several times a week until she ran off to Paris before her sixteenth birthday.

In the quiet of her tiny Paris attic room, Willi had a constant libidinal desire for her father. She had developed what psychoanalysts call an Electra complex.

In view of her long sexual experiences with her Father, it seemed perfectly natural to Willi to try to supplement her meager earnings, only a few francs, as the lowest beginning dishwasher at the Moulin Rouge, by inviting any number of older men back to her cockloft. Willi was after both the money and the sex. She could never get enough of either one.

Somehow, it was all part of her plan to gain the opportunity for an audition as a dancer in the floor show. She knew that chorus girls, especially those at the Moulin Rouge, had a chance to meet rich older men. And Willi wanted one of those 'sugar Daddys' for her very own.

A few years later, about the same time Jacqueline Bouvier married Senator John Fitzgerald Kennedy, the Greek tycoon, Aristotle Onassis, bought a 52% interest in Monte Carlo's Societe des Bains de Mer, which owned Monaco's famed casino, as well as the Hotel de Paris, the Yacht Club, and about 34% of Monaco itself.

In effect, the purchase gave Onassis economic domination over the tiny principality—and an introduction to Willi and Gerhard Von Ribbentrop.

It mattered very much to Onassis to associate with persons carrying famous names. Forget that Gerhard's uncle, an unknown former champagne salesman, who accidentally became Hitler's Foreign Minister, had been hung as an infamous Nazi war criminal. The Von Ribbentrops were still important to Onassis, a people user, and a notorious international social climber.

The Greek and the fancy German couple became the most popular threesome along the Côte d'Azur. Life, in fact, had become the social whirl Willi had only dreamed about. In her mind, she was finally getting somewhere.

For years, Onassis had constantly paraded any number of legends of the world aboard his 315-foot yacht, Christina. From Winston Churchill and Greta Garbo, to young Senator John F. Kennedy and his dazzling French-speaking wife, Jackie.

Not about to take a back seat to anyone, including the Kennedys, Willi and Gerhard Von Ribbentrop increased their social appearances to remain highlighted. The focus was always Willi.

Inevitably, one night at dinner, Onassis made the introduction. "Willi Von Ribbentrop, may I present George Garfield Grey."

Some guests remember the meeting of the suave thirty-six year-old American and the flirty twenty year-old German enchantress as “electrical.” Women blushed at their erotic memories. The men seemed to be mostly jealous. It did not take much encouragement to fire-up the heat of this newly introduced twosome.

Willi, at once on the make for Gar, told him straight out that she no longer cared what Gerhard thought. “I’ll take any damned thing I want. If I want to suck and fuck a guy, I don’t need Gerhard’s permission. In fact, I wish he would go home to Berlin—and stay there permanently.”

Saying these kinds of things to Gar Grey was the same as putting a match to an oil tank. Their heat was combustible.

In Gar’s ship-board quarters, their non-stop frenzy had gone on for more than a full day, causing a famous hard-of-hearing British dowager, not realizing her double-entendre, to shout,

“Can you really do it for such a long time without eating anything else?”

THIRTY-NINE

Having accepted a royal invitation to visit mystical Saudi Arabia, to first meet with his new oil partner, King Abdul Aziz ibn Saud, Gar had decided to make his grandest possible entrance. He would sail into Jeddah harbor aboard his 325ft. white yacht, Emperor II. A spectacular sight, wherever in the world she sailed.

After a private flight from London, Gar embarked at the French port of Marseilles, and headed southeast across the Mediterranean for Jeddah, on the Red Sea. But as history recorded, Gar's meeting with the old king never took place.

On November 9, 1953, as Emperor II prepared to enter the 103-mile long Suez Canal, Gar received an urgent radio dispatch from the Saudi Foreign Minister. The warrior-king, Abdul Aziz ibn Abdul Rahman-al Saud, had died, at age seventy-seven.

Shocked, Gar turned to Captain Giovanni Auriello, "What the hell do we do now, Gianni?" Fortunately, the captain did not have to answer. A radio operator suddenly appeared with a second dispatch from the Saudi Foreign Minister. Gar was invited to attend the royal funeral.

Some second-guessing advisors told Gar if he had chosen to fly to Jeddah, he would have arrived before the king's passing. However, it would not have mattered.

Curiously, he had not been informed that the old king—the oil partner he had so looked forward to meeting—was already enfeebled by crippling arthritis and nearly total blindness.

But then, that's just not what the fates had determined. They had a different story to tell.

Sa'ud ibn Abdul Aziz, at fifty-one years old, succeeded his Father and became only the second King of Saudi Arabia. High on an ambitious list of new government projects, King Sa'ud began to plan for the start-up of the Saudi-Arabian Maritime Tanker Company, a new entity that would have exclusive worldwide rights to transport Saudi oil. It set off storms of protest.

Heretofore, that rich prize was another unassailable profit center of Aramco, the Arabian-American Oil Company, the monopoly that controlled virtually all the production of Arabian oil from its beginning.

The King's plan was for the tanker company to be owned by several partners—one of whom was to be the controversial Greek shipping tycoon, Aristotle Onassis—who had a sullied international business reputation. Foolishly, not a single member of the Saudi royal family was included in the lucrative deal.

Upon hearing this disastrous news, Aramco ran screaming to the openly sympathetic U.S. Secretary of State, at that time, Eisenhower's trusted John Foster Dulles—the former Rockefeller-Chase National Bank-Standard Oil, lawyer.

Of course, Dulles would be sympathetic to Aramco—or anything else that smelled of Rockefeller oil money.

As far back as 1936, both Dulles brothers, John Foster and Allen, who later became the Director of the CIA, were partners in the New York law firm of Sullivan and Cromwell. That prestigious firm represented any number of Nazi-friendly Rockefeller global interests including Schröder, Rockefeller & Company, an investment bank, that Time magazine had called, "the economic booster of the Rome-Berlin Axis."

In this enterprise, the Rockefeller German partners were London-based, Baron Bruno von Schröder, and his cousin, Kurt von Schröder, of Cologne. These men had close ties with the Nazi controlled Bank for International Settlements in Basel, which funneled Nazi-looted gold into the Reichsbank from Belgium, The Netherlands, Czechoslovakia, and other conquered nations.

More ghastly, the BIS handled gold bars, made from melted-down gold teeth, cigarette cases, and jewelry, stripped from condemned Jews in the death camps in Poland.

But Aramco was not the only oil screamer.

Other oil executives were also in an uproar, including J. Paul Getty, who would become the richest man in the world. In that same unhappy oil group, was its newest member, George Garfield Gray, who now had another king as an oil field partner. Another king he did not know.

Getty had a long-standing resentment against Aramco because the cartel never allowed him a foothold in the Middle East. However, at this very time, he was making a last-ditch attempt to secure a new Saudi lease. And already had invested a lot of money—borrowed money.

Not too far south of the greatest oil field in the world, the giant Burghan field in Kuwait, lies an area called the Neutral Zone. Established in 1924, located between Kuwait and Saudi-Arabia, it is 2,200 square miles of unbroken desert occasionally visited by a few wandering Bedouin tribes.

The oil giants had ignored it, but the fiercely competitive, Getty, owner of Pacific Western Oil in far-off Los Angeles, was so convinced there was a vast pool of oil to be recovered beneath the Neutral Zone—and desperately wanted it—that he had paid King Ibn Saud, the, then, outrageous sum of $8 million as a down payment.

World oil was then selling for $1.93 per barrel.

Now, his worries quickly escalated.

The distrustful Getty was sure that Onassis would choose to hold him up over tanker lease rates, or worse—entirely freeze him out. Onassis would simply make no tankers available to transport his Neutral Zone oil. Such a freeze-out, Getty reasoned, might help Onassis soften Aramco's solid opposition to his tanker deal. It takes a thief to catch another.

Unhappily, without another viable option in view, in the summer of 1954, Getty started negotiations with Onassis. What Getty did not calculate was that Onassis, who was most anxious to enhance his still-shaky standing with King Sa'ud, was already trying to develop even greater sources of crude oil—beyond Aramco's vast tonnage.

It was in this connection, that Onassis invited Gar Grey to Monte Carlo for exploratory talks. Talks about transporting Gar's future oil from his yet to be developed field somewhere in the Saudi desert—with a partner he had never met.

Getty—Onassis—and Grey.

Birds of a feather flock together.

Let the world beware.

FORTY

With an insatiable sexual appetite, while on the French Riviera, Willi had an appointment with an important guest at the famous Hotel du Cap d' Antibes, which can only be described as palatial.

Over its storied past it had played host to reigning monarchs, as well as would-be royals and other celebrities, many of whom could no longer remember their humble beginnings.

According to plan, in an opulent suite, the freewheeling Willi Von Ribbentrop, let herself in with a key her host had provided in advance. Now she awaited his arrival.

The famous and aristocratic man of about fifty, was a typical English gentleman in the service of Her British Majesty's Foreign Ministry. A friend turned lover.

Smoking a gold-tipped cigarette held in a long ivory holder, Willi sat sensually slouched—her long legs provocatively crossed. She wore a sheer negligee of black silk chiffon, which exposed most of her ample breasts, as well as most of her milk-white thigh.

She knew her Englishman. In less than a furious minute after his arrival, Willi was in a familiar position—face down. Deeply embedded between his pale white legs, her tongue was creating an impromptu ballet. And judging from her companion's constant moans of pure pleasure, Willi's peerless reputation as a superlative performer was being fully maintained.

Only moments before, in his heat and haste for immediate gratification, the handsome diplomat overlooked the only article of apparel remaining on his otherwise naked body. Comically, he was still wearing one long black silk stocking held up by a trusty elastic black garter. The resulting sight could have been straight from a West End London farce.

At an earlier point in his long and distinguished Foreign Service career, the Brit had been posted to his government's embassy in Bonn, where he had met the wealthy industrialist, Gerhard Von Ribbentrop—years before Willi had ever appeared in Gerhard's life.

With whomever she chose to sleep with, sex with Willi was uniquely memorable. It was as though she used a branding iron on a man's psyche. This day, and this man, were no different. By the end of their afternoon of lovemaking, the Englishman could not imagine ever meeting another woman who could equal the intensity of Willi's sexual performances. No man ever would.

Relaxing in the afterglow, sharing a glass of deep burgundy that matched the color of his silk dressing gown, the diplomat faced Willi, wrapped in the folds of an enormously thick, white Turkish towel.

"You know, Willi, it would be so easy for me to become envious of my old friend, Gerhard. As your husband, of course, he is surely entitled to receive your extraordinary favors, but I wonder—well, quite frankly my dear, I have wondered for some time now—if you might be interested in the three of us sharing each other—intimately. For such purposes, please know that I have a most charming hide-a-way down in the Surrey countryside. It is very private. And, while I have never given him any indication, I have always thought Gerhard a to be a very attractive man. Of course, it goes without saying, my dearest Willi, that you are in a class by yourself. Do you think Gerhard might be interested in such a romp—a bit of fun and frolic?" Looking straight into his dark, anxious eyes, Willi responded, "You don't get it. If this is something *I* want to do, Gerhard has no choice—he will comply. My requests are his commands. The most critical question is will you also obey my commands?"

"I shall look forward with great anticipation to that joyous moment, Willi. When you are quite prepared to make such an appointment, please contact me through the usual channels."

Back at her Cannes mansion, immersed in a scented bath of foamy bubbles, Willi passed off her afternoon of sex in easy fashion. She was already planning an appointment in Surrey.

As she was preparing herself for the evening ahead, she was talking with Inga Torkelson, her young and attractive confidant and personal assistant.

"Now, I'm ready for a big night at Aly's place. It's good that his villa is only down the road. Inga, do you remember that I told you Aly was a great fuck? He keeps an erection harder and longer than any other man I've ever been with. He told me it was due to a discipline that he learned as a teenager—from an old Egyptian doctor in Alexandria. You wouldn't believe how many famous women have been satisfied in his bed.

But, you know what's even more important right now, Inga? I wonder where in the world Gar might be tonight? I miss him, terribly."

Gar had agreed to meet with Onassis at his headquarters in Monte Carlo. He also agreed to a secret meeting with a man named Spiros Catapodis. That clandestine meeting had been arranged at the urging of an Arabian friend, Sheik Omar Arif Akram, whose credentials were first verified and approved by Gar's Liechtenstein lawyer, Dr. Franz Josef Ritter.

Akram was influential, rich, and well respected in international financial circles. He had reported to Gar that Catapodis was a rich playboy, who told anyone who would listen that he was an agent for Aristotle Onassis. Moreover, Catapodis openly bragged that he had set up a fantastic Saudi Arabian oil tanker deal for Onassis, claiming he made the deal through Abdullah Suleiman, King Abdul Aziz' old Finance Minister.

The Sheik's stated purpose for the meeting was for his friend Gar to learn as much as possible about the Catapodis/Suleiman deal before sitting down with Onassis.

Of course, that was only a fairy tale. Gar knew the Sheik's intuitive agenda was the very real possibility of collecting yet another in a long string of multimillion-dollar fees and commissions.

Seeking total privacy for all parties involved, Gar arranged for the meeting to take place aboard Emperor II, anchored just outside the ancient harbor at Monaco. Accompanied by Akram, Gar met with Catapodis in his sumptuous walnut-paneled lounge. To Gar's utter surprise, Catapodis confirmed that the tanker story was true!

The night before his meeting with Catapodis, together with everyone else of social importance, including the now famous Willi Von Ribbentrop, Gar had been invited to a huge dinner party hosted by the super-rich playboy, Prince Aly Khan. Aly was the son of the Aga Khan, the spiritual and temporal leader of the world's Shia Imami Ismali Moslems. They believed him to be a direct descendant of the prophet Mohammed.

In appropriate tribute, on the occasion of his fiftieth birthday, his twenty million followers presented the already immensely rich Aga Sultan Sir Mohammed Shah, with his weight in gold—an enormous 220 pounds. For his seventy-fifth birthday, their gift was expressed in platinum. All of which made him the second best-known South Asian—only preceded by Mohandas K. Gandhi, the father of independent India.

But for Prince Aly, women and racehorses were his great passions—especially women.

Aly's dinner party took place on the broad terrace of his lavish Riviera home, Château de L' Horizon. Near Cannes, it overlooked the Mediterranean. Even though Willi's estate was nearby, she had appeared purposefully late, creating the opportunity for an exclusive grand entrance. Which she did with a bold flourish.

Practically waltzing onto the terrace, Willi was a spectacular sight in a breathtaking blue-violet silk satin strapless gown. Designed by Pierre Balmain, it was an ankle-length sheath which matched her equally astonishing blue-violet eyes. Her long blonde hair softly cascaded down to her exquisitely bare shoulders. Her jewelry deserved a Brinks escort. Willi wore an eye-popping diamond and sapphire necklace with a mammoth pear-shaped cabochon sapphire solitaire drop, which hung from the necklace by a short chain of round-cut diamonds. This magnificence was complimented with matching bracelet, ring, and hanging earrings. The total carat weight could not possibly have been imagined.

Indeed. Even this blasé gathering audibly gasped.

Moreover, Willi had asked the famous Balmain, a superlative designer who was particularly known for his elegant evening wear, to create the illusion that she had had her tall body tantalizingly poured into her gown. Not only did the designer comply with her request, Balmain had not left a stitch of room for undergarments—none. Filling every seam to absolute perfection, Willi's skin-tight gown left nothing to the imagination. One could have counted every last one of her pubic hairs. However, with clean-shaven genitals, she had none. Everywhere a man wanted to touched her, the glamorous Willi was as smooth as glass.

The murmuring had now become palpable.

As Willi had carefully planned, all eyes followed her every turn. As she easily moved from guest to guest, using a martini as a prop, Willi repeatedly sucked on the green olive suggestively perched on the end of a pick. Simultaneously, the fabric of her gown stroked her exposed private parts, continuously bringing her close to her orgasmic edge. The devil-may-care Willi was libidinously tempted to let herself go.

Her revealing appearance had already sent racy vibes through every male body on Aly's terrace. With every intent to fulfill, this lady was hell-bent upon spreading rich promise. Although no man had yet jumped naked into the pool to calm himself down.

Having conquered the sophisticated crowd, Willi was clearly Queen for the night. But it was not all that easy. Any party given by Aly Khan included the most celebrated 'players' in the world—male and female, amateur and professional—as well as many great beauties of all races and colors. Whether a guest was married or single, gay or straight, a wide choice of partners was available. Understandably, long-time wives never felt comfortable during these soirées. It was taken for granted that those who did attend had their own private agendas.

Aly loved throwing a successful party. And in the mind of the jaded Indian prince, 'successful' was only an alternative word for hedonistic.

Obviously pleased to be at the same party, Gar and Willi were softly dancing. Out of nowhere, a man of obvious Middle Eastern heritage, impeccably dressed in a western-style tuxedo with his head wrapped in the familiar kaffiyeh, appeared. Having spotted Willi, the intruder moved quickly to her back. His hands over her eyes.

"So—we do meet again!"

Startled, Willi quickly jerked the unknown hands off her face. Turning to see their source, she didn't quite know what emotion she should exhibit. Before her stood a man she certainly did know—intimately. Sheik Omar Arif

Akram was an unofficial but highly important presence in the Saudi Arabian palaces of King Abdul Aziz ibn Saud. It was known worldwide to highly placed financial officials, even a few in the Soviet Union, if "Ari" appeared, much money was soon to follow.

The accepted rationale was that the Sheik's source of endless resources was the huge Saudi royal family. Ibn Saud had fathered more than forty sons—a long line of overly rich princes. Forget his nearly equal number of daughters. In the Arab world, they simply did not count.

Before Willi had to make a split-second decision, Gianni Agnelli to the rescue. The handsome heir to the Fiat automobile fortune had been nearby with his longtime companion, Pamela Churchill—ex-daughter-in-law of the British Prime Minister. Agnelli aggressively stepped past her to stand almost nose-to-nose with the intruder. But Gar pushed belligerently forward, "What the hell are you doing here, Ari—our meeting is not until tomorrow?"

The kaffiyeh around his head notwithstanding, in perfect Oxonian English, the Sheik replied, "Indeed, that is correct, Gar. And be assured that tomorrow we shall meet at the proper time and place. However, my dear friend, tonight I did not intend to be either monk nor eunuch. More to the point, I did not intend to frighten your lovely lady, whom I have had the pleasure of previously meeting. Mademoiselle, if an apology is in order—"

"Nonsense, Ari, you needn't apologize. It's always nice to see old friends again. And I am even more pleased to see that you and Gar already know each other. Now all three of us can be close."

Ultimately, couples and groups would use all ten bedrooms at the Château. Into the farthest reaches of free love, the night ended in unrestrained debauchery. In a tumultuous all-inclusive group orgy—no one was left standing.

FORTY-ONE

No man with a brain in his head, or at least those who preferred to keep it neatly intact, would ever be foolish enough to cross George Garfield Grey. Certainly not as long as one of Gar's principal partners was the mobster, Meyer Lansky. The Havana gambling czar, in his attempt to find the leak-source of Gar's Venezuelan acquisition from IG Farben, had called upon an amazing network of skilled informers scattered all over the world.

The vast extent of the informer network emerged when a copy of a highly confidential file, from the Washington headquarters of the FBI, was surreptitiously passed on to Lansky.

It read:

"Confidential File No. 100:1202.

Titled "Jean Paul Getty."

It is further identified.

"Character of Case: Espionage—G"

The text went on from there.

According to various sources, it had been reported that during World War II, Getty had made the mistake of openly bragging about his admiration for the Nazi style of government—which he thought to be very efficient. Added to that, was Getty's admitted friendship with the likes of Hitler, Goebbels, and Göring. And there was more.

For some time, within the tightly knit fraternity of international oil, it had been rumored that Getty had tried to sell large amounts of his oil to Nazi Germany. The FBI also knew about his close friendship with Hitler's girlfriend, the German actress, Hilde Kruger, which generated even more attention from the FBI.

Things were not much different with Aristotle Onassis.

J. Edgar Hoover had been monitoring the Greek tycoon since the early 1940s. Not only did Onassis have strong ties to Argentina's fascist dictator, Juan Perón, but also to many who later became Nazi war criminals. In response to the suggestion of inviting the German munitions king, Alfred Krupp, to a ship launching, Onassis replied, "I don't think one more Nazi here or there is going to make much difference to my reputation, now."

Shockingly, Onassis had told an early lover, "Every Greek, and there are no exceptions, beats his wife. It's good for them. It keeps them in line." And that included two beautiful wives, his longtime companion, Maria Callas, the famous opera singer, and his last wife—Jacqueline Kennedy Onassis.

In the case of both Callas and Jackie O., the huge sunglasses provided effective cover. And all of this scandalous information on Getty and Onassis was being funneled back to Meyer Lansky in Havana. Surprisingly, however, when the mobster finally got his first real breakthrough on the Farben deal it did not come from one of his informers. But rather during a visit from Count Carlo of Bergamo, originally a confidant of Lucky Luciano.

"Meyer, you and Charlie know I would never double-cross either one of you—and that goes for Gar, too. But I do think I can help you out of this mess. As I have already told Charlie, I was invited to a small dinner party at the Saudi embassy in Caracas given by two Princes I had previously met in Rome. Senator Warren Bascombe and his wife were also there. The Senator happens to be very tight with the Saudi Ambassador to Washington, who spends many weekends at Bascombe's country place. And, Meyer, I'm telling you that it *was* Bascombe who informed the Ambassador about your Farben deal—which he immediately passed on to his King. Later on, I heard that the Farben story came to Bascombe through somebody on the staff of the senate sub-committee he chairs. Resources and Minerals is plenty powerful. As a direct result, he gets an awful lot of oil buzz from important Washington lawyers and lobbyists who make a living off of his friendship and cooperation. Now, you know everything that I know, Meyer."

All of the information already in his possession, notwithstanding, Lansky continued to have a gut instinct that there was yet a closer link. Calling around the world, he squeezed his resources harder than ever. He was fond of saying, "Ya never know it—till ya know it."

Ultimately, his instinct proved correct. Out of the blue, popped the double agent—Alayne Benning-George!

Not only did Lansky's information finally reveal that Ally was on the payroll of the Saudis, but more specifically, she was on the personal *cash* payroll of Sheik Omar Arif Akram. Akram's secret source book contained four underlined notations regarding Ally.

Attractive.
Bright.
Bi-sexual nympho.
Retainer—plus $1,000 per.

Internationally known for his professionalism, the suave Akram certainly had no time for amateurs. Ally had officially become a high-class whore. Remembering the original close connection, Lansky was immediately on the phone. "And dat's da story, Gar. So now da ball is in yur court, pal."

"Thanks for the call, Meyer. I'll keep you informed."

Replaying Lansky's words in his head, as Gar reached for his still-warm phone, "That sneaky cunt. She *was* playing both sides."

After receiving the Lansky report, Gar issued his instructions. In response, tall, dark, and handsome Umberto Ben-Levi Goldmanni grabbed the first available flight out of Nassau, and arrived at National Airport in Washington.

As soon as he was settled in his suite at the Hay-Adams, across Lafayette Park from the White House, Goldmanni left an ambiguous message for Alayne Benning-George.

"Hello Ally. My name is Umberto Leone. I am from Rome, however I arrived today in Washington. We have never met. Your name and phone number came to me some time ago from a mutual friend who wanted us to meet."

To add authenticity and a bit of mystery, Goldmanni added, "Inasmuch as the Emerald Club is not geographically possible, may I suggest the bar at the Hay Adams." Commandingly, "I have in mind this afternoon—at five. See you there."

Gar had told him two things. "If nothing else, Berto, you'll go mad for her nipples and tits. But, remember, business comes first."

Gar had also assured him that she would show up. As usual, he was right on both counts. Quickly identifying each other, the strangers settled into a cozy corner table in the dark paneled bar. Trying hard to remember that he was on assignment, Umberto said to himself, "Her chest *is* incredible. A guy could get impaled on one of her nipples."

Ally was fully aware of her physical attributes. And did not hesitate to take full advantage. Her very presence in a room, at once established the mood and verbal agenda.

Practically drowning him in the focus of her deeply seductive eyes, "Umberto" she cooed, "what a charming name. And from Rome—oh, lucky you."

"*Wherever* one is born, Ally, is pure luck. È d'accordo Lei?"

"I'm afraid my Italian is pretty much limited to words like 'grazie' and 'ciao'."

Goldmanni knew that Ally didn't know what he said. He wanted her a little off-balance. A tip he received from Gar. "What I said was, do you agree?"

Umberto decided to carry on with word flirting. "Words like 'yes' and 'right,' make good beginning words for our friendship, Ally. 'Goodbye' does not fit in so well. You know we Italians have a famous history for being ardent and long-running lovers. We do not merely hit and run."

"Lovers? What an interesting choice of words. Is there more to this Italian fairy tale?"

With good humor prevailing, the getting-to-know-you-game lasted throughout dinner. Many 'facts' fell into place. Such as fictitious family history to justify his newly adopted last name, schooling, and career. All went well. Shortly before eleven o'clock, Umberto helped the very stylish Ally into a cab. Her skirt rose to mid-thigh. Combining her amazing chest with an enticing length of thigh sent Umberto's thoughts soaring.

Poking his head into the back seat, "It would greatly please me, Ally, if you would make the decision about where we would enjoy having a quiet dinner tomorrow night—then, give me a call. O.K.?"

"I must say, you Romans are very fast—but I'll think about it. Ciao, Umberto."

As the cab disappeared, Ally was already planning tomorrow's evening.

Back in his suite, and pleased with his progress, Umberto made two calls. The first was a report to Gar. At the Savoy in London.

After listening to the details, Gar replied, "Sounds like you made a good start, Berto. Keep me fully updated."

The second call rang in Umberto's apartment on the second floor of the Atlantic Overseas Bank in Nassau. A comfortably naked Victoria Tracy casually rolled her delicious milk-chocolate body toward the phone.

"Hi, honey, I was waiting for your call. Is everything all right? That's good. You know, Berto, you were very evasive about your trip. But, I suppose that it's just more of that secret stuff between you and Gar. I guess all I really need to know is that you're safe—and that you still love me madly. You know my insecurity doesn't vanish overnight."

"But, you have no need to feel insecure, Vikki. I only met four girls today that could replace you in a minute. But give me a little more time."

"That's not funny, Berto. You scare me with that kind of talk. Stop it!"

"Sorry, that *was* a pretty stupid thing to say."

After another few minutes of trivia, "I'll say good night now. I'm totally pooped. If you need me for something important, baby, I'm at the Hay-Adams. Otherwise, I'll let you know when I'll be back. Bye."

As Vikki hung up, lightly clapping his hands as if applauding a superior piece of acting, Gar's New York lawyer and partner, Sal Bellini, casually emerged from the bathroom—removing his robe as he approached Vikki's bed.

"An Oscar-winning performance, lovely lady. Which reminds me, I have some very close connections in Hollywood. Maybe I should send you out there to become an actress. Come to think of it, sweetheart—you're doing a good job of acting right now."

It was not much different in Washington. After some cold water to refresh his face, Goldmanni made a local call. Twenty minutes later, he kept his second female appointment within three hours.

To the older woman, "Rio, you look absolutely sensational. Younger than ever!"

"Thank you, my beautiful, Berto, you always say the most flattering things. Let's have one fast drink—a double Scotch for me. I can hardly wait to get you alone—and strip you bare-assed naked. Then, I have some great plans for us for the next few days. Fortunately, Warren is in the

Middle East on Senate oil business—for a change. I do declare, that strange man loves oil more than sex—at least sex with *me.*"

In London, Gar was unable to sleep.

Looking for some sort of diversion, he dressed and headed for the Emerald Club. Sitting alone at the bar, Gar was still deep into his anger about what Ally had done to him. Out of nowhere, his thoughts were interrupted by a tender hand on his shoulder.

"I don't believe it! Gar Grey in London—*alone?*"

He had not seen Nancy Lee Hendrix since 'that' night. And in this very club room. The night with Ally and the Arab princes. Ironically, here he was again—with Ally occupying his head, and Nancy Lee occupying his eyes. Gar thought to himself, "How strange can life get?"

Putting on his best flip act, "Well, well, well. If it isn't Little Miss Playmate, in the flesh. Or, is that too corny?"

Smilingly ignoring his snide remark, Nancy Lee brought forward an attractive younger man, most likely in his mid-twenties. "Gar, I'd like to introduce a close friend of mine—Ian Hawkins. Ian, this is the famous George Garfield Grey, whom I've told you so much about."

Extending his hand, Gar was caught off balance by the almost feminine handshake of Ian Hawkins. The younger man's soft-as-butter touch sent a hundred red warning lights flashing through Gar's brain.

None of this seemed to make much sense. But then, almost nothing that had occurred the last few days had made much sense.

"Gar—Ian and I are here with a few friends. Since you seem to be alone, would you care to join us?"

"That might be fun, Nan—I'll follow you."

Maybe it was fate. Maybe it was a full moon. Who knows? The old bromide went something like this. "If you spend enough time at the Emerald Club—sooner or later you'll see *everyone* you know—doing *everything* you know."

But, when Gar arrived at Nancy Lee's table, the world suddenly turned totally upside down. As she started to introduce her friends, Gar looked across the table.

Then, "Sorry, Nan, I forgot to make a call. Please excuse me." The sight of a sexy-looking young blonde openly deep-kissing a masculine-featured thirty-something woman—with both parties very much into each other—prompted his quick exit. The greater surprise was that the blonde was Willi Von Ribbentrop. As Gar hurriedly left the table, Willi burst from her chair in full pursuit.

"Gar, wait, you don't understand."

Confused, Nancy Lee reacted, *"Jeez, she's been fucking him, too."*

It was nearly three in the morning, as Gar came through the door of his Savoy Hotel suite. His phone was ringing with an emphasis that seemed to demand an answer.

"Gar Grey here."

"Gar—Zis is Franz Ritter in Vaduz."

"Guten Abend, Franz. Considering the hour, do we have an emergency, somewhere?"

"Keine Notfälle. No emergencies. Vhat I do haf is *good* news—actually *double* good news."

"Great. I can use some of that—especially right now."

"Zho—ze first good news is zhat King Sa'ud is finally ready to discuss your mutually owned oil reserve. Zecondly, earlier zhis evening, a courier personally delivered to me ze final papers on ze Farben purchase in Venezuela."

Lowering his voice as though it would increase the secrecy of the conversation, Ritter continued, "Gar, you should know zhat vee succeeded in getting Vashington's approval for zhis acquisition only through ze good offices of former Ambassador Averell Harriman, whom I haf known for many years.

Before he became a diplomat, Harriman vas ze Chairman of ze Union Pacific Railroad. Az an able und experienced businezzman, he explained to your State Department and CIA people zhat someday ze future national zecurity of ze United States might largely come to depend upon zhese Venezuelan resources. Consequently, it vas essential to have zhese assets in the trustworthy hands of a strong American. All of vhich now makes you a most eminent person. A responsibility zhat you can no longer take lightly."

In a brighter voice, Ritter went on.

"Zho—vee are scheduled to sign ze papers tomorrow in Paris. Zhen—vee go directly to Riyadh to zee King Sa'ud. By ze vay, Gar, ze terms und conditions of zhis deal are thought to be zo confidential in Vashington zhat ze courier vas escorted by two zecurity men from Farben. Zey flew here on a Farben corporate plane. Und I haf been asked to keep ze executed originals in my special underground vault."

"That's one hell of a story, Franz. I congratulate you on a job well done.

Indeed—very well done.

Tomorrow in Paris is fine. Where do we meet?"

BOOK TWO

ZAG

FORTY-TWO

Fifteen Years Later: March, 1969.

To emphasize his extreme positions on most matters, Gar liked to say, "The only middle ground I could ever find always led me straight into a wet pussy."

While comparative anatomical humor had long been a Gar Grey conversational staple—and his crude remark continued to draw laughs from long-time pals—nobody could remember his using it before as a road map.

Yet, in this instance, nothing he might otherwise have substituted would have been more honest and true. No matter where he imagined it led him, George Garfield Grey *was* emotionally unable to find middle ground. On the other hand, his latest obsessive-compulsive scheme contained no humor, whatsoever. It was so outrageous that many friends worried if the world-renowned financier had finally gone over the edge. Quite logically, they reasoned, after the 'plaque' story broke, anything was possible.

Since he had first laid eyes upon it, Gar saw the great bronze plaque as the most powerful symbol of his "immortality."

Not in the least inhibited by the ultra-superiority of his hope for eternal self-life, Gar often spoke to the subject and thoroughly enjoyed embellishing it upon each retelling.

Behind closed doors it was a completely different story. His closest associates questioned, "Could such a brilliantly successful businessman seriously believe anyone could live forever?"

Gar Grey certainly could. *And did!*

His paranormal belief was unfortunately reinforced each day as he arrived at his World Headquarters in New York's Rockefeller Center. There, he passed the huge floor-to-ceiling bronze plaque which had been bolted onto the rose-colored marble wall. Dwarfing the receptionist.

The plaque heralded the sequential creation of Gar's corporate monument, whose excessive size had already been the subject of a curious front-page article in *The Wall Street Journal.*

WORLD HEADQUARTERS
ATLANTIC OVERSEAS BANK OF NASSAU 1953
GENERAL INDUSTRIAL CORPORATION 1953
GENERAL INDUSTRIAL OIL CORP. 1954
GENERAL OIL VENEZUELA 1955
GENERAL AIRCRAFT CORPORATION 1956
GENERAL ARMAMENT CORPORATION 1956
GENERAL FINANCIAL CORPORATION 1957
GENERAL UTILITIES CORPORATION 1958
GENERAL WORLDWIDE CORPORATION 1960

Not satisfied, Gar planned a newer "immortal" symbol, which would generate an even higher level of speculation regarding his emotional state of mind—a psychobiography.

In a secret shared only with his most trusted aid, Irene Henry, Gar had commissioned a noted Italian sculptor to create a life-sized white marble bust of himself.

More than two years later, the finished work was tenderly crated and escorted to New York by the sculptor on Gar's private jet. There, to be installed on its pedestal in his enormous office. This megalomaniacal event occurred at 2 AM, under the safe cover of darkness and a security escort. Much in the same manner and time as gold bullion shipments usually move aboard armored trucks for delivery to the underground vaults of the New York Federal Reserve Bank.

If the comparison struck him at all, in Gar's omnipotent mind even the Fed's gold could not be held as more valuable than his replicated marble likeness.

What followed the installation was the ultimate egotrip. With Gar formally seated at his desk and the pedestaled bust to his immediate right, he summoned Irene Henry with Fabian Bachrach, the ultimate American portrait photographer. Bachrach's reaction was professionally calculated. He knew what Gar wanted to hear. And no way would he lose the opportunity to take this historical first photograph—a photograph that would immediately appear worldwide with credits below. "Courtesy of Fabian Bachrach, New York."

Accordingly, but professionally, the photographer intoned, "The visual dynamics between flesh and stone, Mr. Grey, are truly spectacular."

That response was exactly what Gar had in mind when he first commissioned the bust. Later selected and chiseled from a gigantic block of choice Italian white carrara marble.

He was now convinced that his visitors' reactions would also be spectacular. The word Gar actually had in mind was "overwhelming." The reaction that was comparable to those who traveled to Florence in order to view Michelangelo's unbelievable statue of David.

Badly wanting that comparison to be made, Gar had insisted the sculpture be chiseled from the identical marble and taken from the identical quarry, as used by the famous Renaissance genius.

George Garfield Grey had now forced a dual focus upon himself. While the bust clearly represented his chiseled face, it also had been intentionally sculpted to have the classical Roman appearance of a Caesar.

What chutzpah!

As the talk gathered added momentum, Gar quietly projected the value of the controversial international publicity. "Those stupid bastards don't know a real score when they see one."

Late one New York afternoon, in his lavish private-quarters suite just beyond his office, Gar lay covered from his waist down only by a large white towel. Under the expert hands of Red Atkins, his longtime masseur, the exhausted Gar finally gave in to the inviting relaxation of his daily massage. His last thought was, "Had it all been only a dream?"

In the 1950s, screaming headlines of his giant oil strike had electrified the world!

Almost immediately after drilling began into the oil-rich sands of the Northeastern Saudi desert, at a shallow depth the deeply embedded pressure forced a gusher to explode. The partners had discovered one of the world's largest oil fields! Magically, Gar was rich beyond all imagination. And his Saudi King partner was positively overwhelmed.

During the fifteen hectic years that followed, Gar had moved at lightning speed. With strategic planning, he combined tons of his new oil money with long-term, 30-year corporate bonds, underwritten by the most prestigious Wall Street and London investment banks.

International commercial banks that never would have bothered with him before the big oil gush, now begged him to borrow at rates only basis points above their own real cost of money. A rate never before extended.

Later, some accommodating loans were added to placate those unhappy commercial banks. They all wanted a piece of his far-flung action. Clever Gar left those funds untouched—as free compensating balances. Someday, he might actually need to use those loan balances. In the meantime, frowns turned to smiles.

With this incredible pool of capital at his disposal, Gar turned his acquisition binge into a virtual torrent. Wherever in the world he dealt, he was reported as setting some kind of financial record or precedent. It was all quite mind-boggling.

Out of this frenzy grew his formidable General Industrial Corporation.

Gar's modest original purchase of the Atlantic Overseas Bank of Nassau, the small acorn which held the secret option to purchase the fabulous oil partnership, had grown into a mighty oak. The talk in Beirut, the French-mandate financial center of the Middle East, was that the bank acquisition had been, "L'affaire qui a lancé un Empire." The deal that launched an Empire.

Gar's on-going accomplishments only continued to prove Franz Josef Ritter to be one of the great prognosticators and psychologists of all time. As Ritter had correctly predicted, Gar's new riches forever changed his life. Always a powermaster, his newly found celebrity only exacerbated that innate tendency. In quick order the three dominating features of his psyche were distilled into only one word. *Control. Control. Control.*

Especially so, when it came to the two greatest passions of his life—Money and women.

If he wanted to acquire it, no company could escape his grasp. And no woman in the world was safe outside her Father's house. He no longer just wanted them, he was now driven to control every aspect of their lives. Even when he might be half-a-world away.

Reporters now followed him wherever he went. He was endlessly photographed and quoted on an infinite variety of subjects—most of which he knew little or cared nothing about.

While he gloried in the non-stop media limelight, he bitterly resented the downside. Virtually overnight his privacy had vanished.

"Don't these bastards ever go home?" he screamed at portly Frank Templeton, GIC's Director of Worldwide Corporate Communications. "And, one more thing, Frank. Keep your goddam cigars out of my face. They really stink."

At the beginning of his new public life, even for the likes of the self-centered George Garfield Grey, the headline news coverage that heralded the huge Arabian oil discovery was awesome. The sheer magnitude of his overnight fortune immediately propelled him into the ranks of one of the world's richest men.

While he certainly had been thought of as a boy wonder back in his early law-practice days in Chicago, compared to the world stage where the really big boys played, Gar quickly realized he had only been small potatoes. He was now spoken of in the same breath as Rockefeller, Ford, and Getty. Grand comparisons that were pretty heady stuff.

In every way, Gar flourished in the sweetness of his newly acquired milk and honey.

He thrived to such an extent that friends began to believe he even appeared taller.

FORTY-THREE

London: May, 1969.

Fate? Destiny? Kismet?

Call it what you will.

Most people believe that chance romantic meetings occur only in films. That sophisticated men like Cary Grant and Walter Pidgeon only strolled promenade decks on make-believe ships in those wonderful old movies. Yet, maybe it is not all pure fantasy.

Watch this scene unfold.

Around midnight, after a tumultuous business day, rather than going directly upstairs to his river suite, Gar decided to stop for a nightcap in the Savoy Grill. There, to finally relax over his very dry martini. From out of nowhere, two familiarly scented hands lightly descended on his shoulders. Softly, a sexy voice spoke into his ear,

"Don't move. Don't look yet, either. Just listen.

I understand you know my Mother—intimately."

Astonished, Gar abruptly stood up and found himself merely inches from one of the world's most celebrated faces and bodies. In her German tinted accent, the exquisite international blonde model introduced herself.

"Hello, Gar Grey. I am Ursula Von Ribbentrop."

Slowly, looking her up and down, the still-shocked Gar replied, "Indeed you are."

At twenty-four, Ursula was a clone of her seductress Mother— herself, now only forty-two. Gar could not help staring. Although ogling might have been a better description. When it embarrassingly dawned on him that they were both still standing, "Oh, I'm sorry, Ursula," and, pulling out a chair, "please join me." She sat closely facing him.

"You are correct, of course. I have known your Mother for many years. And I'm sure people tell you all the time that you are the spitting imagine of her."

"Yes they do. And thank you for the compliment. By the way, while you have no way of knowing, she still speaks of you with a certain wistful look in her eyes. Did your affair end badly? Have you seen her lately?"

Recalling the scene at the Emerald Club with Willi in the arms of a lesbian bull dyke, for the moment Gar opted to duck her questions. "No. I've not seen her in some time. But, I'm sure that you and I will get into all of our common ground. And, hopefully, quite soon."

Ever the seductress, Ursula leaned into him.

"Do you promise to be sexually irresistible?"

Outwardly Gar smiled, but her words scored a direct hit. Exploding on-target where she aimed them. Starting in his groin, he felt fresh excitement racing through his entire body. Simultaneously, with an almost hypnotic expression, Ursula suddenly seemed to take emotional leave—to somehow float away—disappear. It was as though she was being mysteriously swept somewhere beyond the here and now.

She heard a primitive jungle beat—intoxicating and sexually stimulating—arriving from a distant place to pierce the deepest part of her imagination. Helpless to resist, Ursula willingly offered herself onto the sacred altar of voodoo witchcraft.

With unrelenting intensity, the beat grew louder and faster. Fifty pairs of bare hands were beating on those jumbo drums. In the most lascivious possible way, Ursula could *see* all those bare hands—even *feel* all those bare hands—sliding into every orifice of her steaming body.

Only one thing mattered now.

Hurtling toward her goal, craving its release, she violently trembled. Her overflowing climax drowned her in supreme ecstasy. Again! Now—total silence. Her drums had vanished. Shhh.

As Ursula receded from her reverie, across the white table linen, Gar was waiting and watching in utter fascination. "Was it a nice trip?" he gently inquired.

"Oh yes—yes it was. I love to slip away into my fantasy world because I can do anything I want there. Perhaps next time you'll share it with me. Do you have a favorite fantasy, Gar?"

Looking deeply into Ursula's eyes, "Of course I do. I'm looking at it right now."

Years later, nearly all of the women present that night seem to remember having heard lightening strike over the River Thames. They believe they heard a blistering charge of electricity having instantly passed between Ursula, a free wheeling, high living, blonde model of eye-popping proportions—from Berlin. And the American, Gar Grey, the handsomely tall, sandy-haired, world-famous billionaire businessman—just past his fifty-first birthday.

Legendary stories are often born of this kind of wishful delusion. In reality, it had been a balmy spring evening in London that night. Not a trace of lightening over the entire length of the Thames.

Lightening or not, whatever the others did or did not remember, it was apparent that the usually cool and sophisticated Gar Grey had been topped. Ursula's instinctive sensuality proved to be far more intoxicating than his martini.

Always the focus of attention, her unabashed seduction of Gar enchanted most everyone in the Grill. Both men and women were silently envious of the scene they had witnessed.

Gar suggestively caressed the palm of her hand. And came straight to the point. "Why don't we just go up to my suite now, and create a brand new fantasy of our own?"

A daredevil since puberty, Ursula claimed to have tried "everything" at least once. But, the deviant scene about to take place was unclaimed territory. To Ursula, the thought of unrestrained sex with her own Mother's lover suggested a kind of incestuous ménage à trois that held great appeal for her. Any threesome did. The mere idea of it set her body on fire and her mind racing madly to explore mysteriously exotic destinations.

Eager to lie flesh to flesh—to kiss and fondle—without a word, Ursula flashed her acceptance by lasciviously rolling her tongue around her inviting red lips. With soaring anticipation, Gar slowly pushed his chair back from the table.

His inevitable control game had begun.

FORTY-FOUR

Only hours after completing a high-level executive search assignment for an Italian pharmaceutical manufacturer, the internationally respected executive recruiter, Cheryl Blake, was preparing to leave Milan. Not expecting any further calls, she was startled by the loud ring.

"Yes," she answered tersely.

"Hi, Cheryl, it's Cliff Blair." Without pause, the usually affable senior assistant to George Garfield Grey ran on. "The boss asked me to deliver a short assignment message. He said to tell you that he will need your help on a previously dead search in Amsterdam. He said you would know what it's about. Since I don't have a clue on this one, I'd say the ball is in your court. In any event, the messenger has delivered the message."

Cheryl Blake, a senior partner in the Los Angeles-based firm of Kramer-Franklin, the largest executive recruiter in the world, was upset by Blair's almost gruff manner. Nevertheless, without so much as a slight change of tone in her voice, "Thanks for the call, Cliff. I'll let Gar know you did your duty."

At Gar's behest, over the years Cheryl had received many assignment calls from Blair. Ever since Gar told her Blair was "an okay guy," meaning he knew the real score, she could always talk straight with him. But not this time. And it upset her.

Blair's message had obviously caught Cheryl off guard. Despite Gar's confident comment to Blair about her knowing what he was talking about, in fact, Cheryl did not know. At least, nothing for sure. Of course, one could never be absolutely sure of anything with Gar Grey.

Pondering, Cheryl decided it probably had some connection with what he had told her a few years back. At that time, in an unusually serious tone, Gar had said, "At some point in the future, Cheryl, with all of my worldwide business activities, it's entirely possible that a set of circumstances might force me to give you an assignment that will be 'different.'"

And it was that word, *"different,"* that Cheryl was recalling. Thinking about it now she thought, "How strange, Gar never mentioned that subject again. I wonder why?"

In the silence of her Milan hotel room, it was the sudden fear of the unknown that was insidiously creeping into Cheryl's mind. She was even more upset than she had first thought.

Encouraged by Gar, over the course of their time together Cheryl had come to completely rely on him for both the solid core of her executive search business, as well as endless rendezvous for their bizarre sexual escapades. Extraordinarily bright, Cheryl had now become the epitome of what Gar wanted all of his women to be.

Smart. Absolutely trustworthy. But, above all—*controllable.* Manipulatable would have been more accurate. In Cheryl's case there was another big plus for Gar. The thirty-two year old raven-haired beauty was very much in love with him.

Minutes later, her phone rang again. This time it was the big guy himself. Calling from London.

"Hey, gorgeous, can you handle a super idea?"

"If that means our spending some time together, you just try me."

"Must be mental telepathy, Cher, cause I really was calling to see if you're free to spend the weekend with me at Lake Como. You've always liked the Villa D'Este."

"Wow! Great sex *and* great scenery—what a quinella! You've got yourself a deal, fella."

Located only thirty miles north of Milan, near the Swiss border, the breathtaking renaissance palace built on the water's edge has long been acclaimed as one of the outstanding resorts of the world.

But Gar had more important fish to fry than spending a perfectly good weekend merely indulging in the many Babylonian-style services the villa offered. Or even engaging Cheryl in some outrageous kinky sex. He could do that anytime. And preferably with a new sex partner. Perhaps some teenager he might first be trying to impress. But none of that for now. He had business to conduct—and business came first. *Always* first.

Gar's weekend invitation to Cheryl was proffered only after he had received an urgent call at his London office. The call had come in on an unlisted number known only to one other person in the world—Wolfgang Amadeus Felsenberg. His Chief of Security.

Not only was that phone line tightly secured, as a further precaution Gar kept the secret phone locked in a drawer in his desk. On the rare times that the number was ever dialed, only a tiny red light flickered near the drawer handle. If Gar was not there, the call remained unanswered.

Felsenberg, a stern, six-foot, no-nonsense man, with an intriguing black patch over his right eye—or where his right eye used to be—was the best of class in his murky kind of business. For many ultra-loyal years, whatever Gar needed Wolf Felsenberg accomplished. Without question or hesitation. For appearance sake, his title was intentionally misleading. "Chief of Security" totally avoided the dark details of his professional specialties.

Espionage. Bribery. Money laundering. Sex pandering. And—when necessary—even murder.

Felsenberg was never in need of many words. No matter how tight the phone security, typically their infrequent calls were brusque. In this case, only a matter of seconds. Straight-out, Felsenberg told Gar, "The Dutch plane is no longer operational."

Without the slightest trace of emotion, Gar replied, "That's too bad."

Both men now shared the same critical information. Oskar Benzinger, Gar's important facilitator in Amsterdam, was dead.

As a facilitator, Benzinger was highly effective. Proving to be extraordinarily adept at procuring military contracts. Lately, and more specifically, fighter aircraft contracts, from the small mostly unarmed NATO countries. Belgium, Holland, Denmark, and Norway.

Oskar's ultimate goal was to push for standardization of all specifications for fighter planes. If accomplished, Gar's General Aircraft Corporation would hopefully win that contract.

Most often, these days, the clandestine meetings between Wolf Felsenberg and his boss, mostly concerned General Aircraft. G.A.C., was the result of an early metal-stamping acquisition, and the restructuring of an unprofitable American airplane manufacturer. Both of which Gar subsequently combined with several discarded subsidiaries of a failed British aircraft company. And under his aggressive leadership, G.A.C. had become a leading international airplane producer and a serious competitor to Boeing, Douglas, and Lockheed.

These three longtime industrial giants all led by strong personalities were now joined by the equally competitive and hardheaded, George Garfield Grey. All four of these companies were embroiled in the do-or-die race for the same fighter plane contract.

Remember, this is post World War II. And from the

beginning of NATO in 1949, the defense capability of their members was at a dangerously low point. Consequently, never before in the relatively short history of aircraft manufacturing had the stakes ever been this high.

It was generally conceded but not too often spoken about, primarily as a matter of national pride, that no matter whose flag would be painted on their tails, one way or another American taxpayers would end up paying for all of these planes.

In point of fact, the entire idea of pushing international sales of arms and warplanes had become the chief financial instrument of U.S. foreign policy—starting in the late 1950s. At that time the Pentagon created a new division called "Military Assistance Planning."

M.A.P. was placed under the leadership of the legendary Henry Kuss, who prided himself on the fact that he was almost solely responsible for selling $2 billion in arms every year. He was convinced this was the right path toward a peaceful world.

The idea of selling American arms picked up even more steam with the election of J.F.K., in late 1961. Carefully taught by his far right-wing father, Joseph P. Kennedy—an outspoken admirer of Adolf Hitler—young Jack Kennedy entered the White House with a great concern over the rising U.S. budget deficit.

His Pentagon, under the tough, business-minded secretary Robert S. McNamara, the former head of the Ford Motor Company, highly endorsed the selling of arms. McNamara thought it far more economically desirable than outright grant aid, which never had to be repaid.

After that terrible November day in 1963 Dallas, Vice-President Lyndon Baines Johnson became President. And any real concern over the budget deficit went the way of the dinosaur. He became a tragic victim of his conflicted Great Society programs and his deservedly hated Vietnam War.

Result: Thirty years of punishing U.S. inflation.

As always, Lake Como was paradise. The Villa D'Este retained all of its magical grandeur.

To suit his own agenda, however, Gar was purposefully acting edgy and short. Thinking in normal human terms, Cheryl thought he was truly upset.

"What is it, my darling? Talk to me. If there is something that you want me to do, just ask. I promise to do anything in the world for you—*anything.*"

"Anything," was the action word Gar was waiting to hear. His *control* word. Instantly turning on his old charm, "Come on, gorgeous, let's get some fresh air out in the gardens." Silently, he scribbled on a night table pad, "It will be safer to talk outside. No bugging." Holding one finger to his lips, he showed the note to Cheryl. She read his words and quickly nodded her assent. Without another word they headed outdoors.

Seated together on a faded-green wrought iron bench in an isolated corner of the magnificent gardens, Gar began to lay the groundwork for Cheryl's latest assignment.

"You and I are about to raise the level of our relationship, Cheryl. From here on we could be compared to a dual trapeze act in a circus—performed without a safety net. Believe me, it will require the most complete trust and confidence that two people can possibly have in each other. Listen carefully, and try to memorize as much as you can. Nothing—absolutely nothing can be committed to writing. Okay?"

"No! Not okay! You're scaring the hell out of me. I really don't know a damn thing yet, but I'm already shaking like crazy—and I can't handle it. And ya know what? I don't want to handle it, either. This just might be the right moment, Gar. So don't say anything for a minute. Let me do the talking now.

You and I have had great fun for a long time, and while I truly love you and appreciate everything you've done for me maybe we should forget our whole scene right here and now. You're taking me in way over my head. And I don't even want to know the rest of your story. How about that for an okay suggestion?"

Naturally, Gar ignored everything Cheryl had said. It simply did not fit into his scheme. There was no way in the world that Gar Grey was not going to vigorously respond to the sudden death of an important cog in his corporate security chain. Especially, a top-rated operative like Oskar Benzinger.

"Steady, honey. Squeeze my hand."

Then, Gar reached for her lowered chin and trembling lip. "Come on, Cheryl, look up at me. If you'll just trust me now, more than you've ever trusted anyone else in your life, you'll do fine. I would never lie to you. You know I've never lied to you. Never."

In an attempt to further mollify her, Gar moved closer—thigh to thigh—putting his arm snugly around her waist. Looking straight into her eyes, he proceeded. "Crucial to the success of many of my businesses, but particularly when it comes to international sales of aircraft, I admit things can get a bit out of hand. Things happen that are extremely vicious and entirely unexpected. It's a rough world out there. And, in that connection, a few days ago I was informed that an important man in my European security division had been found dead—more likely murdered—in Amsterdam. At this point, we have a lot of stories. Lot's of gossip. But, nothing for sure. That's where you come in."

Stunned by what she had just heard, her eyes bigger than saucers, Cheryl stammered, "M-M-Murdered? And you want *me* to get involved in *that*? Jeez, Gar, have you lost your goddam mind?"

With Cheryl protesting all the way, Gar determinedly marched on. "Maybe Felsenberg took Oskar out himself or put out a contract on him. Anything is possible when billions of dollars are involved. I don't know the best route from here, Cheryl, but I absolutely do know that I need you to get close to Wolf. While I have explicitly trusted him for many years, this time he knows a lot more than he has told me. Hell, for all I know there may be a cabal out there plotting to ruin me—or worse. And you're the only person I can possibly trust enough for this assignment.

Right here and now, I'm asking you to take a leave of absence from your firm and work full-time for me. We're a hell of a long way from knowing what really happened to Oskar. And I'll make it extremely worth your while."

FORTY-FIVE

To Gar's Chief of Security, Wolfgang Amadeus Felsenberg, day or night made no difference. They merely represented hours. Totally committed to his dangerous work, sleep was only a bothersome interruption. And most nights a non-event.

"I can sleep all I want—when I'm dead," was a favorite expression.

From their beginning nearly twenty years ago, and about the same age as Gar, "Wolf", as most referred to him, spent about eighteen hours everyday on the outer edge of reality. Courageously, sometimes even heroically, defending the diversified worldwide interests of his employer and friend. Which certainly qualified him for a high place on the endangered species list.

In Gar's best interests, Wolf's undercover activities left him far removed and unconnected from the sensational headlines he often had a major role in creating. Such as the explosive Lockheed Aircraft bribery scandal of the popular Dutch royal consort, Prince Bernhard.

While Felsenberg led the kind of action-packed life most men can only dream about, his principal qualifications for his job were perpetual anger and complete distrust. Derived not from any dream, but rather from a nightmare.

Understandably, in his unusual line of work Wolf could not afford the luxury of any distractions—certainly not from his personal life. Tragically, he did not have any such distractions, because he did not have a personal life.

For the Jewish native of Stuttgart, such normality came to a ghastly end in 1942, at the Nazi death camp at Buchenwald. There, every known member of his family perished in the gas chambers. Felsenberg was left without a blood relative in the world. It was a subject never to be brought up in his presence. *Never!*

Oskar Benzinger had the perfect background to be an international diplomat.

Born in Main Line Philadelphia to an aristocratic and wealthy American family of German descent, his maternal great-grandmother believed she was a Prussian noblewoman related to Kaiser Wilhelm. His Father was a prominent and politically well-connected lawyer.

After Princeton, Oskar studied at Georgetown University's prominent School of Foreign Service. Excellent grades and the best family connections landed him at the State Department. He remained there for more than ten years. Later, Oskar was posted to embassies in Western Europe. Finally, to NATO headquarters in Brussels, where his impeccable manners and custom-tailored appearance easily propelled him to the top of that most glittering of all diplomatic worlds.

A charming bachelor in his mid-forties, Oskar met and became friends with some of the most important personalities in post-war Europe. Greedy men and their extraordinarily ambitious women. The former included Gar Grey.

Among these many highly-placed celebrity friends, Oskar was pleased to count the manipulative, Pamela Churchill. The divorced daughter-in-law of Sir Winston—and perhaps the greatest courtesan of this century—who was now living and loving in Paris. Pam Churchill was now casually sharing herself among several of Oskar's close and powerful friends. She loved her new Parisian life—and all the goodies that were her bountiful rewards.

It was as a friend of Gar's that Oskar was offered the opportunity of a lifetime in Wolf's Security Division. In a later time frame, journalists would not have been kind in describing Oskar's new vocation. It was referred to as "International Relations."

Well suited for his new job, in quick time, Oskar became Felsenberg's chief facilitator. And in a position to cash-in on his VIP contacts, which he proceeded to do without hesitation. The big players were his best friends. And he knew all their favorite personal games.

Oskar's mysterious death now left a gaping hole in Wolf's organization. At the top of the ladder, even Gar seemed to be genuinely upset. But who knew anything for sure about Gar Grey?

Despite the fact that Mother and Daughter could be eager competitors for the same lovers, Willi and Ursula Von Ribbentrop maintained a strangely warm relationship. On rare occasions they even permitted a fleeting allusion to their private lives.

For lunch one London day, Willi invited an old English friend to meet her famous daughter. Willi introduced her with the far-fetched name of Blissful Knight, which she quickly pointed out to Ursula was only her professional name. An ordinary name like Bridgett appeared on her Liverpool birth certificate. But it would never do when she ran away to London at sixteen—looking for excitement.

For a number of years now, and confirming the obvious, countless men of all age groups, many of them in high official positions on both sides of the English Channel, contentedly referred to her as, "Pure Bliss". Mmmmm.

One especially contented fellow even went so far as to have had an 18-karat gold bracelet made for her, engraved with her famous nickname. Bliss wore it as a badge of honor. Repeatedly, she referred to it as, "My Purple Heart."

To a fly on the restaurant wall, these three stunning extroverts all talking at once, stepping all over each others lines, was a show by itself. But the conversation soon took a far more interesting turn.

Bliss confidentially revealed that only a few days ago, "I was asked to put together a special kind of show." Quickly assuring the two Von Ribbentrops that, "It's going to be a really high-class show at a private club in Amsterdam. I suppose it'll last until dawn and no doubt we'll be exhausted from all the activity. But, what the hell, it's just a one night gig. We'll handle it."

The auburn-haired Bliss, a long-legged former cabaret dancer, had known the hungry Willi since her early chorus-line days at the Moulin Rouge in Paris. Before Gerhard and his fortune accidentally burst upon her life.

"By the way Willi, even though it isn't important to you anymore, money is no object here. These guys only want the best of show."

Bliss went on to tell them that her contact was a high government public relations official—no country identified—whose reputation was beyond reproach. A person for whom she had previously fulfilled many special engagements. Both public and private.

"I need at least six girls, maybe even eight, for my part of the entertainment. Would you two be interested in participating?" Laughingly, "And I mean *participating*."

Ursula's fast response was, "I've got to get going on some serious shopping. I'm sure we'll see each other again, Bliss." Kissing Willi on both cheeks, "Bye Mother."

Knowing that Amsterdam was one of the most explicitly open cities in the world, and that Bliss had no inhibitions, Willi was seriously interested.

"You're talking about putting on a sex show. Right? A really kinky orgy. Am I right, Bliss?"

"I guess you might call it that. I'm not stupid enough

to invite the wealthy Willi Von Ribbentrop to anything less than the most lavish of international parties. A party where you will be able to do anything you want. In fact, it will be expected of you."

Willi leaned forward in her chair. Bliss had 100% of her attention. "In fact, Willi, this show can be a new coming-out party for you. Put you back in circulation with some very important people. The kind you like. The big money guys who know how to show a girl their full appreciation."

"So when does this thing take place, Bliss?"

Oskar Benzinger's current assignment, which also proved to be his last, was absolutely critical for Gar's General Aviation Corporation. The same was to be said of NATO itself. The Atlantic alliance was constantly being defined and re-defined. This time the focus was on the urgent financial need for common European military aircraft technology. The buzzword for standardization had become *commonology*.

In 1961, for example, within the countries of NATO, no less than *fourteen* different types of small arms ammunition were being used. The Soviet Union used only one. Secretary of Defense McNamara insisted on unification across all weapons procurement programs—most importantly on aircraft. By far the most expensive item of weaponry.

By now the competition for NATO fighter plane contracts between all of the American manufacturers had heated up to a fever pitch. So much so, that French-speaking Belgians had taken to calling the ultimate reward, *"Le marchè du siècle."* The deal of the century.

In addition to each other, there was another strong competitor. The Americans had to contend with the extremely talented French aircraft firm founded by the concentration camp survivor, Marcel Dassault—who ultimately produced the hugely successful Mirage fighter plane.

For France, gaining the coveted fighter plane contract

was not only economically critical, but also had become a focal point of French national pride. Therefore, Dassault was heavily subsidized by his government. With that kind of money available, the Americans were convinced that the Frenchman was handsomely bribing the NATO procurement officers. Possibly true.

In consequence to the broad picture, Wolf's conversation with Oskar was especially blunt. "Gar emphatically told me to tell you, Oskar, 'No matter what the hell they want—*just give it to them!'* On this point, he shouted loud enough to break my eardrum. So, spread the green stuff around. Make these procurement guys happy. If you don't get the goddam contract, we'll both be in deep shit."

Despite Gar's demanding ways, Oskar Benzinger had never been happier, particularly when he was planning parties. The bigger, the better.

His secretary, Sydney Jerome, inquired, "How large a group do you intend to invite to this dinner party? Is it going to be stag only?"

"You know what's at stake here. Of course, it'll be stag. And only for our "Double A" List."

Sydney pondered, "Well, as we know from previous experience, we should plan to start the evening with approximately three guests for each of the available entertainers. As the evening progresses we know that some of the guests do get bolder. But that's mostly offset by the fact that some of the older gentlemen are easily satisfied. Some even fall asleep.

Of course, towards morning most of the entertainers begin to get tired too—and sore. I can personally attest to that. Not that I would ever complain about too much of such a good thing. In that connection, Oskar, am I also going to be needed at this party?

I do hope you'll want me there—if only for your own personal pleasure."

FORTY-SIX

Boeing, Douglas, or Lockheed. Even a Gulfstream Executive. The make and model of the aircraft didn't matter.

Air Controllers all over the world were familiar with the various planes in General Industrial Corporation's large fleet of gleaming white aircraft with their distinctive red, silver, and blue ornamentation. And they immediately recognized the stylish *GIC* tail logo at their furthest point of direct tower vision. But none of that was for today.

To attract the least amount of attention to this highly unusual flight, all corporate markings had been painted out. The resulting naked white aircraft, now identified only by its navy blue international registration number, was cleared for landing at Amsterdam's small Airport Schiphol—years later to become the world's largest single-building airport. With provisions for last minute weather changes, the chief airport administrator had already given the Control Tower all necessary instructions. Naturally, Oskar Benzinger knew how to get to that bureaucrat. After all, Oscar knew *everybody.*

After touchdown on a seldom-used runway, the plane slowly rolled to a stop inside a cavernous old maintenance building—abandoned since the war. Ten trusted laborers quickly managed to bring down the huge overhead rusted door. At once, the plane as well as the waiting black limousines and chartered buses, all disappeared from any public view. So far, everything was on schedule and according to plan.

The small group of privileged men soon to be wined, dined, and lavishly entertained, would have been thrilled at their first sight of the plane's precious cargo. Led by the vivacious duo of Bliss and Willi, both dressed to the nines, the pair instinctively stopped at the top of the movable stairs to provocatively pose for the non-existent photographers. Old habits die hard.

These two were followed by assorted entertainers of all sizes and races, numerous musicians, and whatever else was considered crucial to a very special dinner party floor show. Seeking a potential aircraft contract running to the hundreds of millions for Gar's General Aircraft Corporation, the dollar cost of this soon-to-be-held dinner party was inconsequential.

Unseen, the limousines and buses left the building via a quiet back driveway with everyone transported to the Amstel Hotel—the best Amsterdam had to offer. Even so, Oskar's office continued to be a beehive of heightened activity.

Despite his extensive friendships and huge popularity as a host, everyone knew Oskar was acting on Gar's behalf. Gar Grey was the de facto host of the dinner. Which meant absolute perfection—beginning with the guest list. Gar wanted to invite every person who could somehow bring influence to bear on the granting of fighter plane contracts.

That would include Their Royal Saudi Arabian Highnesses, the Princes Barkah and Muktar ibn Abdul Aziz, as well as Senator Warren Baxter Bascombe 3rd, Chairman of the powerful Senate Foreign Relations Sub-Committee on Resources and Minerals. The dinner list finally ended with Sheik Omar Arif Akram, whose escalating arms sales commissions were fast becoming a favorite conversation piece of many Western businessmen—to say nothing of the Pentagon.

As an agent, the darkly attractive Akram was now representing several very important American arms manufacturers as well as prominent British and Belgian firms in Saudi Arabia and elsewhere. The international gossip was that he had already earned sums ranging into the hundreds of millions of dollars. Perhaps, not yet in the class of the ultra-phenomenal Adnan Khashoggi, or the merely spectacular Garth Pharaon. But already filthy rich.

That still left unanswered the question of Prince Bernhard, a serious conflict of interest issue for Gar. Wolf had informed him that Bernhard was also an undercover agent for the Lockheed Aircraft Corporation, Gar's major rival for the fighter plane contract.

With this exceptional dinner to be held in his home city of Amsterdam, there had been much conversation between Gar, Wolf, and Oskar about what to do with the popular prince. Surprisingly, the dashing German-born consort to Queen Juliana of the Netherlands carried some heavy baggage. He had been:

—a former probationary member of the German SS before the war.

—an employee of the infamous I.G. Farben Chemical Company.

—a questionable Inspector General of the Dutch armed forces.

Not a squeaky-clean resume for a "royal."

From any point of view, Prince Bernhard was a tight invitational squeeze for his good friend Oskar. And the Prince knew it. In order to avoid awkward embarrassment to any of the parties involved, the Prince wisely suggested that he accept an invitation only to cocktails and dinner. The proposal was quickly relayed from Oskar, to Wolf, to Gar. All agreed.

The crucial evening finally arrived.

The food. Prepared only by the finest chefs imported from all over the world.

The service. Under the discipline of the foremost royal dining hall steward in all of Europe.

The five-hour banquet of endless courses paired great skills with prodigious culinary imagination—served in near sensual slowness, so as to allow the exquisite offerings to touch the senses as well as the stomach. The few guests that survive to this day are still unable to fully describe the splendor—the lavishness—the complete magnificence—of that evening.

After the burning Turkish coffee, aged French brandy, and fragrant Cuban cigars—after extending his ceremonial greetings the smiling Prince Bernhard, with the ever-present white carnation in his lapel, promptly excused himself. With the hour already past midnight, the prince consort was politely trailed by a handful of mostly elderly Dutch guests.

More than an hour later, after time to stretch their legs and freshen up, the guests had reassembled in an entirely different setting. They were now seated in a circular shaped cabaret room elegantly decorated in burgundy, gold, and ivory—with terraced sides that stepped down to what was normally a large dance floor. As a stag affair tonight, the space would be used as a stage in-the-round.

In this configuration each guest was appropriately set apart from each other. Seated throne-like, upon oversized burgundy-colored upholstered armchairs with ornately carved gold and ivory gilded frames.

Confident that Gar had arranged this lavish style of seating especially in their honor, the smiling Saudi Arabian princes looked very much at home.

Throughout the evening, the other guests dutifully came to pay their respects. Not only shaking the princely hands, but also bowing their heads—each according to their individual national traditions.

In point of fact, this homage was being paid to their Father, King Ibn Saud. Not only as a sovereign king and fierce founder of his nation, but to the most powerful oil man in the world. As a consequence of the greatest geographical accident in all of creation, the Saudi king was sitting on the largest untapped oil reserve on the planet—in partnership with George Garfield Grey.

Denominated in American dollars, much of the vast new Arabian national fortune was being directed to the start-up of the Saudi national defense. And in this Amsterdam cabaret tonight, that meant only one thing. Planes—Fighter planes—and more fighter planes. Could there possibly be another game in town?

Over hidden speakers, a voice loudly proclaimed, "Let the entertainment begin!"

On that cue, sensual middle-eastern harem music engulfed the room—setting a tempo of fleshly pleasures. Simultaneously, the huge crystal chandelier, which hung from the top of the gold-domed Florentine ceiling, began to dim. Slowly, the room dissolved into total darkness.

As an experienced showman, the director cleverly used the darkness as an emotional stimulant. For effect, he held the room dark seconds longer than was necessary to intensify every neurosensory cell in the audience.

A wave of palpable expectation engulfed the room.

No one seemed to be breathing.

On stage a soft rose-colored hue barely broke the darkness. Out of the shadows of swirling stage smoke, two naked women appeared. Tonsured and totally shaved of all bodily hair, the two had been sensually gilded in gold leaf paint from head-to-toe. Facing each other about six feet apart, they stood as motionless as statues.

Almost immediately, attention was shifted to a large cage slowly descending from the ceiling. As it came to rest upon the stage, out stepped a tall, large-breasted blonde Venus sheathed in a dominatrix outfit of steel-studded black leather. Typically, a garment worn by the dominating partner in a sadomasochistic relationship. She was standing between the two gilded women. A few in the audience recognized Willi Von Ribbentrop—and were startled.

To invite the most stimulating male response, Willi's outfit had three large circular cutouts. Two cutouts allowed her ample breasts with their tantalizing puffy pink nipples to be completely exposed. The third ample cutout was carved around her genitals—inviting an unobstructed view. And to assure an unforgettable experience, Willi carried an ominously menacing whip!

Without missing a musical beat, Willi drew the dangerous whip high over her head and struck the stage a mighty blow. A loud and clear cue to the two gilded slaves—who immediately moved to comply.

Willi aggressively thrust her exposed breasts toward the slaves who bent to kiss and suck. Instinctively, Willi wanted to feel those slave tongues shoved up to the hilt of her lowest cutout, which by now fully exposed her engorged pudendum.

To achieve that end, she vigorously started to rock her pelvis. Grinding. Undulating. Pushing her horny bottom at the gilded slave girls.

Willi was fire-hot and didn't care who knew it.

Since this did not happen during their rehearsals, the gilded slaves did not know which way to proceed. Neither did the frenzied audience, who certainly had no rehearsals.

Easily able to hear Willi's frantic imploring, her lewd screaming street-talk, the thrill-seeking spectators were vicariously participating. Urging the slaves on. Wanting nothing more than to see them spread Willi wide-open and take turns eating her on stage. Willi could not have agreed more. At that moment she was the embodiment of sheer carnal desire.

Propelled to the critical edge of their thrones, some in the audience were actually experiencing real orgasms. For others, it was surely the closest many of them had come to the real thing in years.

But wait!

Incredibly, there was still more.

Sharp fanfares blasted forth from six glistening trumpets. As they crescendoed, the room seemed to rip apart. Strong staccato drum rolls quickly took up where the trumpets ended—and they kept on and on.

Suddenly, on each terrace level, dozens of seemingly cloned showgirls, dressed identically as Willi, poured forth into the audience. As the deafening drumbeat gained both tempo and intensity, these lovely models leaned their naked breasts into the hungry waiting mouths on each throne. Without a doubt, this was nipple sucking at its outrageous best. One could easily imagine hearing every cock in the room snap to attention.

At least every cock that still could.

For an opening act, Willi accomplished all that was expected of her. But her lingering excitement, coupled with the continuing stimulation generated by her form-fitting leather outfit—which she purposely wore over nothing but her creamy bare skin—left her in great need of some good stiff sex—with whomever. And she fully intended to get it before this night was through.

Accompanied by thunderous applause, at the conclusion of her performance, Willi came off the stage and took a prominent seat at Oskar's front table. The applause continued unabated. Willi took three more bows.

No matter how arousing was the act they had just witnessed, the elite audience could not possibly have been prepared for what came next.

Listen, closely. You can almost hear the sensuous flute notes soaring across the room.

And look.

The background of soft lavender light was slowly revealing the beautiful Blissful Knight, reclining mid-stage on a sumptuous chaise lounge.

The breathtaking Bliss was wearing a multi-colored sheer silk costume consisting of a mini-bra top and a long skirt slit in the rear to her shapely buttocks. Added were the showy black satin opera gloves, whose splendid over-the-elbow length was theatrically effective. And excitingly reminiscent of the legendary Rita Hayworth as she starred in the movie *Gilda*.

Next, a pair of nearly seven-foot, jet-black African men, wearing only white loincloths, carefully walked onto the stage. These were handsome men with washboard hard bodies, gracefully moving on powerful legs and thighs rippling with sexually arousing muscles. Most likely, developed by the daily running from village to village. At least twenty-five or thirty miles apart.

Between them, these giants carried a large covered wicker basket suspended from poles carried over their shoulders. Having carefully set the basket down on the stage, they sat down on the floor with their long legs crossed and their arms resting across their broad chests. Both men had amazingly well-developed mammary glands with extraordinarily long nipples. Illusory or real, their nipples seemed to be lactating.

At once, the music changed beat. The pounding hand drums took a strong lead—and repeated the rhythm over and over. Bliss sensually rose to begin her specialty—a lascivious strip tease.

The satin opera gloves were first to come off.

As Bliss sashayed to the rising tempo, she suggestively rolled them down to her wrists. From where she casually flipped them into the air. When she dropped her bra, wild applause flooded the room. When she vigorously shook her delicious size 38 D's, the room simply erupted.

Removing her skirt was a cat-on-a-hot-tin-roof tease. A marvelous, outrageous obscenity. With hands defiantly on her hips, Bliss stopped, stared, and dared these men not to go crazy. She won. Pandemonium reigned.

Finally, she paraded back and forth in nothing more than a nude-colored G-string. Quickly improvising, she pulled off the damp G-string and flung it into the air.

Oskar ducked just in time. The flying G-string landed on the next head. Unfortunately, that was Sydney Jerome,

Oskar's long-devoted secretary, who wasn't sure what to do with it. Even worse, Sydney had some difficulty getting it untangled from his wavy dark hair. Assuming this was part of the act, the audience roared at Sydney's comedic discomfort. Reassuringly, under cover of the table, Oskar patted Sydney's soft thigh.

Meanwhile, the now totally naked Bliss luxuriated in the bright spotlight that followed her back and forth across the stage. Ending amid enthusiastic applause, she gloriously spread out on the chaise. On that cue, the suggestive music abruptly stopped.

In dead silence, the two black giants carefully removed the cover from the wicker basket. Not one person in the cabaret that night would ever forget the next moment.

Watch, carefully.

From the open basket a dangerous-looking swaying head popped into view. It was not only a live snake—it was a six-foot boa constrictor!

Contrary to popular thought, boas, like pythons and anacondas, are nonvenomous. Nevertheless, they remain terribly lethal killers who strike with lightning speed. By coiling their bodies around and squeezing their prey, boas easily crush out life. Their victims quickly die of asphyxiation.

Nonvenomous aside, this boa's long forked tongue flicking in and out was scary as hell. Many of the onlookers instinctively pushed back on their thrones—putting as much distance as possible between the boa and themselves.

Not that anyone was in any immediate danger.

To cover any emergency, Wolf, seated at Oskar's front table, was never unarmed. His powerful revolver was snugly fitted into his shoulder holster and hung just below his left armpit.

His tuxedo jacket, as all of his clothes, was custom-tailored to comfortably accommodate the side arm. And the same went for a smaller caliber back-up piece neatly attached to his right leg under his formal trousers.

While Gar or Wolf would never have allowed even the possibility of danger to creep into the cabaret, Oskar might have thought an unguarded boa could be a splendidly kinky idea. Oskar did have his bizarre moments.

Despite all of the excitement, the two giant blacks remained unaffected. And with good reason. They were, in fact, the snake's confident handlers. And had been from the moment the reptile was born on a snake farm in their primitive African village. These unruffled men now moved to the sides of the basket.

While snakes do not see or hear in any normal human way, they become agitated and extremely volatile when perceiving a foreign presence in their immediate surroundings. At this moment, the boa remained calm.

The handlers now began to loosen their loincloths. As they dropped to the floor, gleaming nakedness revealed two gargantuan cocks. Easily, each was twelve inches of rare sexual weaponry. Reacting to the new scent, the boa's tongue quickly flicked at each man's huge erection.

Sensing the new electricity, the boa reared five feet—straight up. Perhaps imitating the ultimate erection. Now, free of any restraint, both black cocks were vigorously rising—wondrously or ominously—depending upon your preference. Either way, hungry for human touch. More than willing to satisfy, Bliss urgently grabbed for both cocks. "They're both mine!"

As the houselights dimmed, she quickly stuffed the first jumbo into her trembling mouth.

Not to be left out, the lusting Willi suddenly made a mad dash back to the stage.

FORTY-SEVEN

It was five in the morning, when Oscar and Sydney emerged together from the cabaret. For several hours however, the distinguished guests continued to vanish in the company of gorgeous showgirls of all races, colors, and sexual preferences. In many cases, they left with more than one girl for each guest. But they were not the only ones treated to a night in the flesh.

With so much at stake, the instinctive control compulsion that dominated Gar Grey would certainly dictate his positioning himself somewhere nearby. Certainly, never too far from the important action.

As the steamy big bash was going on, Gar hosted an intimate midnight supper aboard his awesome white yacht, Emperor II. Quietly anchored in the far-reaches of Amsterdam harbor.

Early in the morning, he announced, "All of you are welcome to sleep on board. After all, we are old friends here." In fact, he had invited a few old friends he had not seen for some time. Like the libidinous Rio Roundtree—only by gender disqualified from the cabaret party. Generously, Gar also remembered to include his old college sweetheart, Nancy Lee Hendrix, and her gay lover, Ian Hawkins.

A totally free spirit, Hawkins personalized the idea of drag. He was dressed identically to Nancy Lee—including cosmetics. Strangely, the sexy former southern belle seemed happy.

And how could such an evening possibly be complete without the infamous Alayne Benning-George? She with the nipples that still seemed ready to burst through her blouse. Still as luscious as when they first grabbed Gar's attention at Washington National Airport.

So far this evening, Rio and Ally were the two brightest ideas aboard ship.

Meanwhile, in unusually calm waters, the Emperor II's speedy tender was running fast and furiously from ship to shore and back again. A full load arrived on the first two trips.

By himself, Wolf Felsenberg was next. He whispered something to Gar as he boarded. Then, Sheik Omar Arif Akram and the two Arabian Princes. Much later, all lovey dovey, Oskar and Sydney.

Standing at the top of the ship's stairs, directly above the place where his guests debarked the tender, Gar welcomed his new guests aboard—and introduced them.

"Meet an old and dear friend, Leonard Bernstein. He's the guy who wrote that fabulous music for *West Side Story*." Jokingly adding, "When he has nothing else to do he also conducts the New York Philharmonic."

Having been escorted to the Emperor II's opulent salon, Gar encouraged his guests. "Say hello to each other. Get comfortable. Have a drink or whatever else you want. And there's a breakfast buffet for those who are ready for that."

Drinking and mingling started at once.

As he so often did over the years, Bernstein had been guest conducting in Vienna. And he was still in the Austrian capitol when he called Gar to request a meeting regarding the financing of a new Broadway show being dreamed up by Bernstein and the brilliant choreographer, Jerome Robbins. Along with Stephen Sondheim and

Arthur Laurents, they were the same foursome responsible for *West Side Story*.

After listening to the always-convincing Bernstein outline his story and music, Gar thought it was an idea worth serious consideration. "It's good, Lenny. Real good. I think we should get together with Jerry and the guys when we all get back to New York." Bernstein gave Gar a big hug.

Gar's mind was racing. He knew that his current companion, the model Ursula Von Ribbentrop, would do anything for an important role in a Broadway show.

To himself, Gar thought, "Dangling a Broadway role would be an irresistible carrot. She can't sing a note, but, if I back his show, Lenny will do whatever I ask. Money talks in his key."

Tactfully not mentioned was the well-known fact, that while married and the father of three children, Lenny was a life-long homosexual and indefatigable party guy. His very presence sent a strong signal that by no means was this party over. Ian seconded that idea.

After Oskar and Sydney arrived, the tender returned with only a single female aboard. At last, we revisit the breathtaking Ursula Von Ribbentrop.

While her mother, Willi, and Willi's friend Bliss, were the toasts of the show, they were purposely not invited to this post party event. Although mothers and daughters are highly prized partners for ménage à trois gambols, no worry tonight that this mother and daughter would end up in the same stateroom bed. Other nights might be a different story.

In a mini-short black silk cocktail dress, Ursula was particularly radiant. Even before the introductions, everyone knew who she was. Unquestionably, the international blonde model was the most recognized woman in the world. With such a trophy at his side, Gar never looked happier or more relaxed.

Across the salon, with the evil eye of an experienced seducer, Sheik Ari took one look at Rio and Ally and wickedly smiled to himself. "Gar certainly hasn't lost his touch or his taste for women. These two are prime. Maybe, even together. Could be worth a try."

And while Gar had been an eager participant in many three-way romps, he planned this night of pleasure to be different. And the later couplings certainly were that.

After assuring Ursula he would not be gone long, Gar excused himself and took Oskar into his palatial office for an update on the crucial dinner party on shore.

Oskar was upbeat. "The party was a big success, Gar. We knocked 'em dead. Socko! Most of those fellows won't even begin to think about going home until noon—if they can still walk by then. And based on the remarks made to me during dinner, I think we are in great shape for the final vote on the fighter plane contract."

That was old news to Gar. Wolf had already whispered it in his ear as he boarded. While Wolf had never failed him, nor did any of his world wide staff, Gar was never one to completely trust anyone. He had never forgotten what his old partner, Meyer Lansky, had drummed into his head, over and over.

Having exhibited superior wisdom and calm judgment for decades, proven by the obvious fact that the mob's elder statesman was still alive, was direct testimony to his sage advice. There were at least two versions of his philosophy on survival.

Lansky would tell Gar things like—

"Anybody will try ta fuck ya. So fuck 'em first."

Or, "In dis world, only a real schmuck would ever trust a cunt." And, for sure, Gar Grey was no schmuck.

With an unparalleled musical reputation in whatever setting he found himself, the great Bernstein always had requests to play the piano—especially the sensational music he composed for *West Side Story*.

This group was no different.

And being the quintessential ham that he was, it didn't take much pleading for the maestro to sit down at the grand piano. As the familiar melodies of *Maria, Tonight,* and the other hit songs flowed from his fingers, it was hard to tell who was having the greater moment—Lenny or his listeners.

Ari took the musical interlude as the opportunity to put himself between Rio and Ally. As the three of them sunk deliciously deep into a down-filled sofa, Ari sent his hands out on a search and find mission—both left and right. It didn't matter to him whether the response was the consequence of booze or desire. So long as it was positive.

Ari both searched and found. Neither hand was rejected. To the contrary, both women adjusted their positions to hold on to his roving hand, which had found their Promised Land. Among the three of them, Ari thought the possible body combinations were now endless.

Bernstein finished his music with a triumphal crescendo, throwing his hands high in the air above the keyboard. And luxuriated in the enthusiastic response.

Nancy Lee and Ian were the first to dash to his side. Shortly, engaged in animated conversation, those three left the salon together. Not to be seen again until noon.

Relaxed after their weeks of organizational pressure, Oskar and Sydney, holding hands, said their goodnights and headed off to their stateroom.

Lying appealingly naked on the bed, Sydney begged off taking a joint shower. "You go ahead and shower, Oskar, I'll wait for our nightcaps to arrive." That was Oskar's first surprise. Already in the steaming shower, he couldn't possibly have seen the second.

Surreptitiously, Sydney reached under his pillow and withdrew a previously hidden vial of chloral hydrate in alcohol. Quickly, he emptied the pre-measured liquid into Oskar's waiting cocktail. Sydney was giving his boss and lover a Mickey Finn!

Not lethal, but it would render Oskar unconscious. And taking account of the ex-diplomat's body size and age, he would likely remain comatose for three or four hours.

Then, events moved very rapidly.

Oskar came out of the shower wrapping a huge white Turkish towel around his waist. At the arousing sight of Sydney's total nakedness still spread out on the bed as a luscious feast, he let the towel drop to the floor. Sydney rolled over onto his stomach.

Anxiously downing his drink in one swallow, Oskar's lustful mind was already racing on. The anticipation of the familiar thrill blotted out any possibility of another thought. With his pecs and his cock both hard as rocks, Oskar woozily moved toward the bed. Almost there, his face went strangely pale. As he groped for the blanket to steady himself, he fell forward onto the bed.

Unconscious.

Sydney acted swiftly, according to Wolf's detailed instructions. He knocked three times on a side door to the suite. At the ready, in came two highly trusted ship's officers who had previously worked for Wolf as double secret agents.

In less than thirty seconds, they efficiently wrapped the unconscious Oskar in the sheet and blanket from the bed and carried him out the side door and down the dark steps. They laid him down aboard an unmarked speedboat whose motor was softly idling.

Wolf, himself a former secret agent who seemed to know how to do everything, was already waiting behind the wheel.

So far, so good.

However, as Sydney began to make his way to the top of the steps, he heard voices from the adjoining stateroom. Pausing, he was able to identify the Texas twang of Rio Roundtree.

"I've sucked on a lot of big nipples in my time, Ally, but I've never seen any that come close to the humongous size of your pink devils. I might never stop."

"Forget about stopping, Rio, baby. Suck harder. I love every minute of it."

Hearing another door open nearby, a startled Sydney instantly huddled down in the darkness near the rail—and froze in his place. It was Ari Akram on his happy way to join Rio and Ally. Fortunately, with a delicious ménage à trois foremost on his mind, Ari hurriedly walked on.

Moments later, dressed in freshly cleaned, skin-tight faded blue jeans, navy blue turtleneck sweater, and new white sneakers, Sydney came bounding down the steps and hopped onto the speedboat. Not wasting a precious second, Wolf immediately gunned the engine.

Minutes later, as the powerful speedboat neared the Amsterdam shore, Wolf expertly maneuvered toward an isolated pier. Having practiced this run several times before, at the appropriate moment he cut the motor. The boat continued to drift toward its pre-determined pier where three well-muscled sailors, all dressed in solid black, suddenly appeared out of the shadows and quickly secured the boat to its mooring.

At once, two of the same men lifted the unconscious Oskar off the leather seat where he lay on the boat, and carried him into a drab-looking building on the pier.

Once all hands were inside and the heavy metal door was bolted, a shadowy half-light revealed what looked like some kind of large theatrical set. However, when eyes adjusted to the dim light, it clearly was a fine reproduction of a luxurious hotel room. That set had cost someone big bucks.

In matters of personal urgency, when the high and mighty Gar Grey needed something—*anything*—he never allowed money to be an issue.

With the sheet and blanket he had been wrapped in now removed, the defenseless Oskar was placed in the king-size bed in the replicated hotel room. He looked as if he had been peacefully sleeping there for hours.

From an adjoining space, the two boa constrictor handlers came into the room. The same two men carried the same covered wicker basket they had used in the sexy dinner show. This moment of utter reality had become overwhelming. Already shocked and totally traumatized, Sydney quickly became uncontrollably hysterical. Others also became queasy. And wished they were elsewhere.

Wolf did what he had to do.

Without hesitation, he cleared the room.

Acting on prior instructions, the handlers also knew what they had to do. With unruffled composure they cautiously lifted the six-foot boa from the basket and set the reptile into the bed next to the unconscious Oskar.

The conclusion was forgone.

Instinctively sensing a hostile presence, the powerful boa struck.

It coiled around Oscar's body—and constricted!

The unconscious Oskar never felt a thing.

Death by asphyxiation.

But, why?

FORTY-EIGHT

Long before Oskar's murder, there occurred an improbable period of about twelve-hours. In the dead of night, far beyond any safe speed, two cars raced toward each other on the treacherous Moyenne Corniche.

The Moyenne is the middle of the three coastal roads overlooking the elegant French Riviera. In the French language, the word *corniche* means *ledge*. Indeed, the dangerous roads are but narrow and curvy ledges carved into the Alps mountainside.

The open sides of the corniches lying closest to the Mediterranean offer spectacular views of the blue-green water far below. Likewise, it exposes every car and driver to terrifying drops—especially intimidating to the unfamiliar tourist. In spite of that real danger, miscalculating some of the more deadly corniche hairpin turns causes most accidents.

Wolf Felsenberg, in a determined search for his missing facilitator, was furiously heading East on the Moyenne. Unbeknown to Gar's Chief of Security, speeding directly toward him en route West from Monte Carlo, was the facilitator himself. The urbane, ex-NATO diplomat, Oskar Benzinger.

Ever the most reckless of drivers, at this moment Oskar was light years beyond reckless—befuddled by the liquor, hashish and cocaine he had ingested.

Anyone who knew Oskar had long been aware that under any normal circumstance he would engage in most anything—and as a rule he did. Nevertheless, he was just not the sort of fellow to intentionally put himself at a life-threatening risk. Something was out of whack here. Something far more than Oskar's woozy head.

In his haze, he would have been in grave danger at any speed. At his current clip he was a clay pigeon. Then, in a blinding second, the inevitable happened.

Missing a tight turn, his tires screaming, Oskar's violently skidding car smashed into the mountainside. It was 4:25 AM.

Inconceivable, but true, the first person to come upon the accident scene was the man Oskar was desperately trying to reach—a totally shocked Wolf Felsenberg.

Badly injured, but miraculously still alive, Oskar was rushed to the hospital at Nice, where he was immediately placed on the critical list.

It was hour to hour. Then, day to day.

Weeks passed. So did the crisis.

Oskar finally began a painfully slow recovery from his many injuries and broken bones. But it was his post-traumatic amnesia, the result of serious head injuries, that was proving the most difficult for him to overcome. He would later struggle to recall for Wolf what had triggered his mad dash that night from Monte Carlo.

As Wolf leaned forward so as not to miss a word, Oskar told him that earlier that night at the bar in the renowned Hotel de Paris in Monte Carlo, he was properly introduced to the attractive Angelique Cuvier, now thirty-two.

As a rangy seventeen-year old, the former French international tennis champion had won the prestigious women's singles championships at both the French Open in Paris and at famed Wimbledon near London.

The slender blonde had long athletic legs and small hard tits—never fully developed. Contradictorily, these features were combined with enormous upper-body-strength. Somehow, in her mother's womb her genes were more than a little confused. Was she to emerge a boy or a girl?

At the peak of her game, Angie's blazing serves had become so awesome and her baseline strokes so powerful that her sheer strength was often called into question.

Was she taking an illegal drug? Could a *genuine* female hit the ball so hard as to knock the racquet out of her opponent's hand? On the world tennis tour, stories abounded about her sexual orientation. Was she one way or the other—*or both?*

All these years later, it was Angelique who boldly suggested to Oskar that they continue their conversation in her upstairs suite, mentioning nothing about the timely arrival of a very sexy-looking woman about her own age.

After what Oskar thought was an especially long greeting kiss on the lips, rather than a fleeting airbrush on both cheeks, Angelique introduced her waiting friend.

"Oskar, this is Alayne Benning-George, a very close pal of mine. Over the years, we've done all kinds of crazy things together. Had oodles of fun."

In turn, she identified Oskar as doing some special kind of work, as she put it, "For that rich prick, George Garfield Grey."

Ally's strong cocktail loosened her tongue. In short order, she let Oskar know she was on intimate terms with his famous boss. And that she was also tight with Gar's good friend, Sheik Omar Arif Akram.

Even more surprising, Ally proceeded to wag about important international oil matters, including what he felt sure was classified information regarding Ambassador Harriman's London and Teheran oil conferences.

Since none of that oil talk was of any interest to her, a bored Angelique's eyes became totally fixed on something much more familiar. Ally's famous tits and nipples, riper than ever before, were screaming to be instantly eaten. Fully aroused, the long-legged tennis champ ceased listening and let her imagination take over.

As Angie's breathing grew heavier, highly exciting images were pushing at her. After tennis, threesomes had become her favorite participating sport. Almost imperceptibly, she was also moving her pelvis. Ally was immediately aware. She knew the champ's drive both on and off the court.

"Hey, Angie, where are you?"

Somewhat startled, "I...I'm right here, Ally. Right here with both of you." Ally knew better. Turning to Oskar, "Would you mind if I moved over to sit next to Angie?

"Why would I possibly mind?"

"Cause some people have all kinds of stupid hangups—that's why."

As Ally snuggled in next to Angie, she murmured,

"What you need is some of your big momma."

And to Oskar's utter surprise, Ally quickly freed one of her humongous breasts, and offered it up to Angie's waiting mouth. "Here, baby, come suck on momma's nipple." In mere moments, moaning low, her hips arched high off the sofa, Angie shuddered to a full-blown climax. Ally tenderly kissed her mouth.

Oskar was sure this was not opening night for this highly charged scene. Watching intently, as both his excitement and his giant cock rose to oversized proportions, he proceeded to masturbate himself to orgasm.

Looking up, Ally inquired, "Can either one of us—or both of us—help you out, Oskar? You know we would do *anything* for a friend."

Before Oskar could answer, a tall, handsome, and well-built young man about twenty years old, probably of African extraction, entered through the curtains of an adjacent room. Apparently a love slave, he was wearing scarlet-colored lipstick that matched his robe. Abruptly, he stopped and looked directly at Angelique—obviously seeking her approval. Angie nodded.

Without a word yet spoken the young man casually dropped his bright scarlet silk robe to the floor. Naked, he revealed himself to be a gleaming shemale. Possessing that rare combination of a smooth, hairless body, no facial hair, and fully developed female breasts. Despite these female features, he also had a natural penis, equal to the overly endowed Oskar.

Etienne had a complex background. For badly needed money, his uneducated parents had consented to the questionable experiments of a devious local doctor. The experiments included continuous injections of the female hormone estrogen, responsible for promoting estrus and the development and maintenance of female secondary sex characteristics. The injections, started when Etienne was a prepubescent eleven, continued for five years. Ultimately, the injections also produced his female breasts with large protruding nipples—and a high-pitched voice.

This rare physical contradiction created a serious identity crises for the confused teenager. Desperately looking for solace, nearly four years ago, he had hidden in a tennis club locker room. It was from there that he was rescued and taken home by a deeply touched Angelique. Since then the strange duo were almost never apart.

After emotionally healing, he happily complied with her every wish. She became his dominating influence—and his dominatrix.

Angelique particularly enjoyed cross-dressing Etienne. His good legs in high heels, curvaceous body outlined in a tight blouse and short skirt—all enhanced by perfect cosmetics, made a very attractive female. On the other hand, Angie seemed to be most content when she handsomely dressed as a man.

A perfect night on the town for this flamboyant couple was cruising the sleaze joints of Paris, where Angie took on the additional role of pimp for Etienne. She was very aware of his prized sexual value among certain potential customers. He made such a convincing female that men naturally tried to hit upon him. Angelique urged them on by exposing his deep cleavage and letting them feel his huge erection. Then, it was simply a case of negotiating the price.

The totally naked shemale now turned and headed straight for Angie. In front of her, he knelt down on one knee and bowed his head in submission. In this position his long dark cock dragged wetness across the floor. To fully acknowledge her domination, Etienne kissed her bare feet and lovingly sucked her toes—one by one. Then, he sat with crossed legs as she pushed weighted wire rings through his pierced nipples. In some pain, but not moving a muscle, he awaited her next command. Without hesitation, in her native French, she commanded, "Etienne, sucez son coq! Etienne, suck his cock."

This was more than Oskar could have hoped for. Etienne proved to be superbly talented. Oskar had always considered Sydney exceptional, but Etienne was far and away the best fellator Oskar had ever known. He had been drained dry.

Although this was his favorite way to spend an evening, Oskar had no intention of divulging this part of his Monte Carlo adventure to anyone—including Wolf.

To keep the party going, Angie had Etienne bring in a bag of freshly processed hashish she had obtained in Morocco, where it is commonly smoked or chewed as a narcotic or an intoxicant. Etienne expertly filled three small smoking pipes.

After a few deep inhalations Oskar began to feel giddy. Not knowing that Etienne had added an additional substance—but only to *his* pipe. On orders from Angie, already in league with Ally, Etienne had added crack to Oskar's pipe. It was the best. He had never felt better or higher. His dry mouth was quickly alleviated with freezing-cold, 100% uncut Russian vodka. Later he also snorted a few lines of cocaine.

Now reduced to a contented voyeur, Oskar watched Etienne perform a slightly different encore. This time Angie's ménage à trois came true. Etienne, Angie, and Ally, used each other in every possible way.

Dreamily, Oskar re-entered his own idea of heaven.

Continuing their hospital conversation, Oskar remembered to tell Wolf how he had wondered why Ally had revealed so much private information.

"What was her point, Wolf?" Adding, "Did she have a hidden agenda? Perhaps, there was some kind of a coded message buried in there for me. If so, I totally failed to recognize it."

At some point, he told Wolf,

"Despite my condition, I heard Ally tell Angie that some of her friends were going to teach that arrogant rich bastard, Gar Grey, a lesson he would never forget."

Ally speculated, "I don't know exactly what they meant, but they said Gar could lose something valuable—very valuable. And, Angie, *he may lose it tonight!"*

"When I heard that," Oskar told Wolf, "I knew I had to get to you as fast as I could."

FORTY-NINE

In critical condition in the hospital, Oskar would have had no way of knowing that during the very hours he was being sexually entertained in Monte Carlo—in Vaduz, Liechtenstein a serious forced entry had been made. One or more persons had broken into the basement vault below the office of Gar's lawyer, Dr. Franz Josef Ritter.

Quite obviously, the break-in was what Ally had been referring to when she said that Gar could lose something very valuable. But what was in Ritter's vault that was so very valuable, particularly to Gar?

The original copy of the option that granted the fabulous Saudi oil deal to the Atlantic Overseas Bank was not there. It was nearly four thousand miles away in the secret safe of Sal Bellini in New York. However, except for Gar and Sal, there was not another person who knew the whereabouts of that critical document. Gar did not even trust that secret to Ritter.

Ritter's vault did contain many originals and copies of legal papers that Ritter had worked on for Gar. But those files were minuscule compared to the mountains of paper Ritter had generated over his years in legal practice. For other of his famous clients, those files contained some very juicy secrets—both corporate and personal. Were those files the target of the break-in?

Aside from Ritter himself, only one of his several assistants, the trusted Gretchen, an elderly German lady who had been his first secretary, knew what was in his special vault. Who even cared?

Yet, Ally had to have had inside information from some source to be able to say what Oskar had heard. A source who very much cared.

Within hours of hearing news of the break-in by telephone from Ritter, who suggested they come to Vaduz, mainly for their peace of mind, both Gar, from London in his private plane, and Wolf, from Nice, arrived at Zurich airport within minutes of each other and made the short drive over to Vaduz together.

Looking out the window in the car Gar said, "My gut tells me there's a hell of a lot more to this break-in than meets the eye. Even the possibility that we'll never really know, for sure."

"You're probably right," Wolf responded, without taking his eyes off the road. "I've already got our top people everywhere checking this thing out. Let's see what turns up."

Years before, when Gar's General Industrial Corporation concluded the purchase of the Venezuelan oil business from IG Farben, Ritter had told Gar, "By ze vay Gar, ze terms und conditions of zhis deal are zhought to be zo confidential, particularly in ultra-zensitive Vashington, zhat ze courier who delivered ze final papers to me vas escorted by two armed zecurity men from Farben und flown here on a Farben corporate airplane. Und, az I haf told you before, ze senior executives at Farben haf requested zhat I keep ze executed originals in my zpecial underground vault here in Vaduz."

And those Farben officials were not seeing ghosts in their closet. For years, the slightest corporate move by Farben made world headlines and was examined in endless detail by governments everywhere. News of the sale of their Venezuelan properties would be no exception. The reasons to watch Farben so closely were perfectly clear.

The wealth and power of the deadly combine were beyond calculation. By 1939, Farben had provided the Hitler Nazi regime with 90% of their foreign exchange, 95% of their imports, and 85% of all their military and commercial goods. No western power, including the U.S., had any such dominating company.

Of course, no American company had Farben's spy network either. Known as N.W.7, it operated everywhere and seemed to know everything. Surely they remembered where those transaction papers were kept.

By the time Gar and Wolf arrived, Ritter was able to assure them, "Gentlemen, I am pleazed to inform you zhat ze burglars got nossing. Inazmuch az I keep all my papers in ze vault in blank envelopes inside blank file folders—ze only markings are in my confuzing zpecial code. Conzequently, zhey had no immediate means ov identifying vhatever zhey vere looking for. Zhey alzo had no way ov knowing how little time zhey had.

You see, long ago, my cloze friends at Farben had arranged for zheir engineers to inshtall a lethal gaz system in ze vault. Vhen certain zecurity measures are violated ze gaz isz automatically releazed. Zhat deadly gaz came from ze zame Farben chemical team zhat developed ze cyclon gaz zhat ze Nazis used to kill millions of Jews in ze concentration camps. Ze vord "cyclon" came from ze abbreviation of its ezzential elements: cyanide, chlorine, und nitrogen.

Knowing ze existence of ze gaz zystem izs vhy Farben felt zecure und vanted ze original Venezuelan papers shtored here. Ov course, Gar, not anyvone haz ever known ze existence of your papers—or anyzing else zhat is down zhere. By ze vay, ve haf one of ze burglars—but, ov course, he iz dead. Vhile he had no identification on hiz person, ze dead man iz obviously an Arab. I vould judge him to haf been only in hiz middle twenties. The Vaduz authorities are holding ze body at ze morgue. Under ze circumshtances, it iz unlikely zhat anyone vill come forth to claim ze body."

When Wolf heard Ritter referring to the Farben gas used to murder Jews in the death camps, he instinctively froze. Too painful, this was a subject that was never to be spoken about in his presence. Unfortunately, Ritter had no way of knowing the terrible story that Gar clearly remembered. The six million Jews murdered by the Nazis in World War II, included Wolf's entire family who lost their lives in the gas chambers of Buchenwald. He was the only survivor.

Quickly, Gar changed the subject. Trying to be a bit light-hearted, he smilingly suggested, "Franz, unless the burglars stole all of the illegal gold you were hoarding in your vault, you must still be able to afford to offer us a cup of coffee."

The laughing broke the tension.

That evening over dinner, Ritter suggested, "You know, my friends, vhen vee shtop to conzider ze zcope of my international practice over zo many years now, it iz certainly reazonable to azzume zhat I must have left zome angry people behind—people who vould do mozt anyzing to get back at me. On ze other hand, vee may never know vhat zhis break-in vas really all about."

Gar shot a quick knowing glance at Wolf.

Ritter went on, "I checked your perzonal papers firsht, Gar, und nothing vas touched. Perhaps ze entire incident iz vhat you Americans might call a tempesht in a teapot."

Uncharacteristically, Gar had remained strangely silent. Then, surprisingly agreeing with Ritter, "Maybe Franz is right, Wolf. You don't have a hell of a lot to go on here, anyway."

"Not yet. But, I'm sure whoever was involved here, I don't mean physically here doing the actual break-in—

he, she, or they—are not the important players in this drama. And I don't care about the dead Arab down at the morgue, either. He will ultimately prove to be a nobody. It's the higher-ups I'm after—the strategic planners. I'm sure they will turn out to be important people.

But whoever they are. Wherever they are from. We'll solve this mystery. And we won't give up—you can count on that.

Right now, though, I'm pooped. You guys can stay up and gab if you want, but for me it's off to bed."

Franz Josef Ritter looked terribly solemn.

Cheryl Blake spoke very business-like into her New York hotel suite phone.

"Thank you for accommodating my request, Mr. Rembardt. Our meeting here rather than at your office or in a public restaurant will not only allow us total privacy, but it will also make me feel much more secure. Under the circumstances, that has become of the utmost importance to me."

The self-disclosure prompted a crack in Cheryl's voice. She paused to regain her composure.

"I'm sorry for that, Mr. Rembardt. Surely, you must have concluded by now that I have never done anything quite like this before. Nevertheless, I do look forward to our meeting." Her voice back to near normal, "My suite it is—this afternoon at two. Thank you again. Bye."

Returning the phone to its cradle, Cheryl drifted toward a window and looked out over a surprisingly green Central Park. She had had a bad night. While she always felt secure staying in a high suite at The Plaza, today it would not have mattered where she was staying. Nothing comforted her. She was a nervous wreck—completely strung out.

Cheryl absolutely detested what she was about to do in the next few hours. The very idea ran against the grain of every ethical principle she had been taught since childhood. And now, with time running out, the full impact of the possible consequences that could flow from her action were really getting to her. Cheryl felt her skin getting tighter by the minute—and it was only a little after eleven. Still nearly three hours to go.

Maybe she should take her bath and dress—now rather than later. Then, perhaps, she would just walk across 58th street and duck through the side entrance into Bergdorf-Goodman. For a second, she wondered what might be showing next door at the artsy Paris theater.

"No, I'll be better off browsing around Bergdorf's than going to a movie. I might even find something to buy—and grab a bite of lunch. I think Heidi's is still open over on 56th. Brightening considerably, "Yes, that's exactly what I'll do."

As she headed for her bathtub, the very decision lifted her spirits immediately. And the sound of the running hot water was familiar and soothing.

Before flying back to New York yesterday, she had double-checked with Gar his instructions that he had first given her in the garden at Lake Como.

"Tell me again, right now, Gar, because I have to be very sure. Do you still want me to find out all I can about Wolf? I can't believe that you still question his loyalty after all these years—after all the things he's done for you—most of which I never even want to know about. And, most important, are you really being straight with me now—*I mean really straight?"*

"The answer to all of your questions is an emphatic yes, Cher."

"More than you know, I need you to do an exceptionally thorough job. Pretend it's an executive search assignment for a top client. As a matter of fact it *is*."

He laughed a little. She didn't.

"Look—I know you don't like this job, but I'm asking you, please, don't hold anything back. *Nothing*. Do whatever you have to do, even if you have to do some of it on your back. I want to know the location of every wart on Wolf's body—whichever piece of it comes at you first."

"As you go about this business, Cher, the key thing for you is not to forget how grateful I'll always be to you for undertaking this project. Remember that you can get through to me twenty-four hours a day. So keep in touch, baby."

During the trans-Atlantic flight, what actually remained foremost in Cheryl's mind from that conversation was the fact that Gar had finally said "please" to her. Gar Grey never used that word to anyone—about anything. Looking away from the book she was unsuccessfully trying to read, Cheryl mused, "I guess this Wolf thing must really be important to him. But who knows the real score? That bastard can lie with a very straight face."

Promptly, at two o'clock there was a soft knock on Cheryl's door. To her great surprise, standing in her doorway was a most unimposing man. So ordinary, in fact, that if she saw him again she was positive she would never remember him. Nevertheless, the rich and famous believed him to be the greatest private investigator in the world. So did any number of *Fortune 500* corporations, as well as a few third-world governments.

This was Noah Rembardt, a native Dutchman, who bore a striking resemblance to a somewhat less rotund Alfred Hitchcock. Rembardt had long since become a worldwide celebrity in his own right. His internationally renowned investigative agency, headquartered in New York, operated professionally, efficiently, and most importantly, inconspicuously. In the final analysis, what it all added up to was a single word. *Trust*. It seemed that the entire world had learned to trust Noah Rembardt with their deepest secrets.

With such a high level of respect, his Agency had gained the best inside connections around the globe. It was known and accepted that they could gain entrance almost anywhere.

Slowly, Cheryl outlined what she had in mind for Rembardt to accomplish on her behalf. Given the delicate circumstances, she knew that this was not going to be a quick investigation. And she was prepared to be as patient as possible.

After listening, Rembardt volunteered an extremely important piece of information. Up front he wanted Cheryl to know that the principal subject of her proposed investigation, Wolfgang Amadeus Felsenberg, was a man personally well-known to him. In their earlier years he and Wolf had worked together as undercover agents for an unnamed foreign government.

"Therefore, I can assure you, Miss Blake, that Wolf Felsenberg is a world-class professional. I also know of his highly specialized work for General Industrial, and I am known to his famous boss, George Garfield Grey. Therefore, we will have to take very special precautions in this matter. And I might add, this all adds to the cost of producing the results you require."

As their discussion proceeded, the details were worked out. Cheryl wanted his updates held in his office pending her contact. Adding, "Unless some dire emergency occurs, Mr. Rembardt, I prefer that we not personally meet again."

In London, Gar had assured her that cost was no object.

"Rest easy, Cher. If you put the money out of your mind, I'll put the money in the bank." To that end he had arranged for a large sum of money to be put on deposit in a Swiss bank. And she alone would have access to the funds.

In order to have the famous detective immediately move forward on her case, Cheryl agreed to his steep fee and paid over to a substantial advance in the form of a check she had already drawn on the new account.

Their business concluded for now, the courtly Dutchman lightly kissed Cheryl's hand, re-assured her that her privacy would never be invaded or at risk—and was gone.

The fat was now in the fire.

FIFTY

Fresh in from Nassau by way of British Airways and Heathrow Airport, breathlessly Vikki told him, "Dear precious Gar, you cannot possibly imagine how thrilling it is for me to be here in London, and especially working for you. And this fabulous office—"

She was moving toward him now. Gar was leaning against the front of his desk. She sidled up very close, then provocatively turned her shapely rear end up to him.

"Golly, if you pinch me here do you think I'll wake up and find this is all just a dream?"

Patting her curvaceous tush, he reassured her, "I seriously doubt that you're in any such danger, Vikki."

"Oh, by the way, have you selected an apartment for me, or do I bunk with you?"

"You're all set. I've leased a flat for you in Park Lane. You'll be happy there."

Suddenly, the story of *My Fair Lady* popped into his mind and Gar could not resist a satisfied smile to himself. Of course, the comparison was incongruous. George Bernard Shaw's original Liza Doolittle, while fetching in a Raggedy Ann sort of way, was not even on the same planet with his exquisite milk chocolate beauty, Victoria Tracy.

Wherever in the world Vikki walked, people invariably turned to look at her.

How could they not?

Women looked at her with deep envy. They had all been so badly cheated. Men of every age stared—ogled would be more accurate. A fleeting fantasy and an immediate erection quickly followed. Reaching for the stars since she was a teenager, Vikki's reaction was only to herself. "Eat your hearts out fellas. There's only one guy rich enough to nail this piece of tender black ass. And this chocolate treat will melt in his mouth."

If passersbys could have heard her voice, they would have quickly fallen under the easy charm of her British accent—a natively soft Jamaican dialect of the King's English.

At this point in her life, when Vikki comparatively evaluated all of her personal assets, she full well knew she was in a super-class by herself. Except for Gar Grey, who might very well be unattainable.

No matter what else had changed in his marriage, over the years, Gar had remained close to his father-in-law, Buck McCormack. The generation gap notwithstanding, they continued to enjoy an unusual man-to-man thing. And it had been that way from the first time Gar met Buck.

Their closeness was also nourished by the fact that not only had Gar commissioned hundreds of General Industrial Corporation facilities to be built worldwide, but, without exception they were all built by Buck's giant McCormack Construction Corporation, still headquartered on LaSalle Street in Chicago.

Of all the buildings they had planned and built, both Gar and Buck thought the pièce de résistance was General Industrial's European headquarters located in the ancient area named *The City*—the financial core of London. More specifically, GIC's building on famed Threadneedle Street appropriately across from the Bank of England and the

London Stock Exchange, had become the big buzz in the financial world.

Looking more like a giant trading house, nothing like it had ever been built before. But then, why should so many have been so surprised? After all, that's what it was. A trading house—a *world-class* trading house.

It was now also generally accepted among the most influential merchant bankers and commodity market-makers, that the slickest trader of them all—the one man capable of moving, perhaps even cornering, world markets by himself—was George Garfield Grey, the capricious and controlling Chairman of General Industrial.

Among those who knew Gar the longest, friends such as David Ross and Nancy Lee Hendrix who go all the way back to college days, were very familiar with Gar Grey's obsessively controlling nature. But what the financial world had only begun to realize was that when it came to his commodity trading practices, not only was Gar obsessively controlling, but also secretive to the point where he had become positively paranoid on the subject.

Without any proof of wrongdoing, he now believed that he could not fully trust his own traders, and continued to nurse a deep gut instinct, that for the right price, they would reveal some of his vital trading secrets. And he was emotionally stuck in that make-believe place.

It had gotten to the point where others thought that Gar had even found some perverted joy in saying, "You know, if those guys turned on me they could cost me some really big money. And anybody with any kind of a brain, knows there is nothing in this world as important as money. He who has the gold—rules. Got it?"

Talking on the phone from London to Buck in Chicago, Gar told his father-in-law, "I've gone over the plans you sent me for London, Buck. And I think they're good, in fact, they are very good, especially the trading floor. It's a real knockout. But, right now I want to tell you about the ideas I have for my private office.

I think I've come up with the ultimate privacy concept. To be absolutely sure no one can overhear any crucial orders I place, or eavesdrop on anything else about my businesses, let's start by my telling you that I want my office to be hung in mid-air."

"Where?"

"You heard me right. I said hung in mid-air. I don't want it to be connected to any other room. In other words, it should sort of free-float up there. Your engineers will figure it out. Some steel bars or some kind of steel structure will hold the thing in place—something like that.

Then, I want all four sides plus the floor and ceiling to be soundproofed with cork and a lead sheet underlay. We'll decorate over the cork. And, finally, the whole place should also be anti-static and electronically bug-proof. I think there should be automatic bug sweeps every night.

I even plan on giving the space a name. I plan on calling it the *Control Room.* By the way Buck, I've already engaged Pierre Montaigne, from Paris, to design the interior space. I have always admired his work. So—what do you think about my idea, Buck?"

After a few seconds of trans-Atlantic silence, the old man slowly replied, "Well, I think I've just heard another reason why you're so damn successful, Gar. Honestly, I think your concept is brilliant—simply brilliant. I'll get on it with the engineers and architects right away. We'll probably have some interpretive sketches and specs over to you by the first of next week. So long, my boy. Take good care."

Now picture this.

High over his mammoth new trading floor, the largest private trading floor in the world, there it was. Unbelievably, suspended in mid-air from the twentieth floor triple-height ceiling of the trading floor.

What Buck had built, Pierre Montaigne had exquisitely finished. It was exactly what Gar originally had in his mind's eye.

In order to enter the space, one had to walk across a railed, fairly wide, fifteen-foot hydraulic gangway, which on a key command, magically appeared out of the floor of the space. While it was the only way in or out of the Control Room, two Security Officers dressed in black suits, black tie, and white shirt, were on duty around the clock. One man inside the Control Room entrance. The other never moved from just outside the door to Gar's private suite.

In addition to his gargantuan office, inside Gar's suite was a private dining room to seat twelve, with adjoining kitchen—equipped to cook anything. Then, there was Gar's walnut-paneled conference room connected to a cozy lounge; a complete bedroom with a king-size bed; and a dressing room facility with bath, shower, steam room, and two large massage tables.

A fortune in art hung on the walls throughout the Control Room. Important works by some of his favorite artists: Victor Vasarely, Kenneth Noland, Jasper Johns, and Paul Klee. All of whom reflected his interest in constructive concepts. The same motion detectors that guarded the masterpieces at the British Museum also stood guard over Gar's collection.

Additionally, there was a large and impressive adjoining office for Vikki Tracy, with an inside connecting door to Gar, as well as other more modest-sized offices for various other lesser staff—secretaries and various assistants.

While there could be no real outside windows, the creative Montaigne had skillfully designed extraordinarily realistic look-a-likes. If you didn't know they were fakes, you'd swear they were real windows. Specially sunlit, they decoratively existed along the outside walls preventing any possible claustrophobia. In the middle of rainy London, at least in the fantasy of Gar's Control Room, the sun shined every day of the year.

What Gar Grey had dreamed was now his reality.

And within a few months, he came to prefer his Control Room to any other of his many offices around the world. Even more than his World Headquarters office in Rockefeller Center in New York. The one with the life-sized marble bust of himself.

Hewing to his plan, the Control Room became the secret nerve center of Gar's worldwide financial operations. Of necessity, the overwhelming size and scope of General Industrial's far-flung manufacturing operations, chewed up raw materials of every kind with a voracious daily appetite. This compelled Gar to hedge the price fluctuations of commodities in vast amounts of money—billions of dollars, pounds, marks, francs.

For the most part, these hedging activities were accomplished through the nearby Royal Exchange, the largest in the world. There, frenzied markets and auctions were conducted for every kind of necessary raw material.

Almost maniacally, leaving nothing to chance, Gar had installed one of the first IBM 752 mainframe computers in London. Yet the five phones spread across his desk remained vital.

The same was true with his newly hired traders, all of them MBA's, who had ranked in the top five of their class. Each had been recommended to Gar by the Deans of the business schools at Harvard, Wharton, Stanford, MIT, and Cambridge. Gar had personally interviewed and hired every one of them.

With his deep-seated paranoia, what Gar was mostly probing for during his interviewing process was loyalty. To emphasize his point in a couched format, Gar enjoyed invoking one of the many famous vulgar quotes from President Lyndon Johnson.

"I want the loyalty of men who will kiss my ass and tell me it smells like a rose."

Of course, for LBJ, a ribald Texan, that was not a surprising utterance. With only a single exception, the coarse remark invariably shocked the young men who heard it. At their obvious uncomfortable reaction, Gar would burst into uproarious laughter. But his overall demeanor left no doubt he seriously meant what LBJ had said.

No matter what nonsense wandered around in Gar's distorted psyche, he knew he had put together a bright and gifted group of traders. Naturally, he would never admit how talented a group they were.

Inasmuch as these critical markets follow the sun, commodity trading is open somewhere on the globe twenty-four hours a day. That necessitated Gar's new staff of young traders to work around the clock—in three eight-hour shifts.

Accordingly, Gar issued the following stern directive:

> "In order for us to adequately cover all open markets, it is imperative that no less than twenty traders be on active duty at all times. No exceptions. Work it out."
>
> G.G.G.

Among his new trading crew, that sort of work schedule did not get rave reviews. Especially not from Ramsay Langham-Hawkins, jokingly known to his close friends as Ram Ram.

Hailing from the central midlands, Ram Ram was a close cousin of Ian Hawkins, the surprising current boyfriend of Gar's old college lover, Nancy Lee Hendrix. And heir to a peerage.

Not just another bright guy, upon the death of his father, Sir Archibald Percival Langham-Hawkins, the eighth Earl of Bentonshire and a member of the House of Lords, by the right of succession, the big 6' 3" blond weight-lifter would become the ninth Earl.

A secure fellow with independent convictions, the young blue blood had been the only trader candidate that Gar had not intimidated. His reaction was typically direct.

"It's hard to believe that an American president would say something like that. Did he really say that, Mr. Grey, or are you just fooling around?"

Ram Ram was the quintessential gentle giant whom everyone in the London office took an immediate liking to. Including Gar Grey.

FIFTY-ONE

According to legend, sometime in 1953, Allen Dulles, Director of Central Intelligence, said, "There are no archbishops in espionage." At least none that the CIA has ever admitted to employing. Seriously breaking the laws of foreign countries and, when necessary, killing other human beings, is hardly appropriate work for clerics. It fits others like a custom-made glove.

Such a person was Kermit Roosevelt, whom everyone called Kim. The grandson of President Theodore Roosevelt was a rising star at the Central Intelligence Agency, where he had become a specialist on the Middle East. In the post-war years this was well known to MI-6, Britain's foreign intelligence agency. Not lost on MI-6 was an added attraction. Kim Roosevelt knew every important personage in Washington. And more than a few in London.

As a consequence of his profile, almost a year earlier MI-6 had brought a secret plan to Roosevelt's attention. *The British plan was to overthrow the Iranian government.*

The idea of a foreign power hatching a plan to topple the duly elected government of a sovereign state was totally illegal. In this case, however, Britain felt it had a justifiable reason to get rid of Iran's new Prime Minister, the radical nationalist, Mohammad Mossadegh. In his blinded mind, Britain's days in his country were over. On the other hand, the British goal was to restore Mohammed Reza Shah Pahlevi to his throne.

Among other MI-6 personnel Roosevelt knew from previous cooperations on international intelligence gathering in Europe, were two exceptionally bright young men—neither one yet thirty. But, like Roosevelt they were rising stars. Secret Agents Wolf Felsenberg and Noah Rembardt.

This all came together on July 19, 1953.

On special assignment, Kim Roosevelt, together with Felsenberg and Rembardt, quietly drove from Beirut to Teheran. Yet unknown to the rest of the world, the covert operation, code named Ajax, had begun!

By mutual agreement with the U.S., the British had remained the primary Western power in Iran after World War II. In fact, the U.S. was more than happy not to be involved in that distant part of the world.

At that time, the U.S. was still the world's largest oil producer. Since making the first successful oil strike in Persia in 1909 (Iran in 1935), the British had lifted Iranian oil as if it was their birthright. The original British-controlled Burmah Oil Co. became Anglo-Persian Oil Company, by 1908. In 1935, Anglo-Persian changed its name, yet again, to Anglo-Iranian. Eventually, it become the now familiar BP—British Petroleum. Significantly, owned fifty per cent by the British government.

Starting around mid-century, Iran demanded a more equitable division of the spoils of their valuable natural resource. The authoritarian arrogance of British oil officials, local and in far-off London, sewed the seeds of an unremitting rise in Iranian nationalism.

Another constant reminder of that arrogance was Britain's sprawling embassy compound in Teheran. Covering a massive sixteen city blocks, it also symbolized the unforgiving presence of long-standing British domination.

Adding insult to injury, the lowly Iranians were not even allowed to look at the books kept by the Brits. When that anger turned to outright hostility, the upshot of this deep-seated enmity was not surprising—except to the near-sighted British.

People today don't know and most probably don't care, nevertheless, it was a young British cabinet member, thirty-three year old Winston Churchill, whose mother was the American, Jennie Jerome, who persuaded his government to buy up the original Persian oil concession granted in 1901. Which, by the early 1930s was the world's largest known untapped oil reserve.

In 1911, it was also Churchill who convinced the Royal Navy to convert to oil. Whereupon British foreign policy became fixated on dependable supplies of the black gold.

As the tense Iranian situation unfolded, another key question became where would white-hot nationalism strike next? Unfortunately, the world at large paid no attention to the fact that the militarily weak oil producing countries and the all-powerful consuming nations were on a mighty collision course. Oil barons on both sides of the Atlantic held their collective breath.

They knew only too well that the hugely unbalanced geographical locations of proven oil reserves, primarily in the Middle East, practically guaranteed national conflicts. The old law of supply and demand would repeat itself over and over again. It has not changed to this day.

During the late 1940s, Aramco (Arabian-American Oil Co.), which held exclusive rights to all Saudi-Arabian oil, was selling the invaluable commodity for about 90 cents a barrel, while comparable quality oil was selling elsewhere for $1.28. Both wanting and needing more oil royalty income, the jealous Saudi King, Ibn Saud, leaned hard on Socal and Texaco, the owners of Aramco. Of course, the king received his increased royalty money.

In today's world of more than $30 per barrel for oil, these selling prices may sound utterly ridiculous. If so, try this one when you're filling up at today's prices. The *cost* of lifting Saudi Arabian oil cost Aramco only about *30 cents* a barrel—*30 cents!*

In May, 1951, led by the fiery Mossadegh, the Iranians committed the British unthinkable. *They nationalized Anglo-Iranian Oil.* Simultaneously, abrogating a 1933 concession treaty signed with London. Britain appealed to the International Court of Justice—and threatened military force. And a fearful world faced an unknown international tinderbox. Nothing like this had ever before occurred.

Saudi Arabia, with 25% of the world's proven oil reserves, realized the potential for extraordinary danger. And immediately turned for advice and counsel to its old friend, Franz Josef Ritter, in Vaduz. Ritter concurred on the explosive dynamics of the situation. In turn, he called the world's most influential oil lawyer for strategic consultation—his old friend and colleague, John J. McCloy, in New York.

Unbelievably, McCloy was the lawyer for all seven sisters. And no other single person in the world had better access to the seven largest oil companies.

Under strong advice from McCloy, it was determined that the West was not about to depart Iran in a meek and mild manner. That would send the wrong signal to other exporting countries. In those days, someone in Washington is supposed to have heard McCloy say, "If the Iranians are so damn in love with their oil—*let them drink it.*"

A successful world boycott of Iranian National oil followed. Naturally, all of the oil importing countries unanimously sanctioned the move. As expected, on July 5, the court ruled against Iran.

That ruling, notwithstanding, the extremely left-leaning Mossadegh was not yet finished. His life-long hatred of the British was so deep-seated, it propelled him toward nothing less than total British humiliation. And economic punishment for forty years of exploitation.

To further that end, in October he issued two orders. He ordered all British Anglo-Iranian employees home. Then, he ordered the Iranian army to occupy the vast oil fields and huge refinery at Abadan on the Shatt Al-Arab estuary, which flows directly into the Persian Gulf.

Once Kim Roosevelt, Wolf Felsenberg, and Noah Rembardt arrived in Teheran, each knew what was required of them. Roosevelt set up a meeting with the Shah, who under the circumstances could not easily move around the city. Huddled on the floor in the back seat of an unmarked black car, and hidden under a blanket, Roosevelt was smuggled into the Palace complex. But he never got out of the car. Instead, the Shah jumped into same back seat and also hid under the blanket.

In those close quarters, Roosevelt explained to the Shah that he was the personal representative of President Eisenhower and Prime Minister Churchill. And both countries were committed to returning him to his throne.

In the meantime, Felsenberg and Rembardt used $100,000 of the $1 million in Iranian currency that Roosevelt had brought with him, to rent a street mob out of the gyms and wrestling clubs of Teheran. They would be essential to initiate supposedly spontaneous street demonstrations supporting the Shah's ouster of Mossadegh.

It was not unlike the famed Hollywood director Cecil B. DeMille hiring, "A cast of thousands." The money also bought off key Iranian officials.

Yet, as hard and as carefully as they had worked, much of the detailed planning for Operation Ajax did not go off on time —or at all. And Teheran radio failed to broadcast that the Shah had fired "Old Mossy," as Sir Anthony Eden had called the radical Iranian Prime Minister.

The true facts were that Ajax was so bollixed up, that General Walter Beedle Smith, the new director of the CIA, urgently cabled Kim Roosevelt, "Give up and get out."

But the tide had miraculously turned.

When the pro-Shah forces finally made their move,

the army remained loyal to the Shah. On that cue, Felsenberg and Rembardt took to the streets. Their faces darkened with soot and wearing tattered Iranian garb, the two MI-6 agents whipped their paid mob into near frenzy—directing them ever closer to Mossadegh's residence. Their agitation rose to fever pitch. Fearing for his life, Mossadegh fled.

The Shah received Kermit Roosevelt on August 23, telling him, "I owe my throne to God, my people, my army, and to you!"

Mossadegh was tried and convicted before a military court. He spent two years in prison.

FIFTY-TWO

In the days after the Vaduz break-in, Wolf continued to throw hardball questions at Gar.

"Did Ritter know more about the break-in than he admitted in order to keep us off guard?"

Without waiting for an answer, he went-on. "For chrissakes, Gar, didn't the dead Arab immediately set off flashing red lights? Ritter simply had to have been aware that his old client, King Ibn Saud, had used his vast oil reserves to play both sides against each other during the war. And for sure, that dangerous political game must have left the King plenty of enemies."

All of Wolf's questions and comments were certainly valid. Indeed, prophetic.

To their ulterior advantage, certain high American oil executives had convinced President Franklin D. Roosevelt that the Germans were prepared to pay King Ibn Saud a substantial bribe to insure that the Saudis would supply fuel to General Erwin Rommel's Afrika Tank Corps.

To counteract the German bribe, on July 18,1941, FDR sent the following note to his Secretary of Commerce, Jesse Jones: "Dear Jesse. Will you tell the British I hope they can take care of the King of Arabia—this is a little far afield for us."

Continuing to feign loyalty to both Britain and the United States, it is generally well known that Saudi Arabia had intricate economic and political links to Hitler, as early as 1939.

So, the perfect question should be—how much did oil *really* cost the Allies?

In the meantime, annoyed at the pace of his own agents, and more than ever determined to get to the bottom of the Ritter break-in, Wolf made a surprising decision. He would seek outside help. And without hesitation, he knew exactly to whom he would turn.

Reaching for his secured-line phone in Washington, Wolf was calling New York to enlist the services of the only person he knew who could be completely trusted with such confidential information. His old friend and colleague—the Dutchman—Noah Rembardt.

"Noah, it's Wolf," he began. "How the hell are you, my friend? Long time no see—no talk."

"Wolf, you old rascal, your ears must have been burning. You won't believe how often your name has come up recently in various conversations. So—to what do I owe the honor of this call? If you're in some kind of trouble, you can always count on my help. What's up?"

"As a matter of fact, Noah, you really can help me. It's in regard to a matter of great urgency. Does your schedule allow us to get together—like this week? I'm in Washington so I can meet with you in New York. Great. This Thursday will also work out well for me. Is our usual spot down in Little Italy still okay? Good. I'll meet you there on Thursday at one. Thanks for making the time on such short notice. So long."

In his sound proof office, high above most of the Manhattan skyline, Noah Rembardt slowly put his phone down. His recent meeting with Cheryl Blake and her delicate assignment regarding Wolf was racing through his mind.

"I'm sure Cheryl is only a front for Gar. It has to be his money that is funding my assignment. It's even possible that Wolf already knows what I'm doing. After all, his connections are just as good as mine. Some of them we made together. And most informers will talk—for a price."

With his ever-present pipe, Noah pondered further as he eased back in his leather chair. "Could also be that Gar has gotten wind of something. Plenty of devious schemes backfire. If that has actually happened, that sonofabitch, Gar, wouldn't hesitate for a minute to double-cross Cheryl—and leave her holding an empty bag. Anything to keep his own hands clean. I wonder if she knows Gar cannot be trusted? She might not even believe it if the truth jumped up and bit her on the nose."

As he entered the old fashioned Italian restaurant on Kenmare Street, Wolf smiled. Nothing had changed including the appealing aroma of the fabulous food. His mouth watered with memories.

Of greater importance was the fact that on a slow weekday it was still a safe, out-of-the-way place for lunch. By their sinister appearance, particularly their brown crumpled fedoras, some of the other diners no doubt had the same motivation for lunching there. So as not to be too easily seen.

Only moments later, Noah strode in. After a bear hug greeting, Wolf figured out, "It's hard to believe Noah, but we haven't seen each other for over a year." Noah smiled, "I guess that proves how time flies when you're having fun."

As they settled down with a bottle of Chianti, not wasting any time, Noah questioned, "You said there was an urgent matter on your agenda, Wolf. What's the story?"

"It concerns Gar."

Noah replied dryly, "So what else is new?"

Ignoring his friend's sarcasm, "I assume you still maintain valuable contacts in Central Europe?"

"We manage to keep informed."

"Good. I need your help there. It involves an incident which has me stymied."

After Wolf brought him up-to-date on the facts of the Ritter break-in, Noah responded, "Based on what you've just told me, my gut reaction is that I think you are absolutely right. Ritter *is* lying. And we both know that men of his stature and reputation never lay their professional careers on the line—never.

Therefore, before we consider anything else, the fundamental question underlying the heart of this matter is—*why?* Why, would this internationally prominent lawyer dig himself a hole straight down to hell?"

"You're right, Noah. And that's exactly where I was stuck when I called you."

Noah went on, "An educated guess would have to be that some irresistible source or force is threatening absolute blackmail—the kind that would expose him to ruin.

On the other hand, giving the man the benefit of the doubt, he could be covering up for someone or something—and be completely innocent of any personal wrongdoing. This is going to be one hell of a tough nut for you to crack, Wolf. I sure wish you luck."

"Hold on, my friend. You're not being dealt out of this game so fast. Not by a long shot."

"Wolf, if you had any idea of what my calendar looks like—"

"I don't give a damn what your calendar looks like, Noah. If I didn't need you whole hog on this situation you know damn well that I wouldn't have bothered you in the first place. My regular guys are coming up blank. And I can't wait."

"You always were a clever bastard. Well, at least you were always clever. And I never did learn how to say "no" to you. So—if we are going to start a joint investigative venture, can we at least start off with a full Italian stomach? Waiter—menus please."

Noah, to himself: "What a complicated mess.

I *help* him on this case and report *on him* on the other case. Nobody would believe this conumdrum."

FIFTY-THREE

It was the most elegant French party since Louis XIV moved his court to Versailles.

Paris à son très le mieux. Paris at its very best.

Paul Louis Oppert had succeeded in outdoing himself—if such were possible. With the exception of a summons by the French President to a state dinner, Oppert's vanilla-colored invitation, deeply engraved and addressed in navy blue, was the most sought after of the Paris social season. As always, Paul Louis would have a world-class guest list.

In heightened anticipation, the glittering night arrived. Government officials and foreign diplomats presented themselves in white ties and tails. Some in formal military uniforms. Many were proudly draped in wide over-the-shoulder silk sashes in honor of meritorious military or diplomatic service.

Not overlooked, by any means, were the most important chiefs of the international corporate and banking world. Included in this grouping, of course, was George Garfield Grey.

Their stylishly coifed ladies, some of the most sophisticated women in the world, created a breathtaking display of Parisian haute couture—featuring the likes of Balenciaga, Schiaparelli, Givenchy, and Mainbocher. Displayed and worn to perfection.

And talk about dazzling jewels.

Diamonds, emeralds, sapphires, and rubies, in designs, quality, and amazonian sizes to please the magnifying loupes and discriminating eyes of Van Cleef, Cartier, and Chaumet. The visual delights could only be described as *très magnifique*—which, even in the charming French form does not seem to adequately describe the overwhelming jewels.

The reception service for this glitterati—this ultra beau monde of diplomats and generals, barons, tycoons, and magnates—nabobs all—by the nearly invisible white-jacketed servants was a scene reminiscent of a priceless Versailles painting.

In near silence, these dedicated servants moved among the guests presenting an amazing variety of mouth-watering hors d'oeuvres and exquisite, tulip-shaped crystal glasses filled with the best French champagne.

For years, the now fifty-year old bon vivant, Paul Louis Oppert, slim, dark, and handsome, was renowned for his incomparable entertaining. And his Paris mansion in the Eighth Arrondissment on the Right Bank near the Plaza Athenee, provided a gold and white brocaded setting, accented with pale greens and mellow yellows. The world-famous French silk industry in Lyons seemed to have been invented to fulfill the décor of these sumptuous rooms.

Being the only child of Phillipe Oppert, a wealthy member of the French Parliament from Toulouse, Paul Louis never had to work for his worldly possessions. The huge financial assets of the senior Oppert were accumulated as the result of his having been an original partner of the pioneer plane maker, Marcel Dassault, whose leading French aeronautical firm created and built the famous Mirage fighter planes—and still do.

Family ties also substantially augmented Oppert's fortune. A second cousin, he was a close member of the powerful Rothschild family of international bankers, themselves known to have been extremely family conscious.

And the old saying goes, "Big trees from little acorns," seems most appropriate for them. When the bank was founded in 1801 in Frankfurt, Germany, money-changer Mayer Amschel Rothschild, who had risen from the ghetto, spoke only Yiddish—primarily based on medieval German dialects. Surprisingly, four Rothschild sons expanded their banking business to Vienna, London, Paris, and Naples. In 1822, all were created barons by Francis I of Austria. When all is said and done, perhaps, money is a language unto itself.

Oppert, together with Dassault—born Marcel-Ferdinand Bloch—survived three years of Gestapo imprisonment at Buchenwald. Gaining his freedom, Dassault converted to Roman Catholicism, telling a friend, "Enough was enough." Phillipe Oppert remained a dignified lifelong Jew.

Paul Louis' dinner was a sit-down affair.

With the possible exception of the near six-hundred room Buckingham Palace in London, which housed a ballroom 110 feet long, only Paul Louis' vast ballroom would have been large enough to be converted into a dining room accommodating nearly two hundred guests.

Viewing such a grandiose table set with the best china, silver, and crystal, money could buy, a French minister exclaimed, "*Mon Dieu.*" My God. Paul must have raided the national vault."

Believing her famous German name would be a recognized asset with this elite crowd, Gar had invited his blonde lover, Ursula Von Ribbentrop, to be his dinner companion. Unaware of the possible consequences, the legally unattached Paul Louis had invited the well-connected American headhunter, Cheryl Blake, as his personal guest.

Old friends, Gar and Paul, had warmly greeted each other while the two women, who only knew each other by name and reputation but had never met face-to-face, went to check out whatever it is that women go to check out. Fortunately, they went to different powder rooms.

Because of the large number of guests, place cards on the table would have been difficult. Instead, during cocktails two of Paul Louis' major domos circulated through the gathering and informed the men of their chair numbers—and requested that no chair hopping take place in the dining room. Too much confusion.

When everybody was finally seated, Gar looked around only to see Cheryl seated next to Paul Louis at the head of the table. At that very moment, their eyes met. Cheryl looked quizzically across at Gar. Her expression was pure puzzlement. As if to say, "Who is she? And why not me?"

Her answer hit hard. It wasn't easy to accept the humiliating fact that in making his escort choice for this important evening, Gar chose Ursula. "Maybe it was *always* Ursula."

Humiliated and crushed beyond her ability to conceal, Cheryl noisily pushed her chair back and left the table. The perfect host, Paul Louis, was visibly upset. Realizing all he had at stake, Gar quickly followed Cheryl. Ursula sat bewildered while others looked and whispered about her. The entire world knew who she was. Her deep embarrassment caused her face to flush pink.

Gar and Cheryl were the only two guests standing and moving in the great dining hall. Everyone could sense something very out-of-the-ordinary, even explosive, was in the air! The tension was palpable.

Of course, the French appreciate romantic turmoil more than most other people. And in this case, when you put two and two together—the sum equaled *three.*

"A threesome! Oh, how deliciously French can you get?"

Not wanting to make more of a scene than what had already occurred, Gar caught up with Cheryl in the foyer.

Grabbing her arm, "Not here, but I can explain," he said. Wrenching her arm out of his grasp, snarling, "You miserable shit. You two-timing son-of-a-bitch. How could you do this to me? I always did everything you wanted. I trusted you—even over Wolf."

Gar opened his mouth to explain, but Cheryl cut him off before he could say a single word. "I don't want to hear any of your lying explanation. I'm going back in there now, quietly, for Paul Louis' sake. But don't you even dare to try to speak with me, Gar Grey. I don't ever want to see or hear from you again. Ever. Never. We are through. Done. Finished. Do you understand?"

Never before having been spoken to in this tone of voice, Gar stood dumbstruck. In a final fit of unbridled rage, with all her might Cheryl slapped Gar across his face, hysterically screaming, "*Do you understand me better—now?*"

Turning on her angry heel, the still-enraged Cheryl started back toward the actively buzzing dining room. Only to be confronted by an out-of-breath Ursula.

Cheryl continued to scream, *"And you—you're no better! You're nothing but a slut—an international slut!"*

Summarily, Cheryl also whacked Ursula across the face with such force as to send the German model staggering backwards. And leaving a full handprint on her left cheek.

Gaining her balance, Ursula started back, shouting, "Who are *you* to call me a slut? You're only successful because you fuck Gar Grey!"

The overflowing hatred quickly turned to rough and tumble. The impossible became reality. Cheryl and Ursula actually started to fight. Going at each other like two wild animals. Tearing gowns, pulling hair, clawing. Guests began to take sides. Quarrels ensued. Some sympathized with Cheryl others sided with Ursula. Nobody felt sorry for Gar. He had obviously used both women. "That cad."

The astounded Paul Louis raced into the foyer.

While this theater of the absurd was taking on the spectacle of a sporting event, most guests wanted no part of this madness. And began to push and shove toward the front door. Sheer pandemonium had broken out.

Staring in disbelief at the forsaken dining room—chairs askew, some turned over, table-settings awry, the room in chaos—the Executive Chef broke into tears.

Intricately planned for months, down to the last fresh produce and vegetable shopping this very morning—carefully cooked and timed throughout the day to be at peak serving perfection—the superbly prepared food had now became overcooked. Sauces soured. Salads wilted.

The entire kitchen staff was crushed. There would be no serving tonight.

Paul Louis' dinner party lay in shambles.

FIFTY-FOUR

The next morning the full account of Paul Louis' dinner fiasco hit the world press.

In the absence of war, it became a headline.

A Paris newspaper ran the screaming banner:

BAGARREZ-VOUS À CHÂTEAU PARIS!
BRAWL AT PARIS MANSION!

U.S. papers were just as rough. Especially those in New York, Washington and L.A. Feature stories deeply probed every sensational possibility. Detailed profiles of the principals in the melee were boldly boxed to attract maximum attention.

Quite naturally, the syndicated gossip columnists had a field day. In hundreds of papers coast to coast, the likes of Walter Winchell, Ed Sullivan, Louella Parsons, Dorothy Kilgallen, and Hedda Hopper, squeezed out the last juicy drop from the Paris wire reports.

Because of the involvement of Ursula Von Ribbentrop, a source of national pride, German papers presented more biased coverage. Portraying Ursula as "A young, innocent victim."

Never forgetting Gar's important rank in the corporate and financial world, the story also appeared in *The Wall Street Journal*—albeit in a more subdued version.

Finally, consider the one-day smorgasbord offered to European editors. Two Americans, one German, and throw in a Frenchman. When do you suppose such a front page "dream" would hit the news wires again—in one eye-popping story? Probably never.

Back in his London office, the next day was the worst day in Gar Grey's life. He told Vikki, "No calls—only the usual exceptions."

In late morning, came the first exception. Gar took a call from Paul Louis, who apologized a hundred different ways. "I should have known, Gar, that that there could not have been two such beautiful women left in this world—that you did not intimately know."

"Nonsense, Paul. I could pay you the same compliment. We both get around."

"Gar, if it makes you feel any better, I kept Cheryl here at my home. She was pretty well beaten up. Naturally, she had a bad night. My personal physician came over—cleaned her up and gave her an injection for sleeping. She is still asleep. By the way, I tried my best to harness the news. Having seen the morning papers, I am sorry my people were not more successful."

"Thanks for everything, Paul. Someday we'll have a good laugh over last night."

"Peut-être, mon ami. Un jour. Perhaps, my friend. Someday."

The next call came in person, without so much as a knock on the door. With a distressed Vikki peering over his shoulder, "I'm sorry, Mr. Grey, Mr. Felsenberg just wouldn't listen. I…"

Already in front of Gar's desk, "It's all right, Vikki, we're old friends."

"Bullshit. Not anymore."

"Just close the door, Vikki. No intrusions."

In one unbroken motion, Wolf went to the door, threw the dead-bolt, walked back to the desk—and pulled his gun from his inside shoulder holster.

Gar didn't move a muscle. "You'll never get away with it, Wolf. You know that."

"I might have a better chance than you think. Your security officers will remain perfectly loyal to me—not to you no matter what happens in here. And I won't beat around the bush. I had a call last night from Cheryl. Yes, she was crying. Yes, she was also quite hysterical. But she told me the whole story—everything.

Then, I spoke to my old friend, Noah Rembardt, who confirmed what Cheryl had spilled. You misanthropic bastard. But, I'm not going to kill you—that's too easy. I'm going to do something worse. I'm going to let you live. But without me to protect you, you're as good as dead.

You'll live in constant fear—always looking over your shoulder. Never knowing when or where. Guys like you, the egomaniacs of this world, the control freaks, the power hungry, have no sense of how many enemies you've made over the years. How many lives your deals have left in ruins. Or how many close calls you've had. I don't tell you those alarming details because my job is to shield you. No need to broadcast our secrets to the rest of the world. But, sure as hell, you'll find out now."

Gar could not bring himself to believe what he was hearing.

Wolf went on, "So—I am going to lay this pistol down on your desk. Call it symbolic. Call it anything you want. By any name, it means that I quit. I no longer work for you—effective this minute. Get yourself a new boy. Although that will be one hell of a task. What you'll do for references is beyond me.

As a matter of fact, I don't know anyone in the security business that would accept your job. Nobody will trust you—especially after they hear my story. And they will. I have had two substantial story contracts offered to me already. And it's still only morning. It seems that you are so goddam important publishers think my story is worth a lot of money."

As Wolf headed for the door, Gar called out, "Wait a minute, I can explain. I—"

As he unlocked the door, the former Chief of Security barked over his shoulder, "Fuck you." And went out the way he came in. This time leaving a stunned and totally devastated Gar.

With no response to a soft knock on Gar's door, Vikki Tracy opened it just enough to peek in. She saw Gar head down on his desk. Seeing the gun and thinking the worst, she came bolting in. *"Gar. Gar. Oh my God. Gar can you hear me?"* Then she saw the empty vial—pills spilled all over the floor. Not wasting a moment, she called Dr. Lawton Graham, the in-house physician. "Dr. Graham, please come to Mr. Grey's office. Yes, now—this very second. Bring your bag, but don't say a word to anybody. Hurry!"

As the doctor came through the door, Vikki threw the dead-bolt behind him.

Quickly surveying the scene, "What's going on here, Vikki? What are all these pills doing on the floor." Looking at the label on the vial, "How many did he take?"

"I don't know. He was alone—upset—very upset."

"We'll have to hurry. Get my nurse up here. This medication must be pumped out of his stomach at once. Help me get him into his bathroom. I have everything I need back there."

Dr. Graham was a surprisingly competent physician. Less than an hour later, he told the terrified secretary, "Mr. Grey will be all right, Vikki. Let's get him undressed and into his bed. Good thing he's got an entire house back here. However, he shouldn't be left alone.

Can you stay with him overnight?"

After the scuffle, Ursula was offered a welcome ride back to her hotel in the limousine of the German Ambassador to Paris. No one had ever seen the impeccable model looking as she did. Disheveled beyond belief—scratched bloody and bruised everywhere. Her gown ripped and torn. Her hair a mess.

Completely exhausted, Ursula slumped down in the back seat next to the distinguished Ambassador and his elegant wife. Neither of whom spoke during the short ride. As they pulled up to the hotel, the Ambassador broke the silence—speaking as though Ursula was not present. In her dazed condition she heard or cared little.

He told his chauffeur, *"Helfen Sie Fräulein Von Ribbentrop zu ihrem Zimmer.* Help Miss Von Ribbentrop to her room. If there is a back elevator use it. Don't parade her through the lobby in her current condition. She is a very famous German and must be fully protected. I will call the embassy on the car phone to ask Doktor Hauser and his nurse to privately come over here to attend to her. Stay until they arrive. Don't leave her alone for a minute. We will be safe and will wait right here."

Ursula was stiff and sore the next morning and her lips were puffy. Her primary interest being her career, she ran straight to the full-length bathroom mirror. In order to view all of the damage, she dropped her robe to the floor. The efficient, but embarrassed, nurse followed on her heels.

"None of the marks will leave any scars, Fräulein Von Ribbentrop. Herr Doktor Hauser was very careful with you last night, both on your face and your body. Then he gave you a pill to relax and sleep."

Thus assured, Ursula requested the nurse to go into the living room—and immediately put in a call to Gar in London. She was the third exception. Surprised at how weak he sounded, Ursula aggressively inquired, "Are you sick? What's wrong with you today? You sound like I feel."

Ducking a direct answer, "Frankly, Urs, today is not a good day for a personal conversation. If I send my plane for you tomorrow are you free to come to London?"

"Depends on how I look. At this moment even with dark glasses, I'm a terrible sight. I will spend today resting in bed. Let's talk later this evening. Then we can plan tomorrow."

Cheryl awoke in the early afternoon with an aching body and a throbbing head. She was also completely disoriented.

"Where am I? Whose bed is this? And where did this silk nightgown come from?"

Sensing her confusion, Linette, a gray-haired female attendant, quickly came to her bedside. In heavily French-accented English, the woman told her where she was, and that, "Monsieur Oppert will see you whenever you feel up to it. Even tomorrow would be all right. He does not want you to worry or hurry yourself in any way. You are welcome to remain his guest for as long as you wish. He will take care of everything you need."

"That is very kind of him, Linette. Please express my deepest appreciation."

Remembering last night, Cheryl shuddered.

"Did it really happen? That bastard, Gar."

With her head back down on the square eiderdown pillow, once again she fell fast asleep.

In the early evening, Linette brought her some hot coffee and a warm buttered croissant. Later, a small bowl of clear broth with a pleasant tasting round French cracker. However, just the effort of sitting up to take the light nourishment, Cheryl felt like she had been run over by a train. And philosophized, "Maybe that would have been better."

Feeling a little stronger, she checked for messages at her hotel. The frequency and urgency of the calls from her Los Angeles office caused her to request the latest newspapers.

Forgetting the language barrier for a moment, the sympathetic Linette started, *"Est-ce que vous êtes assurément—"* Noting the blank expression on Cheryl's face, the kind Frenchwoman caught herself. "Oh, I'm so sorry." Starting over in English, "Do you really feel up to reading them now, Miss Blake?"

"Are they that bad?"

"Monsieur Oppert suggested that he would like to bring them in to you when you are ready. Is this the moment, Mademoiselle?"

After Linette lightly dabbed at her face with warm water and brushed her hair, Cheryl responded, "Yes, perhaps it is, Linette. Ask Monsieur Oppert to please come in."

The fallout from the unexpected debacle in Paris was not about to quickly disappear. Important consequences were unfolding—most of which would heavily impact Gar's life.

Back in New York, Wolf received two important calls regarding his future plans. The calls were back-to-back.

The first was from Noah Rembardt.

"Hello there old friend and warrior. I just happen to know that you haven't had much free time on your hands lately. I also assume you've resigned your job with Gar. But aside from becoming published as a world-famous scandalmonger, do you have any ideas about what you'd like to do for a real living."

"Can't say that I have."

"Well, I have. And I've got a great idea that involves both of us," Noah enthused.

"I haven't hung up yet so give it your best shot."

"My idea is for the two of us to become equal partners in my investigative agency."

"Are you are cold sober, Noah? Have you looked at your idea from all possible angles?"

"The answer to both is a resounding yes. We have always worked well together, and I need the kind of practical expertise you would bring to the table. Confidentially, I think it's one of the best ideas I've ever had."

"What kind of money would an arrangement like this require? I've been comfortable in my years with Gar, but I never shared in his windfalls."

"Money? Who's talking about money?"

"I am. If you want me to seriously consider your proposal, Noah, I've got to know the financial parameters of what I'm getting into. Getting in over my head is not my long suit. I'm more of a pay-as-you-go kind of guy. Makes me feel more comfortable. You know that. And by now, you probably know me better than anyone."

"We have total agreement on that. And that's precisely why I'm making you this offer. An offer that I certainly would not make to any other person. Now—the answer to your money question is simple. No money required. Your brain, your experience, and my trust in you, is all the currency you need to make this deal a reality. So—what do you say to that?"

"I guess I'm speechless, Noah. But somehow I'll manage to say that I accept your most generous offer—partner. By the way, if we need to beef up our staff, most of my guys from General Industrial will be available. Nobody will want to stay on with that double-crossing sonofabitch."

When Meyer Lansky's unmistakable voice—a rough mixture of small rocks and pebbles—came through Vikki's line, she was taken by surprise. It had been some time since they were briefly together in Nassau and Caracas. Although she still wore his lavish jewelry gifts and some of the designer clothes he had bought for her.

"Dat you Vikki? Ya sounds real good. Ya mus like livin' in dat rain. I gotta talk ta Gar."

"Mr. Lansky, he's not feeling well today. It would be better if he could call you back."

"Tell 'im he don't have ta talk—jus' listen. Tell 'im. Ya hear me, Vikki? Jus' tell 'im."

"Yes sir. I'll do that."

Almost immediately, a weak Gar spoke into the phone,

"Meyer, I feel like shit today, but it's good to hear your voice. Any trouble?"

"Der's always trouble, Gar. Ya knows dat. But nutin' I can't take care of. I was callin' ta see what was goin' on.

Da papers are killin' ya. I told ya for years not ta trust 'em cunts. Ya jus' don't lissen. What's da real scoop?"

Wolf's second call threw him for a complete loss.

"Wolf, dis iz Meyer."

"Meyer? We haven't been in touch for so damn long, I thought they had put you in front of a firing squad and you didn't have time to say goodbye."

"Naw. Everythin's nice n' quiet. 'Cept for Gar. What da fuck's goin' on wit yur boss?"

"Ex-boss. I don't work for him anymore, Meyer. I quit yesterday."

"Dat's bad, but good. Ya know I can use a guy like ya—now dat yur available. Between yur work for Gar an' MI-6, ya know a lot about a lotta stuff. An—"

"I'm already off the market, Meyer. I made a firm deal just before you called."

"Can ya change yur mind? I'll make it worth—"

"No can do, Meyer. You flatter me, but I'm very pleased with the decision I've made. But that has nothing to do with our personal friendship.

Here's my new number, Meyer.

Don't hesitate to call."

FIFTY-FIVE

Noah and Wolf spent their first dinner together in New York talking about their business future. Big dreams and endless planning. Over desert brandy they reminisced about the beginnings of their long time friendship.

Years back, their eagerness to work for Britain's foreign intelligence agency, MI-6, was based on retribution.

The fact that World War II had been over for nearly eight years made not a whit of difference to Noah, still seeking to inflict as much retaliatory pain as he possibly could on the Germans. The Dutchman would never forget the wartime horrors unleashed on his native Holland.

The Nazis had put to death Wolf's entire family in the gas chambers at Buchenwald. As the sole family survivor, who could have had greater reason for murderous hate in his heart? And convinced as he always would be, that in the deepest recesses of their hearts all Germans were still dedicated Nazis.

Now—wearing headsets and looking grim, Noah and Wolf were closely huddled in the rear of an old, unmarked pickup truck parked just off the Reeperbahn, in the North German Port City of Hamburg. The Reeperbahn was the notorious red light district of Hamburg, world-famous for its wide-open sex shows and outrageous brothels.

In the years before Bangkok achieved its highly sinful reputation, the most jaded of world travelers, male and female, desperate to find one last untried trick with man or beast, first thought of Hamburg as the place where any licentious urge was never more than a glance or call away.

Even locals confirm, "What you don't find here just does not exist—not even in anyone's fantasy. The Reeperbahn never disappoints."

That MI-6 assigned these two agents to the most British city on the Continent, with its private clubs and conservative attitudes, could have been right out of an old Clark Gable, Spencer Tracy movie. But of course, this was stark reality.

In the back of the truck, Wolf and Noah were entirely focused on listening to a 'sneaky', an electronic bugging device they had planted in a second-floor apartment across the street in a lower-class red brick building.

What these two British spies were so intent on hearing were voices they hoped belonged to three attractive Belgian female nationals. All still in their twenties, they were traitors who had been recruited as covert agents for the Russian KGB. A ruthless trio capable of causing serious international incidents. So far as was currently known to the CIA and MI-6, their only two interests seemed to be enraged sex and murder.

Recently, the CIA had managed to connect them to an especially grisly double murder. The victims were two freshman American CIA agents, sadly on their first foreign assignment. Initially, these well-trained but untested agents had worked with the team that designed and built 'catheter', the code name for the vital Berlin Tunnel. Dug under the infamous Berlin Wall, the tunnel was six hundred yards long, six feet high, and fifteen feet underground. It represented a major breakthrough for the CIA who could now tap into more than four hundred hitherto secret Soviet telephone lines—critical lines that connected the Soviet high command in East Berlin to the General Staff and

Foreign Office in Moscow—as well as all major Red Army units in East Germany and all of Eastern Europe.

In what was a serious breach of rules and regulations, the CIA had been able to learn that their two murdered agents had been picked up by the three female KGB agents in a small hotel bar along the Kurfürstendamm, West Berlin's main hotel and shopping thoroughfare. Earlier, they had also been reportedly seen by the doormen at two hotels—the Bristol and the Kempinski.

Undoubtedly promising things that most men would enjoy doing with three women, it seems likely they were lured to a fancy two-bedroom apartment in the Tiergarten Park section of the city—not far from where the new Berlin Philharmonic Hall would be built.

Missing for more than nine hours, the CIA's maximum unreported time, the men were ultimately found. Their throats had been deeply slashed and their penises had been brutally cut off. They bled to death from both ends.

Worse: The amputated sex organs were missing.

Left behind on a night table in the master bedroom was a large 10 x 13 portrait photograph of the world-famous German-American actress, Marlene Dietrich. During and after World War II, Dietrich had unselfishly traveled hundreds of thousands of miles and performed under some very dangerous circumstances to become one of the most popular of all U.S.O. entertainers of American troops.

She had put on spectacular morale-building shows everywhere in the world, including France, Belgium, and Germany. Wherever she performed, she brought down the house. The young G.I.'s simply went bananas for her.

Weird: The glass that protected the photographic face of the stunningly seductive Dietrich, certainly the most outrageous lesbian of her day, had been madly smeared with blood. Perhaps, done in a fit of extreme rage by a psychopath who desperately wanted to force-feed cock into her sensual photographic mouth.

Even alive that would have never worked. During all of her adult lifetime, Dietrich never denied that she preferred to eat cunt.

On one of her numerous trans-Atlantic ship crossings, Dietrich had unsuccessfully tried to seduce a female passenger, who was traveling with her husband. To that married woman, in one of the sexiest voices of all time, La Belle Dietrich had succinctly said it all.

"In Europe it doesn't matter if you're a man or a woman. We make love with anyone we find attractive."

From reliable sources, MI-6 was alerted that the Belgians were reportedly seen in Hamburg. Not surprisingly, on the Reeperbahn.

With London already suspicious that the Belgians might have been involved in the double-homicide in Berlin, MI-6 informed the CIA station chief in Berlin of the new development—and that two of their agents had already been dispatched to Hamburg.

Among the sounds and voices filtering through their earphones, Noah and Wolf suddenly heard something new coming from the apartment.

Wolf heard it first.

"Oh, oh. What's that?"

Pressing the headset hard against his ear, Noah frowned. "I wouldn't be surprised if those bitches might not be alone up there."

"Could be," said Wolf.

Noah: "Those are really strange noises. Something's definitely wrong up there."

"Let's wait a little longer," Wolf replied. "We don't want to blow it to these damn Hamburg Polizei. If we're wrong, London will be furious that we fucked up."

Nodding his head, Noah responded, "That's for sure."

They both refocused on what they were hearing.

Wolf: "Sounds as if there is another person up there. But that other voice sounds like it's muffled or…"

Noah finished, "…or worse."

Suddenly, Wolf ripped off his headset. "Holy shit, man, if you're thinking what I'm thinking—*Let's go!*"

Bouncing off the rear of the truck, they locked their illegal equipment inside. With guns drawn they raced across the street. As they stormed into the building they ran into a middle-aged woman tenant.

Noah yelled at her, *"Gehen Sie jetzt Anruf die Polizei. Im Moment!* Go call the police. Right now!"

Knowing exactly which door opened the apartment they were bugging, the two MI-6 agents hit the door together. They found out that a German door is as solid as a rock. Nothing happened.

Wolf yelled out. "Open up in there. British Intelligence!" Not a sound came from within the apartment. But the commotion caused most of the other apartment doors to cautiously open. Those elderly people were afraid to come into the corridor. The lady who went to call the police opened the door directly across from where the agents were standing. In her thick German accent, "Ja. I called 'em mister. I called the police like you said. They're coming right away. I told 'em you had guns."

With that, both agents instinctively knew they had run out of time. They had to go in. With a sweep of his hand, Wolf put Noah behind him and expertly fired point-blank at the door lock. Wood splinters flew and the door fell back from its lock. Guns at the ready, both men quickly shoved in. Nobody was home.

An open window to a back fire escape and a convenient sliding pole provided a quick answer. "Dammit," shouted Wolf, "We waited too long."

"Maybe not," Noah called back. "Come on in here. I'm sure we rushed them out before they were ready to leave" Following Noah's voice into a bedroom, Wolf stopped short. Looking up, "Oh my God—it's a woman. Think she's still alive?"

From the ceiling, a fully masked but otherwise naked woman's body was limply hanging from an old-fashioned brass chandelier. A rope around and under her arms held her up.

"I'm not sure," said Noah.

When they cut the body down and removed the mask, they found an unconscious young blonde woman. Barely breathing, they rushed her to a hospital by police ambulance.

While she had been badly beaten, the emergency room doctor said, "Für welch moralisch verdorbene Zweck...." He stopped in mid-sentence, apologizing for using the wrong language. Continuing on in his heavy German accent, "For whatever depraved purpose, they mostly used her mouth. But I am confident she will make a full recovery. You got her here just in time."

In mid-evening of her second day in the hospital, with her overworked mouth still very sore, she told them, "My name is Ursula—Ursula Von Ribbentrop. I am German and a model. Those three invited me to join them for a cocktail. I had the time and they seemed O.K. So I accepted. But those bitches put something in my daiquiri—and brought me to where you found me.

As he read the reportage in the London papers, Gar Grey was led to swift action. With good connections, he managed to quickly arrange a private meeting with MI-6 agent Felsenberg.

Not only did Wolf appear right on the minute, he quickly proceeded to impress Gar with his extraordinary range of knowledge. There was also his manly, self-assured bearing—another big hit with Gar. On the spot, he hired Wolf Felsenberg as his Director of Security. Neither man mentioned the young German woman in the story.

Never forgetting that she literally owed him her life, Ursula remained in touch with Wolf. From time to time, in out-of-the-way places, they would meet for an innocent dinner. Ursula felt safe and secure in Wolf's company. A refreshing change for her.

While her climb in the modeling world was upward, decision-making men much preferred to have Ursula either naked on her back—or half-naked on her knees. Sometimes with another woman or man—sometimes *only* with another woman. The number, gender, or even location really didn't matter. Ursula was willing to accommodate any fantasy. Every possible coital position. "I don't care if my ass or my face is up or down. It's all part of my job. My goal is always to be the best at whatever I am doing. And I am the best—the *very* best. You can just ask most *anybody.*"

It didn't take long to find out. On yet another of her many trans-Atlantic voyages, this time on Cunard's famous *S.S. Queen Mary,* the ultimate Berlin beauty, Marlene Dietrich, spotted the younger Berlin model, Ursula Von Ribbentrop—on her first crossing. Without wasting a moment Dietrich introduced herself.

All of her young life, Ursula had idolized Dietrich. Had pictures of her posted all over her bedroom walls—had even managed to have seen *The Blue Angel,* Dietrich's first great film success and Germany's first "talking" picture. A Berlin critic raved, "Dietrich's portrayal of Lola-Lola is one of the most vivid portrayals in all of film history." At last, Dietrich was a star.

Now—to actually meet the great Dietrich, currently the biggest box-office draw in the world—well—the young model was overwhelmed in every way.

Dietrich, dressed as she almost always was in a man-tailored suit, shirt, tie, and crushed fedora, was instantly recognized. Everyone pushed and shoved for her autograph. But the lesbian star coveted only Ursula. In those golden years, what Marlene wanted Marlene almost always got. She was dynamite. The epitome of sensuality.

"Come with me for a glass of champagne in my cabin, my beautiful Ursula." In a state approaching ecstasy the younger one could hardly wait.

Dietrich had the largest and best cabin-suite the *Queen Mary* had to offer. In a starched white uniform her cabin steward brought in a bottle of chilled French champagne—popped the cork, and poured two glasses. As he set them down on a low, round cherry wood table in front of a small sofa, the two gorgeous faces smiled up at him.

"If I can be of any further service, Fräulein Dietrich, please ring my bell." Dietrich, who had a great sense of humor, couldn't resist laughing. Telling the steward, "If we find that we're missing what you've got, I'd just love to ring your bell. But don't hold your breath waiting—sailor."

Alone together, the aggressive Dietrich turned full to Ursula. "You know that I like you very much, dear Ursula. Are you attracted to me?"

Almost swooning, Ursula managed, "Oh, yes, Miss Dietrich. Very much so."

"Just call me Lena, all my friends do. When I was trying to make my way at the beginning, I also was a model. Would you like me to model for you—right now?"

"It would be my absolute pleasure—Lena."

Rising, Dietrich leaned down and kissed the startled Ursula full on the mouth. "I will only be gone a minute or two, my pet. Think something sexy about me. I will think only of you."

The experienced actress used the thought process of a man on the make. She knew she had the young one hotter than fire. Saying to herself, "Stringing her out a little longer will only make later things taste even better."

She took a last glance in the full-length wall mirror, and gave herself an approving wink. Marlene reappeared wearing black patent pumps with five-inch spikes, very sheer black silk stockings which reached mid-thigh, accented by a sexy back seam which gave the exciting illusion of running straight up her ass. A narrow black satin garter belt held up her stockings.

Underneath—only a cleanly shaved, lightly powdered pussy. And the erogenous scent of Chanel No.5. She was bare from the waist up.

Ever the seducer, the licentious Dietrich always made use of everything she had. Among her many physical attributes, she had two enormous rose-colored nipples—which she loved to show. Always leading the parade, Dietrich was among the very first to have had her nipples pierced. Through the tiny pierced hole in each nipple hung 10mm round black pearl nipple-rings.

Spreading her legs, pushing her chest forward, she informed Ursula, "Pulling on my nipple-rings makes me come. It's my favorite way to masturbate."

Dangling her luscious tits in front of Ursula, her voice husky with emotion, "Pull on my nipple-rings, darling. And you can watch me have a giant orgasm." Ursula didn't know how to react to this daring proposal. Cleverly, Marlene eased off.

"Do you like me as a model, precious one? You can have any part of me that you want. I hope you want all of me. I'm certainly going to take all of you."

Without waiting, Marlene took the younger woman into her arms and kissed her in the most romantic French way. Before she knew it, Ursula was bare from the waist up and Marlene was sucking hard on her nipples.

Reacting hungrily, Ursula became the aggressor—dropping her clothing and panties. Totally naked and trembling with desire, Ursula leaned an eager mouth between the famous Dietrich legs. Never before, had Chanel No.5 tasted so delicious.

Waiting was no longer possible.

Words were no longer necessary.

In the middle of the rolling Atlantic Ocean—

Ursula and Lena happily offered their pulsating bodies to each other.

FIFTY-SIX

"You know, I get a migraine headache if I don't get a strange piece of ass everyday."

How typically Gar Grey can you get?

Right?

Wrong.

That raw, very macho remark was surprisingly made by the President of the United States, John F. Kennedy, in an Oval Office conversation with Bobby Baker, then secretary to the Senate Democratic Majority, and a star protégé of Lyndon Johnson, Kennedy's Vice-President.

Baker, a professional Capitol insider, was a sometime carouser with Kennedy back when JFK was still a senator from Massachusetts. Baker also helped to keep the good times going after JFK became President.

At a minimum, he procured the beautiful German prostitute, Ellen Romsetch. And while the stunning Elizabeth Taylor look-a-like may have alleviated Kennedy's migraines as many as ten times, the pleasure was not without its downside risk.

Romsetch, who had come to America in 1961 with her husband, a West German army sergeant assigned to his country's military mission in Washington, was a former member of East German Communist youth organizations.

Her new high-style life, however, had caused a serious new problem. She was not sufficiently tight-lipped about whom she was sleeping with. And she had been intimate with some very important capitol big wigs. Senators, Congressmen—and Gar Grey!

Nor was the brunette beauty reserved about letting her friends know that she was also invited to naked pool parties at the Kennedy White House.

Gar was also present at a few of those wet blasts. He was both an important fund-raiser and a long-time personal friend of John F. Kennedy. Mightily worried about the disastrous Romsetch consequences, Gar took the initiative of bringing her to New York for a private lunch in his opulent Hotel Pierre apartment.

After lunch was served in his large formal dining room, Gar told her, "You're playing with fire, Ellen. Neither Bobby Baker nor I, will allow you to continue going around Washington bragging about with whom you are having sex. If you don't understand what I'm saying, you'd better tell me right now. Frankly, I think you understand everything." After that lunch, Gar never saw nor spoke to Ellen Romsetch again.

Tipped off in July, 1963, that she might even have been a Communist plant, the FBI came to ask Romsetch some questions. Ultimately, two events occurred.

First, the Burcau, with cooperation from certain German authorities, escorted Romsetch back to West Germany. But she was not happy there. She wanted to return to the U.S. to marry an American. When told that would never happen, she began issuing veiled threats.

With the 1964 election only a little more than year away, the Kennedy brothers took her threats seriously. Attorney-General Bobby Kennedy, on behalf of his brother, went so far as to send a personal emissary to see Romsetch in West Germany—with sufficient convincing money. Romsetch sent thanks for the money.

Then, added, "Of course I will keep quiet."

With Romsetch under control, Gar and JFK got a breather—but not for long.

Datelined London, the British tabloid press dubbed the world-shattering news, "The Profumo Scandal!"

The sex-charged story was centered at Cliveden, Viscount Astor's famous country estate. The enormous 400-acre Astor family home at Buckinghamshire, whose renowned mansion overlooked the River Thames, was the setting for much lavish entertaining. Dinners for fifty or sixty guests often took place. And elegant balls for five or six hundred were given two or three times each season for the elite upper crust.

Against that extravagant background, it was at Cliveden that the British war minister, Lord John Dennis Profumo, was charged with having been intimate with a twenty-one year old call girl, Christine Keeler. Stephen Ward, an osteopath friend of Lord "Bill" Astor, introduced Profumo to Keeler while he was quite naked in the swimming pool.

While all the world loves a lover, the world seems to particularly love the juicy tidbits those lovers leave behind. If this breaking story had not been shockingly true, it surely would have made blockbuster fiction. But, of course, some of the juiciest facts were not made public.

As it was, the known bare facts set off a series of international crises that would cause JFK and at least one other world-class womanizer to cool it—to take pause.

True, George Garfield Grey, the "other" man, was still legally married, but he had not lived with his wife, Ellen, for many years. In this case, Gar's main problem was his wounded ego—about to be splattered all over the frontpages. Again.

On the other hand, John F. Kennedy had a problem of far broader dimensions. Not only was he still married to his famous wife, Jackie—he also held down the biggest job in the world!

The first part—the "Jackie" part—did not seriously trouble Kennedy. Whatever it was that Jackie knew had never stopped his bed hopping before. And, since childhood, Jackie had been taught that emotional pain, if there ever was any, was never to be shown to the world outside of Hammersmith Farm, the swanky estate in Rhode Island where she spent most of her childhood. In high WASP social circles, to allow others to witness your pain would have been considered a gauche sign of weakness.

More to the point, Jackie and her father-in-law, Joseph P. Kennedy, had done business before and shared a mutual respect for hard cash. Regardless of source or reason, payment in cash was more like—like unreported earned income. Cheating the IRS is considered quite respectable.

For Jack Kennedy, the explosive part of "Profumo" lay in the political dynamic. Everyone knew that playing with danger had long been a key element in the Kennedy mystique. The consummate political animal, JFK could instinctively sense brewing political trouble. He could almost smell it in the wind. And quickly move to head it off.

But this was a case with a foreign birth certificate—impossible for Kennedy to control. Not only would "Profumo" not go away, there was not so much as a distant sign of relief anywhere on the horizon. Indeed, it had become daily front-page fare. A nightmarish kind of international soap opera, it sold millions of newspapers. So long as readers relished every word, it would be milked for as long as possible.

Hence, the similar profiles of JFK and war minister Profumo—also a young and popular politician, also a decorated war hero, also married to a famous woman—the talented English actress, Valerie Hobson.

All of these coincidental facts quickly grabbed JFK's

attention. He loved political history, especially low dalliances in high places. Forget emotional attachments. Consider only the pure sport of it all.

Perhaps, it was a case of like father, like son. Old Joe Kennedy had always been a cold stone, but simply loved chasing women—of any age. And he had caught more than a few, including the famous actress, Gloria Swanson.

Some women JFK had bedded also complained of his lack of emotional involvement. Never any foreplay. Just slam bam—and thank you m'am. Laughing, Gar once said to JFK, "Jack, you're the only 'Automatic President' in history."

While he never disclosed it to any of his many sexual partners, JFK's fast sexual encounters may have been related to the fact that for many years he suffered from venereal disease. Somehow, he might have thought faster was safer. There was also Addison's Disease, which he always denied having. And his chronically aching back, which caused him to wear an uncomfortable brace.

Under any normal set of circumstances what the world already knew about "Profumo" would have been juicy enough. But wait—what the world already knew only proved to be the tip of much larger iceberg.

Early on, Christine Keeler learned how to play the game and keep score. As a teenager in Middlesex, she had already lost her virginity at fifteen. By sixteen, she was hanging around a London pub called the Angel, and picking up GI's from nearby air bases. At that tender age, Keeler was also frequently satisfying what had already become a fixation—a strong sexual preference for dangerous black men. The bigger the better.

As one thing led to another, Keeler met another dancer, Mandy Rice-Davies. Together they developed a specialty—threesome sex. Under these recreational circumstances, they entertained any number of well-known socialites—both male and female. More good money and good times. As a British national security issue, however, a far more serious fact had been learned.

In addition to the war minister, Christine Keeler was also sleeping with Soviet naval attaché Evgeny Ivanov, a known spy, attached to the Soviet embassy in London. It had been further learned that Ivanov had asked Keeler to find out from Profumo, among other state secrets, when nuclear warheads would be delivered to West Germany. Mind you, not "if", but "when." The Soviets had done their homework.

Ultimately, Profumo confessed that he had previously lied to the House of Commons—and promptly resigned. By October, 1963, the clamor had become so politically damaging, it finally brought down the Conservative Party government of Prime Minister Harold MacMillan.

Although it strains the outer limits of credibility, overlooked in the original hubbub at Cliveden was the startling fact that there was yet another young woman present. Like Keeler, she was also nakedly preoccupied with the much older friend who had invited her—a former Foreign Office minister and a far more important name than John Profumo would ever be.

Considering the enormous fallout from the "Profumo Scandal," the overlook may have been a cover-up for an even worse national outrage. It could also have been a courtesy extended due to the diplomat's long friendship with Sir Roger Hollis, Director-General of MI-5.

The name of this undiscovered sexpot was Ursula Von Ribbentrop, whom Gar already knew. Later on, she became his long-time lover. Ergo, his interest in her presence at Cliveden.

Names of additional international playgirls began making news.

One tabloid shouted,

"THE CZECH AND SUZY CHANG!"

Mariella Novotny was a twenty-two year-old prostitute of Anglo-Czech parentage. She claimed to have been at a party at the Hampshire House in New York, when the

"Senator" took her into any empty bedroom and had quick sex. She said it happened again, later on, at an apartment in Gracie Square. She also detailed a group orgy at the Carlyle Hotel, Kennedy's well-known New York base.

Suzy Chang was an aspiring actress and sometime model, born in Tientsen, China, who traveled in all the right London circles. Kennedy admitted that he took Chang to dinner at the "21" Club in New York. She also received preferential treatment in getting on the China visa quota. For whatever the reason, somebody high and mighty wanted to help Suzy Chang.

Investigative government agencies on both sides of the Atlantic as well as the world press, were aggressively pushing every angle of the "Profumo" case. The key question buzzing around Washington had a central theme—repeated over and over. "Were any American officials involved or even linked to the scandal?" Both the agent in charge of the CIA station in London, as well as the FBI representative there, were being bombarded from Washington.

Find out! Find out! Find out!

And, in point of fact, both Kennedy brothers were being linked. A top-level FBI memo written on October 26, 1963 read, "Information has been developed that pertains to possible questionable activities on the part of high government officials. It was also alleged that the President and the Attorney-General had availed themselves of services of playgirls."

With this kind of dangerous leaking information, things were now rapidly spinning out of control. No longer was there any doubt about it.

The Profumo Scandal was coming to America!

Which begs two monumental questions, even all these years later. If it were not for the fierce intervention of a most unlikely pair—JFK's brother Bobby, the Attorney General, his own linkage notwithstanding, and J. Edgar Hoover, the Kennedy-hating director of the FBI—is it not reasonable to assume, at an irreducible minimum, that the on-rushing Profumo Scandal might have forced changes in President Kennedy's travel schedule?

That said, does it not logically follow that he might *not* have been in Dallas only weeks later, on that tragic November 22nd?

FIFTY-SEVEN

"Noah, there is something terribly important that I alone know. But now that we are partners, we might as well share all of our secrets. Although, this one is not easy for me to admit out loud—even to you. We don't have to look any longer for Oskar's murderer. On Gar's order, I had it done."

Noah asked incredulously, "And that's the whole damn story?"

Assured that it was, "So, what's the big deal? We both know that murder is not uncommon in our kind of business."

"True enough. But, it was the unusual ending that made it so—different." Wolf hesitated, then blurted out, "Oskar was snuffed out by a boa constrictor."

"Well, I guess that settles the Oskar question. It's good to know that you've still got some creativity left in you, my friend. Anything else still leftover from your old agenda that you want to get off your chest?"

"Yes, there is one other important item, Noah. We still don't know *why* Gar wanted Oskar out of the way. Personally, I liked him. He was a good facilitator. Got the job done."

"Do you have a starting place, Wolf—any clues?"

"Not based on anything solid."

"To hell with solid. You worked for the guy for years. You must have some leads."

"That, I do. Franz Ritter, Gar's lawyer in Liechtenstein, is firm in his belief that Oskar's fate is somehow tied-in with a break-in that occurred in his underground vault. Some of Gar's oil documents were in the vault, but nothing was stolen."

"So what's Ritter's rationale for his theory?"

"Two things. One, is that his vault is secured by a poison gas system, designed by his friends at IG Farben. And it killed one of the burglars. A young Arab. That's Ritter's oil connection."

"In my book, at best, that only represents a 'maybe.' What's the other one?"

As briefly as possible, Wolf related the weird story Oskar told him from his hospital bed. Noah listened quietly. Not a word.

Wolf inquired, "What's the matter? You look stunned."

"Stunned might be a bit strong, but I certainly am shocked at the unbelievable coincidence. I'm trying to get this story straight in my mind."

"Shoot when you're ready."

"In this Riviera story you just told me about Oskar, are you talking about Angelique Cuvier the old French tennis champ?

"Yes I am. Oskar told me about Cuvier."

"And she had a black guy with her all the time—I think his name was Etienne. He was her real live sex slave, right?"

"I don't remember anything about a sex slave, Noah. But, what else do you know that I should know?"

"We were able to confirm that this broad, Cuvier, made a lot of dough playing tennis. But she made much more as a whore and a lady pimp for her black slave. As the saying goes, 'She had him by the balls.' He blindly obeyed whatever she told him to do. Never a question. I think he would have jumped off a cliff for her. And that's one hell of a lot of control."

"For sure. But, how do you come to know all of this stuff?"

"That's the crazy coincidence. We had a case, a few years back—a blackmail case. We were retained by a famous Brit who was a member of the House of Lords. Eventually, the whole thing got mixed in with some of the details of the 'Profumo Scandal.' Working for Gar, I know you must remember that one."

"You're right. I remember it in great detail."

"But you might not recall, that Mariella Novotny eventually got married and became London's premier orgy hostess. The man she married was a voyeur—and a friend of Stephen Ward, who introduced Profumo to Christine Keeler. Mariella's husband didn't care how she carried on, or with whom, as long as she let him watch. And Ward was well-known for being able to produce whatever the occasion called for."

"Hold on, Noah. Gar also knew Stephen Ward and believed there was some kind of a past sexual connection between Ward and his Ursula. I was even present once when he confronted her with his suspicion. Of course, she denied any connection with Ward except that they had been long-time good friends. And in her defense Ursula claimed Ward had many platonic women friends. She was not his only one.

In his suspicious mind, naturally, never for a moment did Gar believe her story of how she came to be at the infamous Cliveden pool with Profumo and Christine Keeler."

He accused her again and again, "You were one of Ward's party girls—one of his *popsies.*"

"No. No. No," Ursula wailed. "I tell you the truth, but you still don't believe me. You only want to believe the worst. If I made up a sexy lie that would make you happier."

It really didn't matter. Whatever Ursula said the raving Gar would not let go of his suspicion. In some grotesquely distorted way, it lingered and festered deep in his wounded psyche.

Eventually, the inevitable blowoff occurred.

At an important wedding reception, Gar directly confronted Stephen Ward. And it quickly became ugly. Once he got started Gar was unstoppable. Arms flailing, his face beet red, he was shouting outrageous accusations at Ward. Hurling dirt that he was inventing as he spoke. Prominent names were being trashed. Husbands, wives, whores, lovers, and every kind of pervert were all lumped together. Nobody was spared. Humiliated and infuriated, Ursula left in a rage. The doorman called her a taxi.

"Jeez, Noah, I haven't thought about that stuff in a long time. Then, what happened?"

"What happened in the case we were working on was this. Lord Shetland got horny one night. Looking for some fun, he found more than what he was looking for. In some sleazy dive frequented by some big names who were also out prowling, he ran into this Angelique broad and her black slave friend.

Her sexy French accent and scanty skirt, which barely covered her rock-hard buns when she sat on a barstool, seriously intrigued the nobleman. When she crossed her bare legs, exposing all that exciting suntanned flesh, he was a goner. They started some silly conversation. Bought each other a few drinks. Got a little high.

While Cuvier was a confirmed lesbian, she was smart enough to know that business still came first. She rubbed her tight, slim body against the Brit's front. Simultaneously, Etienne pushed his perpetually hard cock against His Lordship's soft butt..."

"And the rest is history, right?"

"Not quite so fast. Into the same joint up popped the one and only Christine Keeler and immediately went bonkers over this black Etienne guy. The sharp-minded Angelique put two and two together and offered all of them a deal nobody could refuse.

Back in her large hotel suite, the ex-tennis champ provided everyone with some potent dope. In no time, they all became really high—especially His Lordship. Not used to the strong stuff, he was stoned out of his mind."

"Great story, Noah."

"Angelique told Christine she would make it worth her while to be patient. Assuring her that she would get her black cock reward before the night was through.

But first things first.

They undressed His Lordship on the sofa. In a matter of minutes, Christine worked him into a tizzy with her stimulating combination of menthol-oiled hand pumping and hot wet kisses—tonguing all of his erogenous zones. Unsteady with wanton lust and a burning cock from the menthol-oil, the two women helped him into a bedroom.

There, Angelique with a top quality camera in hand, ordered Etienne to do his favorite trick. Immediately, he proceeded to suck on the barely hard, pale white cock staring him in the face. In a his present state, His Lordship begged for more.

Cuvier then told Keeler to sit on his face—and grind her pelvis. His Lordship nearly lost his mind. A weak orgasm followed. Completely underwhelmed, Etienne wanted to try for something much more. But, Cuvier told him, "Anything more might kill the bastard."

Besides, she already had all the pictures she could possibly use. And they turned out to be of unusually good quality."

"How the hell did you get the peer out of this unholy mess?"

"I can tell you, Wolf, it was not easy or cheap. After all, this was about the total character assassination of a famous Englishman. And Cuvier knew the blackmail value of her pictures. Every time we got close to a deal, she nonchalantly jacked up the price. And so far she was winning this dangerous game.

While still properly frightened, Lord Shetland had come to the end of his resources. And come what may, told me the top money he could raise. I convinced Cuvier to take it, or she could do whatever she wanted with the pictures.

Unwilling to leave so much as an extra shilling on the table, Cuvier still attempted to extort even more. She finally sensed the end of the line and agreed to simultaneously exchange pound sterling notes for the pictures and negatives."

The show was over.

FIFTY-EIGHT

After Cheryl had retained Noah Rembardt on the aborted search to determine Wolf's loyalty, Noah felt the need to have a final conversation. He called Cheryl at her Beverly Hills office.

"I'm terribly sorry, Mr. Rembardt, but Miss Blake is not here. However, if you did call she instructed me to tell you to get in touch with her in Paris—at Mr. Oppert's residence." He did.

In the late-afternoon, Paris time, "Noah, I'm so pleased to hear from you. After all that has happened, I was not sure that you would make the effort. What's new? Please, bring me up to date. Yes—Yes, I knew that Wolf had left Gar. It's about time. What? You and Wolf are now partners? Noah, that's great. You two should be fabulous together.

About me?

Well, Paul Louis wants me to stay on here with him. He's so kind and thoughtful, Noah, I've already become deeply attached to him. He tells me that his heart has been waiting for me all of his life. And the magic is that I truly believe him.

In these last days, he talks about marriage. Hell, Noah, I might even surprise myself and say "yes." It's such a far cry from the turbulence with Gar, a girl could get used to this tranquillity.

Oh—By the way, you should know that we are planning a trip to New York and L.A. so that I can begin to wind down my business affairs. It would be great if we can arrange a lunch or dinner. We'll talk some more about it. It really would be great fun.

Well, dear Noah, I can't fully put into words how truly delighted I am that you called. Please give my regards to Wolf. Along the way, remember, if I can be of any help, you can find me here. Don't ever forget, you guys will always be my two best friends."

The mood of another inter-continental phone call was not nearly as cordial.

From his law office in tiny Vaduz, Liechtenstein, Gar's lawyer, Franz Joseph Ritter, was talking on a secure line to a friend—a high-ranking Saudi Arabian prince in Riyadh, the desert kingdom's capital city.

The subject was oil. It was *always* about oil.

Ritter had become an internationally renowned lawyer and advisor to royalty, giant corporations, and wealthy people everywhere, not merely because he was good, he was more than good—he was *the best*.

Someone once remarked, "Franz is only human, surely he must have made a mistake somewhere along the line. It's just that nobody can remember when or what the hell it was."

Ritter continued on his secure line phone conversation. "But, Your Royal Highness, the original option document between your Father and the Vatican made no mention, whatsoever, of Iran, in general, or the Shah, in particular. Therefore, all these years later for you to unilaterally insert Iranian petroleum statistics into an addendum to the original document, I must respectfully inform Your Highness is most irregular. And I might add, is surely not in keeping with your late Father's legendary tradition of a bargain made is a promise forever.

Kindly also remember, sir, at the time the option was granted to the Vatican, using the Atlantic Overseas Bank in Nassau as a front, the Saudi royal family was sorely pressed for the substantial gold funds that the Church readily advanced. And I might add, that it was a most unusual arrangement as between the Mother Church in Rome and a Muslim anti-Catholic nation in the heart of the unstable Middle East.

Moreover, the revelation of his hitherto secret oil statistics would undoubtedly deeply offend and embarrass the Shah. And would be certain to cause irreparable damage to the present stable relationship that exists between Iran and Saudi Arabia. To say nothing of the fact that these revelations would surface so soon after his tumultuous restoration to the Peacock throne.

For these and numerous other reasons, I urge Your Highness not to push further with this sudden and unexpected idea. If we can have concurrence, sir, you have my solemn word never to mention this subject again to a living person."

In the years that followed, the restored Shah had grandiose plans for Iran. Which enormously pleased official Washington.

The U.S. desperately wanted to sell him anything he wanted to buy, including the latest military hardware and aircraft. The Shah's buying spree, generated by his newly found oil revenue, was essential to keep Lockheed, Northrop, and eventually Gar's General Aircraft, up and running. Keep in mind, in post-World War II there wasn't much aircraft business around. Every country lined up for the Shah's checkbook.

Heading that line was Marcel Dassault who very badly needed an Iranian order for his French Mirage fighter planes. Dassault had only been selling a small numbers of outdated planes to Israel. Without many friends, and without much money or credit, the infant

Jewish democracy was willing to buy any aircraft it could procure.

But Israeli Prime Minister David Ben Gurion was more interested in establishing a long-term strategic relationship with Washington. Throughout the Eisenhower years, he was unsuccessful. Secretary of State John Foster Dulles, rich with Arab oil money, made sure of that.

In any event, Ben Gurion didn't trust the long-term prospects of the French—who were still hoping for some kind of economic miracle from their mandate in Lebanon. That never happened.

In the end, the wild card turned out to be Paul Louis Oppert who still owned all the Dassault stock left to him by his Father—Dassault's original partner.

FIFTY-NINE

In the years after the Iranian oil turmoil, and still haunted by the specter of what might have conceivably happened, Gar Grey continued to spend most of his time in London, with occasional short trips to Washington and New York.

Uninvolved in any current personal relationship, the chief benefactor of his almost constant single presence was his London executive assistant, Victoria Tracy.

In order to enter Gar's sanctum sanctorum, one first had to pass through Vikki's adjoining office. And she guarded his private office door with a fierce determination. If she had reason, you might cool your heels a long time before you got in to see the boss. Behind her back, other staffers referred to her as, *Vikki the bitch*. Their envy was palpable. And with little wonder.

Day after day in the Control Room, Vikki was the principal focus. A clothing designer's dream, financially aided by Gar as she had been earlier by Meyer Lansky, the tall, slender, milk chocolate beauty was nothing less than dazzling. Not easily achieved in broad daylight. But then the faux lighting in Gar's hanging office merely reflected the decorating genius of Pierre Montaigne. No matter, Vikki Tracy was stunning in *any* light.

Sheer dynamite in the dark.

And not for a minute was any of Vikki's dramatic sex appeal lost on Gar. *Au contraire.* To the contrary.

However, because of their enormous background differences, Gar seriously thought that any affair with Vikki could never be a long-range proposition. Nevertheless, he enjoyed the casual mental exercise derived from the planning of his Vikki conquest—which he now visualized as a two-act play.

Seemingly content, and at his creative best when he was on the make, most everyday he added exciting new twists to his plot. As he and Vikki went on working closely together, the more he thought about his two-act play, the more fixed he became on a title taking root in his fertile imagination.

"That's it all right—that's the right title. I'll call this play, 'The Proposition.' After all, that's just what I'm leading her up to."

At the end of each day it became more and more apparent to him that Vikki was hesitant about leaving the office. Always stalling. Constantly making excuses for staying longer. Never knowing who might be coming through her office door at any moment, she was always careful to show total respect.

"Will that be all sir? If there is nothing more, I'll be leaving now."

"That's fine, Vikki. Good night."

He knew his indifference was getting to her. Even arousing her. And Gar gloried in that idea. Feeling frivolous and lighthearted about it, he smiled to himself, confident that he was instilling all kinds of doubt in her as to why he was not coming on to her.

After all, all men came on to Vikki Tracy.

But Gar never would have thought in a million years that this time—or anytime—the roles might be reversed.

He was startled as Vikki returned after being gone only about ten minutes. "I'm sorry, Mr. Grey, I forgot to put something away in your bedroom. It will only take me a minute or two. This way, I won't have to remember it in the morning"

"That's fine, Vikki. I have a few things to do yet. Don't rush."

In the next seconds, Gar realized that what he had just said was a double-entendre. He wondered, "Would she hear it that way?" But his instincts alone should have told him it was foolish to have wasted his time. Vikki Tracy was as sharp as they come—speaking of double-entendres. When minutes came close to an hour. He mused, "Where the hell is that broad?"

As he double-locked his two office doors and headed into his private living suite—in his gut, Gar knew. But this was not the way he had been writing his script. "Vikki is stealing my plot lines."

At the very back of his private living suite, his sumptuous bedroom was in darkness—except for the red-orange glow of a burning cigarette. Instinctively, he knew Vikki was on the bed.

"Well, Well—Mr. Grey, do you keep all of your girls waiting this long?"

"That all depends."

"On what, may I ask?"

"On what they're waiting for."

"In this case you already know what I'm waiting for. I've all but put my hot pussy on your desk. But, that's behind us now. What would you like me to do for you, right now?"

"Use your most vivid imagination, Vikki. Act out your wildest fantasy. I'm in a totally cooperative mood."

He heard her get off the king-size bed.

He heard soft things falling on the carpet.

He felt her heat next to him.

"Even in the darkness, I can see you," he said.

She reached for his hand, saying "Sometimes touching can be even better than seeing."

She put his right index finger into her hot mouth and

gave it a quick suck. Then, Vikki put his arms around her naked body.

"Kiss me, Gar. Kiss me so deep down you'll taste my wet cunt all the way up in your mouth."

Kissing her deeply, Gar felt her body sizzle against his clothes. He held her until she ran out of breath. Then, Vikki quietly sat down on the edge of the bed.

"Come here, baby. Let me make you more comfortable. You're all dressed up and there's only one place I want you to go—and it's inside. You won't need any clothes. I'll be in charge of your temperature. As it rises, this chocolate treat will melt in your mouth."

Gar teased, "Like a Hershey bar?"

"More like hot fudge—and you can lick off my whipped cream topping."

"MMMmmm. When do I get to do that?"

"As soon as I tell you tell a fantastic story. My wildest fantasy. I was only a punk teenager but it made a lasting impression. Some older guy who had the hots for me took me to see a private sex show in a plantation mansion on the outskirts of Kingston. It was summer and it was hot. Everybody stripped down nice and naked. The lights went out. And some reggae music began. Mighty sexy stuff, Gar."

"Did you get excited, Vikki?"

"Better believe I got excited—*very* excited. And since I love to dance, I got up alone and started to move to the reggae beat.

A stud got up to join me. He looked just like a young Harry Belafonte—or so I thought then. Do you know what reggae sounds like, Gar?"

"Only in a general way."

"Well, it has three major elements—calypso, soul, and rock 'n' roll. And it's got a strongly accentuated offbeat. Anyway, this young stud not only worked up a great sweat in the steamy room—he also worked up a huge hard cock.

Then, out of nowhere, a pretty white woman, about thirty or so, came on to the floor and joined in our lusty dancing. Of course, she was also naked and well stacked. That made three of us. From the dark shadows a man's voice rang out. "Why don't you fuck them both, big Harry? So we can all watch the double action."

The voice, the music, the name 'Harry', probably the combination of all three, completely pulled her chain. No doubt the size of that potent black porker also had a lot to do with her reaction. I had seen plenty of cock since I was a kid, Gar. Every boy wanted to show me what he had—and I didn't. But Harry's was something else."

"What happened next?" asked a very stimulated Gar.

"That white lady moved in like a cat. In a flash, she was down on her knees in front of Harry and had that humongous porker half way down her throat. That triggered a near panic among several more white ladies in the group who had the same idea. They quickly raced onto the floor screaming, 'We want some of that, too.'

I'll never forget that scene. It was unreal. You'd think that punk Harry had the only black cock in the world.

Lucky for me, the guy who brought me to the show came right out to rescue me from the madness. He told me that I didn't have to fuck anybody—unless I wanted to. And then I should get big bucks. Especially, if I was willing to put on my own sex show. He thought I was the best."

Gar broke in, "Hold your fantasy right there, Vikki, you've already got me on the verge of orgasm. I need…"

Gar felt Vikki's hot mouth engulfing his throbbing cock. He shivered at her touch.

She sucked. She licked.

She pulled on his nipples. She deep-throated him.

Not able to hold back any longer, Gar vigorously shot his cum into her mouth. Load after load, Vikki swallowed every last drop. At last, she kissed him on his lips. It was the first time he had ever tasted himself.

Flipping her over, Gar mounted and shoved his dripping cock in as deep as it would go. Vikki's orgasm was almost immediate—shouting four-letter words.

When things calmed down, Gar turned to her and inquired, "Was it worth the wait?"

"It was great—for an appetizer. But, the night's still young. Let's go out and do something outrageous for our entrée. You game for some good hard stuff, big guy?"

"I can handle anything you can, Vikki."

"Good, let's shower and go get ourselves some down and dirty London."

"Okay, but there are two things I want to do first."

Gar rolled over and took a tender dark nipple into his mouth—putting pressure on it.

Vikki purred, "Delicious, baby. But, I'm crying for you inside."

Gar pushed himself down—face to face with Vikki's cunt. Like a serpent, his tongue flicked. Again. And again.

She screamed, "Now it's my turn to cum in *your* mouth. Like right *nooowww!*"

Great nights.

Lewd and raunchy nights.

Memorable nights.

None of them telegraph in advance. They just happen.

As Gar and Vikki left the Control Room, the Jamaican beauty who had wrapped herself in a white, silk-satin trench coat, with extra-large mother-of-pearl buttons and a double-wide belt, never moved her eyes right or left. She knew the look in the eyes of the security men. She had it memorized in her brain. Now they knew what they had only guessed. Gar didn't care. He knew who signed their checks.

As Gar and Vikki approached his limousine, his driver, Howland, told him that the trading floor was holding on-line—and handed him the car phone.

"Grey here. Yes, Ram, what's up? A run on copper? Interesting. There's no shortage of the metal. Do you guys have any idea of where the buy orders are coming from? Maybe Paris. How high has it run up? I see. Frankly, I think this is a bullshit operation—all show—no muscle.

We were short copper yesterday, right? Well, obviously, somebody has been fed what they think is reliable inside information. And that they've got me by the balls. Ram, did we make an attempt to cover our old short position? You say about half got covered? That's not too bad. Okay—this is what we do now. Start shorting more. You do it, Ram—only you. Don't say anything to anybody else. Offer as many tons as they want—but keep it orderly. I don't want a panic on our hands. When they run out of buying power, we'll make our next move. I'm going to teach the bastards behind this squeeze a lesson they'll never forget.

I'm off to dinner now. Stay in touch with the car. Howland will know where I am."

As they settled into the rear of the limo, Howland inquired, "Your pleasure, sir?"

"Le Jardin."

With that, Gar closed the special barrier between front and back seats. For sure, he wanted to show off his new chocolate beauty. And Le Jardin, perhaps the finest French restaurant in all of London, attracted the most elite crowd.

Turning to Vikki, Gar received a shock. She had unbuttoned her trench coat. Beneath the white silk-satin, she was stark naked.

Unfortunately, the ring of the car phone interrupted the incendiary moment.

"Grey, here. Yes, Ram, it's perfectly all right. What have you got?

"Mr. Grey, sir, I've just been informed by a reliable connection in Paris that our hunch was correct. The copper buying has been traced to an aide of French President DeGaulle. This guy, who is with the Finance Ministry, has been secretly handing off buy orders to commodity brokers all over the world to make it that much harder to trace the real buyer.

And, sir, the strange thing is that, while the copper is being bought by the government finance agency it is not in the name of France—but rather in the name of a fellow by the name of Dassault—Marcel Dassault. Do you know who he is?"

"Indeed I do Ram. I know her quite well, as a matter of fact."

"Sir—I don't mean to be disrespectful, but Marcel is a man, not a woman."

"Right you are, Ram."

Puzzled, but not pushy, Ram asked, "Do you have any further instructions for me, sir?"

"Stand where you are on copper. I'll get back to you."

Picking up the car intercom: "Howland, the plans have changed. We'll drop Miss Tracy at her apartment—then, we're going back to the office."

As soon as Vikki was out of the limo, Gar was back on the car phone.

"Ram, forget what I said before. Short all you can.

A bitch is about to be spayed."

SIXTY

Back in his office, Gar put in a call to Paris.

"Good evening, madam, please excuse the hour. This is George Garfield Grey in London. May I please speak to Monsieur Oppert? Yes, it is a *very* personal call. We are old friends."

"I am sorry, Mr. Grey, but M. Oppert is not here. He is away on his honeymoon."

Gar was shocked. But managed, "How wonderful. It must have been quite sudden. Madam, if you know how to reach M. Oppert, I would appreciate…"

"One moment, sir, I must check something here. Ah, yes, here is your name on M. Oppert's preferred call list. Inasmuch as your name appears here, I am permitted to tell you M. Oppert's current whereabouts. You may reach him at the Beverly Hills Hotel. That is in Los Angeles, California. In the United States."

"Yes, I know where it is, madam, and thank you so much for your help."

"Good evening, the Beverly Hills Hotel, how may I direct your call?"

"Mr. Paul Oppert, please."

Cheryl's voice, laughing: "Go away. Don't you know we're on our honeymoon?"

"Congratulations, Cheryl—it's Gar."

Coldly. "I still recognize your voice. I'll get Paul."

"Gar, what a pleasant surprise. What brings you on the phone tonight?"

"First off Paul, congratulations. I wish you and Cheryl all the luck in the world."

"Merci, Gar. Merci beaucoup."

"Paul, excuse the interruption, but it could not wait."

"It's quite all right, Gar. Tell me what is wrong, my friend."

"I know that it has been years since you were involved in the day-to-day affairs of Dassault Aviation. But, I have a very good reason to ask. Do you still own your Dassault stock?"

"Yes I do, Gar. Never sold a share. Those were my Father's instructions. Why?"

"Something strange is going on, Paul. You know that I hedge all of our commodities. Our worldwide manufacturing needs are so enormous, at all times we must protect our cost basis. The subject here is copper. These days, there is no shortage of the actual metal, and yet copper futures for near-term delivery are under frantic accumulation. You'd think the world was getting ready to start World War III."

"If you are calling me, Gar, you must have some reason to believe that I might know who the buyer is. *Est je corrige?* Am I correct?"

"I'm not just blowing wind Paul, you *do* know the buyer—and very well. A few hours ago, our head trader informed me that we had finally been able to trace the source of the buying. Our trace not only zeroed in on metro Paris, but led directly to a far more serious single source—a financial aide to your President DeGaulle."

"DeGaulle? *Mon Dieu.* My God."

"This guy, reportedly with the Finance Ministry, has

been secretly handing off 'buy' orders to commodity brokers all over the world.

But here's the catch, Paul. The real buyer is not your government at all. The contracts are being bought in the name of your late Father's old partner—Marcel Dassault."

"Dassault? Dassault is not a gambler, Gar. Designer, engineer, pilot—yes. Gambler, no."

"Well Paul, he may not *think* he's gambling. I have the distinct feeling that someone, probably through a third party, tipped Dassault off to the fact that I was short copper. So he probably thinks he can force me to make some kind of a special deal in order to allow me to cover my short position."

"But why, Gar? What is the point of this entire imbroglio?"

"Ultimately, the deal will get around to his Mirage fighters. His planes are the answer to this entire gamble. I am sure someone will contact me about a plane deal. *That* is the point."

"No doubt an educated guess, Gar. Marcel always puts the planes above all else."

"At least that makes some sense. I know Marcel is very tight with DeGaulle. It's their close friendship that allows the French government to be used as a front for this phony copper scam. What's more, in your government's critical financial position, I can assure you they will run out of dollar denominated funds before I do. And French francs will not be an acceptable substitute."

"Right again. It's no secret that France has limited hard currency reserves."

"And Washington will certainly take a very dim view of Paris gambling precious hard currency on a commodity fraud. Especially, since it's the U.S. that keeps France solvent. And Paul, I can personally assure you, Washington will learn about this scheme—and in short order."

"I cannot argue with what you say. Unfortunately, Gar, it is all quite true. And if commodity speculations were to become public information, I fear it would trigger a most unfortunate scandal. And scandals have brought down world governments before."

"I know that Dassault Aviation needs a Mirage fighter plane contract very badly, Paul. We all do. My General Aviation is also running on empty. It's rough and tough these days. The soft condition of the aviation business these days is one more reason why there should not be any current upward pressure on copper prices. At least any natural pressures. And that's the long story behind this call, Paul."

"And it is certainly some story, Gar. It covers so much territory. Do you have a suggested course of action that will be helpful to you?"

"That all depends on how direct an approach you can comfortably make. If you can, you might start by finding out where the leaked information on my commodity trading came from. That's critically important to me. I have an idea, but no facts yet to support it. In the meantime, I don't want to be blind-sided a second time."

"Well, I am the second biggest shareholder in Dassault Aviation—and still a director. I also have many friends there. So—yes, I think I can manage to get some information for you. However, with DeGaulle's office at the Elysée somehow involved, I will have to be most discreet, Gar. Nothing head-on. No matter how well one might be connected, believe me, there is not a single Frenchman who could afford to offend the imperious President of France."

"I understand. Play the song in your best key. When you have something to tell me, I'm in London."

Back in her apartment, Vikki felt sure that Gar thought she was the inside snitch. Her trench coat thrown over a chair, wearing only her high-heeled ankle-straps, Vikki was nakedly pacing the floor. Upset and anxious, pertinent questions flooded her mind.

"How could he believe that I would do such a thing to him? Does he have such a low opinion of me? Doesn't he know how crazy I am about him—that I would do anything for him?"

Still at his desk, by midnight his loss of control in copper futures trading had steadily worked Gar into a towering rage. Only he knew that the loss of personal control was more important to him than any loss of money. Money could be replaced. Control was at his core.

On his intercom, a security guard was saying, "Sir, Miss Tracy is on her way in." The door connecting his office to Vikki's was flung open. There, framed in the doorway, arms akimbo, was one very angry and defiant lady.

"What the hell are you doing here at this hour, Vikki?"

"I knew you would still be here—and steaming."

"Damn right, I'm steaming. Maybe you know why?"

"Hold your fire, mister. That's exactly why I came back. When you dropped me off, I could sense your sudden coolness. That you believed I was the inside snitch."

"Yes I did. And maybe you are."

"Well, you just happen to be wrong. 100% wrong. What kind of low-life do you take me for? In your right mind, can you really believe that I could make passionate love to you, one minute—and the next minute be a double-crossing snitch? Do you rate me that low, Gar? *That* low?"

Her voice choked with emotion. Tears welled up in Vikki's eyes—and spilled over. "Well—I'll prove to you that you're dead wrong about me. I'm not a snitch. And not a low-life, either. I'm just as good as any other woman you know. I may work for you, Gar Grey. I may even be in love with you. But, I don't have to take your personal insults—*and I won't.* Call in security. I want to take a lie detector test. Let's get this over with—*right now.*"

For the first time in his memory, Gar tried to speak but the words did not come. He simply stared at Vikki—

looking as he probably had never looked at a woman before.

In total disbelief at her defiant outburst, he just sat there slowly shaking his head.

In Washington, Alayne Benning-George was deep into a call to Sheik Ari Akram in Riyadh. Akram was speaking. "I can see that you were most successful with my friend at the French embassy there in Washington, Ally. I knew that once he accepted your offer of cocktails at your apartment, it was a done deal. Of course, being an attractive single guy the thought did occur to me that he might be gay. No matter, one way or another, Ally, I always have total confidence in your ability to score."

Mockingly, "Thank you, kind sir."

"In the meantime, as a direct result of your important help copper futures have been going wild. You should also know that we might be able to bring Gar Grey into a bargaining position in yet another way. Copper is only *one* way. Yesterday, I had a long talk with a most influential Saudi oil prince and suggested to him that he try to amend Gar's oil option agreement. Yes, I mean the original one with the Vatican.

I baited him to try inserting some Iranian oil statistics that would make the Vatican's option look deceitful—even illegal. Naturally, I don't know if he will be able to get away with it, but I thought it was well worth the try. We'll know soon enough."

"If these tricks go through, Ari, how much will be in it for me—I mean above and beyond what you normally pay me? I'm not doing all this fucking around for nothing."

"Of course, you're not. While I cannot yet name the amount—you know that. But, when the time comes, Ally, you'll be very satisfied. In the meantime, it might be wise for you to stay in touch with my contact at the French embassy. I cannot think of his name at the moment. Eduard? Right you are. Another roll in the hay might be good insurance. Give that idea some serious thought, Ally. We'll speak again soon."

As he hung up on his call with Ally, Sheik Akram's phone rang. The Harvard-educated oil prince was calling.

"Ari, I have bad news." The prince related his conversation with Ritter.

Akram inquired. "Must you accept Ritter's advice?"

"It would not be advisable to go against him. He has powerful connections all over the Kingdom—as well as all over the oil world. It would be very destructive. When he says that the Iranian insertion at this late date would be illegal, remember that he is the best oil lawyer in Europe. One of the best in the world. What? Say that again, Ari."

"I said maybe Gar Grey does not have an authentic copy of the original. Your father had the original. It is possible that when it surfaced, magically, it had the new language in it."

"Ari, have you lost your mind? Remember what country we are in. If we were to be caught changing the option language, we would both be quickly and publicly beheaded. In the name of *Allah*, such dishonesty would be against every sacred teaching of the Koran. None of us like the American oil companies, Ari—especially Paul Getty, Gar Grey, and the Aramco people. But your idea is just plain suicide. So, forget it."

As Akram put his phone down, he mused, "Maybe I need Ally closer than Washington. Her body seems to be my most effective tool—and it's a steal at these prices. Besides, that's all she will ever get."

Gar did his best to calm Vikki down.

"Don't you dare try to sweet talk me, Gar Grey. I'm dead serious about the lie detector test. After what it took me to get this far in my life—a life you could never begin to understand—it's critical for me to clear my name in your head.

I know there's a lie detector machine down in security

headquarters. Call down and set it up. Tell them to get the guy who administers that polygraph test thing out of bed—and get his ass over here. C'mon mister, let's get crackin'."

All of Vikki's seriousness brought Gar a faint smile, and a huge new level of respect for her. Calling down to security he set her request in motion.

When the test was finished and evaluated, as she had claimed, Vikki proved to be clean as a whistle. The positive recorded results were added to her personnel file.

Back in Gar's office, "What do you have to say for yourself now, Mister Grey?"

"I say, let's go back into the lounge bar and celebrate your victory with a cool glass of champagne. Okay?"

"No. Absolutely not okay. First, I need an apology from you, Gar. You don't have any idea how much you humiliated me. Degraded me. If I don't get an apology from you—right now—I will simply have to quit my job here. That's the way it is. That's the way I am."

"I'll be damned. You're not acting, either. You're serious, aren't you?"

"Go ahead. Try me."

"No. I'll take your word for it. After what we've been through tonight, I would be a fool to lose you now. I've never done this before, but accept my apology, Vikki.

Now, can I interest you in that glass of champagne?"

SIXTY-ONE

On the California shore of the Pacific, near the famous Santa Monica pier, Ursula Von Ribbentrop was dancing up a storm at the decadent La Mar ballroom. La Mar was Hollywood's version of the nefarious Studio 54 in New York. And was already famous for nearly ten years before "54" came on the scene.

In fact, some of La Mar's most dedicated loyalists even had the balls to think that La Mar somehow triggered "54." Of course such a draconian thought surely was never spoken at "54."

Ursula, already the most famous international fashion model, never made a secret of her desire to expand her career into film. Now she was happily in Hollywood to make a screen test at American Studios.

She was up everyday at dawn and busily prepared for her first big film opportunity. Yet, she was out on the town every night having one exciting blast after another. Those who watched her frantic movements on the dance floor, hour after hour, were mighty impressed. However, those who knew her best were not at all amazed at her energy level. It was not a God-given gift. Indeed, it was not a gift at all.

Ursula was on a steady diet of amphetamines—green uppers. The same central nervous system stimulants that provided the seemingly endless energy of Jack and Jackie Kennedy, and other staffers, during the short life of the Camelot White House.

After JFK's tragic assassination, Dr. Max Jacobson, using the same drugs, again helped Jackie get through the tough times. These chemicals were both addictive and illegal. And both Kennedy's were hooked. Ultimately, Jacobson lost his medical license.

Ursula, who naively believed that she had accomplished the screen test on her own merits, had no way of knowing that she was still Gar's star puppet. And had been ever since their chance meeting in the Savoy Grill—their first night of physical intimacy.

Of course, none of this had anything to do with Gar's growing affair with Vikki Tracy. As he told a close friend in London, "What the hell does an interest in one broad have to do with fucking another, or two others—even at the same time. I can do any damn thing I want—*and I do.*"

For Gar, arranging Ursula's screen test was all quite simple. After dangling the possibility of films in front of her for several years, whatever his current whim, once he gave the green light, Ursula's screen test was immediately scheduled. No questions asked. As always with Gar, Ursula's screen test was no mere coincidence.

General Films, a wholly owned subsidiary of Gar's General Industrial Corporation, was the majority shareholder in American Studios. While that was common knowledge in the trade, it was not the kind of information that Ursula would have been interested in knowing.

What she also did not know was that there was a tacit gentlemen's agreement between the major studio heads—Louis B. Mayer of MGM, Adolph Zukor of Paramount, Jack Warner of Warner Bros., Darryl Zanuck of Twentieth-Century Fox, Harry Cohn of Columbia—and Gar Grey.

Therefore, tempting as Ursula was—and she was very tempting—none of these foes, knowing of Gar's deep and abiding interest in the famous Ursula Von Ribbentrop, would dare touch her. With a net worth many times the combined assets of the other studio heads lumped together, a full-blown Gar Grey reprisal was not worth the risk.

Responding to various producers who constantly pushed him to go after Ursula, Jack Warner reportedly answered, "Any guy in this business to go against Gar Grey would simply be a fuckin' idiot. I may be a fucker, but I'm not an idiot."

To the contrary, any time the mood struck his fancy, Gar knew he could make a successful tender offer at a small premium to the low current market price, and gain overnight control of their publicly-owned companies. In their unpredictable roller-coaster kind of business most of the studios were selling well below book value. But, they were all land rich—*Southern California* land rich.

Years back, the huge spreads of vacant land that the studios purchased for next to nothing *per acre*—were now worth a fortune *per square foot*—but were still carried on their balance sheets at original cost. To be sure, Gar was ever mindful of the tremendous real estate profit just waiting to be plucked. Eventually, they all were all taken over.

With her modeling career white-hot, Ursula had continuously wondered why no studio came forth with some kind of screen offer. As she told friends,

"I would have grabbed at anything—absolutely anything."

But she didn't have a clue as to why it never happened.

Even after her initial acting efforts were shot, edited and 'in the can', Gar ordered the first and only print to be sent to him in New York for a private screening. And not until he had seen it was any other distribution to be made.

This was the ultimate power play—the power to make her or break her. In typical Hollywood fashion such power was more the rule than the exception. All of the top studio moguls had it. So did Lew Wasserman, the wheeling, dealing head of MCA. In those days MCA, originally Music Corporation of America, had become the top talent agency in the film business. Overtaking even the venerable William Morris agency.

MCA represented the cream of the stars. Among the many were: Clark Gable, Marilyn Monroe, Bette Davis, Lucille Ball, Jimmy Stewart, Joan Crawford, and for a stormy time, even Frank Sinatra.

Gar Grey and his pal, John F. Kennedy, knew them all. Some, like Monroe—intimately.

Single handedly, it was Lew Wasserman who made Marilyn Monroe into the brightest star in the firmament—only six months after signing her in 1955. When the skillful Wasserman concluded her new contract with Fox, it was the richest that any studio had ever before awarded an actress.

The terms called for $100,000 per picture; unlimited expenses; $500 a week for incidentals; a studio maid; her choice of dress designer, director, and script. And, for good measure, producer Jerry Wald bought her a house that she could pay back "when financially able."

At the crowded press conference called to announce the historical contract, a reporter innocently asked Marilyn what the new contract meant to her. In her famous sexy, half-whisper, baby-doll voice, Monroe's answer shocked the room into dead silence.

"It means—well, it means that I'll never have to suck another cock again."

Understandably, that verbal rocket was never published.

Back in London, Gar prepared for one of his infrequent trips to New York. A few days before his scheduled departure, he shocked Vikki. Almost casually asking, "Are you all set to go to New York. Clothes and everything ready?"

"*Me?* I'm going with you to New York?"

"That's the idea."

"Oh, Gar, that's the most exciting thing I could imagine."

"Good. As you know from my schedule, we leave here Wednesday. But, don't break your neck running around London doing last minute kinds of things. Whatever you don't have, you can buy in New York." Laughing, "I understand they still have a few things for sale over there."

The flight across the Atlantic was smooth. After refueling at Gander, Newfoundland, the nearly fourteen-hour flight aboard Gar's private jet was finally under the control of the tower at New York's JFK International Airport.

In the darkness, as the aircraft slowly descended below an overcast sky, the glittering sight of the sprawling New York metropolitan area was spread out below much like a giant sparkling carpet. Vikki, practically glued to a window, was squealing her delight.

"Gar, look there's the Empire State building! Oh, I can hardly believe it—there's the Statue of Liberty! Oh, Gar!"

After a short helicopter flight to the heliport at East 61st Street and the East River, Gar's limo pulled up in front of his Fifth Avenue apartment building. Central Park was across the street.

Opening the rear door, Nicholas, the uniformed doorman exclaimed, "Mr. Grey, sir, so nice to see you again. Welcome home."

"Thank you, Nicholas. Please bring in Miss Tracy's luggage."

While Nicholas knew that nothing was beyond his famous resident—and he had seen more than his share of Gar's exploits—spotting the exquisite, milk chocolate Vikki, Nicholas lost his speech. Muttering to himself, "I suppose there's a first time for everything."

Ursula continued her torrid California pace. Answering her studio phone one day, her heart skipped a beat. She easily recognized the familiar sultry voice.

"Ursula, darling, this is Marlene Dietrich—Lena. I hope you remember me."

"Marlene! Oh Lena, how could I ever forget you after the great time we had together on the ship. I've dreamed about it over and over again."

As Ursula's recollected excitement spiraled ever higher, unable to get the English words out fast enough, unconsciously she reverted to her native German.

"Es war das größte Geschlecht, das ich je hatte. It was the greatest sex I've ever had."

"Well, my delicious Ursula, I heard only yesterday that you were in town for a screen test—and here I am. I know all of the important people in Hollywood, so how I can help you.

"At the moment I don't need any help, but who knows, maybe I will. Oh, Lena, I cannot begin to tell you how glad I am to hear your voice. I thought that it was just your mood of the moment on the ship. That would not have been so unusual for you. I hear that both men and women throw themselves at you everywhere you go. That you are more popular than even—Greta Garbo."

"Well, there is only one Garbo, darling—and I know her very well. I heard that you have been dancing like crazy every night at La Mar. And that you're driving all the young boys crazy. If you like young boys, I know the best and most beautiful."

"Yes, I have been dancing a lot. I love to dance. And just like your modeling only for me on the ship, I would love to dance privately—just for you. That is if you have the time, Lena."

"Mein Gott! If I have the time? My sweet one, you just name the time."

"Well, I think my hotel would be too public for you. But how about your house, wherever it is. I could make it tomorrow afternoon at five?"

"Das ist gut. I rent a house in Beverly Hills, I'll send my driver for you at four forty-five. By the way, I had too much trouble with men drivers, darling. Instead of just driving for me, they also wanted to fuck me. So don't be surprised, but my driver now is a lovely girl—Heidi—just about your age. Auf Wiedersehen, darling."

For all the sexual experiences she had had since she was sixteen, Ursula was trembling as she put down the phone. She sat down to ponder and to vividly recall her shipboard sex with the great Dietrich. It thrilled her all over again.

Would tomorrow never come?

SIXTY-TWO

In Gar's building there was only one huge apartment on each floor. His sprawling layout consisted of twenty-eight rooms. Not counting his private screening room.

As the uniformed elevator operator stopped at his exclusive tenth floor, and opened the hand-operated elevator gate and door, Gar's elegant Spanish-rose colored marble foyer floor spread out in full view. With the slightest of bows, they were greeted by Gar's English butler—the irreplaceable Henry—waiting to carry Vikki's luggage off the elevator.

"And where should I put madam's luggage, sir?"

"In the master suite, Henry."

"Very well, sir. And may I inform you that I took the liberty of having cook prepare some late supper. After your usual martini, may I serve you in the library?"

"Excellent. And if you keep spoiling me this way, Henry, I may have to move you back to London."

"Wherever I may serve you best, sir.

Miss Tracy, what would be your choice of cocktail?"

"I will also have a very dry martini, Henry. Mr. Grey says you make the best."

The martinis were perfection and the midnight supper was light and delicious.

Through the soft lighting Gar found himself staring at Vikki—soul food for jaded eyes.

Later, in Gar's oversized custom made bed, Vikki said, "This is the biggest bed I ever saw. In Jamaica a family of twelve doesn't have this much space to sleep in."

"Well, we're not in Jamaica, Vikki. Besides, you're too far away from me. Come on over here and cuddle up to your best fella."

Gar felt a hot hand enclose his flaccid cock—which immediately imitated a flagpole. Vikki squeezed harder and received a few drops as a reward. She quickly licked them away.

"See, Vikki—I automatically respond to your every move. It's like—well—it's like black magic."

Ignoring his insensitive humor, Vikki responded, "That's a real compliment coming from you, Gar. Now, let's see what you can do with this."

In one smooth effort, Vikki was up and over him. Her warm thighs cradled Gar's head. He could feel in advance the heat of her cunt slowly descending to his mouth—preceded by the intoxicating scent of Elsa Schiaparelli's erotic perfume. With the union completed, Vikki implored, "Now, I need your tongue, baby. Make it hard—and stick it up my cunt. Fuck me with it. I need to feel it going in and out." Challenging him, "That is if you're man enough to satisfy this piece of sweet chocolate ass."

Gar quickly took up the challenge. His offended ego on full alert. Vikki slowly rocked. With each motion, she felt his hard tongue penetrate deeper. With a sudden violent shudder, she drenched Gar's mouth and face. Her overflow ran down his cheeks. Yet, with her libido not sated, Vikki pleaded, "Don't stop now!

Please, Gar. Once more. Don't stop yet. One more time.

P l e a s e!"

Promptly at four forty-five, Dietrich's silver Rolls Royce pulled into the circular driveway of the Beverly Hills Hotel.

Moments later, Ursula emerged. Stylishly dressed from head to toe in a soft robin's-egg blue—and one long strand of substantial pearls and matching earring's.

Despite the confines of her narrow skirt, with her knees held tightly together she was able to ease herself into the glove-soft leather back seat.

As Ursula settled in, the attractive sandy-blonde driver turned her head.

"Guten Nachmittag Fräulein Von Ribbentrop. Ich heisse Heidi. Ich mache alles für Fräulein Dietrich. Jetzt gehen wir. Good afternoon Miss Von Ribbentrop. My name is Heidi. I do everything for Miss Dietrich. Now we go."

Dietrich's white stucco rented house on Roxbury Drive, set well back from the street, was of Spanish colonial design with a red tile roof. Large and impressive from the outside, it had been built in the late 1920s. A uniformed maid courteously opened the door. However, a quick glance disappointed Ursula. The living and dining rooms were huge, but mostly empty. It looked as though Dietrich had never unpacked.

Suddenly, from the top of the stairs, "I'm waiting for you up here, darling. I live in my bedroom. Come up and join me."

In his private screening room in New York, Gar arranged to see the only print of Ursula's screen test.

With typical arrogance, he had Vikki at his side. And if it bothered her to watch the exquisite Ursula perform on the screen, she never let on. Either way, Gar could not have cared less. The emotional trifles of others, particularly women, were simply not worth his thinking about—and he didn't.

Much as throwing a bone to a dog, Gar told Vikki, "If you don't like what you see on the screen, you can leave at any time. It won't bother me."

The clever Vikki had no intention of leaving.

As opposed to a real movie, a screen test is a film experiment—under highly controlled conditions. Inasmuch as Gar wanted only the best talent to guide Ursula's test, he succeeded in cajoling the famed director George Cukor, who counted *Romeo and Juliet, Camille, Born Yesterday, A Star Is Born, and My Fair Lady* among his many box-office successes, into directing the famous model in her transition to films.

Cukor tried to wiggle out of the assignment, which he secretly felt was beneath him. "Gar, you don't really need me on that test. Anybody else will do it for half." But Gar had his mind set on only one director. Even for a George Cukor, it was too risky to flat out refuse the powerful Gar Grey.

Starting way back with the great Garbo, who fancied herself a boy/man—"Oh, what a funny man I am" or "When I was a young man—" Cukor was known to be able to coax the best performances out of the female stars entrusted to his direction. The rationale that made the Hollywood rounds was that since Cukor himself was gay—and of this fact there was no secret—he probably had a closer emotional understanding of women than most other directors.

Reinforcing the gossip, was that in his personal life Cukor spent most of his lavish $4,000 weekly salary cruising gay bars, picking up stray sailors, and taking them to his home above Sunset Boulevard. It was there that the elite of gay men and the occasional lesbian celebrity gathered.

On cue, Gar's private screening room went dark.

As the test film rolled, romantic music provided full background effect. These white on black words appeared first on the screen.

Screen test of Ursula Von Ribbentrop
Directed by George Cukor
Produced at American Studios
Burbank, California, USA
April 18, 1975
© 1975 American Studios. World Rights Reserved.

The full music level continued behind the first image on the screen. Gar and Vikki, were looking at a full frame tight shot of Ursula's beautiful face.

Cukor's innovative talent immediately took over.

While never done before in a screen test, the background music faded under and a famous radio voice became the 'voice over.' The screen dissolved into a medium length shot of Ursula coming down a Parisian fashion show runway dressed in a breathtaking Givenchy evening gown. The camera panned in. This time *Ursula* was the feature. The Givenchy had become the prop.

Voice-over: "Ladies and Gentlemen, this is Brad Carpenter introducing the famous international fashion model, Ursula Von Ribbentrop, to the silver screen. Ursula, the same face millions of you have seen on the covers of magazines, in newspapers, and in feature stories all over the world. The high cheek bones. The straight, narrow nose. The unbelievable violet-blue eyes. The full red mouth. The mouth every man wants to kiss forever."

Music up full. Next, the screen cut to Ursula in a scant bikini standing at the rail of a white yacht. A bright sun was shining—wind blowing through her hair. On cue, a narrow bra strap broke. Ursula grabbed it—almost in the nick of time. It was the kind of a scene Cukor knew would elicit at least a whistle from any producer in Hollywood. And maybe an offer. It was pretty sexy stuff for its day.

Gar muttered, "That's why Cukor wanted me to put Emperor II into Long Beach harbor. Not a bad scene. Right, Vikki?" Feeling more than a little bit envious, Vikki's response was to put Gar's hand on her naked right nipple.

"If you want my attention, Vikki, I've got a better idea."

With only the two of them in the screening room, Gar unzipped his fly. Vikki didn't need a director.

On the screen, Ursula recreated a famous Garbo dramatic scene from Cukor's smash success, *Camille*. A superb technician, Cukor found the most photogenic camera angles for each of Ursula's close-ups. To show her added versatility, Cukor then had Ursula do a Claudette Colbert comedy piece from *It Happened One Night*. An unknown did a terrific imitation of Clark Gable.

Against a visual reprise of Ursula's bikini scene, the voice-over announcer finished,

"And so we come to the end of Ursula's screen test. Soon, you'll be seeing this famous personality at your favorite theater. Watch for her.

This screen test was produced at American Studios in Burbank, California.

Ursula was directed by George Cukor.

This is Brad Carpenter speaking."

SIXTY-THREE

In New York, Gar received an unexpected telephone call from Ursula—still in California.

"You really are one sneaky son-of-a-bitch. But at this very moment, I may still love you."

"Well. Well. Well. If memory serves me correctly, Urs, that offers all kinds of exciting possibilities. But first, to what do I owe the honor of this call? I hear you're having a ball out there."

"As usual, you're surprisingly up-to-date on me, wherever I am—whatever I do. Do you have me tailed? There are times when I'm sure you do. And I'm probably right. At any rate, after the screen test was in the can, George Cukor told me the entire story. And, of course, *you* were the entire story, Gar. I'll just never figure you out."

"That's the idea. If anyone does, all the fun will be gone. But, I doubt it will ever happen."

"George also told me that you have the only print of my test. So, have you seen it? And, if you have, what's your candid reaction?"

"In complete candor, I was quite favorably surprised—particularly for a first test. Some actors, who have gone on to become great stars, didn't do anywhere near as well as you did their first time in front of a camera."

Laughing, Gar went on, "Of course, Urs, there have been times in our relationship when I've been convinced that you were already a great actress. On a serious note, I've already talked to a number of important Hollywood people about you, and of distributing additional copies of the test. Let's see if that turns up anything interesting."

"Oh, Gar! I can hardly believe my ears. I hope this is not just another one of your crazy mind games. You have the ability to make me quite crazy—and through the years, you've done that over and over again. Please don't do that to me now."

"The film business is too expensive to be a game, Urs. What I'm saying is all quite true."

"Speaking of the film business, why didn't you tell me you control American Studios?"

"It never came up. Besides, I control a lot of businesses you know nothing about. Maybe that's why you never stray too far away. Maybe that's part of my mystique."

"After all we've been through, Gar—who knows? You could be right."

"Urs, I think if you can tear yourself away from your new swinging Hollywood pals, it might be a good idea if you came to New York. We just might get a fresh start here. Paint the town red."

"A fresh start sounds great, but I just love it out here—and almost every day I meet such fabulously interesting people. Be a good guy, Gar, and come out here. I think it's a better idea, and we could have a lot more fun. Is that any kind of a possibility?"

"Always a possibility. I'll give your suggestion some thought and get back to you. In case you're wondering, I know how to reach you. You're staying alone at the Hills."

"Jeez, is there *anything* about me that you *don't* know?"

"Not really. In the meantime, be very careful. Hollywood is a whole new ball game. People in Podunk don't give a shit about models. But they love the movies and their favorite actors. That's why there are fan clubs. And movie magazines are sold by the millions. One slip and you may be finished before you even begin. So, take care."

Despite Gar's warning, Ursula found Dietrich just too incredible to give up. Most often, second-time around sexual rendezvous do not live up to the original scorcher. But, in the scenario of these two beautiful Berliners, such was not the case. Their chance shipboard sexual encounter turned out to be only a lustful appetizer. Both eagerly looked forward to their entrée. And today was the day.

A sexual daredevil since her teenage years, Ursula truly believed, "Everything in life should be explored and tried at least once. After all, everyone has latent homosexual instincts. We all have male and female genes. So why should anything be out-of-bounds? For me nothing is."

Upon arrival in Dietrich's second-floor bedroom, the two fell into each other's arms, and kissed with hungry French abandon. Outer garments were quickly discarded. Bras and panties were also deemed superfluous. Nothing was left untouched or untasted.

To Ursula's naked astonishment, in response to a soft knock at the door and without the least bit of hesitation, Dietrich said, "Come in."

Her housekeeper entered with a light lunch tray and two glasses of chilled champagne. The fortyish woman did not seem at all surprised at the sight of the two magnificent naked bodies. As if they were fully dressed, in her native German, Dietrich casually announced, *"Dagmar, dies ist der berühmte Ursula Von Ribbentrop—auch von Berlin.* Dagmar, this is the famous Ursula Von Ribbentrop—also from Berlin."

Without words, or change of expression, the housekeeper did a slight curtsy to an embarrassed Ursula, set down her tray, and left the room.

With Dagmar gone, Dietrich explained, "She has been my closest friend and mentor since my early days in Berlin cabarets. She was a fabulous dancer—and my first lover. Young, slim, and beautiful. Unfortunately, time has not been kind to her. It doesn't matter, I still trust her explicitly."

Gar purposely left Ursula to dangle in Hollywood. He did not call her back. First things first.

With money being of no importance, he dazzled Vikki with a daylong shopping spree at Bergdorf-Goodman and Henri Bendel. Then, Gar selected a diamond and ruby bracelet from Harry Winston, and a sculptured 24ct. pure gold cocktail ring at the Van Cleef & Arpels salon. Vikki was overwhelmed. And Gar was King of the World.

They dined at such famous French restaurants as Lutece, Quo Vadis, and Le Pavillon. Ruby Foo's for great Chinese. Manny Wolf's for lobster and steak.

On consecutive nights, they saw the fabulous *A Chorus Line* at the Shubert, Stephen Sondheim's *A Little Night Music* starring Hermione Gingold, and *Lorelei* at the Palace with the incomparable Carol Channing.

After theater, Sardi's was de rigueur. Everyone who counted in Gar's world would be there. Enthusiastically greeted by his old friend, Vincent Sardi, Gar wanted everyone to notice his milk chocolate beauty—and they did—with a deadly buzz. Most women thought Gar with a *colored* woman was simply outrageous. On the other hand, most of his male friends were privately jealous.

Tomorrow, Gar and Vikki would be the lead item for the gossip columns of Walter Winchell and Ed Sullivan. In one form or another, snide references would appear in every paper in town. The syndicated columnists also appeared in LA. Would Ursula take the time to notice?

Other Manhattan nights ended with a late supper at The Persian Room in The Plaza, listening to the fabulous Lisa Kirk. Perhaps blini at the Russian Tea Room. Or an apple pancake at Reuben's.

Once, they slummed down to a raucous hole-in-the-wall strip joint in Greenwich Village, where the familiar heavy drum beat and the overheated naked bodies turned the wanton Vikki on.

Over the din, Vikki told Gar, "I could make any of those broads look like nothing," Never one to let an opportunity pass by, Gar replied, "I know the owner. Want to have a go at it?"

The owner said something to the drummer, who switched to a conga drum and beat on the top with his bare hands. With her typical arrogant coolness, Vikki stepped out from behind the frayed curtains. Never one to be ignored, the audience quickly looked up from their tired drinks.

Wearing stiletto heels, the Jamaican beauty started to sashay back and forth. Her perfect hips provocatively shifted from side to side. After merciless teasing she abruptly stopped.

Off came the top to her stunning gold lamé dinner suit.

Never having worn a bra in her life, under the hot lights Vikki's tits glistened with sexy perspiration. Her rock-hard nipples jutted straight out. Wild applause and loud whistles filled the smoky room.

Vikki held out her wet breasts as a sexual offering and posed in a highly suggestive manner. The highly charged audience loved every move she made.

Vikki resumed—only stopping to grind and bump at the sides of the stage. As the whistlers approved, ever the exhibitionist, Vikki outrageously encored the grinds and the bumps.

Back at center stage, very slowly she pulled down her skirt zipper. The expensive skirt crumpled to the floor.

As she stepped out, the audience was totally mesmerized. Without any silk or nylon hose her very long sexy legs were now fully exposed. Her only remaining cover was Gar's favorite—an ultra narrow G-string.

The conga drum grew louder and louder. The whistling guys began to chant, "Take it off. Take it off. Take it *all* off!"

Vikki tried to look for Gar. In the glare of the footlights, it was impossible to see. On her own, throwing caution to the winds, the G-string dropped to the stage floor.

As the stark naked Vikki stood stage center, her legs sensually parted, she performed tantalizing fellatio on a heavily veined, life-like dildo. Every guy in the audience could feel her mouth on his cock. In the melee that followed, a burly security guard forcibly turned back several rambunctious guys who were climbing up the front of the stage.

Reveling in the uproar she had incited, Vikki wondered what Gar's reaction would be to this kinky scene. She had no idea it no longer mattered.

Gar was gone!

He had left a message for her with the owner.

"Mr. Grey told me to tell you something very important required his immediate attention out of town. His car and driver are still waiting for you outside. He'll be in touch soon."

At that moment which was about midnight, north of the city, Gar's private jet was racing full-throttle down the runway at Westchester County Airport.

Next stop—LAX. Los Angeles International.

From somewhere over the Rockies, Gar called Ursula to tell her the good news—he would be at the hotel within a few hours.

With each futile attempt, his resentment grew. His last unanswered call was placed when his plane was already circling out over the Pacific in preparation for its final approach to LAX. Gar muttered to himself, "Where the fuck is that broad at this hour?"

Upon his arrival at the Beverly Hills Hotel, where he permanently leased a two-bedroom bungalow, Gar was instantly recognized by the night manager. In violation of house rules, the young night manager escorted him to Ursula's large second-floor room. Using a passkey, he stepped back and allowed Gar to enter.

Tired from the long trip, Gar installed himself in an oversized lounge chair—feet up on the ottoman. And waited in complete darkness. At about four in the morning, two female voices awakened him from a deep sleep.

With only a small bedside lamp lit, in the deep shadows Gar remained alert but undiscovered. After a quick shower, in high spirits Ursula and her guest leaped into bed. In a matter of minutes, Gar had heard more than enough lesbian lovemaking—and switched on a bright lamp. Shocked at the unexpected light and that they were not alone, Ursula and her young partner disbelievingly jumped up. Only to hear Gar sarcastically question, "Is this a private game, or can anyone play?"

True to form, not at all ashamed at being found in this compromising position, Ursula chose to simply ignore it.

"Gar—honey—why didn't you let me know you were coming?"

"I did. At least four times from the plane. If your schedule was so damn tight, I don't know why you invited me to come out here. Remember—you said it would be more fun. Is this what you had in mind. And who is this young lady in your bed?"

"This is—uh—oh, I'm really sorry, but I forgot your name."

"My name is Jane. Just plain Jane."

Gar cracked, "Jane is obviously a very old friend of yours—I'd say at least for an hour or two. How old are you Jane?" Jane looked helplessly at Ursula.

"Tell him how old you are. I never asked, so I don't know. And you better tell him the truth or he'll ask to see your driver's license."

"Well—next November—next November—I'll be—sixteen."

"But right now, even with all your clothes off, you are just fifteen. That's right, isn't it?"

"Yes, sir. That's right. Tonight, I'm just fifteen. But, I'm very experienced for my age. My mother taught me *everything* when I turned twelve. I looked like I was eighteen. She used to be in the movies, so she knew a lot of tricks. If you want to take your clothes off, sir, we can have a threesome, and I'll show you just how experienced I really am. All my clients, but especially my female clients, are very satisfied with my work. They invite me back over and over again."

"I'm sure you're very good at what you do, Jane. But, what you obviously do for a living is against the law. You're also a minor—a more serious law. Now, I want you to put your clothes back on and quietly leave. And don't stop at the bar to pick up another client. Got it, kid?"

With plain Jane gone, Gar turned to Ursula who had returned from the bathroom in a fetching nude-colored negligee—more off than on—and erotically sidled up to Gar.

"Why don't you put this horny baby on her back?"

"First things first, Urs. Did you hear one word of what I told you on the phone?"

Pleading ignorance, "About what?"

Angrily, Gar screamed, "About *what*? About your new film career—*that's* what. I told you to be careful about what you did, and with whom you were seen. Are you going to seriously tell me now that you don't remember one word of those warnings? Not one goddam word?"

"Oh, *those* words. I guess I heard some of them. Were they so important?"

Ursula was playing a two-handed game. On the one hand, she was successfully getting Gar's mind away from her interrupted lesbian affair with Jane. On the other hand, knowing how bright Ursula was, playing stupid was making Gar all the more furious.

Having had a belly full of her nonsense, Gar grabbed her by an arm and roughly sat her down on the edge of the bed. "Now, hear me, Ursula—*and hear me good!* I will not lower myself to continue to have this inane conversation with you. If you think you're playing with some kind of a goddam fool—you should know better than that. So stop this bullshit stupid act.

Besides, right now, it's more important for us to talk about my warnings to you about your potential film career—an opportunity for which you've been angling for a very long time. I didn't bite before because I never thought you were mature enough to handle it. That may still be the case.

You don't have to be very mature to be a star supermodel. Films are much tougher to conquer. A film camera can strip you emotionally naked in seconds. But, it's your life and your career. If you are going to continue to ignore what I tell you—and think that you can defy all the unwritten rules of the industry, you are wrong—just plain wrong.

Always remember, Urs, this business is not about reality. It's about perception. And you can ask people who tried to break the rules."

Ursula stammered, "I—I don't have the vaguest idea of who you're talking about."

"Well, you can ask the great Garbo, who thought of herself as a man—and definitely preferred women over men. She retired from films early on. Not to be alone—as legend has it—but mostly to cover-up her lesbianism from the public. She also was burdened with an Electra complex—an unconscious libidinal desire for her father. She intensely disliked her mother.

Or you might ask Stanwyck, who, despite her lavender marriage to the weak Robert Taylor, stayed in the closet for all of her acting career, mostly with her publicist, Helen Ferguson.

Try Kate Hepburn, whose relationships with socialite Laura Harding and film editor Jane Loring, lasted longer than her six-week marriage to stockbroker Ludlow Ogden Smith. Despite her years with the married Spencer Tracy, whom she used as a beard, Hepburn said, 'In my relationships, I know I have qualities that are offensive to people—especially men.'"

And, while you're much too young to remember Fatty Arbuckle, Urs, he made $7,000 a week as a silent film comedian back in the 20s. *Big* money. Yet, his career was ruined after the mysterious death of a young woman at a wild drinking party in San Francisco. He died broke at forty-six. It's a list almost without end—and no happy endings."

Letting it all sink in Ursula responded, "Gar, this time I heard every word. My only excuse is that I felt like I was on cloud nine and couldn't fall off. Like I couldn't do anything wrong. Now I see that I acted foolish and immature. And I want you to know I am truly sorry."

"Sounds good, Urs. The real question is will you remember *any* of it tomorrow?"

Hurt and confused, Vikki languished for a few days in Gar's New York apartment. She never left the building. The phone never rang.

With her frustration escalating by the minute, in a fit of total anger Vikki threw a book against a wall—picked it up and threw it again—even harder.

Without the expected call from Gar, the chocolate beauty said thank-you to the servants—and boarded a flight back to London.

A day after her London arrival, Gar called from California.

"I wanted to explain…"

"I don't need or want your carefully thought-out excuses, Gar Grey. They are just words to you—and mean even less to me. My resignation is on your desk. I quit."

In Gar's ear, the line went dead.

Vikki snarled, "That no good son-of-a-bitch.

It may take me a while—but this affair is not over."

SIXTY-FOUR

Much as he would have preferred not to lose Vikki, Gar took her leave in his normal confident stride.

"Of course, the irreplaceable person hasn't been born yet—but her loss sure does screw up some great plans I had in mind for that broad."

Coincidentally, only moments later his long-time New York assistant, Irene Henry, was on the phone. "Mr. G., you might find this hard to believe, but your new London secretary is already at work at her desk in the Control Room."

"Come on, Irene. You know better than to pull my chain."

"I'm really telling it as it is. I took the liberty of filling your vacancy the minute I confirmed her availability."

"Irene, since you take such good care of my needs, may I at least ask her name?"

"It's a person you already know. It's my sister, Martha. Martha Henry. She's been living and working in London for two years, now. And just thrilled to be working for you."

Ursula, meanwhile, had moved into Gar's luxuriously decorated bungalow on the grounds of the Beverly Hills

Hotel, while Gar took over a large corner office with a secretary, at American Studios in Burbank. Nevertheless, because of the huge time differences around the globe he was constantly on the phone from the bungalow—running his worldwide business affairs. He did make one important concession to his present geography. For the first time, Gar began to take a genuine interest in his subsidiary film company.

Over the years of their love/hate relationship, it was now Ursula's acting career that had aroused this interest. All of Hollywood knew he was her sponsor and benefactor. The town also knew his reputation as a man who got what he wanted—and waited with bated breath to see how the saga would play out.

As Gar had previously told her he would, he had additional prints of her screen test hand delivered to all the studio heads—as well as important producers and directors. To assure prompt action, right next to the name of the addressee, in bold red block letters he had stamped,

CONFIDENTIAL
SCREEN TEST ENCLOSED
FROM GEORGE GARFIELD GREY

It read almost like a command. In fact it was.

Yet, nothing happened. If everyone was waiting for Gar to make the first move they didn't have long to wait.

Typically, after only two days, "They can all go fuck themselves. Sure as hell, I'm not going to sit around here just waiting for the phone to ring like some star-struck kid from Tulsa."

With sheer delight, Ursula could see that he was taking over. "Just imagine," she squealed to a girlfriend, "One of the most important men in the world, Gar Grey, is really acting as my agent. It's unbelievable I tell you—*absolutely unbelievable!*"

But, Gar Grey, the perfectionist, had only begun.

If he was going to do it all by himself he muttered, "By God, I'll make Ursula the best there is. Whether she is or not."

After consulting his top executives at American Studios, in a single day Gar hired a drama coach, and singing and dancing instructors—assured that this trio was the best money could buy. If Ursula had any natural talent at all, these three top professionals would find it, develop it, and polish it to perfection.

And to place Ursula's name in all the right spaces and places, he also retained the legendary Darcy Dunne—for nearly twenty years the most effective publicity operator in the business.

Back in her early twenties, Darcy started in the publicity department at M-G-M under the imperious Louis B. Mayer. At the time, she had been more beautiful than many of the female stars she later made so famous. There were those whose recollections still included the graphic story, true or false, that Darcy was unexpectedly interrupted on her knees, servicing her contented boss. And had to stay cramped and silent under L.B.'s desk for more than an hour.

With Gar's A-team now in place, Ursula's training days had become exhausting. However, at night the handsome couple was in constant demand. The important power brokers wanted to be up close and personal. And they knew how to score points.

Jack Warner, whom Gar considered his best friend in the film industry, invited them for a dazzling epicurean banquet. The dean of Hollywood agents, Jule Stein, the founder of Music Corporation of America, and wife Doris, threw a rare dinner party for them at Misty Mountain, their palatial mansion atop the Hollywood hills.

Lew and Edie Wasserman hosted a lavish reception for more than two hundred of the cream of Hollywood at their Foothill Drive estate. And the invitations continued to pour in.

To catch their breath, Gar and Ursula finally took a weekend off and drove down to Palm Springs, the long-time desert hide-a-way only 100 miles southeast of L.A.

Legendary Hollywood names like Bob Hope and Frank Sinatra already maintained huge estates there with adjacent streets adorned with their names. Everyone of note had some kind of playpen in the desert. Or they stayed at Charlie Farrell's chic Racquet Club on the northern edge of the oasis. The handsome Farrell, who starred opposite Janet Gaynor in the 1927 film hit *Seventh Heaven*, ultimately made a fortune developing the raw desert.

In the typical Palm Springs weekend fantasy, turquoise-bottomed swimming pools, perfectly manicured golf courses, and har-tru tennis courts replaced offices, sound stages, and editing rooms. But nothing changed the mores of Hollywood. A mere hundred miles was certainly not going to change the Sodom and Gomorra behavior of the mostly loose acting crowd.

Ursula and Gar were the guests of honor at a sumptuous Saturday night dinner at the sprawling home of a famous star—that unexpectedly turned into a full-blown orgy. Booze was far more appealing than food. And drugs were a steady and acceptable shortcut to unwinding from the week that was.

Not unusually shocking, on a glass-topped coffee table in the middle of a large California Room, were multiple lines of pure white heroin—happily being snorted. On another nearby glass-topped table an erotic drama was playing to an enthusiastic audience. At the peak of a mind altering rush from the potent heroin, a world-famous star just past thirty, had stripped naked.

Cheered on by her husband and best friends, the gorgeous blonde who still had a drop-dead body, announced loudly that she would take on all comers, male and female alike. Putting her naked body down on the cool glass and spreading her legs wide, she screamed, "Who's first? Step right up boys and girls. Don't be shy. This cunt is free for the taking!"

While it sounded real enough, in reality, it was the heroin talking.

A bit tipsy from the champagne she had consumed, Ursula was greatly tempted.

"Gar, honey, I really do have the hots for her. Before you came out we spent several sexy evenings together. Could we take her back to our guest house for some fun?"

"I have no objection to whatever you want to do in our own privacy, Urs. If you're in the same horny mood when we're ready to leave, you can ask her if she would like to join us for a nightcap at our place. Her husband too. Anything goes in private."

When the solo piano expanded to six pieces, those still able to stand and move danced to the old standards and familiar Broadway show tunes. When the tempo stepped up to disco and rock, the still-naked star put on another show. In her stoned state of mind, free of all her usual hang-ups, she gave the most believable performance of her career. Turning slowly away, a famous director said,

"How sad. How *very* sad."

SIXTY-FIVE

When Gar picked up the phone to take a call from Paris, there was no mistaking Paul Louis Oppert's French accent—which didn't fade under the brilliant California sun.

"Gar, my friend, I have not at all forgotten our last phone conversation. We returned to Paris only recently and my mission on your behalf was the first serious task I undertook.

"You have my full attention, Paul."

"After several unproductive discussions with certain employees, it was clear to me that I had to confront Marcel directly. He, alone, knew the full story.

Up front, I told him that we had spoken. That surprised him. After ducking some of my direct questions, ultimately he confessed. And Gar, your supposition proved to be correct. The copper futures trading was merely a ploy to weaken you."

"It was stupid, Paul. Should never have happened."

"You and I know that, Gar. But Marcel hoped he would gain some leverage to use in later bargaining with you about an airplane deal he had in mind. And he was fixated on the idea of somehow getting you on the short end of the stick. I told him that he had made a terrible miscalculation. That you were too strong and diversified to be brought down by a copper sham. And for him to have thought otherwise was surprisingly naïve."

"That's for damn sure."

"When our discussion moved on to the involvement of the French government—well— that gambit, I told him, was not only painfully ill-advised but also internationally dangerous. On that score, Marcel finally did admit that De Gaulle had been most reluctant to proceed. And that he did not want to personally know any of the details.

As a matter of fact, Gar, I don't know where Marcel got the irrational idea in the first place. We did not touch on that, but I can tell you from past experience he is not a financially sophisticated person. A great engineer—yes. But, my father was the financial brains when he was alive."

"I have heard that from many sources, Paul. And those great Rothschild connections."

"So, you can see now how embarrassed I am to tell you that the entire complicated operation, which you know better than I spread quickly around the world, was basically simple and plainly stupid. If it had not been combined with more serious realities, it would have been almost comical. By the way, Marcel's final word was that if you are ever interested in joining with him in some kind of a combination or co-venture, he would warmly welcome a call."

"Well—I'll think about that. Who knows what strange things the future may hold? In any event, Paul, I can't thank you enough for your help. I trust your trip to the States went well. My regards to Cheryl."

"Au revoir, Gar."

Only days later near the concierge's desk at the Beverly Hills Hotel, a stranger stopped Gar in the hotel lobby.

"Mr. Grey, it would be easier if you would step outside so that we can talk."

"I'm not going anywhere. Who are you—and what do you want?"

"At this point, I am only authorized to tell you that Wolf sent me."

Incredulously, but quietly, *"Wolf Felsenberg?"*

"Yes, sir."

At the mention of Wolf's name, Gar was more than willing to listen.

"Okay, let's step outside—but not together. You go first. Walk down toward the pool. I'll follow in a moment."

To the concierge who had witnessed the scene, but could not overhear the conversation, Gar quickly said, "Have security follow me—*right now.*"

Gar caught up with the stranger who was waiting under a large palm tree near the pool. The security guard stayed back. Out of direct sight.

Gar asked, "How do you know Wolf, and what message do you carry?"

"My name is Gerard, Mr. Grey, I work for Wolf and Noah Rembardt's International Investigative Agency—in their Paris office."

"So?"

"Well, sir, I happen to be assigned to a certain open case that contains a considerable amount of information about you personally, as well as your aircraft sales activities with NATO in Brussels. That was during the time the late Oskar Benzinger was on your staff. By the way, our client in this matter also happens to be NATO.

Among many other assignments on your behalf, Benzinger hosted an elaborate party in Amsterdam for an elite group of NATO officers. Wolf was also there. To say the least sir, the sex details of that party were quite spectacular. There are also various references to the sales tactics of the French aircraft manufacturer, Marcel Dassault—as you know a most vigorous competitor."

"Gerard, rather than engage in a long conversation out here in the open, I think we should go for a walk along Sunset Blvd. I could use the exercise."

The Beverly Hills Hotel sits on the northwest corner

of Sunset Blvd., where it meets Coldwater Canyon. The canyon road twists and turns as it first rises up and over the Santa Monica Mountains, before descending into the San Fernando Valley.

An experienced operator, Gerard knew why they were going to take a walk. What Gar wanted was the reassurance that the traffic noise along Sunset would overwhelm any recording of their conversation, in the event Gerard was wearing a wire.

True to form, the late afternoon bumper-to-bumper traffic on Sunset created a deafening noise that made any sort of conversation impossible—forget about recording it. To say nothing of the noxious fumes.

As the two men slowly walked down the hotel's curving driveway—halfway down—Gerard abruptly stopped. "Mr. Grey, before we inhale those exhaust fumes from hell, there are some other personal messages that I have for you from Wolf."

"Great. I'd like to hear them."

"Wolf, emphasized the importance of the first one."

"Which is?"

"He wanted you to understand that he was sending me here on a friendly mission. Nothing adversarial. In spite of the fact that your parting was less than cordial, he holds no rancor. He has chosen to remember only the good years you two spent as a team."

"Well, Gerard, I'm very pleased to hear that. We did share many victories."

"So, Mr. Grey, let's skip the smelly walk down on the sidewalk. I'm not wearing a wire." Opening his jacket, "Here, you can check me out. I'm clean. Let's go into the bar and have a chat."

Comfortably seated in the Polo Lounge, with drinks and snacks, Gerard started. "Mr. Grey, we have all the information we need on you, personally—after all Wolf knew everything that went on in your companies during the years he was your Chief of Security. If I may say so, sir, you have led quite a unique life. Most people never get your kind of opportunities."

"That's true. On the other hand, one has to know when and how to seize those opportunities. For the most part, they come around only once in a lifetime."

"Going forward, Mr. Grey, we do have some blanks in the case history of Oskar Benzinger. We know all the routine stuff. Born in Philadelphia, good family, Princeton, etc. But the State Department is unwilling to disclose certain facts contained in his personnel file. And Wolf feels that Oskar held back certain parts of his encounter with the ex-French tennis champ, Angelique Cuvier."

"If Wolf doesn't know the full Cuvier story, Gerard, nobody does. Oskar was in the hospital and nearly dead when he talked with Wolf. It seems highly unlikely he would have withheld anything at that point. If he did, I wouldn't have the vaguest idea of what it might have been. But it no longer matters. Whatever dark secret he may have had is safely buried with him."

"Both Wolf and Noah concur with that, sir. Although, I gained the impression they were hoping for some kind of unexpected bombshell from you."

"Tell the guys I am sorry to disappoint them. Now—let's move on to other things."

"Before we do that, sir, let's review what you remember about the elaborate sex party in Amsterdam. It was held on your instruction, was it not?"

"No, it was not. Oskar, working directly for Wolf, had come up with the idea as part of his sales campaign to secure a NATO fighter plane contract for our company. It was an intensely competitive fight for a crucial contract. Every aircraft manufacturer pulled out all the stops on that one—including the Frenchman, Dassault.

In that connection, I will always be convinced that the Paris government had given him a blank check. Dassault's men were spreading enormous amounts of francs around like it was play money. We even knew some of Dassault's beneficiaries. Many NATO officers were more than willing to take bribes from more than one source. Nothing embarrassed those guys.

And while it's true that I approved the expenditures, all the details, including entertainment, were left entirely in Oskar's hands. He knew everybody's secrets."

"Regarding the lavish entertainment, Mr. Grey, I have already interviewed Willi Von Ribbentrop and her friend, Blissful Knight. They were both fully cooperative and their memories were flawless. I have long tapes from both."

Then, laughing wholeheartedly at what he was about to say, "However, I must confess, Mr. Grey, not one word has been heard from the boa constrictor."

As the two men were about to call it quits, Ursula came in looking for Gar. "So this is where you're hiding? I've been looking everywhere for you."

"Hi, Urs. This is Mr. Gerard. He works for Wolf and Noah, out of Paris. Gerard, this is Ursula Von Ribbentrop. You have already met her mother."

Gerard looked stunned. Had he seen an apparition?

"Your eyes are not deceiving you, Gerard.

They could easily pass for sisters."

SIXTY-SIX

Alone in their New York office, without prelude or preface, Noah turned to Wolf.

"I just don't get it. After all this time, you suddenly come to the conclusion that Oskar's Monte Carlo story with Cuvier has blank spots in it—why?"

"It's not suddenly at all. When we talked in the hospital, Oskar was still suffering from posttraumatic amnesia, the result of his head injuries. It was a struggle for him even to recall what had triggered his mad dash that night from Monte Carlo. That being the case, it was not at all far-fetched for me to assume he also left out other details. Purposely, or otherwise,"

"So far, Wolf, I probably buy what you're selling. But, if you had lingering doubts about the Cuvier story why did you let the boa finish him off? There was no escape from that scene."

"There were several reasons. And they all revolved around Gar."

"What else is new?"

Wolf chose to ignore Noah's sarcasm.

Continuing, "Knowing Oskar's sexual orientation, I have always assumed that what he chose not to tell me had occurred earlier that night. And had something to do with Cuvier and sex. Or, somebody else and sex. With Oskar it was a safe bet that it would always be about sex."

"And if I took one king-size guess, after that you let your imagination run completely wild. Somehow, you managed to connect Gar with Oskar's omissions of that night—or possibly other nights. And after the many kind and generous things he had done for you, including monuments in Stuttgart to your family's memory, you were not going to leave anything undone that might reflect badly on him. No matter how extreme your action would have to be. Am I close?"

"Unfortunately, on the button."

When Private Investigator Gerard caught up with Angelique Cuvier she was at the U.S. Open Tennis Championships at the famous West Side Tennis Club in Forest Hills, Queens—one of the five boroughs of New York City, not far across the East River from Manhattan.

As a former Wimbledon and French open champion, Cuvier was always extended the courtesy of a courtside box at the U.S. Open.

With no advance information to guide him, lucky Gerard hit the jackpot. Like ducks sitting in a row, the three other Americans on his list of people to interview were all sitting in Angie's box. Her long-time playmate, Alayne Benning-George, Rio Roundtree, an old friend of Ally's, who came up from Washington, and the handsome Umberto Ben-Levi Goldmanni, in from Nassau—a close friend of Rio's. And the man who ran Gar's Atlantic Overseas Bank there.

This attractive foursome gained attention and a big round of applause when the still-popular Angie was introduced to the crowd before the women's final match. Still trim in a short white tennis dress, Angie stood and removed her sunglasses—then smiled and waved in response to the applause. These devoted tennis fans had not forgotten her championship accomplishments.

Gerard mused, "I wonder what this crowd would think if they saw her put on one of her prodigious sex shows in the middle of center court—with Etienne as a bonus? But, enough of this wishful thinking."

He patiently waited for most of the crowd to leave after the final match. Then, he slowly made his way toward Cuvier's box, where Angie was busily signing autographs.

At last, "Miss Cuvier, it's important that I see you in private." Without even knowing who this man was, "Good. Can all three of my friends watch us?"

Meanwhile back in their hotel suite, left alone without a clue as to how he should dress, or what time Angie would get back from Forest Hills—Etienne was comfortably lying naked on the king-size bed. As always, he would await her orders.

Only moments later, the hall door abruptly opened, and he heard voices. Etienne grabbed his favorite sheer pink dressing gown with a matching feathered shawl collar, and happily rushed into the living room. Angie was back—but not alone. She had Gerard with her.

In a slow motion rerun, Gerard looked up and saw Etienne in an all pink blur. Dark breasts were exposed at the top—and a black penis peeked out from beneath an unclosed overlap of gown at the bottom. A freeze-frame quickly developed in the camera. Nothing moved. Not knowing where to put his eyes, a stunned Gerard broke the silent scene.

"Obviously Mlle. Cuvier, this a not a good time for us to have a serious chat. I'll call tomorrow for another appoint..."

"No, no—Gerard," Angelique broke in. "There is no reason we cannot talk now."

Looking first at Etienne, and beseechingly back at Angie, "But Mlle. Cuvier..."

"Really, Etienne is no problem. He is my constant companion. I don't go anywhere without him." With that Angie walked over and whispered in his ear. Etienne looked dubiously over his/her shoulder at Gerard. Angie alone with a man, disturbed him. It had never happened before.

"It's okay, Etienne, Gerard is not here for sex. He's an investigator. We have some old things to talk about. Go into the bedroom and watch television for a little while."

Seated now in a comfortable lounge chair, but still shaken by the shemale image of Etienne, Gerard forthrightly asked Angie, "Have you ever had sex with George Garfield Grey?"

"Gerard, this may surprise you, but the closest I have ever been to Mr. Grey was at a London reception after a Wimbledon tournament, hosted by the Duke of Edinburgh. Who, quite naturally, gave us a proper introduction."

"Mlle., do you happen to know Oskar Benzinger?"

"Why? Do you also know him?"

"I think we can finish this much sooner, Mlle. Cuvier, if I ask all the questions."

"Certainement. Certainly."

"Do you happen to know where Mr. Benzinger is now, mademoiselle? Have you possibly seen him recently?"

At this point, exasperated beyond containment, Angie exploded. "Inspector Gerard, do you take me for some kind of a fucking idiot—or would you prefer that I continue to string you along some more? Oskar is dead—and we both know it. Therefore, your questions are ludicrous and insulting. You've seriously overstepped your boundaries here and this interview is over. *Right now?"*

"Mademoiselle, I was simply trying to do the best job I was hired to do. My sincere apology. Now, I bid you good afternoon."

Etienne immediately reappeared—this time totally naked. His massive erection was just what Angie needed to calm her down. With a warm embrace, she led him back into the bedroom where she pushed him onto the bed. Using his especially strong erection as she would have used a pump handle, Angie vigorously pumped him all the way. But that was only the beginning. Their eroticism escalated wildly from that point.

Two hours later, Gerard met Ally, Rio, and Berto, together, in the Peacock Lounge of the Waldorf on Park Avenue. Once more, he identified himself and his mission.

"Miss Benning-George we believe that on a certain night in Monte Carlo, you told Angelique Cuvier that George Garfield Grey could lose something valuable. Indeed, that he could lose it that very night. What did you mean by that statement?"

Before this get-together, in a quick telephone call Angie had told Ally that she didn't tell Gerard anything—and that she threw him out. With that assurance, Ally responded to Gerard, "She didn't tell you that because I never said it. You're on a fishing expedition, and you're not going to catch anything—at least not from me. You're a sneaky snake. And this is interview is over."

Looking at Rio and Berto, a disappointed Gerard said, "Without asking, I know you two also will have nothing to say to me today. But—there will be other days. Other days, when all of you will find it to your benefit to stop stonewalling me and refresh your memories. Good afternoon."

Back in her room, Ally immediately put in a call to Riyadh. She wanted to update Sheik Omar Arif Akram. After waiting more than an hour to get the call through and with the Saudi phone system primitive by any standard, he sounded oceans away.

"Ari? Ari can you hear me?" she shouted. "Okay, that's a little better. I wanted you to know that the situation with Gar is heating up. I'm in New York for a tennis tournament and was just visited by a private investigator. He wanted to know if I told Angie something about Gar losing a valuable item."

"Did you actually tell her that?"

"Yes I did—but we covered for each other. He didn't get anything."

"Do you know who he was—or where he comes from?"

"He works for Wolf and Noah Rembardt. In Paris."

"Ally, that's bad news for us. I know them both very well. And you should know that they are the best in the business. They must be on to something they think is substantial. And you can be sure that they will be back. Is there anything more?"

"Well, he was asking Angelique funny questions about Oskar. Questions in the present tense—like maybe Oskar was still alive. Angie threw him out of her hotel."

"That wasn't too smart of her.

Well—keep me informed, Ally. And keep your wits about you twenty-four hours a day. Those guys can be all around you and you won't even know it.

I repeat—they are not going to go away. Not until they have solved this case."

SIXTY-SEVEN

Ursula was right. In Hollywood she did meet the most interesting people.

Nevertheless, it had been many years since any couple had taken the movie capital by the sheer force of their magnetic personalities. Now, it was equally true for both—Ursula and Gar.

In most previous Hollywood captivations, excitable levels of fan and trade interest had been primarily due to good old-fashioned hype. The kind that was whipped-up—mimeographed—and handed out by hard-grunting publicity departments. In point of fact, most of the old handouts were pure fantasy. And for good reason.

With few exceptions, the realities of the stars were no different from the people in Lubbock or Keokuk, who flocked to see their heroes and heroines on the silver screen.

Some had been elevator operators, or garage mechanics, or sales clerks. Most never got that far. Even their original names would have been marquee disasters. From the silent film beginnings, in 1910, of seventeen-year old, Canadian-born, Mary Pickford, 'America's Sweetheart', whose real name was Gladys Smith, to the macho superstar John Wayne, who started life as the not-so-macho Marion Morrison—and walked so fairy funny.

Or, you might prefer Barbara Stanwyck as Ruby Stevens; Robert Taylor as Spangler Brugh; or the perfect "10" star, Bo Derek. Not very sexy as just another Mary Cathleen Collins.

If they wanted to fulfill their ambitions, the screen stars America knows and loves willingly allowed themselves to become manipulated puppets. Off camera and behind the dark sunglasses, they were re-created—out of mostly blue sky. 'Exploit' has long been an accepted part of the Hollywood vocabulary. It goes hand-in-hand with the movie industry's well-oiled publicity machinery. But even the best in the business sometimes get unexpectedly fouled up.

For example, Marilyn Monroe did everything she could to further her career. Whatever publicity wanted—publicity got. When she married baseball's classy Joe DiMaggio, he tried to break that manipulated mode. The traditional and private DiMag raged over the famous Monroe photo showing his wife's skirt blowing sky high—exposing her panties for all to see. That was not the old Italian way of Joe.

Unable to reconcile these very real differences, their marriage was a brief affair. Perhaps it was doomed from the beginning. Joe was a star seeking privacy. He knew who he was. Marilyn would spend the rest of her short life desperately searching for herself. She lost everything.

This time the circumstances were completely different. Here were two fully experienced international personalities, Ursula and Gar, real pros who knew just about all there was to know about gossip, spotlights, and front-page headlines. And both gloried in the attention.

This high level of fishbowl comfort allowed their unique personal qualities to always hold center stage. Ursula's breathtaking beauty and cool confidence, which complimented Gar's rugged handsomeness and preeminent financial prowess. Cachet on this grand scale had never before been available. And was eagerly embraced.

As the epicenter of all the important tinseltown social

action, they had every host and hostess desperately hoping that some of their glitter might rub off. In that pursuit no stone was left unturned to make each gathering a special occasion—the peak happening of the season.

The extravagant reception motifs and the dinner party themes grew to rival film sets—with predictable consequences. Entertainment costs and planner's fees escalated wildly. Much as the L.A. area real estate on which these ultra-lavish events took place. Sooner or later, someone would top them all. It happened sooner.

Gar's worldwide business calls were unexpectedly interrupted by the arrival at his hotel bungalow of a private Oriental driver—dressed from head to toe in black.

"Mr. George Garfield Grey?"

"That's me."

"My instructions are to put this envelope directly into your hand—only yours."

Gar glanced at the unusual black envelope he now held. Looking back at the driver, "In that case my good man, you have fulfilled your obligation."

As Gar stood framed in the doorway, the driver said, "Thank you, sir." Bowed slightly, turned on his heel, and was gone as quickly as he had arrived.

Back at his desk, Gar took a long look at the jet-black envelope. Addressed to both Ursula and Gar, it had been hand-penned in white ink by a top-notch calligrapher. The dramatic white on black contrast made an emphatic statement. It commanded Gar not to tear it up, or rip it open. But rather to open it carefully. Which he did.

Gar slowly removed an invitation, an R.S.V.P card, and matching small envelope. All with appropriate tissues and also printed in white ink on jet-black papers. No question, it grabbed his full attention. The invitation was actually only a two-line date holder—in the form of yet another command.

"Don't make any other plans for Saturday, October, 18th. Or you'll miss the party of your lifetime."

Gar thought, "The party of my lifetime and no one signed it? What's this bullshit all about?" He hated bullshit. Unless he created it. Nevertheless, he promptly returned the RSVP card.

When he told Ursula about the strange goings-on, she was not at all surprised. She had heard that the entire Hollywood "A-list" was already agonizing over the suspense—inundated by delicious rumor and gossip. And loved every minute of it.

Days went by without another word. It was like waiting for the other shoe to drop. On the seventh day, the same driver, still dressed in all black, suddenly returned.

He repeated the same routine. Only this time he handed Gar a slightly bulky 5 x 7 black envelope. Same white calligraphy. Same, "Thank you, sir." Same slight bow. Again, he was instantly gone.

As he closed the door, Gar smiled to himself. He told Ursula, "When we finally know the details of this gigantic put-on, I'm going to hire whoever is behind it. To make this kind of simple social bullshit work in a town famously known all over the world for practically inventing bullshit, is Pure Genius."

Much as an excited child, Ursula urged his attention back to the 5 x 7. "Hurry up, honey. I can hardly wait."

As she hovered over his shoulder, Gar removed a white, full-face mask made of papier-mâché. Then, an invitation printed in white ink on jet-black card stock.

You Are Hereby Commanded To Appear At
A Masked Costume Ball
Saturday Evening, October Eighteenth,
Nineteen Hundred Seventy-Five
Cocktails: At Nine
Dinner: Sometime Later

Details Will Be Forthcoming At The Appropriate Time
Attire: Character Costume
No Guest Will Be Admitted Without Wearing The Mask

What Gar did not know yet was that he had *already* hired the Pure Genius. Darcy Dunne was working for him as Ursula's Publicity Counselor and overall mentor. And, Darcy Dunne was the best.

To avoid any later misunderstandings, upon her hiring, Gar had made everything perfectly clear.

"Because we don't know each other from the past, up front Darcy you should know that in whatever I undertake, I never settle for less than the best. *Never*. Including my own performance. Now, I also want the best for Ursula.

Everyone I've talked to has assured me you are the best in your business. If that proves to be true in this case, you'll earn every dime you've asked for. So I agree to your terms. Who knows? Maybe you'll even earn a bonus. I hope I'll owe you one.

Next. About your budget.

For you to help me make Ursula into a movie star, and I mean in the shortest possible time, you have unlimited resources. That gives you enough rope to get the job done—or hang yourself—whichever comes first.

So, dear lady, unless you have something further, the clock has started to tick. From here on, I only want to see asses and elbows."

Always ready with a quip, Darcy retorted, "I can't promise you any elbows."

While a similar party must surely have been done before, nobody in Hollywood remembered where or when. That being the case, in creating the Masked Costume Ball concept, Darcy was breaking new social ground. While spending Gar's money at racing speeds, she also felt highly confident.

She knew, "When the "A-list" realized that Ursula, still only a fashion model, had successfully carried off the most realistic acting performance as Hollywood's secret hostess, Gar's fierce determination on her behalf will have been highly rewarded. Without exception, the top tier of studio management will instantly recognize that Ursula already is a valuable film asset. And pushing Gar to strike out on his own on her behalf, was a costly blunder."

Then, Darcy Dunne, who knew Hollywood as few others did, took her thought one step further.

"The blunder admission will be quickly set aside. Offers will pour in. Studio bosses don't agonize long over their many errors of judgment. Those mistakes are quickly buried in the broad meltdown against 'gross profit.' Along with every other expense item that the most creative accounting teams can dream up."

And those accounting extravaganzas have stood up against the IRS for decades—procedures that remain the tax-advantaged financial core of the movie industry.

An anonymous Hollywood financial official once remarked, "Maybe we've got this whole thing set-up backwards. Perhaps, the *Oscars* should go in the opposite direction."

It's an accepted Hollywood fact, with very few exceptions, that regardless of box office 'gross take', no picture is allowed to ever turn a 'net profit.' Accordingly, actors have been unmercifully burned on 'net profit' contracts that disappear into thin air.

This all stems from the same source of deep wisdom as the legendary, "location—location—location" bromide in the real estate business.

Regardless of a great location, no private builder or developer has ever been caught making a profit. At least none that they would ever publicly admit.

Yet, it would be impossible to build mansions, join exclusive country clubs, or send your children to the top-rated colleges and universities, from just 'breaking even'.

'Depreciation' and 'Amortization' are the eighth and ninth wonders of the world.

When Darcy decided that she had squeezed most of the drama out of the suspense angle of the Ball, and before going any farther, she requested a private meeting with Gar.

"What's our agenda, Darc? You know I hate surprises."

To herself: "Mister, you don't have any idea of what a surprise *really* is."

Out loud, "I'll tell you the reason for the meeting when I see you."

Darcy suggested that just the two of them should meet in an abandoned sound stage on the back lot of Gar's American Studios. She would bring two ham and Swiss and coffee for lunch.

He joked, "If it's bad news, I'll lose my appetite. You'll have to eat both sandwiches."

"Keep a stiff upper, Gar—you're a survivor. I'll see you at one o'clock inside the sound stage. Don't ask anybody for directions. If you don't find me, I'll find you. I remember my way around back there."

When they met, her opening shot was like out of a cannon. "You are the first to know, so I warn you in advance. Don't fall off of your chair."

"Remember Darc, I told you that I don't like surprises."

"Then, hold on especially tight. And hear this.

The Masked Costume Ball is going to be held at the La Mar Ballroom—unless you like this place better."

"And just how do you happen to be in possession of such privileged information that most of this town is torturing themselves waiting for? Besides—what the hell do *I* have to do with it?"

"Because we are partners in this—sort of. The concept is all mine. But, the money is all yours. That's why you have *everything* to do with it."

"Well—I'll be a…"

"Listen, fella. You told me that you wanted to make Ursula a star—and *fast.* You said a bunch of nice things, too. Like you had heard I was the best in the business. Like you were not going to negotiate my fee: And that my budget was unlimited. True?"

"All true."

"Well, Gar, I *am* the best. Only this time, you didn't get fucked. For a change, how does it feel to get your moneys worth—standing up?"

"Darc, I have to hand it to you. This caper ranks right at the top of the greatest promotions I've ever known. To turn this jaded town into a group of anxious little kids waiting for Santa is…well—unreal. My congratulations. Urs is in for a big shock."

As they rose from their folding chairs, Gar leaned forward to give her an airbrush kiss on the cheek. But he got more than he bargained for. The still-beautiful and slim Darcy put her arms around his shoulders and gave him a long, deep kiss.

As she sensually ground her sexy bottom into him, "Ursula gets all the good stuff. I'll settle for a few good well-placed crumbs."

"Darc, I…"

"Please—don't respond right now…I've been a grown girl for a long time, Gar. I know exactly what I said—and I meant it. For you, my door will always be open. But nobody is forcing you to walk through it. Tuck it away in the back of your mind. You and I both know the future can have a very fickle finger."

Gar was at a complete loss for words.

"Now, enough love and kisses. Let's sit down and finish our business.

The key questions are:

Where? The choices are:

La Mar Ballroom.

Somewhere here on the lot.

Or do you have a better idea?

Security will be critical that night—wherever we do it. Do you want me to arrange for private security, or will you want your own people to be on guard?

When do you think it will be safe to tell Ursula? It would be a shame to blow the whole bundle now if she can't hold it.

I have the up-to-date A-list for you to review, Gar.

After you supply some answers, I think I've covered your ass. But, be careful of your mouth. Know what I mean?"

SIXTY-EIGHT

Darcy and Gar thought it best if the two of them, together, told Ursula the secrets of the Masked Costume Ball. To that end, Gar had dinner brought to the bungalow that evening. Darcy, the shrimp cocktails, and hello kisses—arrived simultaneously.

Earlier, after Gar had added and subtracted from Darcy's A-list, precisely 262 guests were invited to the Masked Costume Ball, which would be held at the Lar Mar Ballroom in Santa Monica. Those guests would soon be receiving the remaining details regarding, "the party of your lifetime."

Ursula had a few incidental questions for Darcy—and quickly received answers. In a quiet voice, Gar casually brought up the subject of the Masked Costume Ball. "Urs, there are a few details about the Ball that you should know."

"And from whom did you get such hot inside information?"

"From the lady who conceived the idea of the Ball—*just for you.*" Then, in exaggerated formality, "May I present—Ms. Darcy Dunne."

Ursula's first reaction was beyond surprise. Acute shock would have been more accurate—as evidenced by a brief mental numbness. In this condition, Ursula dropped a shrimp loaded with red cocktail sauce. And watched it tumble all the way down the front of her white sweater. It left a messy red track.

At last, Gar's words sank in. With eyes big as saucers, a disbelieving Ursula shrieked, "*Darcy did what for me*?"

Still trying to keep Ursula calm, Gar maintained his equanimity. "You heard right, Urs. Darcy conceived the Ball as a big promotion. Part of the P.R. and publicity work I hired her to do to push your movie career as fast as possible."

Darcy stepped in. "You know, Urs, sometimes an idea whose time has come, ignites by itself—takes on a life of its own. Unexpected things like that happen in the crazy fashion industry all the time. Well—that seems to be what's happened to my Masked Costumed Ball idea.

I was sure I had a good idea to start with. A glitzy publicity party—a vehicle to launch you into the film business. No matter how or why, it took off like a rocket. Now, we've got a major social production to organize and control."

As usual, listening with only one ear and still unsuccessfully patting cold water on her badly stained white sweater, Ursula swore, "Damn. Oh well, let the dry cleaner worry about this." And pulled it off over her head. Not the least bit embarrassed that she wore nothing underneath.

Darcy took one look at Ursula's perfectly formed nipples and tits—the same ones that Playboy and Penthouse had tried for years to nakedly photograph—and had a novel suggestion.

"Hey, Urs, maybe this bare view might be all the costume you need for the Ball. You could wear a jaunty angled beret as a Berlin prostitute looking for a John. And for the night, we'll change Gar's name to John." The two women thought the idea hysterically funny.

Gar did not. "Okay, girls—enough."

Turning to Ursula, "The waiter will be in again soon—

cover yourself up with something. And let's get back to discussing the Ball. That's what we're here for."

As she pulled a pale-blue cashmere sweater over her head, Ursula was back, saying, "You two know everything. I don't even remember when the damn thing is."

Gar replied, "Saturday, October, 18th."

"Where?"

"At your favorite place. The La Mar Ballroom."

"Jeez—That's a big place. How many people are going to be invited?"

"We finally ended up with 262 guests."

"Wow—the real crème de la crème. And they will all need costumes!" Indeed they did.

As soon as those 262 privileged guests were notified, they quickly generated a land-office business for every costume maker in L.A. and New York. To say nothing of the worst nightmares for every wardrobe department at the various studios.

Imagine the pressure these very creative costume makers were under trying to suggest, design, cut, sew—and custom fit, 262 *different* costumes—all at the same time—all to be worn on the same night—to the same party. Every costume shop was sheer pandemonium.

And talk about the implications of power....

"Edith, my husband told me if it's not perfect, you'll never hear from his studio again."

And—"I don't want anyone else showing up in my costume, Helen. Be sure it's *my* original."

Things were a little different for the host and hostess.

Gar knew his London tailor had his up-to-date measurements. The same for Ursula. All the famous European fashion designers knew her numbers from memory.

Citing urgent business, and surrounded by deep leather comfort, the couple flew back to London on Gar's jet to have their costumes quietly made there.

SIXTY-NINE

As Gar came through the door of his London office for the first time since Vikki left, subconsciously he still expected to find her at her desk. That was only to be a memory. Instead, his new administrative assistant, Martha Henry, graciously greeted him.

A tall, slim, pleasingly attractive woman in her late thirties, Martha had sensuously long chorus girl legs and stylishly cut brown hair, Gar recalled that she had never married—whatever the reason. And his roving eye predicted that her tits were on the small side—but with good nipples. Overall, he found Martha quite appealing. It was obvious she was in immediate awe of Gar.

"Welcome back, Mr. Grey. You may not remember me—I'm Martha Henry."

"Hello, Martha. We haven't seen each other in a very long time. You look great and you sound great on the telephone. Looks and sounds are very important to me. I'm glad Irene got this brainstorm. I'm sure it will work out just fine—for both of us."

"Mr. Grey, I wanted very much to remain here in London. I feel much more free and happier here. Your unexpected opening popped up at just the right moment. It was like…well, sort of like…fate. And I'm very flexible. In whatever way I can possibly please you, I'll do anything you want me to do."

Proceeding to his desk, as was his habit, Gar opened the top drawer first. There, he found a brief note in a familiar handwriting:

"Gar:

I want you to remember that I really am just as good as any other woman you've ever known. Given the chance, we could have been something special. Please look in the left pocket of your blue silk robe. It's hanging in the back of your wardrobe closet. I wish you well.

Vikki."

Following her instructions, Gar was unprepared for what he found. In that pocket was all the jewelry he had bought for her on that fabulous shopping spree in New York. In his hand, the precious stones started to naturally warm and sparkle. Before Martha came looking for him, Gar quickly opened a hidden wall safe and placed the jewelry safely inside.

Yet, Vikki's image continued to dance in his head. It was in here, in this very same room, that their intense relationship began. He smiled at the glowing memory of her cigarette in the dark. But, Gar Grey was not one to ever allow yesterday's nostalgia to spoil today's opportunities.

Still pumped from the Hollywood scene, Gar and Ursula were ready for anything. They were regulars at all the trendy new London restaurants and nightclubs. There were also a few special places—reserved for the right mood and moment. Late one night, more than normal alcohol produced the right mood and moment.

Entering his limousine, Gar said the coded, "Mayfair."

Howland, his ever-reliable London driver, knew the exact location. And drove them to a brothel in Mayfair, which catered to upper-class sadomasochists.

The madam silently nodded her recognition as Gar and Ursula came through the door on their way downstairs. In the brothel's basement was an elaborately equipped torture chamber containing every kind of pain-inducing mechanism man could invent.

With Gar and Ursula comfortably seated in overstuffed chairs, all of the available bodies were paraded in front of them for selection. Gar quickly noticed a blond, teen-age boy with a smooth hairless body, and thought him to be particularly attractive. The young man immediately started to get an erection, Gar stared as it grew to amazing proportions.

As he looked to Ursula for possible confirmation, an attractive redhead—a twentysomething female—aggressively pushed forward. "Please, sir. I haven't had a satisfying whipping in more than two days. And I desperately need one today, so that I can have an orgasm. Choose me for either you or your beautiful lady. I beg you, sir—oh, please choose me."

Taking his time, Gar chose a vicious-looking cat-o-nine tails with fine thongs of thin leather strips—and the redhead. As the disappointed young man turned away, he said to Gar, "Come back for me another time when you're alone. I'll show you the time of your life."

Without another word, the keeper of the dungeon swiftly hung the chosen girl by her arms so that her tiptoes barely touched the floor. Turning to Ursula, and handing her the whip, Gar said, "O.K., baby, here's your chance to get even with those three Belgian bitches in Berlin." And she did.

Ursula used the whip with extreme vengeance. Across the woman's back and thighs, the pale flesh turned from pink to bright red. With great force, Ursula laid on stroke after stroke.

In the dark unconscious recesses of the mind, pain is a first cousin to ecstasy.

The redhead screamed, "Do it harder—much harder. I'm almost ready to come."

Happy to oblige her victim, Ursula swung the painful cat-o-nines again and again. Several of the deeper welts began to break open.

The sight of blood and the redhead's continuous pleadings were getting Ursula excited in a strange new way. It was the domination. The absolute control. Maybe Gar was right all along. Control was good. She liked it.

Nearly exhausted, Ursula swung the whip one more time as hard as she could. And got the response the victim had been craving, "Oh yes! I'm coming! I'm reeaallly commmming!!!"

With her victim cut down, contentedly bathing in her own juices, Ursula stared at this woman who had begged to be beaten bloody in order to attain orgasm. The very idea of achieving climax through pain was a new and different experience for the international German beauty. "Gar, honey, after she gets washed and cleaned, can we have her privately. I find her sexy."

"Not here, but, I can have her sent over to our place. What do you think about the young blond boy?"

"You know me. Anything that arouses our curiosity should be fully explored."

Gar thought about curiosity again the next day. His attraction toward Martha Henry was irrefutably curious—but remained confusing.

He had known many far more beautiful women. And while he could not put his finger on it—there it was. Something about Martha appealed to a secreted dark part of his core—never touched before. But, at this point in his life?

As he twirled the fantasy of her around in his mind, he felt sure it was connected with what she told him on that first day he was back.

"In whatever way I can possibly please you, I'll do anything you want me to do."

Martha's words magnetized Gar's imagination.

Speculating deliciously, "Could she possibly be an obedient submissive?"

Gar concluded that the entire Martha fantasy most likely was linked to his life-long nemeses—*control.* Unadulterated dominance. His insatiable need to be the master of all he surveyed.

And now, most of all—to be Martha Henry's absolute master.

SEVENTY

Gar often repeated, "I've always been able to juggle more than one toy at a time."

These days that ability served him especially well.

Wherever else his mind may have been involved, Gar and Ursula were busily engaged in planning their Masked Ball costumes. After discarding a dozen ideas, Gar told her, "It's not that complicated, Urs. You're making a mountain out of a molehill. I think you're a queen, so why not dress as one for the Ball?

"Could I be Marie Antoinette of France?"

"You can be any queen you want to pretend to be."

Ursula clowned a command, "On your knee, slave. Kiss my ring."

"Kiss my ass, Urs. Don't get carried away too far with this queenie thing."

Ursula ran to Gar's extensive library, wanting to learn, "What was the famous Marie Antoinette all about?"

Gar decided to be Don Juan—an obsessively extravagant seducer of women. And who could possibly be a more perfect profligate?

Of course, he would be obnoxiously overdressed as the ultimate dandy.

In full breeches of ivory silk, gathered and banded just below the knee; matching free-flowing blouse with a wide ascot collar; heavily brocaded silk vest; white stockings; black patent-leather shoes with silver buckles; topped off with a garish, overly-wide brimmed hat sporting a long plume of white heron feathers—worn rakishly. An altogether flamboyant costume.

Further, as Don Juan, Gar would be overly perfumed and wear thick powdered make-up. And to successfully carry it all off, he would act in a properly overbearing manner.

As Ursula teased his tailor at his final fitting, "You made him look too damn good for just a one-night stand. We'll have to figure out another night where we can wear our costumes again."

Gar responded, "That's a great idea Urs, because I'd like to take you to dinner at the Dorchester or the Savoy in your Marie Antoinette outfit. With your bare tits showing, you just might incite another revolution on this side of the English channel."

With both costumes now carefully packed to carry on Gar's jet, this mission was nearly over. And nobody was more aware of Gar's dwindling London schedule than Martha Henry.

Without exchanging so much as an intimate word, Martha extravagantly hoped that she held some appeal for her new employer. But that hope was fraught with uncertainty.

After years of listening to her older sister, Irene, secretly brag about her many clandestine romps with her famous boss, it occurred to Martha that what she felt for Gar might be nothing more than an unconscious sibling rivalry. Yet, in her mind she knew, "Gar is so handsome, so virile so...so...*dominating*. And he's so *masterful*. He's all the manly things I find most appealing."

To sort it out, Martha reasoned to herself, "Yet, in reality, if this is only a fucking contest between Irene and me, I would make a complete fool of myself if I made an explicit move on him—and he had no interest in me.

Yet, on the plus side, he's still married. With my orientation that's always better. My deepest sexual satisfaction has always been with dominant, married men. I know that's also true with Irene. We've tried sex the same night—with the same man. But not as a threesome. One of us always was the voyeur. We surely enjoy watching each other. I just adore my sister Irene.

If Gar somehow picks up on the real me, I just know that he'll come flying back to find out what he might have passed up. If not—hell, it could cost me my job.

Then what?"

Back in Hollywood, Darcy was up to her eyeballs in the details of the Ball. Not the least of which was the all-important matter of security. With the fortune in jewels that would be on display that night, security had the highest priority.

In response to her original security question, later on Gar told her that as long as the Ball would not be held on studio property, she should arrange for the services of the top private security agency.

After consulting the Chief of Security at American Studios, Darcy did just that. She contacted the best security firm in the L.A. area, *Situations Security Management,* whose head honcho, Jim Hazelett, was a man with whom she had worked on many previous assignments. Hazelett carefully listened as Darcy laid out the entire Ball evening.

After which he suggested that his on-duty people would best blend in as servants and other staff, wearing various unattractive costumes. They would be stationed both inside and outside the La Mar Ballroom—and they would be armed!

Darcy still had more questions. After more back and forth, Hazelett concluded, "Having worked that particular venue any number of times before, Darcy, we'll be covering familiar territory. No question, your 262 guests and their valuables will be completely safe. And in appreciation for your referral, that night I will personally be the on-site commander."

A reporter and photographer for the L.A. Times were at the private terminal area at LAX when Gar's jet touched down. The attractive three-column photo of the famous pair made first page, second section.

By now, an old hand at this interviewing game, Gar tersely told the reporter, "Always happy to be in L.A. No further comment."

His limo was waiting.

As the days flew by the hectic pace accelerated.

With eighteen-hour days, Darcy and her staff were pulling the diverse elements of the Ball into place. With the caterer and menu resolved, and the music and entertainment also set, her biggest remaining problem was the dinner seating placement—more difficult than for a shotgun wedding in moonshine Appalachia.

Dealing with the superegos of Hollywood, a town of overflowing self-importance, required Gar's personal involvement. When they finally sat down together at Darcy's Wilshire condo, she and Gar went over the entire list—for the zillionth time.

Darcy projected, "To seat 262 guests at tables of eight we'll only need 32 tables. No matter the occasion, inevitably we'll have a few no-shows. Losing six bodies is par for the course. That's okay. And the ballroom has six fully staffed permanent bars. By the way, Gar, the bartenders are union. Any problem?"

"No problem, Darc. It's only a party, we're not going to remake *Gone With The Wind* there. So far, it sounds as though you've got the whole shebang under control."

"Not quite. Now comes the crunch, Gar. Let's spread out 32 pretend tables. And *you* start placing names at those tables." Laughing, "If wars or revolutions break out that night—just remember who did the placements. Oh, maybe you'd like to know that I heard yesterday that it's gone beyond panic at all the costume shops. Jeez, what kind of a monster did I create?"

"A good one Darc—the best. No matter what happens that night, Hollywood will remember this party for years. And I will be eternally grateful to you. By the way, I never did ask you. What's *your* costume for the big night?"

"I've got it right here in my bedroom closet. Give me a minute, and I'll give you a sneak preview. Pour yourself a drink in the meantime. I could use one too."

"How about double Scotches?"

"Pour your heart out. The Glenlivet is in the crystal decanter."

Gar never heard Darcy come back from the bedroom. When he looked up—there she was—dressed like a ten-year old little girl.

Short, pink, baby doll dress—with adult-sized protruding breasts; black patent Mary Jane shoes; pink anklets; and a large pink ribbon on top of her head. She was licking a pink lollipop.

One good look—and Gar spilled his Scotch.

Darcy said, "No matter the costume, every gal there is going to try to look sexy. My costume revives an old male fantasy—fucking an innocent little girl."

Walking toward him, and lifting her skirt, "But a hot, naked cunt is my own twist. Maybe yours is to fuck my brains out—right now!"

"It's not everyday that I get such an erotic offer."

"You can fuck an innocent little girl as you see me dressed now. Or, give me a few minutes and you can fuck an experienced lady who has dreamed about balling you since the day we met."

"I'll meet you in your bed in ten minutes."

With only five minutes having elapsed, Gar walked purposefully into the bedroom au naturel, carrying the two double Scotches.

He found Darcy also naked—just finishing three prominent lipstick markings.

She had drawn a red circle around each nipple—and a long red arrow pointed down to her pussy.

Darcy explained, "Call it my sex map. Since you've never been over this particular territory before, I wanted to make sure you found all the popular attractions—and didn't get lost." Gar had not laughed this hard in a long time.

Still smiling, he handed over her Scotch, and proposed a toast. "To Darcy's experience, wisdom, and inspiration. May she continue to accumulate many more of these attributes—and always include me as her inside man."

Glasses clinked.

As they drank their Scotches, Darcy, smilingly asked, "Do you remember when you told me to get cracking on the Ursula assignment—after which all you wanted to see was asses and elbows? Do you recall saying that?"

"Sure I do."

"I told you then that I couldn't promise you any elbows. Well, here's the rest of your request." That said, Darcy turned her inviting bottom in Gar's immediate direction.

Extending Gar another raunchy invitation, Darcy handed him a life-like lubricated dildo. Fully aroused and always ready to deviate from the blandness of normal love-making, Gar reached out for the dildo—and this sexy lady.

As he rolled Darcy onto her stomach, he slowly inserted the slippery dildo—which had been a frequent experience for her since her early twenties. Under Gar's skillful touch, she purred with satisfaction.

As the substitute penis reached full penetration, Darcy produced a monumental orgasm—not an uncommon reaction in the theory of psychophysiology. Occurring when the correlation between mind, behavior, and bodily mechanisms is closely synchronized.

Content and relaxed, it pleased Darcy to leave the dildo in place. Thus, Gar turned her on her back.

Hardly able to wait, Darcy eagerly spread her legs.

SEVENTY-ONE

Bright and balmy, the big day finally arrived.

October 18, 1975.

To nobody's surprise, for the exhausted Darcy it did not arrive a day too soon. So far today, the big surprise was a very uptight Ursula. An unlikely reaction for a model so experienced on the most sophisticated runways in the world.

Calling Darcy every few minutes, she confessed,

"Darc, this is different. No matter whose designs I wore on a runway or a photo shoot, I was still me. Today, I don't have the vaguest idea of who I am. I've had that damn queen whore's costume on and off ten times today—and it's only noon. With that enormous white wig and my tits sticking way out, I...."

"I understand, Urs. I know where you're coming from. I've been through similar situations with a number of actors in their early days, who are now some of the world's biggest stars. So, for your own good, listen to me—I mean *really* listen. Not like you ordinarily don't. To start off on the right foot tonight, you have to play a good game of *Let's Pretend.*"

"I haven't done that since I played with my dolls as a little girl in Berlin."

"I'm sure that's true. But tonight, you must pretend that the Marie Antoinette costume is just another famous designer's outlandish creation. That the other female guests are also models wearing more far-out designs from the same haute couture. And that the entire affair is merely another fashion show in Milano. And forget about your bare tits. For this game, they're not important."

"Darc, that's almost like living some kind of a lie."

"Wrong! It's *nothing* like a lie. Whatever you do Urs, don't start wrapping yourself in a cloak of piousness. Next, you'll be talking about chastity and virtue. With your flirtatious history, a *real* lie would be talk like that coming from you. More than a lie, it would be fraud.

"But it's…"

"No! This is *not* about lying, Urs. It's called acting. Remember *acting?*

That's what this whole damn party is all about. Getting you into Hollywood—into acting. When you act you're really playing make-believe—pretending that you *are* the character you're portraying. Pretending for the camera. Pretending for the people who come to see the movie. And you're still pretending when you make personal appearances to promote the movie.

And when you give an extraordinary performance—a brilliant pretending job—and you have me ringing all the right trade bells for you, your peers vote to give you an 'Oscar'.

Think about Liz Taylor, Greg Peck, or Sidney Poitier. Think about some of the other film greats. Bergman, Tracy, Gable, Dietrich, Bogart—all the way back to Janet Gaynor, the first Oscar winner in 1928, and pioneers like Mary Pickford and Lillian Gish. Each was a first-class pretender.

But, the word 'pretender' would never go over with movie fans. So we call them 'actors' instead. But it's really the same. *It's still pretending!*

And, while the marvelously talented scenic designers and art directors have made make-believe easier than ever to accept—nothing has changed. Pretending is still the name of the game.

You did the same thing as a fashion model, Urs. Sashaying down the runway all dazzled out in a divine Givenchy gown—but you had just left your real cut-off jeans in the dressing room."

"I never thought about acting or modeling the way you're describing it to me now, Darc."

"Well, this is as good a time as any to start. I didn't mean to give you such a long lecture, Urs, but there's a fortune riding on your success tonight. Don't blow the chance of-a-lifetime."

"I guess you're right."

"Trust me. I've watched the passing parade out here for a long time. I know the ones who made it big—doing great pretending for the cameras—and the ones who merely pretended on their backs and knees. I also remember those with a great deal of potential talent—who never learned to play the pretend game at all. And never made a picture, either."

Ursula scrunched her face in disapproval.

"I don't know if you ever heard the story that I got my first break under Louie B. Mayer's desk. Well it's true. I did what I had to do. Nothing was going to stop me. I would win anyway I could—and so should you. Except that with Gar's power and money behind you, there's no reason for you not to end up a big star. Be smart. For your own sake—tonight—play *Let's Pretend."*

One by one. And two by two. The first of the 262 crème de la crème guests started to arrive about nine-thirty. To be early was a social faux pas. In costumes and masks, they signed a guest register—a *"Who's Who"* of the movies. Lemmon, Douglas, Holden, and Fonda—

Crawford, Dunaway, Bacall, and Bette Davis.

Watching from behind some scenery, Ursula jumped for joy. Gar smiled. He knew them all.

From the moment they arrived, the guests strutted about in their costumes like preening peacocks. To be sure, the costumes were a sight to behold. To even attempt individual description would be impossible. They were all immensely creative and outrageously expensive.

While the costumers were undoubtedly exhausted, they also had raked in a ton of money. Every Hollywood woman had gone all-out to be the belle-of-the-ball.

As the guests were busily engaged in cocktails, hors d'oeuvres, and local trade gossip, their attention was commanded by rolling drums and shrill trumpet blasts. An offstage voice said, "And heeeers, Johnny!"

As he did on his famous *The Tonight Show,* through a break in the background curtain, out strutted the smiling, good-looking, Johnny Carson.

As a special favor to Gar, the star of late-night television had agreed to act as M.C. A popular figure in the entertainment community, the applause was loud and long.

At the microphone, the witty Carson opened with, "Good evening, ladies and gentlemen—or *whatever* you are tonight."

Laughs and applause.

"When I told Gar that I don't work Saturday nights, he lobbed a typical Gar Grey firecracker. He said, 'O.K. Johnny, I can't force you to do something that you don't want to do. But if you don't work *my* show—then, I'll have to *buy* yours.' That man can be *very* convincing."

Carson's gag hit the bullseye with this knowing crowd. Many had been in that situation with Gar Grey, *for real.*

Johnny went on, "Now let's give a big round of applause to your hosts. May I present first...Don Juan...my pal, *George...Garfield...Grey!"*

Gar entered smiling, bowing, and swaggering, as befitted his Don Juan character. And aggressively shook hands with Carson, who continued, "His co-host...and tonight...the world's most exotic queen...in her Hollywood debut.

Welcome one of the most famous faces in the world... the internationally known cover girl, *Ursula... Von... Ribbentrop!"*

Ursula entered bathed in three crossed spotlights—two magenta, one nude-white. Her three-tiered white wig was spectacular. It grabbed first attention.

Carson led the applause—followed with an exaggerated curtsy and the faux kiss of a queenly hand.

When eyes got better focused, the guests could see Ursula's great naked breasts thrusting through the open front of her Marie Antoinette costume—and her equally naked long model's legs. An audible gasp fell over the ballroom. The crowd was obviously thrown for a loop.

Gar never wavered. In a show of solid support for both Ursula and her half-naked costume, he moved to hold her hand. Together, they acknowledged an even louder round of applause. With her proud chest held high, Ursula's imperious gaze circled the room.

She looked everyone straight in the eye. She smiled. She remembered Gar's original words. "This business is not about reality. It's about perception." *And she would pretend!* Vowing, "This is *my* Hollywood coming-out party. They will perceive me on *my* terms."

She also recalled a quote from a sexy female star.

"In Hollywood, a cunt with a willing attitude is a sure prescription for success."

Having both, Ursula would use them. It wouldn't be the first time. "I've played this game all my adult life. So what was I so upset out about this morning?"

At the end of a long drum roll, Ursula shouted a queenly command, "Let the fun begin!"

As the guests were trying to figure out who each of them was under the costumes and behind the masks, Jack Warner walked over to Gar.

Always right to the point, the Warner chief said, "After seeing Ursula's bare breasts, I know why you never let any other studio get close to her. You must be the original dirty old man."

Gar replied, "I see it didn't take you very long to get a good look, Jack—speaking of dirty old men." To which they both heartily laughed.

"You're a lot younger than I am, Gar. But, I can tell you from personal experience, the law of supply and demand changes. My supply is increasing—but my demand keeps shrinking."

Reflecting on that sober comment, Gar opined, "Here's another one, Jack. As we get older some things get harder to do—but some things don't get hard anymore at all."

William Holden, dancing with Ursula could feel the warmth of her bare breasts. "In this kind of an outfit young lady, you can play opposite me in the next film I make—whatever the hell it is." They were interrupted by Stefanie Powers, Holden's long-time companion.

"Ursula, I'm Stefanie Powers. I just want you to know two things. Your costume is sensational. Second. You're an absolute knockout. If you're going be in Hollywood long, I'll have to take Bill back to Kenya—for safekeeping."

Out of nowhere, there was another vigorous burst of applause. Back from New York earlier than he had planned—in tuxedo but no mask, a beaming Frank Sinatra had just walked into the Ballroom. Ol' Blue Eyes' smooth charisma immediately enveloped the room.

The evening moved seamlessly along. The fact that everyone was hiding behind their masks proved to be great fun. Couples were dancing, but for the most part they were not sure who their partner was—the unknown factor added rare spice. A few assignations were set for nearby days.

But an entirely unscripted surprise had already begun developing, which would forever change the historical reference of Ursula's Masked Ball.

It's beginnings were set in place when the La Mar Ballroom was built atop huge timber pilings, and triphammered into the sandy loam of the Pacific shore near the Santa Monica pier.

That La Mar actually extended out over water and afforded magnificent views, particularly at sunset, was one of its great original attractions. In those days romantic young couples held their dancing partners close. Later, a cocktail on the huge outdoor terrace overlooking the ocean.

As the years passed, the mores and the music of young dancers dramatically changed. Hollywood became flooded with stories of drugs and kinky sex that took place in the remote darkness of what became the *infamous* La Mar terrace. Despite the prevailing gossip, or, perhaps, *because* of it, La Mar, like Studio 54 in New York, never lost its popularity or its singular sophistication. Velvet ropes were still required nightly to control the young people clamoring to get inside.

The clear day had given way to dark clouds blocking out the light of the moon. In the darkness, a rusted freighter, her peeling name lost to the constant exposure of wind and sea air, appeared on the horizon.

Her motors fell silent. The flukes of its dropped anchor dug deeply into the ocean floor. When the dark of night was total, the mysterious ship launched four black rubber rafts with no visible markings. Each raft held six men who wore black, skin-tight, wet suits to protect against the freezing cold ocean water—topped with both waterproof aquahoods and balaclavas—additional hoods that completely covered their heads and neck.

To eliminate any possibility of later identification, these erstwhile frogmen wore black nylon stockings pulled over their faces. To retain the lowest possible profile, the rafts had their power turned off—propelled only by the combined swimming efforts of their six passengers, three on each side, who wore scuba fins for extra propulsion power. As the rafts came onshore they were lashed to the pier.

These twenty-four men were international outlaws and jewelry pirates. They knew why they were here and what they had come for. Down to the last diamond stickpin.

Principally based in Hong Kong, jewelry piracy had been rampant since the days of the boat people desperately fleeing the Vietnam War. Piracy became so profitable it quickly ballooned into giant syndicates.

In turn, these syndicates came under the control of cruel but highly knowledgeable international professionals from Hong Kong, Indonesia, Malaysia, and Singapore. A few had been educated at the best American universities.

In order to obtain advance information on where in the world the richest collections of great jewels might be concentrated—such as at any single function—the syndicates employed hundreds of undercover spies. And thousands of ragtag snitches. Self-serving insurance publicity to the contrary, there were many such functions. And rare gems of untold value are often worn in public.

Ursula's Masked Ball was but one example.

Princely gatherings on the rocky heights of Monte Carlo or the Riviera. Or any number of important ceremonials at Buckingham Palace and other rich and royal nestings throughout the world.

Without the slightest hesitation, to get their information, these murderous thieves would stop at nothing. In the end, advance information was the mother's milk of this hideous business.

Currently, a note was thrust into the hand of a woman on Canon Drive in Beverly Hills. The male teenager who delivered the note then ran toward Wilshire and was quickly lost in the crowd. The recipient was Darcy Dunne's senior staff assistant—Ming Jade.

She nervously read. "Your father has advanced life-threatening diabetes. We are holding him in solitary confinement. He will not receive insulin, or any other vital medication, until you provide us with the details of your Masked Ball.

We want date, time, place—and detailed guest list—including home addresses and phone numbers. Be in the phone booth at Canon and Wilshire at noon tomorrow. Have the information with you for delivery. If you value your Father's remaining life, don't do anything foolish. This note is signed with a drop of his blood. Don't spill any more. We are very serious people."

As intended, the note panicked Ming Jade who had been regularly sending money home to Hong Kong ever since she arrived in California— fifteen years ago. A loving and devoted daughter, she immediately complied with the note.

Near midnight as everyone sat down for a Masked Ball gourmet dinner, underneath the Santa Monica pier all twenty-four pirates were in place and ready to move. As with every other robbery they had committed anywhere, they had rehearsed this jewel heist to perfection.

Compared to what they could legitimately earn in their third-world home countries, these killers reaped unmatchable financial rewards. As in all extreme imbalances, there was a trade-off. In this case, the bright side of the money was offset by the dark acceptance of the penalty for any mistake. A violent and horribly slow death by group clubbing with diabolically equipped American baseball bats. These bats were implanted with nails, sharp screws, and jagged pieces of glass—anything capable of pulverizing human flesh. Thusly beaten into a mass of bloody pulp, the remains were pushed over the ship's side as food for the man-eating sharks.

Their evil-minded overlords considered any other form of ultimate discipline to be of insufficient fear to be effective. And these annihilators did not soon forget. Ergo, mistakes were an infrequent occurrence.

The twenty-four black-clad pirates quickly climbed to the outside terrace of La Mar. Stealthily, they took out the security guards Jim Hazelett had provided. Generous amounts of chloroform, combined with a heavy oriental liquid chemical momentarily held over the faces of Hazelett's men, rendered them immediately unconscious. Hazelett himself, had been gagged and tied—then put out with the same chloroform combination.

With security gone, the pirates crouched beside the four sets of double French doors already open to the balmy Fall air. On cue, the brigands came storming through the open doors, quickly fanning out around the perimeter of the dining area in the Ballroom—brandishing an assortment of machine guns, pistols, knives, and blood-stained machetes.

Awaiting their appetizers, predictably, the diners panicked in their seats.

"Oh my God, they're going to kill us all," screamed one bejeweled dowager—who promptly fainted.

Moving to keep things calm, using a voice-distorting bullhorn the pirate leader, in oriental accented English, warned the jewel-rich crowd, "Don't move and nobody will get hurt. Just stay in your chairs. Don't anyone move your hands. Keep them both on the table. All we want is your jewelry and cash."

Gar stepped forward. "Without going any further, you can have whatever amount of cash is in this room."

"Shut up, smart-ass man. We'll take what we want."

With that, half the bandits started to remove jeweled watches, rings, bracelets, necklaces, and brooches. Anything that looked like valuable jewelry—and all the substantial available cash.

Everything was thrown into heavy, dirty-white canvas bags which closely resembled those used to make large bank deposits. Now they were being used to make heavy withdrawals.

A husband moved to reassure his wife—and a machete instantly came crashing down on his table. Glasses, dishes, and silver went dangerously flying. The unhurt man turned a ghastly white and crumbled to the floor. He had a well-known heart condition. His wife screamed.

The leader screamed louder, *"Nobody move!* It's no big deal. Just another fat old rich guy. The next machete will not miss. Somebody will lose a hand."

The robbers busily continued to remove every gem in sight. And more cash.

Against the leader's orders, Frank Sinatra bravely stood up and walked toward him. "Listen, pal, I'm Frank Sinatra. Maybe you've heard of me. If you stop now and give everybody their valuables back, that man," pointing toward Gar, "and I will give you ten million dollars. Right now. Tonight."

The leader warned the singer, "Don't take another step, man." And wasted a burst of machine gun fire into the ceiling.

Jeering, "You think you big man, Mr. Frank Sinatra. I know who you are. I hear you sing songs on records."

Another burst of machine gun fire tore another giant hole in the ceiling.

"Now, you sit down you little shit, and shut your mouth. Or, I have your throat cut and you never sing again."

Famous as a man with a short fuse, the enraged Sinatra looked as though he was thinking of rushing the leader. Gar, his Don Juan costume awry, quickly grabbed the singer's arm. "Don't even think about it, Frank. This guy would do anything!" Still steaming, a very reluctant Sinatra had to be forcibly restrained.

Having made an enormous haul, the plunderers were finished. Their booty stuffed into many canvas bags.

Through his bullhorn, the leader shouted, "All men back to the boats—except Sung Lee."

As the burglars left the same way they entered, the roughest-looking participator stepped forward to the leader's side. A huge, sweaty, muscled man, perhaps six feet five, with arms the size of piano legs, Sung Lee carried a wicked-looking machete.

With a lecherous grin, the leader walked over to the half-naked costumed Ursula—and pulled hard on an exposed nipple. With a loud scream, hurt and humiliated, the would-be actress turned away.

With an affirmative nod from his chieftain, Sung Lee grabbed Ursula in a suffocating arm lock and laid his cold machete against her exposed breasts. Too scared to move—the feel of the cold steel sent shivers down Ursula's spine.

Again on his bullhorn, "Okay, we ready to go now. We take this girl with us for insurance. We like lots of insurance. After I leave with the girl—nobody still not move. Phones lines cut—so forget calling police."

The chieftain and Sung Lee, with Ursula as a most unwilling hostage, followed the other bandits. Fearful for her life, Ursula did not put up any additional struggle. When the three of them got down under the pier the other men were already in their rafts. But the horror was not yet over. With one swipe of his machete Sung Lee left Ursula stark naked. She trembled. Widely grinning, the huge pirate quickly exposed himself. Her head spinning with fear, the naked Ursula felt faint.

As he approached her, holding his huge erect cock, she turned to run.

It was futile.

She didn't have a chance.

The next day Ursula woke up in St. John's Hospital in Santa Monica, with Gar and Darcy at her beside.

Her shattering physical and emotional experience notwithstanding, the doctors had assured Gar and Darcy that Ursula would be just fine. But would need a period of rest and quiet.

Thus relieved, her two visitors had been scanning a dozen Sunday papers. Ursula's Masked Costume Ball certainly would not be remembered as the three of them had planned. It was the jewelry heist angle that made front-page news. And captured millions of dollars worth of free publicity!

Seeing that her eyes were open, Gar came to her side and took her hand.

"Well, Urs, you surely look much better today."

"I don't even want to think about last night, Gar. But, I do remember what happened."

"Put it out of your mind. Pretend it never happened."

"Pretending is what I seem to be mostly doing these days. Right, Darc?"

"That's true. But this time it has already paid off. Jack Warner couldn't reach Gar, so he had Ed Roth, his chief of development, call me earlier this morning. Hold tight, Urs.

Warner, who talked with Gar about you last night, has offered you a major supporting role in an important new production. He's sending the script over this afternoon.

And—there's more.

You danced with your new male lead only last night.

It's William Holden!"

SEVENTY-TWO

All the Hollywood hullabaloo was over.

Ursula had physically recovered and was busily engaged in her first film effort, which served a dual purpose. She was gaining important film experience, but most of all, it helped her emotional state of mind, which was shaky for some time after her unfortunate encounter.

Still outraged at his loss of control at the Masked Ball, Gar was back in New York. By comparison with what he had been through on the Coast, Gotham suddenly seemed peaceful and quiet. Naturally, that didn't last. The hectic pace continued the very next day.

Irene Harvey, who had been in and out of Gar's private office, like a revolving door, at least twenty times during the day, finally suggested,

"Why don't you leave something for tomorrow, Mr. Grey? There's no law that says you've got to finish everything today. If it will calm you down, I'll be happy to stop by the apartment later."

"We'll see, Irene. If I'm up to it, I'll call you."

Gar had his driver drop him off at The Regency.

He entered the bar as a conquering hero. Old friends greeted him left and right. Everyone seemed to have a comment on the Masked Ball jewelry heist.

Even the bartender, quipped, "Mr. Grey, if you're broke now after the robbery, Mr. Tisch told me to serve you whatever you wanted at no charge." Another bout of laughter.

As the maitre d' seated Gar at his usual table, the waiter immediately brought his favorite cocktail. A chilled, very dry martini—with two olives.

Unannounced, a slightly younger man, tentatively slid into the empty chair at Gar's table. Whoever he was, this man was quite obviously angry about something. Acting fidgety, he seemed to be just another off-the-wall nut.

As Gar moved to signal the maitre d' to remove him, the man frantically grabbed his arm.

"Don't do that! Don't call the waiter. It's important that we talk."

"Who the hell are you?"

"You don't know me. But I know who you are. I've *always* known who you are. Your name and your pictures are slapped all over the newspapers and magazines. It would be hard *not* to know who you are—George Garfield Grey. We even have the same last name. And that's not just a coincidence.

"What?"

The stranger quickly withdrew an old photograph from his wallet and handed it over to Gar. It was a picture of a man and a boy of thirteen or fourteen, more than likely, father and son.

Gar looked closely at the photograph.

Without question, the man was his father. He had a picture of his own in which his father struck the same pose.

Then, another look back at the man across the table. The family resemblance was unmistakable. The man also handed Gar his drivers' license.

"My name is Lucien Smith Grey, Jr. I'm your half-brother!"

Numbly, Gar dropped the photo and the license on the table and sat back in his chair. He felt as though someone had just thrown a medicine ball directly at his stomach.

Trying to catch his breath, Gar repeated in a monotone, "Lucien Smith Grey, Jr."

These were not easy words for him to say. In fact, he was having a difficult time making this entire revelation properly connect in his brain.

"Lucien, you're right. We do have a lot to talk about. But not here in a public place. Let's go back to my apartment. Nobody's home. I only got back in town last night."

Cynically, Lucien responded, "So I read in today's newspapers."

Darkness was setting in as the two men alighted from Gar's limo in front of his Fifth Avenue apartment. Nicholas, the regular doorman was off tonight. Gar did not recognize his new replacement. The elevator stopped on ten—opening to his sprawling twenty-eight-room apartment. The sole residence on the tenth floor.

With his frantic day at the office demanding any number of worldwide decisions, and now coming face-to-face with an unknown half-brother—all tagged onto the Hollywood madness—Gar was pooped from the bewildering goings-on. And from keeping each subject in its own compartment in his mind.

Leading Lucien, Gar said, "I think we'll be fine in here. After pouring them both a glass of wine, the two new siblings sat down for a lengthy conversation in a small cozy reading room—decorated in various shades of green chintz. They were not too far from Gar's master bedroom suite. A long walk from the elevator foyer and main drawing room.

Surprisingly, the fine Bordeaux seemed to have a contrary reaction. For Gar, taking small occasional sips, the rare vintage was relaxing. Lucien drained his glass in one swallow and intently glared at Gar. His unexpected opening set the tone for the remainder of their conversation.

"First off, you might as well know that I hate your guts. And I have since as far back as I can remember. You and your selfish father have stolen most of my life from me, so you have only yourselves to blame for my hatred."

"Hold on, Lucien. I don't know a single fact about your life. I didn't even know you existed until an hour ago. So I can't refute a single thing you say—except to tell you that I am sorry you have suffered for so many years. By the way, if we are half brothers—who was your mother?"

"Not *was—is*. She's still very much alive. I won't tell you her name, but she is still a beautiful, sweet, southern woman. Back then, a gorgeous southern belle with great sex appeal—from a solid family. She and our Father met when she came up to work in Washington and he was already there. Early in the first Roosevelt administration.

She remembers it as love at first sight. I've never talked to him about it. Since your mother had already moved back to Chicago, the two lovebirds spent an intimate weekend at the Greenbrier. Unfortunately, I am the misfit result of that weekend of lovemaking."

"I cannot condone my father's conduct, Lucien, but you shouldn't paint me into the same frame. I didn't do anything to you—directly or indirectly."

Lucien's eyes turned wild.

"Of course, that would be your high and mighty selfish version—it sure as hell is not mine. You've had everything in this world—but if you didn't exist it might have been all mine. Maybe it still could be mine."

Startling Gar, the erratic Lucien pulled a pistol from a hidden shoulder holster. Without saying a word about his dangerous weapon, he simply laid it on the table. And went rambling on.

"Dammit, I even had to go to court at twenty-one to

get my rightful name. Have it changed to what it is now.

And while you've had everything handed to you on a silver platter since the day you were born, I haven't had a happy day that I can remember. And, you're so goddam uppity snobby you can't fathom what the hell I'm even talking about. And that dirty sonofabitch of a father is no better.

He made my mother and me cry our eyes out for him. We sat for hours just holding hands and crying together. That went on for years. But it didn't do us any good. We didn't mean a thing to him. He didn't give a shit about our broken hearts. He was too busy running his damned bank—and giving money to you. Money that could have and should have been—mine!

Why should you have gotten it all? *And I got none."*

Gar could see recalling his sad life only made Lucien more and more angry. A break here might be a good idea.

"Lucien, I've got an important call that I must make before it gets too late. If you'll excuse me, I'll make it as short as possible."

Over many years, Meyer Lansky, his Mafia connections notwithstanding, had been Gar's friend, partner, and confidant—offering many words of wisdom. As Gar sat alone in his library giving Lucien time to cool down, his thoughts turned to some of the best advice Lansky had ever given him. That Gar should know how to cross-dress.

"Lissen ta me Gar. Ya never know when ya might have ta sneak out of a joint in a hurry—and not be recognized. I done it myself plenty times—or I wouldn't be here ta tell ya dis. An' if *I* could cross-dress an' get away wit it, ya can too. Yur sure a lot better lookin' den me. So, come on down ta Havana. I've got a broad dat's a make-up genius. Does all da show people. She'll show ya how to do all da make-up stuff yurself 'an she'll also take ya ta places where ya kin buy all the broads kinda clothes.

Ya'll need a lot a stuff, cuz ya should keep a secret closet full of it in New York an' London. Maybe on yur ship too."

Years back, Gar took Lansky's advice and spent some time in Havana learning all the things that Conchita Garciapapa taught him. He became a pretty good make-up man. And learned how to properly dress as a female under many different scenarios. Putting on lipstick was easy. Learning to walk in high heels was another matter. Nearly broke his neck more than once.

Having learned from Inspector Gerard that Wolf still had friendly feelings, Gar called Wolf Felsenberg's New York office knowing that his home phone would be connected to the office switchboard. He was right. After two rings, Wolf answered. After a brief up-dating on old loose ends, Wolf asked about the Costume Ball fiasco.

"I'm glad you brought that damn Ball up, Wolf. That's the reason for my call. I want to retain you and Noah to go to the Far East and see what you can find out for me about the syndicate behind the heist. You can use my office in Hong Kong as your base. Report back as soon as possible. I feel like a fool about the entire mess. You're right—total loss of security. How about total loss of *control?*

You, above anyone else, know how I feel about that."

With the call concluded, Gar headed back to the reading room where he had left Lucien. His pistol was still on the table—but Lucien was not there.

"Lucien? Lucien, where are you?" Getting no response, Gar thought his newly found half-brother was so upset that he picked himself up and left.

"Oh, well. Maybe it's better that way."

Figuring the night was finally over, Gar headed for the bathroom in his master suite—and got the shock of his life.

The spotless almond marble room was a shambles.

Every cabinet door was open.

Every drawer pulled out or turned upside down.

Some bottles had broken. Tubes and vials thrown everywhere.

The bathroom looked as though it had been hit by a tornado.

Gar knew as soon as he walked into his bedroom. Sprawled on the carpet was his newly found half-brother. Gar felt for a pulse.

Lucien Smith Grey, Jr. was dead—a suicide.

He had obviously ingested handfuls of every kind of pill he could lay his hands on in Gar's bathroom. That kind of mad combination would only produce a deadly result—*and it had!*

Whatever Gar intended to do, he would have to act fast. He decided on a quick call to Meyer Lansky in Havana.

"I'm sorry, sir. Mr. Lansky is in an important meeting and cannot be disturbed."

"Just tell him Gar Grey is calling from New York. It's an emergency."

In seconds, Gar heard the familiar gravel voice,

"Whadda fuck kinda 'mergency ya got, Gar?"

"Meyer, my whole world seems to be falling apart these days. I suppose you read about the jewelry heist at a party I gave in California the other night?"

"Ya I did. Somebody made a clean heist—and ya looked like a big schmuck."

"No question about that. Well, I'm back in New York now, and some weird guy sat down next to me in a bar. He told me he's my half-brother that I never knew I had. So we came back to my place to talk. While I made a few calls, he O.D'd on some of my pills and I've got a dead body on my hands—right here in my apartment.

Meyer, if this story gets out before we have a smart solution, coming right on the heels of the California shit—our stock will get beaten down to zilch. It could develop into a very serious matter. Any suggestions?"

"I gotta great idea. Yur one lucky bastard."

"What's your great idea."

"Conchita Garciapapa—ya member da make-up broad?"

"Very well. Terrific girl."

"Well she's been visitn' her mother up in da Bronx. I'll have 'er over ta yur apartment in less than an' hour. I'll give 'er complete instrukshons of what ta do. Yur problem is solved. Jus' stay da hell outta any more truble. An' take good care of our stock. For crissakes, we all hav ta make a livin' ya know. Sa long kid."

In about forty-five minutes, the doorman announced the arrival of a "Miss Garciapapa." Moments later this six-foot, drop dead-looking hooker walked into Gar's apartment carrying a make up bag big enough to carry out a body. And that was Gar's first thought. But he was wrong.

Conchita said, "I have all the instructions we need from Mr. Meyer. We're going to make up this guy to look just like you. So it will be 'you' that gets buried—but not really.

I'll start the make up first, while you bring me one of your dark suits. Then, start to undress this guy. Remove his wallet and all other identification. Substitute your wallet, but leave your I.D. inside. And don't forget to put your watch on his wrist.

After that go into your locked closet and pick an outfit that's close to what I'm wearing. I remember buying it for you in Havana. Put on a long brown-haired wig, earring's, and high heels—the works. Look as glitzy as possible. I'll make you up as soon as I finish this guy, whoever the hell he is. We don't have too much time, so get moving. There's a long night ahead of us."

After all of Lansky's orders were complied with—they left Lucien as 'Gar.' And Gar's cross-dressed outfit looked amazingly similar to Conchita's.

The big Cuban woman stopped in the small reading room. With a handkerchief she carefully picked up Lucien's gun and dropped it into her bag. She did the same thing with his wineglass. With a furniture polish-cleaner, Lucien's fingerprints came off of the chair, table, and other woodwork. Gar's prints were left untouched.

Having given the scene a last once-over—and finding everything copacetic—the two hooker look-a-likes casually walked out of the lobby into the Fifth Avenue night.

Gar's senior maid came on duty at 6 AM. After three rare days off, she had plenty of work to catch up on. Twenty-eight rooms are a lot of responsibility.

Making her first rounds, the open door to Gar's bedroom immediately grabbed her attention. Instinctively, "Something must be wrong. Mr. Grey always keeps his bedroom door closed. With great caution, she approached the door and slowly peeked in.

Lying face-up on the floor, directly in front of her, was a sight she would never forget for the rest of her life.

"Mr. Grey! Oh, dear God. Mr. Grey!"

And immediately did what Gar had always told her to do. "In an emergency—before you do anything else—call Irene Henry."

In fifteen minutes, wearing a blue jogging suit and no make up, Irene Henry was in the apartment. When she saw the body in the familiar dark suit, she began to sob—but quickly regained her composure. Without wasting a precious second, she dialed Sal Bellini's unlisted number at his nearby town house.

"Sal, it's Irene—I'm at Gar's. He's dead. The maid called me. I got here in minutes and found his body on the bedroom floor. Yes, you heard me right. His *body.* And there are all kinds of pills and vials scattered all over. Of course I felt for a pulse. He's cold and he's dead. What should I do?"

Bellini was not the kind of man to get easily flustered.

"I can hardly believe what you're telling me, Irene. But, let's get going. I know some of the guys at Gar's precinct station. I'll give one of the detectives there a friendly call. You better stay until they come over."

Sal slowly hung up the phone. An era had ended—and an unusually close thirty-year friendship raced through his mind. "Gar, a suicide. I never would have believed this could happen. Must have been something that he forgot to let me in on."

Dialing the precinct, "Good morning sergeant, this is Sal Bellini. Is Keenan around? Good. I'll wait. Hello, Keenan? Sal Bellini here. Keenan, I need you to help me out of a delicate situation. No, nobody was caught in a strange bed—it's much worse.

I've just been informed that a famous client of mine—you remember Gar Grey of General Industrial? Right, the same guy who was in yesterday's papers. Well, he just committed suicide in his apartment on Fifth. And it's urgent that we keep this as quiet as possible—his wife doesn't even know yet. Then there's the stock market—it'll be opening in a few hours. All the usual stuff.

Keenan, I would appreciate it if you would go over there right now, with just one or two others. The body is still there, but I'll have Mallory & Malone send a hearse over. And I'll tell the coroner's office there's no need to cut this guy apart in an unnecessary autopsy. If you can confirm that with them, it might make them more comfortable. Got the picture, Keenan?

I can consider it done? Great. Call me back if there are any complications. Next week the two of us will have dinner."

Next. Mallory & Malone, the celebrity funeral directors. More good friends.

"Good morning. Sal Bellini calling for John Malone. Can you connect me with his home? It's urgent.

Hello, John. Sorry to bother you at this early hour. Don't let it out yet, but our mutual friend, Gar Grey, just committed suicide. Yeah, I'm shocked too.

John, here's what I need for you to do—and fast.

Send a hearse to Gar's place on Fifth and bring the body back to your mortuary. Prepare it for burial in the same dark suit you'll find him in—and that's strictly according to Gar's final instructions. So this is absolutely critical, John.

No, there will not be an autopsy. The police will confirm that it's a suicide. And since I know the funeral will be at St. Pat's, I'll call the Cardinal to make the arrangements.

On this next point—and you well know the size of Gar's ego—under no circumstances did he want anyone to see him in death. No wake. No viewing.

And there are to be no exceptions, John—not even his wife and children. Lay him out in the best bronze casket—and seal it shut. Put a lock on it, if necessary. I'll call Irene Henry at the apartment and tell her your hearse is on the way. She'll wait there until everything has been taken care of. We'll talk again later in the day. Many thanks, John. Gar would be grateful, too."

At 8AM, the day doorman relieved the night man at Gar's apartment building.

"Anything interesting happen last night that I need to know about, Pat?"

"Interesting? Would you believe Mr. Grey committed suicide last night, Nick?"

"Mr. Grey? Get along with ya. Mr. Grey, of all people. Not in a million years."

"Well you're wrong this time, Nick. The cops were crawlin' all over the place. Then a hearse from Mallory & Malone came to pick up his body. I tell ya, Nick, it was one hell of a busy night. Lucky you were off duty. An' lissen to this bit of inside information."

"What big secret are ya going to share with me now, Patrick?"

"Earlier last night, a knockout of a broad—I'd say an expensive Latin whore—came to visit Mr. Grey. But, I guess she was not enough for 'im."

Taking a fast look left and right, the night doorman leaned close to the day man's ear.

"Wouldya believe I only saw this *one* broad arrive—*just the one*—mind ya. But it was *two* broads that left. No question 'bout that. There was *two* of 'em.

An' I tell ya somethin' else, Nick.

I sure would have liked to fuck that *second* one."

ABOUT THE AUTHOR

Robert Paul Miller, a native of Minneapolis, has always been surrounded by words. Starting out as an eighteen-year-old Midwestern radio announcer, later newscaster, broadcasting seamlessly brought him into advertising and public relations, as well as much pioneering in TV writing and production. After nearly forty years of living on the fast track in New York City, he writes about the corporate and financial worlds in **Zig / Zag**. He now makes his home in Scottsdale, Arizona.